I0735260

EMBRACE ME DARKLY

A DARK ALLIANCE NOVEL

KIRA JAMES

EMBRACE ME DARKLY

A DARK ALLIANCE NOVEL

KIRA JAMES

For exclusive content and updates,
visit KiraJamesAuthor.com
to join the Elite Readers Group!

THE DARK ALLIANCE SERIES

Crave Me Roughly (prequel novella)
Embrace Me Darkly
Torture Me Gently
Tempt Me Deadly
Crush Me Tenderly (prequel)
Hold Me Wickedly
Claim Me Sinfully
Hurt Me Sweetly

The vampire stood in the shadow of a massive oak, watching as the human hurried down the sidewalk, passing lawns littered with tricycles, wagons, and other hallmarks of a happy suburban life.

Frank Constantine. An academic. A diplomat.

A fool.

A man who had opened the door to a world he thought he understood, but never truly had. Now, he never would. Because in less than five minutes, the human would be dead.

Electric streetlights provided spotty illumination to the sidewalks of this Silver Lake neighborhood, and a low growl escaped the vampire's throat as Constantine moved closer, stepping in and out of the shadows as he swung a shopping bag and sang to himself, the sound so soft that no human could have heard it from this distance.

The vampire could hear just fine.

"Happy birthday to Sara. You're my sweet little dear-a."

As the dead man sang, the vampire changed location with preternatural speed.

"Now you're eight and I'm late. Happy——"

Constantine stopped in a circle of light, his forehead furrowed, his breathing irregular. The vampire caught the enticing scent of adrenaline. He growled, hating what he had to do even as he craved Constantine's fear-laden blood.

"Who's there?"

The vampire remained perfectly still, well-hidden in the shadows.

Constantine released a nervous laugh, then lifted his shopping bag. "Nerves," he told a pink teddy bear. "Occupational hazard." He cleared his throat, then began walking again. "But Sara is going to love—"

He didn't finish the sentence. Instead, he spun around, his eyes going wide as the vampire swooped in and drained every last drop of blood from the human's body.

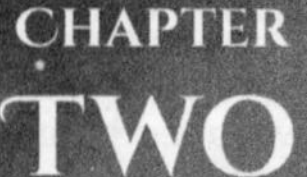

CHAPTER

TWO

*T*wenty Years Later

Back straight, Sara told herself. *Eyes forward. Don't fidget.*

It was one thing to stand in front of a judge or jury. To cross-examine a defendant or parse out a story from a nervous, confused victim. Opening statements and closing arguments were her métier, and responding to opposing counsel's objections was a hell of a lot more fun than a night out drinking with her friends.

As for putting away a vile, fucked up serial child-killer like Xavier Stemmons? Well, that was even better than sex.

But this? Standing on the steps of the courthouse as she faced reporters and onlookers? This was pure hell, even when all those staring eyes were full of congratulations and relief.

Beside her, Andrew Porter easily fielded the barrage of questions from the gathered press. Los Angeles County's polished and popular District Attorney, Porter was a brilliant lawyer who seemed built for the public eye. He'd given Sara, an Assistant District Attorney, the Stemmons case and all of the press and public appearances that went along with prosecuting the Baby Doll Killer. By all rights, she should be standing up here alone, and she was grateful to Porter for standing beside her now.

"—verdict remarkably fast," a tall, thin reporter shouted. "Did that surprise you?"

10

"Not at all," Porter said smoothly as thunder rumbled across the cloudy sky. "Ms. Constantine presented an airtight case. She's a credit to this office."

"This was your first time as the lead attorney in a capital murder, not to mention such a high profile case." The familiar voice rang out as reporter Andrea Tarrant maneuvered through the crowd until she was directly in front of Sara, sunglasses balancing on her head amid short, choppy hair. "Were you concerned about your lack of experience?"

Sara met her friend's eyes, grateful to Andy for tossing her the kind of softball question that could segue into a tidy wrap-up of the press conference. "Not at all," she said, glancing at Porter as the first fat raindrops began to fall. "I was trained by the best, and the evidence spoke for itself. My only concern was presenting the strongest case possible so that this office could get a conviction and justice for all those little girls."

More reporters' hands shot up as others shouted questions on top of each other. "That's it for now," Porter said smoothly as reporters called Sara's name, and she blinked against the sudden onslaught of camera flashes.

"I meant every word," Porter told her once they were safely back inside the courthouse. "You did this office proud."

"Thank you," she said, meaning it. Porter didn't give out unearned praise.

"Now get out of here. No cleaning up your office. No digging into your other files. Go celebrate with your friends, Constantine. You deserve it."

She bit back a grin. "Yes, sir." She hesitated before walking away. "There's a group of us meeting at Probation. Join us?"

He scoffed. "Are you kidding? I need to clean up my office and review some other case files."

She rolled her eyes, then started toward the exit.

"Constantine."

She paused, turning to look back over her shoulder, her brows rising in question.

"You should call your mother. She'll have heard by now. And she'll be proud."

"Sure," Sara said, then turned and hurried away, wishing Porter hadn't mentioned her mother. Not today when Sara was riding high on the verdict. Her mother had never once commented on Sara's career, neither to congratulate or intervene. As far as Sara could tell, she wanted as far away from the world of criminal law as she could get. Which meant as far away from Sara, too.

So, no. Sara wouldn't be calling. If Deborah Constantine wanted to congratulate her daughter—hell, if she wanted to give any sign that she remembered she even had a daughter—she could make that call herself.

But it would be a cold day in hell, Sara knew, before that would happen.

As far as Sara knew, the local dive bar, Probation, had been tucked away on Hill Street since the beginning of time. Or at least since the first courthouse was built in downtown Los Angeles. With its narrow etched-glass windows, dark wood exterior, and heavy doors engraved with the scales of justice, there was no mistaking the place as anything but a hangout for attorneys and cops.

For Sara, it had become a second home, a place her mentor had brought her after that first exhilarating day as an intern at the District Attorney's office back when she'd been a 2L. The bar had been the icing on an already tasty cake. A respite from the intensity of the work, but still surrounded by people who understood her drive and dedication. Her need to guard the lines that kept the world safe. And to punish those who crossed them.

Now, Probation was as comfortable as her own condo. And since it was only two blocks from home, at least as convenient. She tugged open the door, then stepped over the threshold as she closed her umbrella, laughing and smiling as everyone in the bar started to call out various incarnations of *Way to go, Constantine!*

She did a self-congratulatory spin as the room burst into applause, but it was Petra Tsang who topped off the celebratory cake when she let loose with a piercing whistle guaranteed to get every-one's attention. "To my bestie," she shouted, gesturing toward Sara with a gloved hand that extended from a long-sleeved tee. "A kickass lawyer who got a jury to convict in two hours. That's barely enough time to elect a foreman. And boom, smash, Xavier Stemmons goes doooown. This woman is amazing. I'd marry her if she weren't so damn tall!"

"Get in line!" That from Manny Hernandez, her office-mate since her first day on the job, and he'd made no secret that he was attracted to Sara. It wasn't mutual, but considering how much her body was humming with victory, the allure of a little friends-with-benefits action couldn't be denied.

"Don't even think it," Petra whispered as she reached Sara's side. Sara rolled her eyes. They'd met during Sara's sophomore year of college, when Sara had interned for a Legal Aid organization, and Petra had been doing volunteer PI work, clocking hours as she worked toward getting her investigator's license along with a degree in criminal justice. They'd hit it off, and the friendship had blossomed from there. Usually, Sara thought that was a good thing. Right then, she thought that Petra knew her too damn well.

"Not going there, and you know it." Over the last three or so years, the thrill she used to get from self-medicating with a one-night stand had faded. Sara knew that was a good thing, but that knowledge didn't ease the constant ache inside her, like the pain of a phantom limb.

"Not with Manny, maybe," Petra continued, cocking her head so that Sara followed her further away from the table. "But I wouldn't be your bestie if I didn't point out that *he's* here again." Petra said the last with a flourish and a significant nod toward the bar.

Sara followed her gaze, her chest tightening when her eyes found the man sitting on the other side of the dark room. Unlike most of the men in Probation, he wasn't wearing a suit. Instead, he wore jeans and a crisp white button down. His dark hair had a hint of curl, and was just long enough to graze his shirt collar. It gleamed in the light, and Sara could imagine the feel of the strands, soft between her fingers. The fantasy was so tactile it felt like a memory, and she held her breath as he turned to look right at her, his face chiseled perfection. She held his gaze, then looked away, unnerved by her body's visceral response to this man.

"A friend of yours?"

Sara jumped at the familiar voice behind her, then turned to face the man. "Dan. Hi. I wasn't expecting to see you tonight." A lawyer with a football player's body, Dan Cummings had spent the better part of her career asking her out. He'd finally worn her down, but after three months of dating and stress-relieving screwing, she'd ended it right before Stemmons' two-month-long trial began. And before he could start making noises about getting serious.

His dark eyes studied her. "Do you think I'm that petty? You blew it out of the park."

"That's high praise from a public defender." She shrugged out of her suit jacket and tossed it over the back of a chair, relishing the cool air on her bare arms, revealed in the silk tank top.

"Yeah, well, I'm glad he wasn't my client. Stemmons was garbage. A monster. He—"

"*No.*" The word came out with more force than Sara had intended, and suddenly all eyes at the table were on her. "No," she repeated, softer but with no less force. "Don't you dare give him an excuse. A monster? There are no monsters."

Dan laughed. "Hello? Aren't you the woman who wrote your undergraduate thesis on vampire folklore?"

"I did. There's a wellspring of insight into humanity hiding in tales of the supernatural. But that's fiction. Monsters? Please. The monsters hiding under your bed are just the personification of our human fears and guilts. Stemmons is as human as I am. As you are. And he's evil."

She held his gaze, silently daring him to argue. A moment passed, then Dan sighed, shaking his head. "You're right. But what he did to those girls...." He shuddered, the horror thick in his voice. "I do my job because everyone deserves representation, not because they're innocent. But if Stemmons had come to me, I wouldn't have taken his case."

Thick tension hung over their table, the eyes of the other attorneys on them.

"You would have," Sara finally said. "Because you're good at your job, and that's how the system works. And you know I respect you for it."

"Sara..."

She turned away, recognizing the heat in his voice.

"Hey, Danny-boy," Manny said, thankfully breaking the tension. "Got a whiskey here with your name on it. You, too, Sara."

"I've got Sara covered," Petra said, gesturing for Sara to return to her side. Sara did, shooting the others an apologetic look. It was, frankly, a minor miracle that Petra had come to Probation to celebrate. As a rule, the private investigator didn't like crowded places —too many possibilities for accidental touching. And Petra had a skin condition that was exacerbated by even the lightest of touches.

At least, that's what her friend had always told her. Lately, Sara had begun to wonder if it was more phobia than physical.

"You should go order yours at the bar," Petra said, pulling Sara from her thoughts. "Save the bottle we already ordered for the rest of us."

"Pet…"

"Don't even try to act like you're not interested. I know you are. And he damn sure is. He keeps looking over here, and we both know it's not me he's looking at."

"I'm supposed to be celebrating with my friends."

"So? Go *celebrate* with a new friend."

Sara fought to turn an amused grin into a scowl.

"Come on," Petra prodded. "You know you want to. And he does, too. This is, what? The fourth time we've seen him watching you in the last two months?"

"Fifth," Sara said.

Petra broke into a wide grin, and Sara cursed, realizing her mistake.

"Just go. Enjoy your victory."

"I do need a drink. I mean, it's my party, right?"

"That's the way to justify. Go."

Petra twirled her hand in a hurry-up motion, and Sara gave up protesting. It had all been for form, anyway. She knew what she wanted. She may have only noticed him five times, but it felt like she knew him intimately. As if she'd been waiting for him. Expecting him.

That, of course, was ridiculous. But it didn't change the fact that she was curious. With a quick nod to Petra, she took a breath, then headed toward the mythological god at the bar, smiling and waving in response to the calls of congratulations volleyed toward her by the other patrons.

"This one's on me," the bartender, Melanie, was saying to the god as Sara settled on the stool next to him. About Sara's age, Melanie had been working the bar for as long as Sara had been coming to Prohibition.

"That's really not necessary," the man said to Melanie. There was a hint of amusement in his voice, coupled with an accent that Sara couldn't place.

"Of course, it isn't necessary," Melanie retorted. "But it's still on me. Seriously, Luke, you saved my ass."

Luke. She let the name roll through her thoughts, and decided that it suited him.

"Not that many nice guys walking the streets these days," Melanie continued. "A couple of drinks isn't even close to sufficient thanks for what you did." She turned her attention to Sara. "Yours is on the house, too, Sara. Great job getting the riff-raff off the street. The usual?"

"Sure. And thank you." She grabbed a handful of peanuts out of one side of a scale of justice put to a campy new use, then set them on a bar napkin.

"Sara's our rock star," Melanie said.

"I know." Luke turned a bit in her direction. His eyes were amber, an unusual color that made his steadfast gaze seem predatory. He glanced up at the muted television that hung above the bar. Her own face filled the screen. "Congratulations," he said, returning his attention to her.

"You followed the trial?"

"Of course."

"Are you an attorney?" she asked. "Or maybe a cop?" Both were good bets considering the bar's usual clientele.

He took a sip of his drink, a hint of a smile dancing at the corner of that exceptional mouth. "I'm neither. But I do believe that evil must be fought. We don't always win, but we have to try." He put his glass down and faced her more directly. "You tried. And you won. You're an impressive woman, Sara Constantine."

"No, I'm—" She cut herself off, drew a breath, then said, "Thank you."

"Why is it so hard to accept praise?"

She laughed, then took a sip of the Macallan that Melanie had slid in front of her. She glanced meaningfully at the bartender, then back to Luke. "I assume that question is meant for you as much as me?"

"Indeed." He lifted his glass, and she met his toast with hers, the *clink* settling strangely warm in her belly, especially when she noticed the silver signet ring on his right hand. *Not married*. Always a good sign.

She studied his face as temptation tightened in her chest. She'd noticed how attractive he was months ago, the first time she'd seen him watching her from across the bar. But he was even more gorgeous close up, with a strong jaw and well-defined cheekbones. A scar bisected his left brow, and that single flaw seemed to lift all his other perfect features to an even higher plane. She'd thought of him as a mythological god before, but that didn't really do him justice.

"What case will you tackle next?"

She laughed. "What? Don't I get a rest?"

"You don't want one."

"No," she admitted. "I don't." She traced her finger over the rim of her glass, surprised that he saw her so clearly. "Tomorrow I'll finalize paperwork and clear out my office. After that, I guess I'll see what comes up on the docket."

"An excellent way to live," he said. "Never knowing what's coming next, but always at the ready. It keeps you fresh."

"Some people can't handle it. But I love it." She tilted her head, trying to place the accent coloring his subtly formal pattern of speech. "Where are you from?"

"I've traveled all over the world, but I've spent a lifetime in Los Angeles." He took a sip of his drink, then glanced quickly over his shoulder toward the back tables.

"You're really from LA? You sound…"

He returned his attention to her. "What?"

She wanted to brush off the question, but found herself answering honestly. "Exotic," she said. "God, that sounds so rude."

"Not at all. From you, I'll take it as a compliment."

"You took my compliment much easier than you took Melanie's."

"Did I?"

"What did you do for her?"

"She found herself in need of a place to stay."

"And you're letting her stay with you?" An annoying niggle of jealousy tugged at her gut, and she was grateful he'd turned away to glance over his shoulder again. She thought he was watching a dark-haired man, head bent as he read the paper, and was relieved that he wasn't keeping tabs on a woman.

"My asshole ex kicked me out," Melanie said, coming up to refill the nuts. "Luke found me a new place in under an hour. No credit check. Reasonable rent. No first and last months upfront. Great location. He totally saved my bank account. I was afraid I'd have to hole up at some rat-infested hotel. Or drive all the way to Riverside and stay with my mother. Seriously, this man is the coolest. Be right with you!" she added, waving at a couple who'd just settled in on the far side of the bar.

Sara took a long sip of whiskey for courage, then met Luke's eyes as he turned back to face her. "You've been watching me."

"Yes," he said simply. "I have."

She leaned back, surprised by his honesty, then lifted her drink. He reached out, capturing her arm before the glass met her lips.

"What is this?" His thumb brushed lightly over the soft skin under her wrist, skimming over the characters inked there:

吸血鬼.

"Just a tattoo."

"An interesting choice."

She hid her frown by taking another sip of her drink. "You know what it means?"

"I do. It holds some special meaning to you?"

"You read Hanzi?"

"I have a knack for languages. And you, it seems, have a fascination with vampires."

His thumb was still on her wrist, just beneath the word, and she tugged it back, his understanding of that one little word making her feel weirdly exposed. "My father was into folklore. Paranormal stuff. He passed the fascination on to me."

That much was true. But the tattoo had come much later. Only about three years ago, actually. She'd been feeling at loose ends for months, unable to get a handle on what was wrong with her. Then she'd stumbled across the Hanzi word in a graphic novel she'd been reading during an afternoon at the beach, and from that moment on, she'd been obsessed by it. An obsession that had only been relieved when she'd finally found an artist to permanently ink it on her wrist.

Strangely, once the word was on her wrist, she'd felt more like herself. Not fully—she'd still wake up crying and grasping for something she'd lost, though she had no clue what it was—but the daily malaise faded. She told herself it was a remnant from her childhood. Her father had been brutally murdered by someone pretending to be that very bloodsucking fiend. Of course she had issues.

True, but that explanation never felt quite right. Eventually, her workload grew, and she'd decided it didn't matter. There was no therapy in the world better than taking down bad guys, after all.

She finished off her drink. "So tell me why you've been watching me."

The corner of his mouth curved up. Clearly he knew this was her ploy to change the subject. She fervently hoped it worked.

"I already told you," he said, signaling for Melanie to refill their glasses. "You're impressive."

"You were watching me even before this case. I've seen you five times, including today."

He put his hand over hers, the point of contact stealing all of her focus. When he finally spoke, his voice was low and smooth, rumbling through her like a warm caress. "It's the work that's impressive, Sara. The passion. Not simply the Stemmons case. You stand as champion for the weak. So do I. And," he added with just the hint of a smile, "I've watched you six times before today in this bar alone. Not five."

"Oh." She swallowed, suddenly aware of her pulse pounding in her veins. She told herself his attention should feel creepy, but she didn't believe it. Strangely, weirdly, it felt right. Even familiar.

She took a sip of whiskey to ease her suddenly dry mouth, and when she spoke, she didn't meet his eyes. Her, who was usually so bold with men. Something else that was baffling. "Is that all you want?" Her words came out as a whisper, and she forced herself to lift her head and look into his eyes. "To watch?"

His brows rose, and she could tell he was fighting amusement. Her chest felt tight, and she had to work to breathe. She wasn't certain how they'd slid into this sensual dance, but she was enjoying it immensely.

"No, Sara," he said. "It's not." He leaned forward, his lips brushing her hair as he murmured in her ear. "I want to celebrate with you."

Her heart stuttered as she remembered the way Petra had used that word, and all the heat that had been building within her settled between her thighs. "I do have reason to celebrate," she said, pulling back so that she could see those hypnotic eyes. "Big case. Big win." Her voice was breathy.

"Indeed."

She plucked an olive from a small bowl sitting beside a single rose in a bud vase, enjoying their flirting. Even more, enjoying the warmth that now flowed through her body and the way her skin tingled with awareness. She lifted the olive to her mouth, then drew it in, her eyes never leaving Luke's as she sucked, then chewed, then swallowed.

"Do you like olives?" she asked.

"More and more with each passing moment."

She stifled a laugh, then took another olive from the bowl, this time brushing the slick surface over his lips until they parted and he drew in both the olive and her finger. He sucked, and it was everything she could do not to moan aloud as a ribbon of heat ran from the tip of her finger, through her chest, and all the way down to the juncture of her thighs.

She tugged her finger free, her heart beating wildly. "Luke."

She'd meant the words as an admonishment to slow down. Instead, it came out as a plea.

His eyes skirted away, skimming over the back area of the bar. When his attention returned to her, there was nothing but panty-melting desire on his face.

She felt lightheaded, and not from the whiskey, although she downed the last of it for both courage and the buzz. She turned to look back toward the entrance. She caught Petra's amused gaze, and saw Dan's disapproving frown, but the rest were lost in conversation, heads bent over the table.

After a deep breath for courage, she slid off her stool. "Count to five, then follow me."

She didn't wait to see if he'd obey. She simply headed toward the hall that led to the restrooms and storage area. She leaned against the wall, breathing hard, fear that he wouldn't show warring with fear that he would. She wasn't a stranger to picking up men—to burning off that energy and need as if she was chasing demons or something—but that was usually all it was. With Luke, it was more. It was tangible. It was *want*. Need. A craving like nothing she'd experienced before, and the possibility that he might not show felt like ice in her veins.

She saw his shadow first, and warm relief flooded her body. Then he stepped into the light at the end of the hall, his broad shoulders seeming to fill the space. Now that he was standing, she realized how large he was with his broad chest, massive arms, and muscular thighs. He stood for a moment, and she soaked up her fill of him, the vision alone enough to make her feel a little drunk. Then he was beside her, the speed of his approach almost dizzying. His hands were on the wall on either side of her, caging her in. Their eyes locked, and though she expected a wild, rapturous kiss, he didn't move. "Luke," she whispered. "Please."

"Yes." The word was the softest of whispers, even softer than the brush of his lips over hers that followed. She wanted more. Harder. Claiming. But his soft tease was even more intimate, and when he drew kisses down over her jaw and to the soft skin of her neck, she thought she would melt with pleasure.

"Your pulse beats with the passion of a warrior. Is there anything that scares you?"

"Yes," she murmured. "But not you."

He pulled away, and she gave a soft moan of protest that changed quickly to a gasp when she saw the intensity of his gaze, full of heat and need and, strangely, gratitude. "Luke?"

She could still taste his name on her lips when he swooped in, finally claiming her mouth with his, the bruising kiss wilder and deeper than she'd anticipated. A kiss she could get lost in. And right then, she desperately wanted to get lost.

At first, his touch had seemed cold. Her own nerves, she assumed, but he was like fire against her now, their combined heat flowing through her as if they were twined together in flames.

He drew away, and she whimpered in protest, silenced only when he took her hand and tugged her though the door to the Ladies Room. He caged her against the door, keeping it firmly closed as his mouth claimed her again and one hand grappled to untuck her silk tank. She used one of her own hands to yank it free, the other to cup the back of his head, silently urging him to kiss her harder. Deeper.

He took her wrists, thrusting them above her head and pinning her against the door so that she was helpless against the onslaught of sensations that crashed over her as he played her like a fine instrument. He used only one large hand to hold her wrists, and with his other, he teased her breast, then slid his fingers slowly down until he was inching up her skirt. She'd abandoned her hose in her office before coming to the bar, and now his fingers on her bare thigh were sending her spiraling into a sweet oblivion. When he reached the elastic of her panties, she was certain she would melt right then.

She wanted this. Oh, please, yes, this was exactly the kind of celebration she'd been craving. But not here. Not pressed up against a public bathroom door. Not when she wanted to feel this man naked and on top of her, his body pressing her against her mattress as her head swam with lust and desire.

"Luke," she whispered, fighting to get the word out as his fingertip found her slick core. "Not here. My condo's just a block away."

His fingers slid inside her, and the desire to grind against him and explode in his arms was so compelling she could barely resist. "Can you truly wait a block?"

"No," she admitted, her voice raspy. "But anticipation is a potent aphrodisiac."

"So it is," he murmured, freeing her. He took a step back and it took all her resolve not to change her mind. To beg him to put his hands on her again. "With me," he said as she straightened her clothes.

He took her arm, then led her back to the bar, where he tossed a crisp hundred dollar bill on the polished surface. He plucked the rose from the vase, then handed it to her, a red ribbon tied around the stem.

"I just need to say goodbye and grab my jacket."

He'd turned to glance at the back of the bar, and now she followed his gaze to see the back door that led to the alley swinging shut, and the table he'd been watching was empty. When Luke turned to face her again, he was frowning. "I'm so sorry, Sara. I'm afraid I can't tonight." He brushed the pad of his thumb over the curve of her jaw. "You almost made me forget," he whispered, the words full of wonder.

With any other man, she might have believed it was a brush-off. A lack of nerve. But not with him. He wanted her as desperately as she wanted him; of that much, she was certain. Quickly, she grabbed a napkin and the pen from the tray with the bill, then scribbled her address and phone number. "No pressure," she whispered, pressing the napkin into his hand. "But I hope to see you at my door."

His fingers curled around the napkin, and for a moment she thought he was going to give it back. Then he flashed a small, sad smile before sliding the napkin into his pocket. "I want nothing more than to stay with you, but I cannot." He took a step away, then stopped.

Slowly, he turned to face her again. "Be careful, Sara Constantine. There are things in the world more dangerous than the likes of Xavier Stemmons."

THREE

Sara watched as the door swung shut behind Luke, fighting the disappointment that swelled within her. She told herself it didn't matter. That she probably wouldn't see him again. After all, he'd been watching her for ages, but now that he had a real chance with her, he'd vanished. Despite his pretty words, the odds were good he was done. Saw. Caught. Conquered.

Except he hadn't conquered. Not really. Not yet. And although she told herself that she was naive to believe he would call her, she truly did believe it. Maybe tomorrow. Maybe next week.

Hopefully tonight.

"Well?" Petra whispered, meeting Sara halfway as she returned to her friends' table.

"I'm heading home."

"Oh?" Petra's tone rose with her eyebrows.

"Not for that. He had to go. Some sort of appointment."

"Okay, hold up a sec. I saw you two disappear into the back. Didn't you—"

"Nosy much?"

"Um, yeah. Details, please. I need my vicarious smoochies, you know."

She spoke casually, but with Petra's touch issues, Sara couldn't help but worry. She knew Petra had dated in the past, but she doubted her friend had ever had sex. And she definitely wasn't dating anyone now. Not that Sara's wild child ways were something to be emulated, but she hated the thought of her friend not making that connection.

Like you do? As if all those men you used to pick up were mix-and-match soulmates?

Sara frowned at the thought, accurate and cutting as it was. She'd told herself time and again that she wasn't that girl anymore. And yet she knew damn well that if Luke showed up tonight, all bets were off.

Still, she wasn't going to bank on it. She knew too damn much about loss and disappointment to truly be optimistic about an unknown future.

"Earth to Sara..."

Sara shook herself free of her thoughts. "Sorry. Smoochies, yes. But then he said he had someplace to be, so..." She trailed off with a shrug.

"He wasn't lying," Petra said firmly. "He'd be an idiot to just blow you off. And the guy's clearly hot for you, so that means he's not an idiot."

"And that's why you're my best friend," Sara said, meaning it.

"Back at you." She cocked her head toward the table filled with attorneys. "We've still got nachos and whiskey. Come on back and enjoy being the toast of the town."

"I think I'm going to say goodnight," Sara said.

"Seriously? It's not even ten. There's still plenty of celebrating to do."

"I'm wiped. I've barely slept since we picked the jury. I've been running on adrenaline, and I can feel the crash coming."

Petra frowned, but she didn't argue. How could she? The words were technically true, even if the bigger truth was that she hoped Luke would come by her place later.

"Alright. Fine. But at least tell me he has your number."

Sara just smiled, then headed to the table to grab her jacket and say a general goodbye to the others. By the time she pushed through the doors, the rain had slowed to a drizzle, and she didn't bother with her umbrella as she walked the short distance to the Plaza Towers.

Thirty-four stories tall with balconies in every unit, it had been the fifth floor rooftop bar and pool that had drawn her to the condominium. She'd seen a photograph on a flyer and had called a real estate agent that day.

That had been three years ago during a month when she'd been feeling decidedly unsettled. Every day seemed foggy, and she struggled with the sense that she'd forgotten something but had no idea what it was. The moment she'd seen the flyer, though, the feeling ebbed. For years she'd been thinking about moving out of the family home she rented from her mom. Now the universe was telling her to do it.

Real estate lust, Petra had called it, but Sara didn't agree. It wasn't the craving for the condo so much as the desire to leave the Silver Lake house. There were too many memories there. Too many ghosts. And far too often, late at night, she had the feeling that inside that home, a part of her was missing.

Her father, of course. What else could it be? Maybe he was still looking out for her, telling her it was time to move on.

So she had. She'd settled on a spacious studio, then made a huge down payment using the money from the trust that had been established twenty years ago with the life insurance proceeds after her father's murder.

A shudder passed through her as she opened the door and saw the pink teddy bear on her unmade bed. Her eighth birthday had been a nightmare, and her mother had never understood why Sara had kept the bear that her father had been bringing home to her when he'd been killed, his throat ripped out as if his attacker were a monster from some shitty B-movie.

Deborah Constantine had advised her daughter to throw out the bear. The bear was a reminder of a bad day. Ergo, the bear should go. But to Sara, the bear was a good memory, despite the bad day. A sign that her dad had loved her. That he'd gone out of his way to search out such a silly, goofy present, knowing that his daughter would love cuddling on the couch with it when she watched cartoons.

No, her mom hadn't understood why Sara had kept the bear. Or any of her father's books and journals, for that matter. Then again, Deborah had never understood much about Sara. Mostly because she'd never tried.

"I got Stemmons, Daddy," she whispered. "Someday, I'm going to get your killer, too."

It was still early, but Sara was bone-tired, the tension of the day finally catching up with her. Still, she took the time to put the rose into a bud vase, which she then placed on her desk that sat perpendicular to the wall of bookcases. She gave the rose a place of honor, right next to the photograph of her at seven standing next to her father. He had his hand on her shoulder, his other arm hanging free despite the fact that he was standing right next to Sara's mother. She tried to remember if she'd ever seen them touching. She didn't think so.

Frowning, she grabbed her phone, then opened her text messages. She scrolled down to find the last text with her mom—almost five months ago—then tapped. *Can you talk?*

She hesitated, then slowly backspaced her way out of the message. After all, they really had nothing to talk about.

With a sigh, she leaned against the desk as she wrapped the ribbon around her finger while she took in the overstuffed shelves. Hundreds of books, many of them fiction or legal studies. But most had been her father's. Mythological tales about supernatural creatures. Supposed eyewitness accounts of vampires and other ghoulies that he'd found in various antiquarian bookstores. Notes from the lectures he gave as a professor of folklore at UCLA. And, of course, his journals.

As a child, she'd never known where he kept them, but she'd found them as a teen when her mother agreed to let Sara have her father's old study as her own. Sara had found a hidden cubbyhole behind one of the bookshelves, and it had been filled with a treasure trove of journals.

The notes were cryptic, and clearly related to his folklore research. Notes and scribbles about various creatures, including hints of a war brewing between vampires, werewolves, and demons. Her father used to tell her stories about the creatures' bubbling discontent, about how one day they would break free from the shadows. Not in a scary horror movie way, but to take their place in the world. The thought was both exciting and terrifying to young Sara, but he would brush off her eager questions, telling Sara he was working on a novel, and that she could read it when it was finished and she was older.

Now, Sara assumed the journals were his working notes. Scribbles of plot and character notes that popped into his head. The kind of thing that made sense to the writer, yet meant very little to anyone else. Certainly Sara couldn't interpret any of it. *Tiber and D*, for example. Was he referring to the river Tiber? And what about *Dragos— Italy?* Wasn't the Tiber River in Italy?

So many cryptic notes littered her father's journals, most of which she didn't have a chance in hell of interpreting. She supposed it didn't matter, though. Whatever story he'd intended to write had died with him. But the bottom line was that she'd inherited her father's love of supernatural lore. She had his books, she thought as she twisted the red ribbon in her hands. And she had her few, fuzzy memories.

But it wasn't enough. One thing was missing. His killer.

She'd find him. If it took until her dying breath, she would hunt down the bastard who had stolen not only a good man, but her childhood. And once she did, she wouldn't rest until she'd put the bastard behind bars forever.

Enough with the pity party. She'd done great today. One more bad guy put away. One more stand-in for her father's murderer.

With a shuddering sigh, she crossed the room, stripping as she did, so that she left a trail of clothes on the path from her desk to the bathroom. She went through her evening ritual, but ignored the oversized tee she usually slept in. Instead, she slid naked between the sheets, the pink bear shoved to the far side of the double bed.

She hadn't bothered to turn on any lights, but a soft glow from the various downtown high-rises filled the room, the illumination coming in through the sliding glass door. She had no curtain; on the twenty-fifth floor she didn't need one. And the dim light didn't bother her. She liked it, this feeling of floating above the city.

Now, she closed her eyes, wishing that Luke had come home with her and wondering if there was any chance in hell that she'd ever see him again.

The judge's body lay sprawled on the wet ground, his eyes still open in surprise and terror. He'd known what was to befall him in his last seconds. Known that his betrayals had finally been avenged, his crimes soundly punished.

Without thinking, the vampire licked his lips, still able to taste the bitter flavor of Braddock's fear. Fear, but no remorse. Of all the monsters that moved in the night, Marcus Braddock had been among the most vile.

He was dead now. Justice delivered. Fate sealed.

It was over.

The vampire took one last look at the Los Angeles police officer, standing stiff in his uniform and talking rapidly into the radio on his shoulder as the lights from his patrol car painted the drizzled night in red and blue. Nearby, a female sobbed, one of the two joggers who'd discovered the body and called 911, setting the wheels in motion.

Soon detectives and crime scene techs would descend. And then the others would come. The ones who would understand what had truly happened here tonight.

The ones who would search for Braddock's killer.

The vampire needed to be gone before they arrived.

And with that thought, Lucius Dragos took a step backwards, turned, then melted into the rain-soaked night where he belonged.

Luke's scent filled Sara's head, her body tingling from the brush of his fingertips over her skin, his lips on her mouth, her breasts, her thighs....

She moaned as she rolled over and clutched her pillow, trying to fight the need to wake. Trying to ignore the persistent ring of her phone.

Ring! Ring!

And then silence. Blissful silence.

Her entire body relaxed as she said a silent thank you to the genius who invented voicemail, then tried to slide back into her glorious dream.

It didn't work. The damn thing started ringing again.

She grappled for it, fully intending to throw it across the room, then sat bolt upright when she saw the caller ID.

"Sanchez?"

"I thought about not pinging you," Detective Renata Sanchez said without preamble. "You're not the ADA on call, and I figured you'd be off celebrating the Stemmons verdict. But this DB's got a neck wound. And I know you—"

"It's mine." She was already out of bed and stumbling toward her dresser for panties and a bra. "Location?"

"Elysian Park. A couple of late-night joggers found the body. I'll text you a GPS pin."

"Got it," Sara confirmed as the text flashed on her screen. "I'll be there in fifteen. Less." She ended the call without bothering to say goodbye, then shimmied into her favorite jeans, slipped her feet into a pair of flats, and pulled on a turtleneck. She grabbed her raincoat from the rack by the door along with her purse, then bolted for the elevator.

She had the directions on her phone by the time she reached her car and was standing beside Lieutenant Renata Sanchez at eleven-forty, a mere thirteen minutes from the call. The hood of Sanchez's windbreaker was down despite the steady drizzle, her short hair flattened against her thin face, making her eyes seem even wider. She blinked against the rain, then pointed to where a medical technician was working the body under lights set up to augment the full moon, still high in the night sky.

"What have we got?"

"Not much," Sanchez admitted. "This rain isn't helping the situation." She scowled up at the dark, misty sky like a parent noting bad behavior. Then she nodded toward a uniformed officer who was talking with a male and female jogger, both of whom looked close to losing their shit. "Those two found the body. We're taking statements, but they don't know much. Hell, they don't know anything."

"Jogging this late in the rain?"

"Apparently it's some social media challenge. So many miles every day. Break the pattern, lose the challenge."

"And that's why I avoid social media," Sara said. "And jogging."

"You and me both. They found him about twenty minutes ago. No TOD yet, but the rain hadn't completely washed away the footprints around the body, so I'm thinking they stumbled in pretty soon after our vic died."

"You got lucky on the footprints. Right here, the ground's a mess." Sara frowned at the muddy, trampled turf. "And we've got trees on the perimeter and a paved road into the park. Hard to know where the perp came from or what direction he took when he left."

"I don't disagree. I've got a K-9 unit on the way, but I'm not optimistic. Lot of traffic through here every day, and the rain only makes it harder. And we both know the odds of matching a shoe print are slim. Especially in these conditions"

"Tell me about the vic," Sara said, as they continued to walk toward the body.

"Marcus Braddock. A mediator. Sometimes court-appointed, but primarily does private dispute resolution. Part-time. The guy doesn't need the money. We haven't dug deep yet, but his bank account is healthy. Probably family money. Does a lot of volunteer work, especially with troubled teens and young adults. And somebody decided to play like they're a B-movie bad guy and take a bite out of him."

"Which is why you called me."

Sanchez looked at her sideways. "Yup. You ever going to tell me why neck wounds get your juices going?"

"I'm a prosecutor, remember? All murders get my juices going."

Sanchez shot her a *yeah, right,* look, but Sara just shrugged. Maybe someday she'd tell Sanchez about the way she'd found her father's body, his neck ripped open, his sightless eyes staring at the dark, moonless sky.

Maybe.

But not today.

"Rain," Detective Severin Tucker said. "You wanna tell me why we're always getting called out in the goddamn rain?"

"Clean living," Ryan Doyle answered, eyeing his partner with amusement as he slid his '63 Pontiac Catalina in beside an LAPD black-and-white. The flashing lights cast eerie shadows over the thickly wooded park, illuminating an ambulance and two unmarked piece-o'-shit vehicles that had homicide written all over them.

"I just got this dry-cleaned," Tucker continued, his fingers running down the lapel of his perfectly tailored suit.

"Screw your wardrobe," Doyle retorted as he slammed the gearshift into park and killed the engine. "For once I'd like to do our job without the humes getting the jump." He shot Tucker a sideways glance. "No offense."

"None taken." His partner reached into the backseat for a slicker, *Division 6* stenciled on the back. He slipped it on before exiting the car. Doyle didn't bother. Wasn't as if he'd melt in the drizzle.

They circled the car, falling in step together as they left the pavement for the squish of the park's damp grass.

"My date last night has a roommate."

"Are we in a fraternity?" Doyle growled. "Don't make me put in for another partner."

Tucker flashed his most charming smile, which was pretty damn charming. "You know you love me."

Doyle scowled. They'd been partners for going on five years, and no one was more surprised than Doyle at the way his so-very-human partner had grown on him.

"Just pick up the pace," he chided.

Tucker fell in step beside him, and they slogged toward an officer in a rain-soaked slicker who was standing in front of the crime scene tape. The officer stiffened as they approached, his eyes widening like a deer caught in the headlights as he held up a hand. Like that could keep them out.

"You might want to step aside, junior," Doyle said, not bothering to slow as he lifted the tape and started to slide under.

"I'm sorry," the officer said. "No one passes."

"We got authority here," Tucker said, staring hard at the guy, his eye color flickering from brown to green. "So come on, rookie. Get off our backs and let us through."

The officer's face went through the usual jumble of confusion before smoothing out. He smiled, all polite cooperation, then lifted the tape so Tucker could slip under.

Doyle followed, unable to stifle his grin. His partner might be human, but the boy definitely had gifts. "And that's why I keep you around."

"You wound me, man," Tucker said, pressing his palms over his heart. "I'm seriously wounded."

"You'll want to speak with Lieutenant Sanchez," the now-compliant uniform said. He pointed to a dark-haired woman in an LAPD windbreaker. "She's in charge."

"Not anymore." Tucker and Doyle continued toward the crime scene, even as Sanchez marched toward them, her Noxema-fresh face pinched. She wore black trousers, a matching blazer, and the windbreaker with the hood hanging down despite the rain. For that, at least, Doyle gave her points.

Another woman with honey-blond hair, a wide mouth, and at least four inches on the detective, marched beside Sanchez in jeans, a black turtleneck, and a raincoat. They intercepted Doyle and Tucker about midway to the body.

The detective spoke up first. "You want to tell me who you boys are and what you're doing at my crime scene?"

"I'm Agent Ryan Doyle. My partner, Agent Severin Tucker. And it ain't your crime scene." He pulled his shield from his pocket.

She peered at the shield and ID, but it was the tall blonde who spoke. "Division 6? Why's Homeland Security involved? There's no federal jurisdiction here."

Doyle tilted his head, studying her. "Who are you?"

"Sara Constantine. Assistant District Attorney."

"Yeah, well, you need confirmation, you just call this number." He pulled out a card and passed it to her. Ask for Nikko Leviathan."

Constantine barely looked at the card before passing it to Sanchez, who studied it, then shot a scowl between him and Tucker. "This is a crock of shit."

"You really should make the call," Tucker said, his eyes doing that thing as he concentrated on Sanchez, who frowned, then said, "I probably should go make that call."

Constantine's eyes widened as the lieutenant stepped away. She turned, her narrowed eyes going first to Tucker and then to Doyle. "Homeland. This case. Seriously?"

"'Fraid so." Technically, it was true. The North American branch of the Preternatural Enforcement Commission had been formally set up as a department within Homeland Security. A secret department, but there nonetheless. And considering the type of terror the PEC chased, there was a certain beauty to the ancient organization's modern cover story.

Constantine turned those sea-green eyes to Tucker. "Is he shitting me?"

"No, ma'am," Tucker said. "We at Homeland Security do not have a sense of humor of which we're aware. And now we're going to go see our victim."

Her feet stayed planted, but she tilted her head and sent Tucker a scathing glare, because despite the pretty face and wide smile, she was clearly a hard-ass.

"Step aside, counselor," Tucker said, those eyes of his turning on that sweet, inescapable persuasion. "Just step aside."

Doyle fought a grin. Sara Constantine was about to get whammied.

Constantine cocked her head. "Not until you explain exactly how a Federal agency is claiming jurisdiction in this murder."

Doyle caught Tucker's eye, but his partner only shrugged.

Well, hell. Guess he had to pull out the big guns.

He took a step toward Constantine, stopping only when he felt the pressure of his partner's hand on his shoulder. He glanced up, saw the quick shake of Tucker's head, followed by a nod at something behind Doyle. He turned to see Lieutenant Sanchez returning.

"It's theirs," she confirmed to Constantine, shooting both Doyle and Tucker the kind of glare that could freeze water. "I talked to Porter himself."

"What have I been saying?" Doyle flashed the women a triumphant smile, then led the way toward the med tech, Tucker right beside him as the two women hung back, probably whining about mean old Division 6.

He froze when he saw the body. "Fuck me," he said. "Intel was right."

"Marcus Braddock." Tucker sucked in a breath. "This is gonna get messy."

Doyle peered down at the ghostly pale form of retired judge Marcus Braddock. By all accounts, the man had been a shape-shifting son of a bitch, but that didn't mean Doyle would wish murder on him. And this particular cause of death was the worst kind of murder. The draining of a human or para-human was a Class Five homicide in violation of the Fifth International Concordat, and punishable by public execution. Bad shit all the way around.

Tucker was squatting near the body, his hand reaching for Braddock's collar when the rat-faced little med tech shoved his hand out of the way. "What the hell are you doing? You aren't gloved."

"Careful," Tucker said mildly. "Do that again, and you'll lose a few brain cells."

The rat hesitated, confused. Then Sanchez stepped up. She signaled to the rat with a jerk of her chin. "Go ahead. Show the Feds what they want to see."

Ratboy's eyes narrowed, but he used his gloved hand to tug the collar down, revealing the ripped flesh and brutalized muscle.

Bloody vampires. Despite the Concordat and the strict laws against contact feeding, it seemed like every time Doyle turned around one of the fuckmongers had sucked somebody dry.

He clenched his fists at his sides, hating their weakness. Disgusted by their lack of restraint. And, yeah, he'd seen all the damn statistics that showed that the vast majority of vampires could control the darkness within. That they didn't feed on humans. That they didn't kill. That they obeyed the law.

That they weren't the walking, talking incarnation of pure, fucking evil that Doyle knew they were.

Statistics be damned. As far as Doyle was concerned, the only good vamp was a dead one.

Marcus Braddock may have been a Therian prick—on and off the bench—but Doyle was going to make sure that the rogue vampire who sucked the life from him went down—with either a stake through the heart or an ax to the head.

"I would have said serial killer until you boys showed up," Sanchez said, her comments pulling Doyle back to the moment.

"No, ma'am," he said. "This is much worse."

"Worse how?" Constantine asked, her eyes on the wound rather than Doyle.

"That's something I'm not at liberty to say." He conjured a smile. "Federal jurisdiction, remember?"

She shot him a rage-filled glance, but to her credit, she said nothing.

The rat looked to Sanchez, and when she nodded, Ratboy cleared his throat. "We found this under the body," he said, holding up a clear evidence bag.

Doyle took it, his eyes not needing the illumination from the flashlight that Sanchez politely held up. A silver signet ring, caked in mud. Despite the dirt, the intricate craftsmanship stood out. A delicately carved dragon with a ruby eye, the body forming a circle as the beast consumed its own tail.

Tucker stood, leaning in for a closer look. "Isn't that—"

"It is," he said, his smile cold and hard. The Dragos crest, straight from the finger of Lucius Fucking Dragos. Finally, after all these years, he had his old friend's balls in a vise.

Doyle tilted his head to look at his partner. "I need to see if there's more."

Tucker shot a glance toward the humans. "You really want to deal with the paperwork?"

Doyle thought of the stack of reprimands and warnings that already peppered his file. But there was no time to clear the scene as per regulations. "Can't wait for authorization," he said. "Body's not getting warmer."

"Is there a problem?" Constantine asked.

"Not yet," Doyle said. To Tucker, he added, "You know I have to do it."

"Aw, hell," Tucker said, then rolled his shoulders in defeat. "Fine. Go for it. What's a little official reprimand between friends, right?"

Tucker sighed as he stood up, then looked deep into the eyes of Lieutenant Sanchez, who wandered away, suddenly remembering she had an elsewhere to be.

"Lieutenant? Renata?" Constantine looked between Sanchez and Tucker. "What the hell?"

"She's fine," Tucker said, his eyes on hers as he laid on the whammy. Or tried to, anyway.

"What exactly is fine about this situation?" Constantine demanded.

"Again?" Tucker snapped, looking at Doyle in frustration.

"Seriously," Constantine continued. "What are you two up to? Because—"

"I'll tell you," Doyle said, taking her hand, feeling the hum rise inside him, that electrical buzzing like tinnitus on crack. Beads of sweat formed on his brow as he used almost all of his energy to focus. To keep control. When he was certain he wouldn't lose it—wouldn't go too deep—he gave her just the hint of a nudge then backed away fast.

"Oh," Constantine said. "Excuse me." She turned, then crossed the field toward Sanchez.

Doyle shook himself, releasing the rest of the buzz.

"What the hell is going on?" Ratboy asked, his eyes darting between Doyle and Tucker.

"I can explain," Tucker said, crouching as he met Ratboy's eyes. After a moment, the med tech rose and wandered away to join the women.

"What is it with her?" Tucker asked, turning to frown at Constantine.

"Right now, I don't give a fuck." Doyle knelt by the body, his hand against Braddock's forehead. "Keep everyone else away."

"Will do, but you better find it fast."

Doyle nodded, but didn't speak. He was in.

Darkness. Surprise. Pleasure.

At least until it turned. Shifted.

Then the fear came.

A mishmash. Horror. Pleasure. Pain.

Black. Red.

A pulsing vein.

A woman's breast.

Blood on lace.

A growl.

Fangs.

Men's shoes, running, pounding through the mud.

The sky.

But none of it coming together, none of it coalescing into an image.

Just confusion. A jumble of confused emotions and reactions. Nothing to grab.

Nothing to hold on to.

"Come on, come on," Tucker said, his voice sounding a million miles away. Doyle closed his other hand over the body's heart, trying to get purchase on the fading aura.

Dizzy. Gone.

Remorse.

The fingers of death, so cold and familiar.

And then, finally, a face.

The last image before death won. The last conscious thought.

Doyle looked. And in his mind he saw Lucius Dragos, fangs bared, as he bent close to suck the last vestiges of life from Judge Marcus Braddock.

Doyle's teeth chattered and his body shook as he pulled free of Braddock's mind. But he had Dragos now, had him dead to rights.

Exhausted, he tilted his head up to face Tucker. "We finally got him, partner. And we are going to nail his ass to the wall."

Ural Hasik stood in a copse of trees, looking at the activity inside the crime scene tape. He'd been monitoring the humans' police band radio when he'd heard the call. Joggers. A body in the park. A neck wound.

He'd reported it immediately, of course. As he expected, he'd been ordered to come. To watch. To stay hidden. And then to report what he learned.

Now, he pushed the button on his phone, knowing that his report would make Gunnolf very, very happy.

"Dragos," he said, when the Therian leader answered the call. "The para-demon says that Lucius Dragos killed the judge."

FIVE

Doyle stumbled, losing his footing as he shuffled from the muddy ground to the asphalt of the parking lot. His body was wrung out, every movement akin to pushing his limbs through pudding. And the miners with pickaxes whacking at the inside of his skull weren't helping the situation.

Tucker thrust out his hand. "Keys."

"Fuck you."

"I mean it, man. You're spiraling. No way are you getting behind the wheel."

"The hell you say," Doyle retorted, but it was only for form. He was ripped up, and right then all he wanted was to collapse on the Catalina's bench seat and close his eyes.

"Keys," Tucker repeated.

"Only to shut you up." Doyle tossed him the keys. Or tried to. They made it a few inches, then clattered to the pavement.

"Fuck it, Doyle." Tucker bent to grab the keys. "Give it up and let's get you what you need."

Doyle gritted his teeth and shook his head. "Be fine," he managed, sliding into the passenger seat and closing his eyes. "I'll sleep it off. You drive to Malibu. I'll be fine."

"Bullshit," Tucker retorted as he slid behind the wheel. "It's me, remember? I've gotten to know your sorry ass pretty well over the years."

Doyle lifted his head to tell his partner to fuck off, but found he didn't have the energy.

"Okay. That's it. We'll hit Dragos's house after. But first, I'm taking you to Orlando's."

"No." He hated that his partner knew what he went through. Hated more that Tucker had been sucked into helping each time Doyle sank deeper into the mire.

"I don't see that you have a choice, buddy," Tucker said, fastening the seatbelt that Doyle was struggling with. "You're fading fast. When was the last time you had yourself a Happy Meal?"

Too long, and he hated that he needed the hit. Needed to feed.

The weakness in him shamed him. He was only half demon, dammit; he should be able to wrest more control. Should be able to function without taking, without feeding.

And it wasn't just the weakness that plagued him when he didn't feed. He lost his gift, too. How was that for fucked up? He could see the dead's attackers, but only if he fed. If he made himself a monster.

When he fed, his demon side surfaced. Claimed. Wanted.

Yes, he'd have strength. He'd have power. He'd have his visions.

But he'd also have the dark fury of a demonic temper fighting for release.

The constant battle exhausted him. And in his darker moments he even understood why some demons lost control. Why so many vampires let their darkness take over. So much easier to just stop fighting. To give in to that base, inherent nature.

No.

He'd lived that way once, and he wasn't going back.

He wasn't a thing. Wasn't evil.

He wasn't Dragos.

And if he had to battle his own nature until the end of time to prove it, then that's what he'd do.

His body jerked forward, then slammed back, and Doyle realized his eyes were closed. He opened them, but nothing he saw made sense "What the fu—"

"I told you, man. You're bad off. You haven't fed in over a week. You went too deep with Dragos on too little mojo."

"Had to. Had to look for..." He trailed off, unable to even remember what he was looking for. "Where are we?"

"Skid Row. Roll down your window."

"You ... said Orlando's." He almost smiled. At least he remembered that.

"Fuck that. There's no time."

Doyle fumbled for the handle, then heard Tucker's soft curse.

"Never mind. This will take a decade if I wait for you." He scooted over on the bench seat, leaned across Doyle, and cranked the window down. One sharp wolf whistle and he'd caught the attention of a rail-thin streetwalker who looked to be putting all of her profits into crank.

She pasted on a smile, adjusted her tiny skirt, then tottered toward them from her station under a streetlamp.

"Your lucky night, boys," she cooed. "I'm running a two-for-one special."

"Save it," Tucker said. "I'm just here to watch."

Her brows rose slightly. "That'll cost you extra." When Tucker didn't protest, she turned her attention to Doyle. "What's he want?"

What Doyle wanted was to get the hell out of there. But that thought was barely formed in his mind; he sure as hell couldn't put it in words.

"Do you kiss?"

"What? On the mouth? Shit, no."

"What's your name?"

"Sally."

"Well, Sally," Tucker said. "That's what he wants. And he'll pay extra."

"How much?"

"Whatever it takes."

"Yeah?" She looked at Doyle with respect. "That a fact?"

"Get in," he croaked, his voice thin, his lips barely moving as he forced the words out.

Her brow furrowed, and she took a step backward. "Your man's sick. No way I'm getting whatever he's got."

"He's not sick," Tucker said.

"Kiss my ass." She turned and started walking away.

Doyle reached up and clawed at the door handle. Tucker was right; he needed it—needed her—and he needed it now.

"Wait," Tucker called. She turned, hands on her hips and a scowl on her face. "Kiss him," Tucker said, and Doyle didn't need to see his partner's eyes to understand. "Kiss him nice and hard."

She teetered a bit on her heels, then sauntered back to the car, her eyes glassy and slightly confused. "Got a freebie for you, sickie-poo," she said, leaning into the window so that the shelf of her breasts balanced on the window ledge. "Come to Mama."

He did, leaning into the kiss and opening his mouth wide.

Opening and sucking and feeding and—

Oh, fuck yeah ...

Her soul filled him. Nourished him. And, yeah, it roused the darkest parts of his demonic half.

Right then, he didn't care. The strength flowed back, and he wondered how he'd ever given it up. How could he have thought to exist without this? Weak as a kitten and docile as a bunny?

This was it. This was good. This was power and strength and—

Beneath him, the woman made a mewling noise. Tucker's bond had broken, the soul that remained within her insufficient to accept the suggestion.

He needed to back off. Needed to leave her some. With even a scrap, she'd heal. Wouldn't be hollow. Wouldn't be a shell. A casing for one of the incorporeal creatures to fill.

He knew all that, yet he clung to her, the taste of the power flooding him too sweet to resist.

He felt Tucker tug at his arm. Heard him mutter words of protest, his tone frantic, but his words indistinct. Then he felt another poke, and—holy fuck—the asshole was inside his head.

Let go.

Doyle did, releasing the whore in an instant, minute scraps of her soul still intact. He rounded on Tucker, his hands to his partner's throat, his blood boiling as he pressed the traitor up against the driver-side window.

"Never," he said, slowly. "You do not fucking get inside my head."

"You were ... destroying her," Tucker said, gasping for air.

"Who the fuck cares?"

"I thought you did."

That got through, and Doyle released Tucker, shooting back against the car door, horrified by what he'd just done. "Tucker, I—"

Tucker held up a hand to stave off the apology. "You together now?"

Doyle took a breath and clenched his fists, fighting, concentrating, until he felt his demon side slip reluctantly beneath the surface. "Yeah," he said, wiping beads of sweat from his brow. "Sure."

"She'll be okay?"

Doyle thought of the strands of soul he'd left her. They'd grow back, sure. But he'd stolen from her. Cheated her. And that left a mark.

"Doyle?" Tucker pressed. "We need to get to Malibu. Search Dragos's house."

"Malibu, then." He glanced out the window to where Sally lay curled up on the sidewalk. "But we make a stop first. Orlando's."

"—Homeland swooped in and took over. It's bullshit, sir." Sara held the phone to her ear as she paced the short distance from one side of her condo to the other as Porter's voicemail listened patiently at the other end of the line. "And I logged into the docket when I got home. They've done the same thing in over a dozen cases in the last year alone. Taking over murder investigations where there is absolutely no basis for Federal jurisdiction, and if we just put up with it—"

A sharp *beeeeeep* interrupted, signaling that the message had cut off, and she cursed. She considered calling the DA back, but she'd already told Porter everything she knew. At this point, she was just venting.

With another soft curse, she tossed her phone onto the bed, then went into the kitchen to pour a glass of wine. It was almost one in the morning, but she was too worked up to sleep, and she knew the wine would help relax her. Some, anyway.

She took it with her as she headed into the bathroom, stripped, then took a quick shower—just long enough to rinse the day off and leech some of the chill out of her bones. Not from the cool night air, but from what she'd seen. Braddock's pale face. The ragged wound on his neck.

And, in her mind, her father with a similar gaping wound.

She closed her eyes, then pressed her forehead against the tiles, letting the waves of sadness and loss wash over her. Her mother had always been distant, but her dad ... well, her dad had been her best friend.

No.

The word rang sharp in her thoughts. She was not going to roll around in grief. Not now.

Instead, she turned off the water, dried off, then slipped on her bathrobe. She stepped out of the tiny steam-filled room and into the main area, taking a sip of her wine as she moved toward the sliding glass door. The rain had started again, and so she kept the door closed then turned off the overhead light so that the only illumination came from the cityscape.

A mist had gathered on her porch, swirling on her balcony. She watched it, mesmerized with the way it seemed to move, not with the wind, but in spite of it. She took the final sip of her wine, then turned to set her glass on the small table by the balcony door. As she did, something flickered in her peripheral vision.

Luke.

She moved closer to the glass, chastising herself as she did. She was on the twenty-fifth floor. Of course, Luke wasn't standing outside. And yet somehow she could feel him. The remnant of an attraction she hadn't expected, but seemed so familiar. As if something lost had been found.

She drew in a breath, then untied the belt and shrugged the robe off her shoulders. It pooled at her feet, leaving her naked in front of the door. This high, there was no one to see her, and yet she felt deliciously exposed. Watched.

Turned on.

She knew she should pick her robe back up, turn away, and ignore whatever erotic fantasy had started to play out in her mind. But the truth was, she didn't want to. Something about Luke had called to her in a way that was both new and familiar. And the disappointment when he'd left had been a visceral thing. Like losing a limb.

She'd lost the thrill of his hands on her earlier tonight, but she could still have the pleasure. The fantasy.

With a soft breath, she closed her eyes, then slid her hands down over her body as she imagined that he was out there, standing on the balcony, craving her. His own body hardening in response as he watched and wanted. The fantasy was intense. Desperately real. And as her hands stroked her breasts—as her palms grazed her sensitive nipples—she gasped, so caught up in the fantasy that her legs could no longer support her.

Unsteady, she moved forward until she reached the door, then pressed her palm against the glass to steady herself. In her mind's eye, she saw him lost in the mist, his eyes fixed on her, his expression rapturous as she slid her free hand down her belly, then lower still to find the slick heat between her legs.

She swallowed a moan, her neck arching back as she teased her clit, imagining his touch. His fingers. His mouth. She wanted him kneeling before her, his hands steadying her hips as his tongue sucked and teased. In her fantasy, he removed one of his hands from her hip, then thrust his fingers hard inside as his tongue continued to tease and torment until her knees buckled. And in the moment that she cried out Luke's name, her body shook, the orgasm that crashed over her sending her tumbling to the ground in a wash of wild, pure ecstasy.

Slowly, Sara opened her eyes, surprised to find that she really was on the floor, her body tingling. She closed her eyes, suddenly self-conscious. A ridiculous emotion since she'd been her only witness. But still, to lose herself like that to a man she'd met only once. A man who wasn't even there.

A man she might never see again.

She pushed the thought away, then climbed to her feet, clutching the robe. She started to put it on, then froze. *Why?* Why should she feel self-conscious in her own apartment? Hell, that had been a better orgasm than she'd had with most of the men she used to drag home, desperately trying to burn off some wild energy she didn't understand.

Own it.

She glanced once more at the balcony. The mist was gone. The moon hung low in the sky, as if skimming the top of the downtown high-rises.

She smiled, then let the robe fall back onto the floor before striding naked to the bed and, hopefully, to a slumber filled with dreams of Luke.

A fine mist swirled lazily twenty floors below Sara's balcony. At almost two in the morning, the deck was empty. Then the mist grew thicker, easing into the shape of a man.

When he was whole, Lucius Dragos sat hard on the raised edge of the hot tub, his constant craving for Sara on overdrive after what he'd just witnessed. And his name on her lips had only intensified that hunger.

Luke. He closed his eyes with the memory, his body tightening with longing.

He had only himself to blame. He should never have started this. Should never have watched her from the shadows all those months ago, and he certainly shouldn't have let her catch sight of him. It wasn't carelessness, though; he was far too good at his job for that. No, Luke's sin had been a combination of greed and hubris. He wanted her, plain and simple. Had craved her for years.

And he was arrogant enough to believe he could have her.

But that wasn't possible. Not now.

Not with what was coming next. And certainly not with what had come before.

Unless...

There was a chance. A thin one, but he had to take it. If it meant he could stay in Los Angeles, it was worth the risk. He took a quick glance around, making absolutely certain there was no human on the deck with him, then drew out his phone to call the one man in all the world who had both the power and—hopefully—the will to help him.

"Lucius." The low timbre of the ancient vampire's voice seemed to vibrate through the phone, the pleasure in his tone undeniable. "Are you in London?"

"I am not. I'm calling as kyne for the repayment of a debt."

"Speak, then. As is your right," Tiberius responded, using the ancient form proper to a request from one of the kyne, a secret brotherhood sworn to do the bidding of their leader in the Alliance, often undertaking missions without official sanction and which would be loudly and strongly denied by every Alliance representative.

"Judge Braddock is dead. Unless I run, I will be arrested, something that will inconvenience you as well as me, since if I am incarcerated or dusted, I will be little help to you."

"You request a pardon."

"I do."

A moment passed, then another, and Luke knew the answer before the vampire leader spoke. "This I cannot grant. The life was not taken in service as kyne."

"No," Luke agreed. "But without the pardon, my usefulness will be limited. And there is also the bond of friendship to consider."

"Luke." The speaker was no longer the great leader, Tiberius, the Alliance representative for the vampires and governor of the Southern California territory, among others. Now, it was Tiber, the friend, and his regret was palpable. "You know I cannot. Not now, with the power struggle between the Therians and the Vampires balancing on a knife-edge." The shapeshifters—particularly the werewolves—were a constant thorn in Tiberius's side, and like little yipping dogs, they kept howling that they weren't treated fairly within the Alliance.

"To do this thing for you could mean sacrificing all that our kind have gained over the last two centuries," Tiberius continued. "Were Braddock's life lost in service to your role as kyne, then I could perhaps make an exception. Otherwise, I am sorry, my friend."

"As am I."

"You will contact me when you can?"

Despite the circumstances, Luke grinned. Tiberius clearly understood that Luke had no intention of being incarcerated or dusted. And, if he could help surreptitiously, he would.

"I will," Luke said. "And thank you."

"Good luck, my friend," Tiberius said, then ended the call.

Luke slipped the phone back into his pocket, forcing himself to ignore his disappointment. Lingering on it would do him no good.

With measured steps, he moved to one of the chaise lounges, then sat, his mind whirring as he sorted out what came next. He'd always known that disappearing for a century or two might become a necessity, and he always kept an escape route open. Now it was time to put the wheels in motion.

When he'd worked through the details in his head, he once again pulled out his phone and dialed, grateful when he heard the deep voice at the other end. "It's time to repay your debt," Luke said. "Let me explain exactly what I need."

Less than an hour later, he had the path laid out, the various tasks assigned to either trusted friends or those eager to no longer be indebted to Lucius Dragos. Soon, it would be time to play his part.

Soon, but not quite yet. There was still one thing to do before he stepped into his role.

Slowly, he laid back against the lounger, his eyes open to the night sky. The lights of downtown Los Angeles had snuffed out the stars, but it didn't matter. He knew each intimately, and he could picture their patterns above him. The constellations grinning down at him, calling him a fool.

They were right, too. He should walk away. Despite the ache in his chest that cried out that Sara was his, he knew that he should leave. To see her tonight would only torture them both.

And yet he knew that he would go to her anyway. How could he not? She was his obsession. His everything. Perhaps it made sense that he should be her tormentor, too.

With his own castigation playing in his head, he crossed the pool deck and entered the fifth floor lobby through the etched glass doors. He picked up the courtesy phone and punched in the number for Sara's unit, then listened through four harsh beeps before he finally heard her soft, sleepy voice on the other end of the line.

"Yes? I mean, hello?"

"I woke you. I'm sorry," he said.

"Luke?"

Something like relief laced her voice, and he smiled. "My errand took longer than planned. But I shouldn't have—"

"Come on up."

He hesitated as the elevator doors slid open. Once again, he told himself to walk away. Instead, he stepped into the car.

The ride to the twenty-fifth floor was swift, and when the doors opened, she was standing in her doorway across the hall, wrapped in the now-familiar bathrobe. He wondered idly if she'd put something on under it. He hoped that she hadn't.

"It's late," he said. "And you surely have to work tomorrow."

"I'm a big shot prosecutor, remember? I think I can go into the office late if I want to."

They shared a smile. "Then you should know that was my last attempt at chivalry. I've wanted you since the moment you walked into that bar tonight."

The corner of her mouth quirked up, and she stepped back, holding the door open for him. "We both know you wanted me long before that."

"And that doesn't scare you?"

"It probably should, but no."

He took her hand, then pulled her toward him as the door swung closed. Gently, he stroked her hair, now hanging in waves around her face. "Why not?"

"I don't know." Her eyes searched his face. "Is it crazy to say you seemed familiar?"

"No. Not crazy at all."

She studied his face, then frowned. "You feel it, too."

He considered the question. He had watched Sara Constantine since she was a child, her sworn protector. Of course she was familiar. And yet...

And yet for a while now he'd felt a sense of loss when he was around her. The feeling that—even though he could see her clearly—she'd been taken from him. A foolish thought, yet he couldn't deny its power, and he tilted his head in acknowledgement. "Yes, Sara. I feel it, too."

"I didn't think I'd see you again. Not really. I'm very glad I was wrong."

"Sara, I—"

"Just kiss me," she said, then didn't bother to wait for him to comply. Instead, she moved forward to press her lips against his. As soft as a whisper at first, then harder. Wilder. A claiming kiss that reflected his own desire. The years of wanting. Of needing. Of waiting for this woman he had first known as an innocent child needing his protection, but who had grown into a woman he admired and desired.

She cupped his head with her hands, as if holding him in place, never willing to let him go, and he moaned against her mouth, his own arms pulling her close until their bodies were one, her heat flowing through him. Her heartbeat pounded like the most enticing of promises, her blood the most alluring of drugs. The urge to take her—to taste her—was overpowering, and he pushed her roughly away, then turned toward the balcony door, afraid that she'd see the truth of what he was in his face.

"Luke?" From behind him, she pressed a hand to his shoulder. "What's wrong?"

"I want you more than I should," he admitted. "And in ways that I shouldn't."

"Oh."

He heard the swish of material as her robe fell to the ground, and it was all he could do not to moan with frustration and longing. Then he felt the press of her body against his back, and it took all his effort not to claim her right then.

"You can have me however you want," she whispered, and that unexpected offer ripped the cry of her name from his lips even as he spun to face her, drawing on all his self-control not to slam her up against the opposite wall and take her right then in every way possible.

She stood straight, her chin lifted and her eyes on his so that he was the first to look away. How could he not, when she was standing there in stunning, naked perfection, her skin both pale and sun-kissed? He reached out, slowly tracing the lines on her upper thighs, then on her arms, as she bit her lower lip in a way designed to drive him crazy.

"Tan lines." She tossed the words out like a shrug. "It's either that or jog naked."

"You jog." It was something he didn't know about her. There was, in fact, so much he didn't know. So much of her life he'd never been able to observe.

"I aspire to jog. Mostly I walk. And only on the weekends when my caseload is light. I like to go to the beach and run in the surf."

"Perhaps you'll walk there with me some evening."

"I'd like that," she said as his fingers traced over the curve of her hip and then up to cup her breast. Her nipple was hard, and he teased it between two fingers, watching the way her areola responded. Her breasts were lovely, full and firm, and as she arched back, her lips parted with pleasure. He forced himself not to think about marking her there. Tasting her. Making her truly his.

"Please," she murmured, the word like an answer to his thoughts. Instead, he eased his fingers down, exploring the texture of her ribs under her skin, feeling the excited, rapid beat of her heart beneath his fingers, then the soft texture of her abdomen as he worked his way slowly down, relishing the way her breaths came faster and faster, culminating in a little moan when he reached her pubis. She was waxed, her skin slick, but he didn't move his hand any lower, even as she whimpered in his arms.

"Luke."

He closed his eyes, fighting the urge to slide his fingers over her slick heat, then toss her onto the bed and lose himself in her. But he couldn't. She deserved the truth, though not all of it. Perhaps he was a coward, but he feared that she'd despise him if she understood what he was. What he'd done.

But she should know the rest of it. The fact that they could only have this night. He had to leave this place, and by the time it would be safe for him to return, she would be only a memory. But even if he stayed—even if he were not a wanted man, they could have no future. Not really. And yet he knew that he would live on this night forever.

And what will she do?

He closed his eyes. Yes, she deserved the truth. Or as much of the truth as he could tell her.

"Luke?"

"I must leave before morning," he said, wishing he could lose himself in the stormy sea of her eyes. "I don't know when I will be back." He cupped her cheek. "I may never come back."

"You're married." Her voice was dull. Flat.

"No. For work. There is no one else."

"Then why don't you know when—?"

He shook his head. "I will stay or I will go, and I cannot tell you more. But the choice is yours, Sara. Shall we share one night? Or shall I go right now?"

His body went tense, and it seemed as though the sum of every moment of happiness he had ever experienced hung in the balance of her decision.

She said nothing. Instead she moved closer, pressing her body against his, her head tilted back as her lips brushed his in a sweet kiss that could have been either in farewell or welcome. When she pulled back, she met his eyes again, and her single word sent the world tumbling beneath his feet. "Stay."

Despite being surrounded by businesses that reflected a booming economy, Orlando's exterior was dull and drab, with peeling paint and a neon sign that flickered, showing nothing more than *Or do* instead of the establishment's actual name.

Despite its shabby appearance, the parking lot was full, and Doyle knew that the inside would be packed. He shot a look toward his partner. "Ready?"

"The place gives me the wiggins. No offense, man, and I get why we're bringing her here. But soul-trading...." He trailed off with a shudder.

"You think it's my happy place?" Doyle snapped, then wished he could call back his words when he saw the regret on his partner's face.

"Shit, Doyle. You know I didn't mean that."

"Yeah. Sure," Doyle said. "I know." Except really, he knew no such thing. Why shouldn't Tucker despise a place like this? Doyle did. Hated that he had to take souls to survive. That the demon inside needed them to live, to hell with what the human half wanted. To be a man and not a monster. But it was the souls that gave him the strength to battle the demon back down. That fueled the gifts that made him one hell of an asset to the PEC.

And how was that for the universe throwing some fucking hideous irony his way?

"Gotta be done," he said, opening the passenger-side door and causing the light to illuminate the Catalina's interior. He swiveled, looking into the backseat where Sally was spread out, her eyes moving in panicked motion under her closed lids. "Wait here if you want," he added to Tucker as he slid out of the car.

"Screw that," Tucker said, and got out as well.

It was easiest to just carry the woman, and Tucker took that on, as if to reinforce the apology. They entered together, moving from the shabby exterior to the clean, contemporary decor of the bar. He started toward the stairs, knowing that was where Lissa kept her office, but was stopped by Marco, the head of security for the soul-trading bar.

Marco sniffed, then his eyes narrowed. "A human? And her soul in tatters? What the hell are you doing bringing her here?"

"We need Lissa's help."

"She's not running a charity or a hospital."

He took a step forward, his temper rising. "Dammit, Marco. As often as I come here? As often as I look the other way?" He noticed the slight widening of the security guard's eyes. "I'm just saying that I'd think you'd cut me some slack. At least let me talk to her." He spread his hands and grinned. "I mean, come on. I'm practically family."

In front of him, Marco looked ready to spit nails. But Doyle couldn't tell if he'd convinced the gatekeeper or not.

It didn't matter. He recognized the voice that spoke from behind him. "It's okay, Marco."

He turned to see Lissa, standing calm and poised as always, her pale blue eyes studying him. Without a word, she gave him her back, then started heading for her office, her blood red gown sweeping the floor as she moved past the bar and the dancers toward the back rooms that were so damn familiar to him. She didn't go that far, instead climbing the stairs that hugged the north wall.

They followed, Tucker silent behind Doyle, and Sally's breath coming in ragged gasps in his arms.

Lissa opened the door to her office, her arm sweeping in invitation. "Put her on the couch." She indicated a silk sofa that complemented two armchairs as well as an ornate wooden desk.

She settled into one of the chairs, crossed her legs, and waited.

"I took too much," Doyle said, hating the words, but not willing to dance around the topic. He nodded toward Sally, now half-sprawled on the sofa between him and Tucker.

As he spoke, her eyes fluttered open, then narrowed when she saw Lissa. "The fuck are you?" The words were barely a whisper.

"I'm Lissa." Her voice was soft, as gentle as a breeze.

"Oh. Okay, then." The eyes fluttered shut again.

"I didn't mean to," Doyle said, forcing his voice to stay steady. "I was working a case, and—"

She held up a hand. "You don't have to tell me. But I do want to know why you brought her here. She's human. There's nothing I can do for her, and we both know her soul will grow back."

"Maybe. But fast enough?" Doyle asked. "She's a streetwalker."

He saw understanding in Lissa's face. Humans abused their souls all the time. Sally had most likely burned through most of hers even before Doyle came along.

"What's her name?"

"Sally," Doyle said as Tucker leaned forward, then added, "Can't you help her along?"

Lissa shook her head. "There's nothing I can do for a human except take a soul. Only she can restore it." She glanced toward Sally, her eyes full of compassion. "But I can give her a job. Keep her here. Nurture her until she is whole again. And then she can decide if she wants to stay or go."

Doyle forced himself not to show the extent of his relief. "You're a good woman, Lissa."

She arched a brow. "Am I?"

"In my book you are. You ever need anything, you know you can count on me."

A smile touched the corner of her mouth. "And you know I never count on anyone but myself."

CHAPTER

SEVEN

Stay.

Her voice hung between them in the room, her head tilted back though her body was pressed hard against his.

"Sara, are you—"

She pressed a finger to his lips. "If tonight is all we have, we don't have a moment to spare." Heat flickered in his eyes, then he bent to kiss her. Not hard and claiming as he'd done in the bar. This kiss was sweet. The soft brush of his lips over hers, so tender that it made her heart ache. She didn't understand it—the connection she felt with this man. Simple lust, probably. The pent-up need from having gone so long without a man in her bed.

Except she knew better. There was something there. Something intangible. It was right there, as close as a memory and just as fleeting. If she could only stop—just breathe—then maybe she could catch it. But how could she when he was trailing kisses down her neck, the rough palms of his hands sliding down the sides of her body?

He stopped at her hips, his hands tightening to hold her steady as his tongue teased the little hollow between her neck and her shoulder, the sensation as erotic as if his tongue were on her clit. More, she thought, as a wild tremor went through her, and she moaned, wanting him to never stop touching her like that even as she wanted to feel him inside her.

That incredible mouth of his moved lower still, his lips trailing over the swell of her breast as he brushed his palm softly over her other nipple, sending fingers of fire shooting through her. Making her even more wet. Making her crazy.

He pushed her back until she fell onto the bed, and she squirmed, trapped between the mattress and this man, and all she wanted was him. His hands, his mouth. Everything.

"More."

She saw the heat flare in his eyes before his mouth brushed over hers. She felt her body tremble, and she stifled the little moan of pleasure that bubbled up when his lips grazed her cheek, her ear, her hair.

"Sara," he whispered, and pulled her close, his hands in her hair, his body hard against her.

Ready, so ready.

"Luke," she managed. "Please."

And then his mouth was on hers, and she lost herself in the kiss, her pulse tripping as his hands explored her body and his mouth moved to dance kisses along her neck even as he murmured soft words that seemed to shoot straight through her, making her warm and wet and ready.

"Sara," he murmured. "By the gods, Sara."

She melted beneath his words, her mind knowing only a desperate, urgent desire. She thrust her hands into the back pocket of his jeans and urged him closer even as his kisses turned so wild it seemed as if he wanted to consume her.

So help her, she wanted him to.

He grabbed her wrists, holding them above her head as his mouth dipped to her breast. His tongue teased her nipple before pulling away, the sensation of cool air on damp flesh intensely erotic, and she writhed with need, silently begging him to touch her, to take her all the way over.

He needed very little encouragement, and he slid down her body, making her gasp as he pressed his hands to the inside of her thighs, the pads of his thumbs teasing her mercilessly. His mouth soon joined in the torment, the magic of his tongue making her breathless and desperate.

She buried her fingers in his hair as her body writhed with pleasure, but still seeking more. "Luke," she murmured, wanting to feel him on top of her, inside her. Wanting to feel his lips, his tongue. Wanting to taste him and tease him. "Luke, please."

She eased him up, then took his mouth hungrily in hers. She

hooked one leg around his waist, locking him in place, wanting him, all of him.

"Please," she whispered, sliding a hand between them to struggle with his fly. Beneath her hand, his erection strained, and he growled low in his throat, the desire she heard making her crazy.

"Sara," he whispered, his voice raw, as full of need as she felt. He moved off her long enough to strip, then returned, his eyes full of question.

"Yes," she whispered. "Oh, please, yes."

He kissed her then, wild and deep, his cock finding her core even as his mouth ravaged her. She opened her legs wider, rising up for him, needing to feel him inside her, craving the connection. She gasped as he filled her, then rocked with him, their bodies moving in a glorious dance as they rose higher and higher until, finally, she seemed to burst into starlight in his arms before settling back, contented, on the mattress, warm and safe within his arms.

"Sara," he whispered as she snuggled close, wishing they could stay like that forever.

"I must go," he said minutes later, when sleep had almost claimed her.

"Can't you wait until morning? It's not even four yet."

"I cannot." He brushed his thumb over the line of her jaw. "I desperately wish that I could."

She forced a smile, hoping he couldn't see her desperate sadness. She'd known that he would leave; it wasn't fair now for her to make him feel guilty. "I understand."

He shook his head. "No, you don't. But I appreciate that you trust me." He bent forward, then pressed a kiss to her forehead. "There is no one else, Sara, and if I could stay with you, I would." He pressed his forehead to hers, and when he spoke, she could hear the pain in his voice. "I will never forget you."

She wanted to beg him to stay, but she knew that he wouldn't. Whatever obligation called him away, he would honor it. She didn't know him well, but she was certain of that much. Luke was a man who kept his promises.

"I don't have your number," she said as he slid from the bed and began to dress. "I don't even have your last name."

"When I return," he said.

"You mean that you might not return."

He tilted his head in acknowledgement, and a shiver of fear ran through her.

"You know what I do, Luke. I have connections. Is there something I can help you with?" She'd acknowledged the possibility that he was in trouble when he first told her that he would leave before morning. She'd pushed it aside because she'd wanted this, and all the rules and honor and justice had faded under the sweet spell of lust.

Now, though…

Now, she studied him, watching his face as she pressed the point. "Are you in some sort of trouble?"

The corner of his mouth twitched, and he reached for her hand. "I swear to you, Sara, there is nothing about my obligation or your job that intersect. But I must go. And I cannot tell you why."

"Will not, you mean," she countered, and was impressed when he nodded. "All right, then." She let her shoulders rise and fall. It wasn't as if she had the right to press. He'd been honest from the beginning, and she had no claim on his personal business. "Will you do me one favor, then?"

"If I can."

She slipped out of bed, still naked, then moved to stand in front of him. "I'm going to go take a shower and get ready for work." He glanced at the clock, and she laughed. "Why not? I'm already up. Will you please go while I'm getting ready? And whatever you do, don't say goodbye."

He inclined his head. "As you wish."

She drew a breath, telling herself that was for the best, then turned toward the bathroom. She paused at the door and allowed herself one backward glance. Then she stepped inside, closed the door, and sank to the floor as she hugged her knees to her chest.

When she heard the subtle click of the front door closing softly, she forced herself to her feet, turned on the shower, and told herself that it was time to begin her day.

"Nice digs," Tucker said as Doyle parked the Catalina in front of Luke's sprawling Malibu house. It boasted three stories, backed up to the beach, and took up at least half a city block.

"We're not here for *Architectural Digest*. If you're gonna start waxing poetic about his damn kitchen, you can wait in the car."

"That was one time, and I was in the middle of a remodel,"

Tucker said as he slid out of the car. "And like it or not, that Viking range and oven was sweet. Too damn much on my salary, but sweet."

"Spare me," Doyle said as he started up the sidewalk that led through a manicured front lawn to the entrance. Tucker caught up with him, and Doyle used the knocker to rap hard on the carved wooden door. A moment later the door opened, and Doyle found himself staring at a short, round man who wore his butler's uniform with infinite dignity.

"I'm sorry, Ryan," Melton sniffed. "He's not home."

"That's Agent Doyle to you, and his absence would break my heart if this were a social call. Since it's not, I'll just ask you to step aside."

"I'm not sure—"

Doyle spread his arms and grinned. "Melton, man. It's me."

"That, *Agent*, is the problem." But he didn't press another argument. Just stepped aside and ushered them in.

"Seriously nice digs," Tucker said, then held up his hands as Doyle shot him a hard glare. "Just saying."

"It's a house. There's marble and glass and art and furniture."

"You really need to broaden your perspective," Tucker said, earning him another glare.

As Melton frowned, Doyle headed up the stairs, his partner right behind him.

The floor had a study and a bedroom. The study was locked, and Doyle didn't bother asking Melton to let him in. Not only would the butler surely decline until Doyle had a warrant, but Doyle knew too well that Luke wouldn't leave anything obviously incriminating lying around. This trip wasn't about gathering evidence so much as it was about reacquainting himself with an old friend.

Tucker entered first and Doyle followed into the sparsely furnished bedroom that had only a huge bed, a dresser, a fireplace, and a wall of bookshelves.

"There's never a coffin," Tucker quipped. "What happened to tradition?"

Doyle ignored him, heading instead to the ledge above the fireplace where several antique photos were prominently displayed. His gaze roamed over them before stopping at one that made his stomach clench. Four men standing in front of a copse of trees on a brightly sunny afternoon in the mid-1800s. Not that the photograph said as much, but Doyle remembered the day. A day when the four men in the photo had been the closest of friends.

Doyle, Luke, Nicholas, and Sergius.

That, however, was a long time ago.

"That you?" Tucker said, looking over his shoulder as Doyle realized he had picked up the photo, and now his finger was tracing over the glass.

"It's nothing," he said, hurrying out of the room. "Come on." He started up the stairs to the next level. A few moments later, Tucker caught up with him.

"You never talk about that."

"And if you think I'm going to start now, you don't have the brains to be my partner."

Silence hung heavy, then Tucker pushed open one of the doors. A guest room, apparently, as it looked as if no one had lived in it for years. They tried the other door, and Doyle let out a low whistle. "Here we go."

"It's a little girl's room," Tucker said, looking around at the pink bedspread topped with antique rag dolls.

"His ward. Tasha. And she's not young. Body stopped aging at seventeen, but the girl's got centuries on you."

Tucker picked up one of the dolls as he nodded. "Right. I remember hearing about that. He violated the Concordat when he turned her. She wasn't in her right mind after some head injury on her farm or something."

"He knew he shouldn't, and he turned her anyway. Almost got them both staked. Shoulda been, but fucking Tiberius granted them a pardon, and the damn PEC didn't challenge it."

"Was that what—I mean, you guys used to be friends. Was it because of Tasha that you're not?"

Doyle shook his head. "No. That was later. I knew the girl. He watched over her. Treated her like a daughter. Kept her out of trouble and helped her keep the darkness down. But I knew from the beginning he'd never manage to keep her muzzled forever. There's a reason children and the unstable aren't turned. Fucking vamps are dangerous enough as it is. Add another layer of instability to the mix, and that is some seriously bad shit."

"You think he took her on the run with him?"

"I do." Lucius Dragos might be a prick, but he'd sworn to protect Tasha. And if Doyle knew the vamp—and he did—he also knew that Luke wouldn't break his word.

"They've surely skipped town already."

"Maybe. Maybe not. A Seer's working off the signet ring. With luck we'll have a location soon."

"Dragos must know by now he lost it. He'll know we'd use a Seer. And he'd get the hell out of town at least until the aura fades."

"Maybe," Doyle repeated, then slowly smiled. "Or maybe he's playing a much longer game."

"What are you talking about?"

Doyle didn't answer. Instead, he met his partner's eyes and grinned.

EIGHT

Luke cast his gaze around the cavernous room, lit only by the glow of the monitors that made up the security feed. Right now, all was clear. That was good. But the clock was ticking down. Doyle would learn where he was soon enough, and there were still things to be done.

Despite the need for action, he didn't yet reach for the telephone. Instead, he closed his eyes and leaned back in the leather-upholstered desk chair, his thoughts not on his plans but on Sara.

Sara.

Were it not for her, he would have no qualms about what he was about to do. He knew how to disappear, and he knew better than most of his kind how much changed over the course of the centuries. He could wait, and when he emerged from hiding, no one would care about the events of tonight. He would be free to come and go as he pleased.

And Tasha would still be alive and safe.

Sara, however, would be dead and buried.

The thought burned inside him. For the last twenty years, she had been his constant. First as her sworn protector, later as a woman whose vibrancy and passion aroused his senses even as much as the way the moonlight played across the hollows of her cheeks or the honey-gold of her hair.

He knew her grief, her dedication, her resolve. And, yes, he loved her. But before tonight, he never thought he could have her. Now, to have touched her on the very night that he must run...

Well, Fate truly was the cruelest bitch of all.

Stop.

He closed his eyes, forcing himself to heed his own order. Sara was not his problem at the moment. Escape was. And it was time he got down to business.

With renewed purpose, he rolled to the closest bank of monitors, the ones that showed various angles of the interior of the Security Mart, a home and business security retail establishment that filled the space above him. A business owned by a holding company that was owned by a corporation that—beneath layers and layers of business filings and legal documents, was owned by Luke himself.

He'd realized long ago the value of owning both real estate and retail establishments through corporations that he ultimately controlled. Stock as well. It made the use of accumulated wealth after a span of time longer than the average mortal life that much easier.

As far as Luke was concerned, any creature alive for more than a century who didn't have an overflowing portfolio was either doing something wrong or was a fool. Probably both.

He used the joystick to move the camera, once more carefully inspecting the exterior view as the side street off Hollywood Boulevard began to glow in the early morning light. Mentally, he went through his checklist. He'd been busy in the last hours before dawn, and the property was ready.

He put on the headset. There was one last thing to do.

"Tell me she's safe," he demanded, the moment his oldest friend, Sergius, answered the video call.

"Please," Serge said, his blond hair standing on end, as if he'd run his fingers through it. "It's me."

"And that's why I ask," Luke said, equal parts joking and serious.

"She is safe. The journey was fast, though exhausting. Traveling incorporeal for two—that was a hell of a thing."

Luke nodded. Mist, the incorporeal state available to vampires with more than a few centuries behind them, allowed for the swiftest of travel. Tasha, however, didn't have the ability, despite her age. She'd piggybacked on his power more than once, and Luke knew how draining the travel could be.

"Where is she now?"

"Settled in the spare bedroom. Where are you?"

"Better you don't know."

Serge nodded. "But you will be here tomorrow? I will do whatever you ask as my brother and kyne, but I cannot take on a ward." His voice turned serious. "Lucius, you know that."

"I do. And I owe you a debt for what you have already done for me and for Tasha."

"You don't. Never."

Luke nodded. Between the two of them, there were no debts, only the tight bond of friendship.

"So tomorrow?"

"That depends on Ryan Doyle and his pretty boy of a partner."

"Doyle's sharp," Serge said. "You need to be ready."

"I am."

"And you're sure? You could leave now, be here in two hours."

"I cannot."

"Why the hell not? You're going under anyway."

"Because nothing says guilt more loudly than running. And I want them to be certain it was me who took that son-of-a-bitch out."

"Luke…"

"Trust me. I'll find someplace safe, and I'll send for her."

Serge shook his head. "Don't underestimate him, Luke. We both know Doyle. He'll put everything he has into catching you. One slip, and—"

"I won't slip."

"Dammit, Luke, you have to come for her."

Luke laughed. "And here I thought you were concerned for my well-being."

"Fuck your well-being," Serge said, but with a grin. "Right now we're talking about me."

Luke leaned back in the chair, amused. It had been far too long since he and Serge had been in the same city. "Are we?"

"No." Serge's voice took on a harsh edge, and a tendril of worry twisted in Luke's gut. He loved Serge like a brother, and he was the only one Luke could trust to keep Tasha safe until Luke could get there. As an attorney, Nicholas wasn't an option. He was loyal, yes. But he'd also taken oaths. And Luke wasn't inclined to have his friend break them.

Serge had been his only option, and Luke hoped it had been a safe one. With Serge, these things often weren't certain.

"I mean it," Serge said. "Don't underestimate Doyle."

"I don't."

"If he puts you in a cage, you know he won't stop until he's found her. And you know what will happen then."

"Then I am fortunate to have you at her side."

Serge's jaw tensed, but he nodded. "Yes," he said. "She will be safe with me."

For a moment, silence hung between them. Luke was about to ask him to call Tasha to the phone, but Serge spoke first. "What about Sara?"

Luke tensed. "What about her?"

"Do you expect me to believe you're just going to walk away from her, too? I know you too well."

"I should," Luke admitted. "I had no right to touch her, no right to even want her. Not after what I've done."

"We've all done things, my friend. We all battle it down. For some, the battle is harder."

Luke nodded, knowing perfectly well the internal battle that Serge waged every second of every day.

"One night," Luke confessed. "I craved her in a way I've craved no other, and I succumbed to the call of pleasure."

"And now?"

"Now I regret that I can have her no more. Serge, there are no words for the way she touches my heart. It is more than the years I've watched her. There was something tangible between us. Even the feel of her skin beneath my fingers felt familiar, and I can only assume I am feeling Fate's punishment. Because though we shared one perfect night, that is all we can claim from the universe. And certainly more than I deserve."

Once again, the realization that he was leaving her forever swept over him, and he closed his eyes only to be lost in the memory of the night when he first saw her, so young and so innocent. So scared, and so very alone.

He deserved to suffer the pain of leaving. She did not. It would have been kinder to stay away. But he was weak where she was concerned, and he always had been. Even now, he wanted to dial her number, if only to hear her voice before he ended the call. But he couldn't. Luke knew the extent of his own strength, and he also knew that even a whisper from her now would break his resolve.

"There is something I must tell you," Serge said. "You made me swear not to—not ever. But now I think that is an oath I should break. I will leave you to judge that, and to take whatever payment you wish if my decision is wrong."

Luke frowned, struck by the unfamiliar formality in his friend's voice. "Go ahead."

"Three years ago, you were intent on protecting Sara. She was going to meet a witness she believed would shed light on her father's death, and we caught up with her. Your instincts were right. It was a vampire attack, and we were able to save her. We followed her back to her house. I stayed hidden in case there was trouble. But, Luke, you went inside. You took her to bed."

Luke shook his head. "No. Serge, this never happened."

"That morning you were attacked. Young vampires, still able to walk in the sun. I was there. I'd been hiding in the garage, but I entered the fight. I heard what they called her—Abomination."

"Abomination?"

"To this day, I don't know why. But the connection between you and Sara was palpable. If it was not love, I don't know what is. It made my heart ache to think that the bonds of love could tighten so fast, and I confess I was jealous. I am well acquainted with lust. But love has never touched me."

"Serge, I—"

"Let me finish. One night, you were with her when the Shades came."

"Shades?" The creatures were few, thankfully, as they survived entirely on darkness. To task a Shade was no small matter.

"They bound you in hematite, and they took Sara's memories."

Icy fear crept over Luke. Fear, and the first, faint whispers of memory.

"And mine? They took mine next?" He knew they must have, as he remembered none of this. At least not until moments ago as Serge told the story.

"No. They let you keep them."

Luke shook his head, frowning. "But—"

"You summoned the Shades yourself a year later. You were miserable. You wouldn't feed. You were weak. Lovesick," he said. "Who knew a vampire could feel emotions so deeply?"

Luke knew. And despite his words, Luke knew that Serge did as well.

"I had them take my memories." He closed his eyes, flashes of that year coming back to him. The fight behind a coffee shop, saving Sara from a vampire. The two of them in her bed. The young vampires attacking in her kitchen. "I remember. By the gods, I remember."

Serge's brows rose. "Interesting."

"You recounting this to me must break the spell."

"Perhaps." Serge tilted his head, considering. "There are some who believe the Shades' gifts don't fully work on a vampire. It is an interesting question to ponder. But that's for another day. My only point was to say that this connection you feel to Sara Constantine is real. You once called it love. Perhaps it is. Or perhaps love is nothing more than an illusion, and you two are walking a circular path, lost in the heat of a mirage."

Luke took a few moments to gather himself as Serge went to get Tasha from the room he'd made ready for her. She slid into view, as graceful as a dancer crossing a stage.

"Are you coming," she asked, facing the camera with a pout, her auburn curls framing her lovely round face that still retained the air of childlike innocence.

"Not yet," he told her. "Serge will watch over you until I get there. Do you understand?"

"But you can come, too. Fast. Fast as the wind. Faster, even."

"I can't. Not right now. I need to take care of things first."

"I can be the wind. Let me come home to you."

"You know you're not able. And even if you could, it wouldn't be safe for you here. Stay with Serge. I'll be there soon."

She swayed, as if in time to music that was only in her head. "They say the neon lights are bright on Broadway," she sang. "But there's no magic, Lucius. I wanted there to be magic."

"You're in San Francisco, Tash. And I'll be there soon to get you, and we'll move on." He watched her expression turn into a pout, but she nodded. "Yes, Lucius."

"I need to go, but I'll be there soon."

She nodded. "Where did you go?"

"I need to go now," he clarified. "I need to end the call."

"Before," she said. "Where did you go before?"

He frowned, not understanding.

"Last night," she said. "I saw you. You were with him, and then you weren't. I thought you would come home, but you didn't. Was it her? The one you've watched for so long?"

A chill ran up his spine, as disturbing as the touch of a Shade. "You've been spying on me?"

"Why do you watch her?"

"You didn't answer my question."

Her lower lip protruded. "You promised to protect me always."

He sat back, his shoulders relaxing as he realized that she wanted only reassurance. "I will. I am. That's why I sent you with Serge. But I'll be there soon."

"What if they come to take me away? To hurt me?"

He stiffened. If they found her, they would do exactly that. "They won't."

"Then why did I have to leave?"

He laughed. "I'll see you soon. Just put Serge back on, okay?"

She nodded, her face sliding out of frame as she passed the phone. "Tomorrow," Serge said, as Tasha began to twirl around the apartment behind Serge, the skirt of her nightgown flaring as she moved in and out of the frame. "Get your ass here tomorrow."

By the time Manny arrived in their small, shared office, Sara had already cleared her desk of all the leftover paperwork from the Stemmons trial and had pulled out the private file she kept locked in her desk. The one she only allowed herself to study in that short space of time between closing one case and returning her focus to the never-ending list of others.

The copy of her father's cold case file that she'd requested after her first year in the DA's office.

The self-imposed limits on her time were necessary; it would be too easy to slide into obsession, going down every rabbit trail over and over again, searching for that elusive clue she must have missed. She opened it, then slowly flipped through the pages. She knew them all so well, she could have recited every word or recreated every photograph. It didn't matter. Sometime, someday, she would see something she'd missed.

"Still riding high?" Manny said, slouching into the chair behind his desk with his sunglasses on.

She raised a brow, amused. "I'm just settling in for work. Looks like you're the one who spent the night partying."

"Just with a bottle," he said, blinking as he tugged off the glasses, tossed them carelessly on his desk, then ran his fingers through his coal black hair. "From what I could see, your celebration was a bit more ... active."

She drew in a tight breath, then focused on the documents in front of her. Or tried to. *Shit*. She looked back up. "You have something to get off your chest?"

"No. Sorry, no. Or, actually, fuck it. Yeah. Yeah, I do. I'm just wondering why you prefer strangers to what's right in front of you."

She shook her head, anger rising. "Sharing an office doesn't make you my shrink, and it sure as hell doesn't give you the right to judge me."

He lifted his hands as if in surrender. "I'm not. But shit, Sara, come on. You think I don't see it? You broke up with Dan. You turned me down—"

"We *work* together."

"—and then you get all hot and heavy with some stranger. I mean, hell, it wasn't like you were playing tic-tac-toe on the wall by the restrooms, right?"

"Don't go there, Manny. Do not even think of going there."

"Why? You know it's true. I care about you, Sara. Really care. As a friend even if there's never any more. You know that. And because I do, I hate watching you do this to yourself."

She started to interrupt, but he was on a roll. "You chase danger. Probably because you found your father's body. A violent crime, and you were just a kid, so of course it's all twisted up inside you. But now you seek it out. You lobby to work on cases with the worst kinds of perps. And for a while there, you were going home with strangers. What? You didn't think I noticed?"

"I don't do that anymore."

"No," he agreed. "It's been awhile. But I'll bet you dollars to donuts you hooked up with that guy after he left."

She felt her cheeks burn, and not just from her fury. "There is no way in hell I'm justifying myself to you. And you have no right—"

"Yeah. I do. Because we're friends. And because I understand the why. You take risks. Face danger. And every time you walk away without dying, it's a big fuck you to whoever killed your father."

Infuriated by his words—and by the truth buried in them—she shoved away from her desk and stood. "Fuck you, Manny. An undergrad degree in psych doesn't give you the right to—*fuck it.*"

She grabbed her tote and spun toward the door.

"Shit, I'm sorry. Sara, please."

She paused in the doorway, her back to him.

"Where are you going?"

She didn't have a clue. What she wanted was Luke, but she wasn't about to admit that to herself or Manny. "Coffee. For some reason, I've developed a headache. And I want it gone before my meeting with Porter."

"Aw, hell. Sara, you know I'm an asshole."

"Yeah, you are." She hesitated, then looked back at him. "But it doesn't mean you're wrong."

She flashed him an apologetic smile, then headed out. Now that she'd said it, grabbing a latte from the outdoor kiosk sounded like one hell of a good idea.

She made it almost to the building's main entrance when she heard her name. She paused, scouring the area, then found Petra hurrying toward her, her brother Kiril keeping pace beside her.

"Slumming at the courthouse?"

"Research in the clerk's office." Petra made a face. She much preferred fieldwork.

"Hey, Kir," Sara said, nodding toward the Goliath of a man who, Sara assumed, played football in high school. If he hadn't, his alma mater had seriously missed out. A private investigator and Petra's boss, Kir had always seemed like more of a bodyguard, having taken over the head-of-household role after their parents' deaths.

"You got a sec?" Petra asked, then edged Sara to the side and away from Kiril before Sara could answer. "Well? Did you meet up later?"

Sara only grinned. "A lady doesn't kiss and tell."

"I knew it. Tell me everything."

"Everything would take longer than we have. I need a coffee, then I'm supposed to meet Porter. He shot me an email this morning."

"But you like him?"

"Porter?"

Petra's brows came together above her nose. "Do not even pretend not to understand me."

Sara felt the smile on her lips as she said, "Yeah. I really do."

"Name?"

"Luke."

Petra twirled her hand in a *gimme more* motion, but Sara just shrugged. "You're shitting me. You didn't get his last name?"

"Sorry."

"Seriously? You're a prosecutor. You didn't think to run a background check?"

"Hello? Where was the caution when you were shoving me in his direction? Besides," she added with a wicked grin. "I like to live dangerously."

"That's a figure of speech, not an actual life plan."

"And again I point out that you were my number one enabler."

One of the courtroom doors opened and a cluster of attorneys swarmed out. Petra edged Sara away from the flood. "Vicarious living. I need details. And do you want me to dust your place for prints? I'll run him for free."

"Petra! Chill."

"What? It's important to be thorough."

"God help the next guy you go out with."

"First."

"What?"

"First guy," Petra said, looking more at her feet than at Sara.

"No way. You went on dates when we were working at Legal Aid."

"Technically, I pretended to go on dates. It's just ... you know. With my condition. Well, he'd have to be a special guy to put up with that."

Sara's heart actually broke a little. "Pet...."

"Don't you dare feel sorry for me. Just tell me when you're seeing him again, and I'll live vicariously."

"I'm not. He's leaving town," she rushed to add, before Petra could give her the same lecture that Manny had been warming up to. "Work."

"You believe him?"

"I do," Sara said, surprised by her own certainty. "He left me flowers," she added, as if that somehow underscored his sincerity. It didn't, of course, but the bundle of tulips she'd found on the doormat when she'd left for work that morning had considerably brightened her day. She'd never been given flowers before, hadn't even realized there was a hole in her heart until his gift had filled it.

There was no note, but it didn't matter. Of course she knew that Luke had left them. They'd marked each other. Gotten in each other's heads.

And, despite what he'd said, she was certain she'd see him again. For the first time in a long time, she wanted a second date. And a third, and a fourth. With luck, that would happen.

Now, she slipped her right hand into her blazer pocket, her fingers finding the red ribbon coiled there. It wasn't enough—not nearly—but it was all she had, and she let the memory of last night roll over her. He'd moved her. And damned if she hadn't wanted to be moved.

"Petra!" From where he was leaning against the wall, Kiril raised a hand, pulling Sara from her thoughts.

"Gotta book," Petra said. "Call me."

"Will do." She glanced at her watch. "Shit. I have to go, too. With a quick wave, they took off in opposite directions, Sara only slowing when she was within two doors of Porter's office. She paused, made certain she wasn't gasping, then casually entered the antechamber.

"Oh, good, Sara," his assistant said. "He just finished a call. Head on in."

She found him sitting behind his desk frowning at a pile of briefs, but as soon as she sat, his attention turned to her. "So how are you feeling today? Still flying high?"

"A bit," she admitted. "Right now, I'm irritated with Division 6 grabbing our cases. I'm sorry if my voicemail was a rant, sir, but I just don't understand how they're claiming jurisdiction when—"

"Stemmons is being transferred to San Quentin tomorrow. He's not appealing."

"Oh." Sara sat back. "Why on earth not?"

"Maybe your case was too tight."

Sara smirked.

"It was tight," Porter said. "And it got you noticed."

"Noticed?"

"By Division 6," he said, clearly fighting a smile. "You have to love the irony."

She shook her head, not quite sure she heard him right. "Division 6? What does that have to do with me?"

He stood. "Let's take a walk."

A few moments later, they were waiting by the elevator and Sara was goggling at her boss. "They're *recruiting* me? Why?"

"You should be flattered. They only recruit the best."

"Yeah? Well, they're going to have to impress the hell out of me. Their agents are assholes, and they're edging in on our cases."

"Don't judge too swiftly." He shot her a sideways look, something like amusement in his eyes. "I think you might be intrigued."

She said nothing as she followed him into the elevator. He used a key to open what looked like a utility panel, but turned out to be access to a series of sub-basements. He hit the button for sub-level ten.

"I thought Homeland was based on the sixth floor."

"Not exactly."

She frowned. "What does that mean?"

"It means you're about to get an education. I'm sorry you're getting tossed in like this. As the liaison to Division 6, I should have given you a proper orientation."

"Why didn't you?"

"Leviathan wants you expedited."

"Who?"

"Nikko Leviathan. The director here," Porter continued, when Sara only shook her head, entirely clueless.

"Okay, but why?"

Porter shot her a grin. "He wants you on the Braddock case," he said as the elevator slid to a stop. "Get ready. You're about to go down the rabbit hole."

The doors slid open, and Sara took an involuntary step back, not able to believe what she saw, but also unable to deny her own eyes.

Outside the elevator lay a whole new world. A world where a wolf slunk across a reception area, becoming human by the time it reached the far side. A hulk of a man with pale orange skin and cloven feet stood at a granite counter calmly filling out a form. And the woman behind the counter had blood red eyes and some sort of mist swirling around her.

There were humans, too. At least they looked like humans. But they really weren't the ones drawing her attention.

"A little overwhelming the first time, isn't it?"

Hell yes. Her heart was pounding so loud she could barely hear herself think, and her palms had started to sweat. The rabbit hole, he'd said? Try a wormhole to hell.

She looked at Porter, calling on every ounce of self-control to keep her voice from shaking. To keep from revealing how much her world had just tilted. "This is for real?"

"You okay?"

She forced a bright and perky smile. "Absolutely." And then, just to prove the point, she stepped out of the elevator and took a deep breath. Since nobody with fangs rushed to assault her, she took another tentative step, then looked around.

And the truth was that despite the rather bizarre appearance of some of the beings occupying the space, the room had a familiar feel. The hustle and bustle of the criminal justice system at work. "This is a reception area?" she asked.

"You got it, but it's appointment-only or under escort. There's no public access. That's on the sixth floor for humans and creatures that pass as human. Or the other creatures capable of hiding their true form with a glamour. They're escorted down by staff. Creatures that would stand out are brought in through an entrance off the parking structure. One of the reserved levels.

He shot her a wry smile. "As you might imagine, a number of the creatures who pass through this office would cause a bit of a stir if they marched through the building's main lobby."

"Yeah. I guess they would."

"Bottom line is that no one comes past reception without an escort." He studied her face. "You're really okay?"

She nodded slowly, letting this new reality sink in. *It was real.* The creatures that had fascinated her father. The stories that she'd analyzed in college. It was all real. All hidden in plain sight. "Yeah," she said, feeling more and more like Alice with each passing moment. And, oh, how she longed to explore Wonderland. "Yeah," she repeated. "I'm fine. It—it makes sense."

His eyes lingered on her a bit longer. "When you leave here, the world will be a bigger place."

"No," she said. "Not bigger. Just revealed."

"Very true." He pointed to a door over which hung a logo that seemed vaguely familiar, though she couldn't place it at the moment. A triangle inside an ornate circle, the three spaces filled with each of the letters P, E, and C. And in the center of the triangle, the familiar sword and scales of the goddess Justicia.

"PEC?"

"Preternatural Enforcement Commission," Porter said. "It's an ancient organization. Homeland Security is the cover story for Division 6, the arm that covers this portion of the US."

She nodded, processing that. "The evidence was right in front of me," she said as they passed through the door and into a hallway lined with a long counter topped with a number of odd-looking devices. "I never saw it. What kind of prosecutor does that make me?"

"The evidence? Sara, you couldn't possibly have known. Very few do."

She thought of her father's neck wound. "I should have," she said as Porter gestured for her to take a seat at one of the desks.

A harried looking worker behind the counter signaled that she'd be right there, and Sara used the wait to look around more. She twisted in her seat, wanting to take everything in, and noticed two men—or they looked like men—heading down the hall with lanyards boasting what looked like a QR code and a bold letter V.

"—same thing last week," one was saying. "It's going to get worse."

"Therian pricks," the other said as they continued past Sara and Porter. "Speaking of, I heard Caris dropped into town. Traitorous bitch."

"Therians?" Sara repeated, her voice a whisper. "That's shape-shifters, right?"

Porter's brow rose. "I see why you caught Leviathan's eye."

"Okay, let's get you checked in," said the worker, the words going straight into Sara's mind without being voiced.

"Thumbprint," said the voice in her head, and she put her thumb on the electronic pad. "Now look here," she said, and when Sara complied, her face was suddenly dotted with light. "Face mapping," the worker said in explanation.

She peered at a monitor. "Sara Constantine. Designation? H?"

"Uh?"

"Yes," Porter said from behind her. "Human."

The worker rolled her chair back, retrieved something that was emerging from a machine, attached it to a lanyard, and passed it to Sara. A QR code and the letter H.

"Keep that on at all times. Corridor A. Blair will meet you."

Sara slipped on the lanyard as she stood, then looked around, not having the slightest clue where to find Corridor A.

"This way," Porter said.

She fell in step beside him. "Who else knows about this?"

"In Los Angeles? The only non-Division 6 employees are me, the federal prosecutor, and you."

She paused to stare at him. "Seriously?"

He lifted a shoulder. "So I'm told."

"Why me? Why now?"

"The truth?" He shook his head. "I haven't a clue."

They continued in silence down the hall, the counter soon replaced by offices, many with open doors. In one, Sara saw a guy in a suit leaning back, his boots on his desk the way Manny often did when he settled in to read. The familiarity of it made her smile, though it quickly disappeared when they passed the next office. There, a red-faced creature pounded on a desk as he yelled into a phone, sharp protrusions extending from his face.

She looked away. "So, um, this is a judicial system?"

"Exactly."

"And, what? My job would be prosecuting who? Vampires?" She felt ridiculous even voicing the question.

Porter shrugged. "And werewolves, demons, fairies. A whole plethora of creatures. All those stories you thought were only the stuff of nightmares or stories told to scare children or populate horror movies. All those things are real. They're real, and they're out there, and some of them are just as evil as Hollywood has portrayed them."

"Some of them?"

"A small percentage, actually. When you get right down to it, it's not that different. Like humans, most of the preternatural are law abiding. It's the ones who break the Concordat that Division 6 is concerned with."

"Concordat," she repeated. "That's like a covenant. A law."

"Exactly."

She eyed Porter. "You're awfully sanguine about all this."

"I wasn't at first. You're taking it with much less shock than I did, I assure you."

"How long have you known?"

"Since I became the DA."

She nodded. "So Einhart knows, too," she said, referencing his predecessor.

"No."

She frowned. "What?"

"The knowledge is available while necessary. After that..." He trailed off with a shrug. "I understand the process is simple and painless."

"Oh." She cleared her throat, feeling awkward. "So, um, there are others, right? This is Division 6, so there must be at least five more?"

"Correct. All over the globe. They fall under the jurisdiction of the PEC, and the PEC hides in worldwide governments. Very secret. Very need-to-know."

"Right. Hide in plain sight. That makes sense."

He stopped walking when they reached an intersection of corridors, their path blocked by a set of doors. Above the doors was painted an inscription: *Judicare Maleficum.*

"To judge the evildoer?"

His smile seemed proud. Almost paternal. "Sara, you're going to do just fine." He gestured at the door. "This is where I leave you. Your pass and the facial scan will get you through."

"You aren't coming?"

"Not authorized. An escort will meet you on the other side."

"Right," she said, her stomach choosing this moment to get fluttery with nerves. She was going past that door alone. And who knew what that meant. "Well, I guess, thank you."

"I imagine you'll be tendering your resignation to me soon, Sara. I hate to lose you."

"Sir, I—thank you. Thank you for everything."

He extended his hand, shook hers, then turned and walked back the way he came. Sara drew in a breath, then another, trying to center herself. Then she held her lanyard in front of the scanner, watched the light on the door turn from red to green, and walked over the threshold into Wonderland.

TEN

There was a balance to San Francisco, Sergius thought. Wants warred with disappointments. Pain complemented pleasure. And darkness was beaten back by nothing less than the sheer force of will and electric generators.

He belonged here in this penthouse of steel and glass just as he belonged in the deep, windowless den he'd acquired deep in the ground with the subway tracks. A home in the dark, far away from prying eyes.

He pressed his palm to the glass, then looked out at the Golden Gate Bridge sparkling in the distance under the afternoon sun.

The glass had been manufactured to his own specifications. Glass that allowed him to stand in the light.

It pleased him to stand there now, looking down at the humans scurrying like ants thirty-two stories below. Did they have any idea of the horror he could wreak upon them should he choose? Did they know the effort it cost him to stay here, behind glass, fighting the urge to take and to kill? To rend and become?

Every day, the battle within him grew more fierce, and every night he fought to remain inside, to keep himself far from the scent of blood. And not just blood. That was the deepest craving, yes. But it sparked others. Sex. Violence. Passion.

Blood.

They were all one, and he wanted to revel in them. In it. To take. To rend. The dark serpent within him craved chaos, and that need was seeping into his dreams and his thoughts, threatening to burst out. To run wild and free.

He had told no one of his growing hunger, not even Lucius, his closest friend.

Soon, though, he would have to reveal his secrets. Either that, or he would have to kill.

And then, of course, he would have to run.

"Will we go out come nightfall?"

Tasha's reflection looked back at him from the glass, and he watched as she approached him, gliding across the polished wood floor. Her auburn hair hung in loose curls to her waist. She moved in front of his floor lamp, and for a moment, she was illuminated from behind, a halo of red and gold dancing around her, her hair crackling with unknown power. A vision. A goddess. Something untouched and pure, her face carved by the gods themselves, her fiery red lips seeming to call to him. To lure him in. Begging the beast inside him to discover if the purity was only an illusion.

She wore a gown of white silk with nothing under it, and he clenched his hands tight at his sides, fighting his body's reaction to her soft curves and moon-white skin. She had walked this earth for over five centuries, and yet she still had a seventeen-year-old's body. A saint with a seductress's form and an innocent mind that had no cognizance of her own allure.

He bit back a curse. She was Luke's ward, as close to him as if she was his own daughter, and she was innocent. He would never touch her. And he damn sure shouldn't desire her.

"Serge?" she said, the press of her hand turning his blood to molten lava. "Will he be okay?" Her lips curved into a little pout, and tears filled her eyes. He turned and met her eyes, the serpent within him starting to sway. Craving. Wanting.

"He'll be fine," Serge said, forcing the darkness back down. "He's been in tighter scrapes."

She pulled back and blinked blue eyes so pale they had almost no color at all. "It's because of me," she said, in that singsong voice. "Me, me, me. Shouldn't have told him. Naughty girl, telling secrets." She pulled away from him and moved to a black leather armchair, curling herself up so small she looked like a child.

Her suffering moved him. She was a victim to a world that had hurt her. An innocent beauty whom Luke had rescued and sworn to protect. Now, he'd entrusted her to Serge. And Serge would not break faith. He would battle the beast within. Force it back. He owed as much to Luke, and so much more.

With a sigh, he turned his attention back to Tasha. She was everything he was not. Everything Luke was not. And yet the horrors of their world had spilled over on her.

Not for the first time, he felt a pang of regret that Luke had turned her at all. Serge had been there, of course, on that snowy night in France. The farmhouse, burned and raided by a band of werens, the inhabitants brutally slain. The girl herself huddled in the barn, crying and injured, her head bashed in by a spooked animal.

He understood why Luke had turned the girl. His friend had looked upon Tasha and seen his beloved Livia. He'd seen the dying girl and believed he could quell his nightmares by snatching her from the arms of death.

He'd been a fool, of course. Her mind had been broken by both trauma and injury, and she barely survived the Holding—the ritual that every vampire must go through in order to control the *Azag Mahru*—the dark serpent—and bury it deep within.

From that night on, she'd become Luke's responsibility. His talisman, even. But Serge couldn't help but wonder if Luke truly saw redemption when he looked upon her sweet face. Or did he instead see guilt?

Perhaps, Serge thought, his friend saw both.

"Watching me," she sang. "Pretty, pretty me, and you're a naughty boy for looking."

He released a breath that was almost a laugh. He despised himself for the many times he'd looked at her with naughty thoughts over the centuries. Now was not one of them. "I was thinking of Luke."

At the mention of his name, she frowned. "His eyes don't touch me like that." She stood, arms out, naked beneath the soft film of her gown. "He doesn't let me see the way his pulse burns for me."

"It doesn't, Tasha. Not like that."

"No?" She tilted her head, studying him, then stepped closer. "But yours does, yes?" Her whispered words tickled his ear, the lavender scent of her hair wreaking havoc with his self-control. "Does your blood throb with desire? Do you want what you cannot have?" Her eyes dipped down, and he was certain she could tell that his cock had sprung to attention and was now straining against the tight confines of his jeans. "Naughty boys," she murmured, her voice low and singsong. "Naughty boys want their toys, and pretty girls have them."

"Tasha." His voice was hoarse, but firm. "Sit down." He wouldn't do this. Not to her. She didn't understand. Didn't have a clue, really, what she was playing at. Despite all the years behind her, she didn't understand.

And above all else, she was under Luke's protection.

Serge had done a lot of regrettable things in his long life, and he was certain that he would rack up more in the future, but never would he stoop so low as to count fucking his best friend's ward among them.

"Don't want to sit. Want to play." She slid her hand down over her belly, over the mound between her thighs, and the only thought in his head at the moment was that Luke had damn well, damn well, better value their friendship, because the serpent was coiling inside him, stirring up all those dark cravings, and fighting it back was using all of his willpower. Every last drop. "Don't you want to play with me, Sergius?"

"You don't know what you're asking," he said, forcing the words out. "I need to get some work done." He made to move past her, felt her fingers close over his arm. "Let go, Tasha. I need to get out of here." Talk about an understatement.

"But I do know," she said, sidling closer, her gown brushing against him, her soft thighs pushing close. "He showed me," she added, cupping her palm over his frustrated, desperate cock. "He showed me how to play."

Warning bells sounded like Klaxons in his head, and he stepped back, gripping her shoulders and looking firmly into her face. "Who?" he demanded. "Who showed you?"

"Judge not," she giggled. "Lest ye be judged."

"Judge not?" he repeated, not understanding. But as he looked at her and saw that glint of sexuality spark in her eyes, he knew. He knew what had happened to her.

More than that, he now understood Luke's motivation.

"Braddock," he said, the name like a curse on his lips. The judge had always been oily, and for decades there had been rumors of bribery and blackmail. If Serge was understanding Tasha right, Braddock had gotten his hands on her—and had gotten himself killed for his trouble.

He looked down at Tasha, unable to conceal his fury. "What did the bastard do to you?"

"Do you want me to show you?" she asked, pressing herself up close, her body swaying dreamily from side to side. "I promise to only share the part that felt nice. So nice. All soft and sweet." She scowled and shook her head, her brow creasing. "But not the part that hurt. That's the secret part. Not for sharing. And I don't like it. I don't like it when it burns. No pain," she added, the vixen shriveling to reveal a terrified child. "Please, no pain. Not again."

She fisted her hands in his shirt and looked up at him with wild, terrified eyes. As she whimpered in his arms, he wished that he'd been there to help Luke take Braddock down.

"Tasha," he said, wishing he could extinguish the fear in her eyes. "You're safe. He can't hurt you anymore."

"No more pain..."

"No."

"Only pleasure..."

"That's right."

"I can make it stop," she whispered, her dreamlike voice working on him like a trance. She lifted herself onto her toes, her hands still lost in his shirt. Her lips brushed lightly over his. "I know things I'm not supposed to. I know things about making the hurt go away. About turning pain into pretty, pretty pleasure." She tilted her head back, her smile as convincing as any whore he'd taken to bed during his youth as a human. "Do you want me to show you?"

"Tasha." He ground out her name, his hands closing over hers, pushing her away. "Don't."

"Don't what?" She moved closer, the gossamer gown caressing curves that his fingers ached to touch.

A lump formed in Serge's throat and he tried to swallow back the rising serpent. He would not bed his friend's ward. He wouldn't. He couldn't.

And yet as she moved ever closer—as his body tightened with need and the darkness raged in his blood—he feared that no matter how hard he fought, in the end, he would betray his friend.

Sara passed through a wall of light as she crossed the threshold, realizing it was a facial scan to verify her identity. She stood a moment, soaking in the strangeness and wondering where her escort was, when she heard a flapping sound approaching from the dimly lit hallway.

A moment later, the source of the flapping appeared—a woman with flowing dark hair, a pale complexion, and wings that spanned almost the entire width of the tunnel. She landed a few feet from Sara, her head bent, her wings folding back, then seeming to disappear all together.

She lifted her head, a brow raised as she studied Sara. Sara did the same. She had high cheekbones, pale blue eyes with cat-like pupils, and she held herself with complete confidence.

The woman—or whatever—cocked her head. "Well? I haven't got all day." She turned and started to walk down the hall, back the way she'd come. Sara hurried to keep up. When they reached an intersecting hall, her escort extended a hand, pointing. "Investigation to the right, prosecution to the left. Detention on sub-15. Questions?" she asked as they turned left.

"Yeah. Who are you?"

"I'm Blair." She stopped, her eyes roaming over Sara. It didn't look as if she liked what she saw. "I'm the one who can destroy you with a song and kill you with a kiss."

Deliberately, Sara crossed her arms. "Is that your official title?" No way was she showing intimidation. She glanced at Blair's lanyard, searching for a clue as to what this woman was, but the S she saw there didn't mean a thing.

Blair almost smiled. "I'm your paralegal. For now."

"Oh, will I be getting someone else soon? Pity."

"No, it's a permanent assignment. Permanent being a relative term, since I'll move on when you do. If you even decide to take the job."

Sara took a step closer, then looked Blair up and down, exactly as the paralegal had done. "You think I'll flame out?"

Blair shrugged, and Sara fought the urge to dance with victory when she moved a step backward. "Eh, you might last longer than the last one."

"Last one?"

"Last human prosecutor. That was two—no, three—years ago."

"What happened?"

Blair's eyes narrowed, and she smiled with delight before saying, "Took a swan dive off a building."

"Oh. I—"

"He moved to Tulsa." The words, spoken in a deep, melodious

voice, came from behind her, and Sara spun to find herself facing a tall and debonair man in a dark suit. He looked to be in his fifties, with graying temples and a stern but kind face. "That's all for now, Blair. You two can bond later."

"I'm counting the minutes," she said, then turned, extended her wings, and flew off down the hallway. Sara watched, and when she was sure she wasn't gawking, turned back to the man.

"Her bedside side manner leaves a bit to be desired. Still, I won't lie. It's a different environment down here. You may not be warmly welcomed at first, but do good work, and you will be accepted."

"You're Nikko Leviathan."

He inclined his head. Like everyone else, he wore a lanyard. His, however, had no bold letter.

"So, um, what are you?"

"I'm the Director of Division 6 and head of the Violent Crimes Department."

"Right." So apparently that wasn't an Emily Post approved question. "It's a pleasure to meet you. May I ask you a question?"

"Of course."

"Why me?"

"You have well-placed advocates," he said, beginning to walk.

"Advocates?" She hurried to keep up.

"Let's just say that your skills have not gone unnoticed. The Stemmons case is an excellent example. And I need good people."

"So does Alexander Porter. So do the victims of criminals like Stemmons. All those little girls."

"What about that little girl who found her father murdered on her eighth birthday. Do you stand for her, too?"

She came to a dead stop. Leviathan paused as well, then looked back at her.

"So it's true? A vampire killed my father?"

Leviathan only nodded, but it was enough. Her stomach twisted and her knees went weak. She forced herself not to crumple to the floor. "Do you know who? Was he punished? That's what you do here, right?"

"It is what we do, but no. I'm afraid the matter of Frank Constantine remains a cold case in both your old world and you're new. But now, at least, you know the true nature of the defendant."

"No, sir," she said firmly, forcing her chin up. "That's not true. I've known since the night my father died that the man who did that to him was something monstrous and inhuman. Knowing his murderer was a vampire doesn't change my perception of him at all."

Leviathan nodded, his expression one of approval. "I presume you will want to see the file?"

She closed her eyes, trying to stay calm. Trying, but she wasn't sure she was succeeding. "Yes, sir," she said, opening her eyes to meet his. "I would like that very much."

When he continued walking, she hurried to keep up. "And you will be able to. If you accept the position." He paused, then swept his arm, gesturing for her to enter the office they now stood in front of.

It was empty, with the exception of a desk and office chair, a computer, a bookcase, and two guest chairs. She circled the desk, then saw that the familiar logo—a circle with the letters PEC embedded inside—twisted and turned as the computer's screen-saver. *Where had she seen that before?*

She pushed the question away and focused on the moment. "Is this my office?"

"If you accept the position."

She clasped her hands in front of her and couldn't deny that she was interested. An office to herself. New challenges. The possibility of answers after all these years, and the appeal of working in this hidden, dangerous world. "Why do you want me so much that you're dangling my father's murder as a carrot?"

"It's not a carrot, Sara. Just the truth. You decline the job, and you will have nothing."

"Except I'll know there's something. I can still look."

"No," he said, then sat in one of the guest chairs.

"No, I can't look?"

"No, you won't know that there is something."

"But I..." She paused, feeling suddenly cold as she remembered Porter's words. "If I don't take this job, you'll make me forget."

He lifted his hands in a Gallic shrug, but said nothing.

"You can really do that? You can take my memories?"

"I? No. But there are creatures who can. It's very surgical, I assure you. You'll remember chatting with Mr. Porter. Nothing else. As far as you'll be concerned, you spent the day at your desk reviewing memos and such that you'd pushed aside during the Stemmons trial."

"I see."

"Division 6—the entire PEC—is confidential. And we intend it to remain so. Think carefully, Sara. The secrets will weigh you down, and the lies will change you. Only you can decide if the tradeoff is worth it."

She swallowed. "Okay, then. How long do I have to decide?"

"As long as you need. But you can't go back upstairs until you do. At least not without forgetting today."

She stood, then sat down again. She understood the implications. There would be no talking about her caseload with Manny over a drink. No settling in with Petra to trade gossip. She'd be able to tell them only that she worked for a division of Homeland, and that she couldn't talk about her work.

Could she live with that?

The answer came swiftly. *Yes.*

If it meant finding her father's killer—if it gave her the opportunity to learn firsthand about the world she'd come to know so deeply as fiction—then hell yes, she could.

She faced Leviathan, prepared to tell him exactly that. But what came out instead was, "Why me, really? Is it because of my father?"

He chuckled. "No. Though knowing Frank's love of what the outside world calls the supernatural, I imagine that being his daughter left you better prepared than most."

"Then why?"

"Your mind resists most forms of suggestion, Sara. It's a handy skill for a prosecutor to have when many of our kind can manipulate thought."

She sat back, her thoughts spinning. "You're saying that I—wait. That agent last night. Tucker. He was trying to get into my head?"

"He tried. You resisted."

She pressed her fingers to her temples, equal parts fascinated, relieved, and entirely pissed off. "Is he—I mean, is he a vampire?"

Leviathan chuckled. "Human, actually. He has a gift. Some do."

"Oh. Well, I'm glad he couldn't get into my head. That would be—"

"He didn't. Doyle did. He's a demon, by the way. Well, half-demon."

Her entire body went cold. "A demon. And he was in my head. What the hell did he do?"

"His job," Leviathan said. "He sent you away so that he could use his gift to find a killer."

"Wait, what?" It wasn't until she reached the wall that she realized she had stood up and started pacing. She stopped, faced him. "You're saying he knows who killed Marcus Braddock?"

"He does. He's already filed an affidavit."

"But that's—" She truly had no words. It was all too much to take in at once. "How?"

"You'll learn soon enough. And while things may seem odd here at first, I assure you that our process—and the parameters of your job—are very similar." He flashed a half-smile. "Humans borrowed the setup of their judicial systems from ours, after all."

She still had a million questions, but she voiced the only one that truly counted. "So who killed him?"

"An ancient vampire. And if you agree to join us, you'll be prosecuting this case and have access to all the details. Does that scare you?"

She put her hands on the desk and leaned forward. "I haven't said yes, yet. Does that scare you?"

He chuckled. "Today will be long. Ready?"

She thought of the stories she'd been weaned on, of the long nights doing research in college, surrounded by books of folklore and modern fiction. She thought of her father the way she'd found him, unmoving in a pool of his own blood. She thought of the answers that would be at her fingertips. But she also thought of Stemmons. Of all those dead little girls. The ones who needed someone fighting for them. For their families.

She thought of secrets and silence. Of never being able to fully share her life again. Of slipping through a curtain and ending up in another world that looked like hers, but wasn't. She was looking behind that curtain now. Having looked, could she ever choose to go back?

She didn't know, but maybe right now it didn't matter.

"Yeah," she said, eager to see what else he would show her even if, in the end, she forgot it all. "I'm ready."

Luke paced in front of the monitors, his mind in a muddle as the memories flooded back to him.

Sara.

She'd been his. Truly his. Just as he had been hers.

And then the Shades had taken it all away from her, leaving him to wallow in his grief as he tried to learn who had tasked the Shades to steal her thoughts. He'd never found the answer.

So many questions. How could he leave with so many damn questions?

Because you must.

The answer rang in his mind with the force of truth. Tasha needed him, but Sara was strong. More, the past three years had proven that there was no lingering danger.

Safe. She was safe. And though it did not satisfy, the knowledge would give him some small comfort when he was away.

Frustrated, he pressed his fingers to his temples. He had no time to think about Sara or to mourn her loss a second time. The wheels for his plan were in motion, and soon Doyle and his team would come to hunt him.

He checked his phone, a new one and untraceable. But there was no message. The team was not yet on its way. Perhaps Doyle wasn't as clever as Luke remembered.

Which meant there was some time, after all. He could go to her. Enter the courthouse from the system of subterranean tunnels. Find her in her office. And then—

But no.

He already said goodbye, and he'd spoken the truth when he told her he had to leave. He would torture her by showing up only to leave again. And he certainly couldn't invite her into hiding with him and his ward. She had a life, a human life. And he must let her live it.

He considered summoning a Shade to take his memory of her as he had the first time.

But no. He'd been a fool then. This was his cross to bear, and he must.

He'd tried to forget her once, and fate had brought her back, giving him a fresh taste before he had to leave. Giving him the knowledge that she was truly his, and though he could never have her, he also would never forget her.

ELEVEN

"'...At which point Agent Doyle identified the silver signet ring as belonging to Lucius Dragos. He then made the determination to examine the victim's last mental image in order to confirm suspect's identity.'" Sara looked up from the one-page summary she was quoting. "Examine the last mental image?"

In the guest chair across from her, Blair glanced up from the fingernail she was examining. "Problem?"

"Could you elaborate on that?"

"With any other prosecutor down here, I wouldn't have to. That's why we call that a summary."

"You do realize that if I take this job, I'll be your superior? And that means that I'll be able to make your life as least as hellish as you make mine."

Her perfect brows rose, and those fascinating pupils turned to slits. "I've yet to meet a human with that much imagination."

Sara leaned back in her chair, her fingers steepled. "You must not have met that many humans. If you had, you'd know that we excel at making life hellish for others."

Blair released a loud laugh, then clapped her hand over her mouth. Sara just smiled sweetly, hoping the dam had finally cracked. "Truce?"

The woman—or whatever—didn't answer. But she did explain about Doyle's gift of seeing the last thoughts of the dead. "He can't do it for every corpse. The images fade over time. But get him fast to a crime scene, and it is sweet. This one especially. For him, anyway."

"Why's that?"

For a moment, Blair stayed silent, and Sara feared the dam hadn't cracked after all. But then Blair shrugged. "Long-standing feud between those two. Doyle and Dragos, I mean. I'm pretty sure as far as Doyle is concerned, getting Dragos behind bars is better than sex."

"Why the feud?"

"No idea."

Sara studied her paralegal, but as far as she could tell, Blair wasn't holding back. She put the summary back on the desk that might soon be hers.

"So what are you?" She remembered Leviathan's odd reaction to that question. "Or is that question considered rude?"

"I'm a siren," Blair answered, and Sara forced herself not to do a victory fist bump. Apparently, she really had broken through Blair's wall.

"A siren," she repeated. "So, based on what I've seen you must really have to turn on the charm to reel in the men." She held her breath, hoping she'd been right and they'd broken the ice enough to tease each other.

Blair stood, then circled Sara's desk, humming as she walked. As she moved—as the sound filled the office, Sara started to feel a little tipsy.

"Well, look at you," Blair said, and immediately Sara's head cleared.

"What did you do?"

"Nothing like what I meant to. You were supposed to be begging me to fuck you on your desk, but you weren't even close." She cocked her head. "Not sure if you're impervious or if you've got someone locked tight up here," she said, tapping Sara's head. She bent close, then sniffed near Sara's ear. "A bit of both, then," she added as she returned to her chair and crossed her legs. She smiled at Sara. "Oh, and in case it wasn't clear, I don't limit myself to men."

"Yeah," Sara said. "I got that."

"Just a demonstration so you're familiar. It's a class two violation to pull out the glow at work. Or without consent."

"That's probably a good thing."

"So who is he?" Blair asked. "The guy I can sense in your head."

"I wasn't thinking of a guy." That was true, but at the same time it wasn't. She hadn't been actively thinking of Luke. But he'd been on her mind since—well, honestly, since the first time she'd seen him watching her. He'd been there all that time, hiding just under the surface. But now he was out, filling her thoughts, touching her soul. No wonder Blair could sense him.

Too bad Sara never would again.

"He's—he doesn't matter. I won't be seeing him again." The thought made her ache inside. But she had to acknowledge one good thing about him leaving. With everyone else, she knew she could keep the secret of Division 6. With Luke, she didn't think so. She wanted no secrets between them. And this was as big as secrets came.

She glanced down at the report on PEC letterhead and once again noticed the logo. With a start, she remembered where she'd seen that symbol.

"Blair," she said as she rose. "Take me to Director Leviathan's office."

"You're in?"

Sara didn't answer, just motioned for Blair to hurry. She followed the paralegal to the huge office at the end of the hall, then burst inside despite the frustrated howl from Martella, his assistant, seated in the alcove outside his door.

Leviathan looked up calmly from the file he was reading.

"My father knew about the PEC, didn't he? I've seen the crest in his journals. Is that why he was killed?"

He gestured for her to sit. She ignored him.

"He knew, yes," Leviathan said. "But he wasn't killed because of it. He worked here."

"Oh." She dropped into the chair he'd indicated, then heard the click of the door behind her. She turned and saw that Blair had discreetly left the room. "But—but he was human, right?"

Leviathan smiled. "He was. He was exactly the man you knew. He simply worked for us."

"Doing what?"

"What did you understand his job to be?"

"He taught folklore at UCLA. I remember that. Then I think he left. My mother mentioned something about a research grant. That was after he died, though. I never asked for details."

"We are the details. A cover story to have handy for those in his world who might ask about the source of his income."

"So what was he really doing?"

"Exactly that. Research. Archival work. He wrote several historical volumes. He was a good man, Sara, and an asset to the PEC."

"Can I see his research? His papers? Any journals he left here and not at home?"

"You can, yes. Once you accept our offer. I doubt you will come to any more understanding than we have. The vampire who attacked him may have had no reason other than to feed. Bad things happen, Sara, sometimes for very little reason. As a prosecutor, you know that."

"Honestly, sir, I'm not sure I know anything anymore." Her thoughts were spinning in her head, and she felt as if she would drown under the waves of new revelations that kept coming and coming. "Nothing except that I'm staying."

"You're taking the job?"

She nodded.

"I'm very pleased."

She forced herself to lift her chin and meet his eyes. "I need to be honest, though. I may only be doing it so that I'll have access to the information about my father's killer. And so that I can work the cold case."

"And you think that would disturb me? To find and bring a killer to justice? If that truly is your primary motivation for joining us at Division 6, why should that disturb you? Hasn't your father's murder defined the course of your career even without us? Wasn't his murder the impetus for your decision to practice law? Don't you pull out his cold case file upstairs every chance you get? Now is no different. It's just a few stories beneath the ground. And perhaps your co-workers are a bit more colorful down here. Otherwise, not much has changed."

She had to admit he had a point.

"But Sara, our case is cold, too. Your father's file is not a treasure trove of leads for you to follow. You may learn nothing more here."

"I know. But I have to keep—"

"Yo, Director," someone said in the moment that the door burst open and two men stepped in. Sara recognized them from the Braddock crime scene. Doyle and Tucker.

"Got a lead on Dragos's location," Doyle continued.

Sara hadn't paid much attention to Doyle's appearance last night. Now, she studied him, the asshole who'd poked around in her mind. He was a lanky man with a rugged face and the kind of broad shoulders that suggested tight muscles hidden beneath the ill-fitting clothes. He walked with the swagger of an old-time sheriff, and his eyes were cold and flat. Beside him stood his partner, looking well-dressed and snappy.

"I'm so sorry," Martella said, her heels clicking on the tiles as she scurried to the door. "I couldn't stop them."

"I don't doubt it for a second," Leviathan said, with a sharp look at Doyle. "Don't worry, Martella. It's fine. Shut the door, would you?"

As soon as she did, Sara stood, marched to Doyle, and slapped his face. "Stay the fuck out of my head," she hissed, as Tucker practically threw himself at his partner to keep him from lunging at Sara.

"Enough," Leviathan ordered as Doyle yanked himself out of Tucker's grasp, his eyes hard on Sara.

"I do my job, you do yours," Doyle said. "My job is making sure your kind don't know I'm doing my job." He cut a glance toward Leviathan. "And what's she doing here, anyway?"

"She's prosecuting the Braddock case."

Doyle's face went pale. "That's not funny."

"It wasn't meant to be. She's our newest prosecutor, and I expect you to play nice."

Doyle shifted to look at her, his eyes so sharp they could have cut glass. "Not worth the effort. Haven't had a human prosecutor since Crawford. And he's, what? Growing wheat in Tulsa now? No way can she handle it."

She took a step toward him. "I assure you I can handle it."

"You are so fucking green, sweetheart. And human."

"So is your partner," Leviathan pointed out.

"Tucker's different," Doyle said, and Sara heard genuine affection in his voice. "And he's solid."

"Gotta love the praise," Tucker said.

Sara took a step closer to Doyle. "I'm solid, too."

"Guess we'll find out." He shifted his attention to Leviathan. "We need to act fast. He's still in town. Can I toss this presentation to your wall screen?"

At Leviathan's nod, the plain wall behind Leviathan turned into a screen with the PEC logo. As soon as it appeared, the logo faded, leaving an image of a map. A grid of streets, a large green space, and many office buildings.

"This is the Hollywood Forever cemetery," Doyle said, drawing on his table so that the greenspace on the wall was circled. We figure he's going to bolt from his location, so we've got a team in place right now using sonar to find his tunnels. We'll have teams at all exit points."

He circled one of the buildings next. "This is where he's holed up. Plans show two basements. Place was built in the thirties, and he was the first owner, and we figure he spent time constructing tunnels to the crypts, especially the ones he owns in various names."

"Oh." Right then, that was all she could manage.

He turned his attentions back to Leviathan. "Got a team drilling down on all that. Looking for plans. Any signs of additional construction, hidden exit points, sewer access, that kind of thing."

"Excellent," Leviathan said. "And you're certain of the location?"

"Dead on." The screen changed again, this time to show a photograph of the silver signet ring found at the crime scene. Sara hadn't gotten a good look at it, and now she frowned. It had a dragon with a ruby eye, the creature consuming its own tail.

She felt the cold sweat break out under her arms. *She knew that ring.* She'd seen it last night at the bar. It had been on Luke's finger.

"Who—" she began, then swallowed the question. Doyle had answered it with a photograph. And there, splashed across half of Leviathan's wall, was the man whose hands had brought her skin to life. Whose tongue had laved her. Whose cock had filled her. Whose urgent thrusts had left her moaning and begging for more.

The man who'd left a bundle of tulips on her doorstep. Who'd filled her thoughts and eased her dreams.

"Lucius Dragos," Doyle said, his voice practically giddy. "It's going to be a hell of a day."

She had no time to process, no time to realign her reality with this new perception of the world. Luke was a murderer.

A vicious, cold-blooded killer. The very epitome of the evil she'd dedicated her life to putting behind bars.

There had to be some sort of mistake.

And he wasn't simply a murderer. No, he was also an in-your-face, straight-out-of-your-nightmares vampire. The exact kind of creature that had murdered her father.

She closed her eyes, fighting tears. Determined not to show any reaction while she was in this room.

It was outrageous. Unbelievable.

Mortifying.

He'd had his hands on her. He'd touched her—he'd claimed her —and surely, surely she would have known if she'd been sleeping with a killer.

She remembered, though, the strength in those powerful hands and the determination in his amber eyes. She'd seen control there along with an undercurrent of violence that had both scared and excited her. He'd practically thrummed with a potency and raw carnality that had wreaked havoc on her. She'd wanted him, yes, but he'd wanted her, too, and he was a man who took what he wanted.

He'd taken her, leading her to where he wanted her to go and then watching with unabashed rapture as she'd shattered under his touch.

He was dangerous, all right.

She'd seen it, and she'd simply ignored it. In his arms, she'd felt no risk. The opposite, actually, because he'd made her feel more secure than she ever had in her life.

She fought a shudder. If it had only been sex with a murderer, she could handle that. But she'd felt something for him. More than something. Being with Luke had felt like coming home. Like they belonged together. Now all of that had shattered. Now, she felt like a fool.

And the worst of it was, she'd never seen it coming.

"Constantine?"

She noticed that someone had turned off the screen. She blinked, turning her attention to the director. "Sir?"

"Are you okay?"

She nodded. *No.* "Yes," she said. "Yes, I'm fine. It's just strange. After years of thinking it was all fiction, to see a photo of a normal-looking man and learn that he's a vampire." She looked again at the screen, as if Luke's face was still there, but saw only her own reflection. A storm of feelings raged inside her—anger, confusion, even longing—but she saw nothing in her face that would give away her secret. Nothing that would reveal that she'd been thrown.

It was the face of a trial attorney, and a damn good one. A prosecutor who could get the shit kicked out of her by a witness in front of twelve citizens good and true and make it look like the witness said the exact right thing to put the final nail in the defendant's coffin. It was, she realized, the face that had gotten her this job.

Her job.

She shouldn't be working this case. Not with the baggage she was going to be lugging into the courtroom. She should tell Leviathan the truth right now.

But she said nothing. Later, when he was in custody. Maybe she'd talk then. If she told them now, they'd surely shut her out. A frisson of fear cut through her as she realized that they might even erase her memories and send her back up to Porter. They could do that, and then she'd never have her answers.

She couldn't take the risk. She needed to do this. Needed to prosecute this case. To put away a murderous vampire. For justice. For Braddock. And for her father.

She might never learn exactly who had taken Frank Constantine from her, but she could walk this path. She'd hold on to her memories no matter what the cost. And, yeah, she could prosecute the monster who had taken her body and toyed with her heart. The killer who'd gotten under her skin.

It might not be closure, but it would be close.

With determination, she forced herself to recall the crime scene. The body on the ground. The neck ripped open, just like her father's. "He killed a human?"

"A Therian," Leviathan said. "A shapeshifter. In this case, a were-fox. Considered a para-human for purposes of the Concordat, and violence against a human is the most egregious of crimes."

"Which means that once the jury comes back with a guilty verdict. Dragos gets a stake through the heart." Doyle didn't even try to hide his smile. "About time. The serpent rides high in that son-of-a-bitch."

She frowned, wondering about the glee she'd heard in his voice. She'd always celebrated her wins, but only with Stemmons had her emotions felt both gleeful and personal. Why, she wondered, was this case personal to Doyle?

That wasn't a question she was prepared to ask. Instead, she said, "Serpent?"

"The Holding," Doyle said, as if that explained everything.

Leviathan gestured for her to take a seat, then began speaking as she did. "In pop culture, vampires are usually portrayed as the dead come back to life. The idea being that the human soul has moved on, and what is animating the body is some sort of opportunistic demonic entity that moved in. Do you agree?"

She nodded. "That tracks with most cultures' definitions, yes."

"That's not the way it works. In fact, the human soul or essence or spirit—whatever you wish to call it—is part of a duality. The soul embodies the good, but it is paired with darkness. With evil. In most people, the good wins out and the evil is suppressed. In some, that isn't the case."

"Stemmons."

Leviathan nodded. "When a person is killed by a vampire—their blood drained almost to death and the vampiric blood ingested—the person doesn't simply awaken as a vampire. Instead, a vicious battle begins inside the body. The two forces fighting for control. We tend to call the good side the soul or the light. The dark evil side is the *Azag Mahru*—the serpent presence, sometimes simply called the darkness."

He paused, his eyes on Sara. She nodded that she was following, and he continued.

"The serpent is strong, and the battle is fierce. It seeks to grow, to feed. To become. It wants power, and it feeds on pain. In ancient times, the serpent almost always won, and vampires wreaked havoc upon the earth. But over time, a blood ritual was developed. It calls forth a spirit—a *Numen*—for strength and assistance in wresting control away and restoring the prominence of his good."

"So the serpent completely disappears?"

"Once released, it will never completely be gone. But most vampires can adequately bind it and they live ordinary lives, blending into the population."

"But only at night."

"Only when they are older. Young vampires can walk in the sun."

"Okay. But you said *most*?"

"Some do not prevail at the Holding," Leviathan said.

"Those are the rogues," Tucker added. "The PEC's got teams that hunt down and kill rogues. Nasty business."

"Is Dragos a rogue?" She had to know, had to understand the man as well as the vampire. "Is that why he killed?"

"Why do humans kill?" Leviathan asked. "Not every murder can be blamed on the serpent."

Sara licked her lips. "Of course not."

"Dragos is not a rogue," Leviathan said. "But I fear that the Holding was not entirely successful with him."

"I don't understand."

"His darkness is exceptionally strong. It seeks release even now, and Lucius Dragos must constantly struggle to keep it at bay. To be honest, that is not unusual. Most vampires struggle at times. Some, though, struggle more than others. That is why it is a crime to change children and the mentally infirm. They do not have the mental acuity and strength to fight the serpent. Even if they prevail in the Holding, they invariably succumb to the serpent."

"So what happens to them?"

"They are executed. As is their sire."

"Oh." She felt sick.

Leviathan's expression softened. "For centuries, bands of vampires who had fully succumbed to the *Azag Mahru* swarmed Europe, leaving destruction in their wake. Trust me when I say that we only do what is necessary."

Doyle snorted, but said nothing.

Leviathan turned to him. "You have something to add."

"Dragos may have the dark under control—mostly, anyway—but he and his ward both should have been staked when he sired her. She'd been kicked in the head not long before he found her. She wasn't all there, and you damn well know it. She should have been staked along with Dragos."

"Considering she was turned over five centuries ago, and the girl's serpent has not taken control, I think that question is moot. But even if you do not, Agent, that is not for us to judge now. We were explaining to Ms. Constantine about what happens when a vampire is sired."

"I think I understand," Sara said. "The serpent is bound, but it's always fighting to get out. So what happens if Lucius Dragos's serpent gets free?"

"He would undergo the Holding again if he is able. If not—or if he has harmed others under the serpent's influence—then he would be executed."

Doyle snorted. "Or else he'd be pardoned." He turned to face Sara. "We live in a harsh world, Constantine. But it ain't always a fair one."

"He's not stupid," Tucker said. "He might not know you popped a vision, but the guy's gotta know he lost the ring. So why would he still be hanging around LA? Maybe he figures the sheen wore off before we got it to a seer?"

"He wouldn't assume shit," Doyle said as he stepped into the RAC jumpsuit. Not standard procedure—broke about a dozen regulations, actually—but no way was he hanging back and letting the Recon-and-Capture team go in first. With Dragos, Doyle intended to be front and center. And close enough to see the hate in the smug SOB's eyes when Doyle snapped the binders around his wrists. "He's got a plan. Dragos doesn't do anything without a plan."

"Got a clue what it is? Because if he's just sitting pretty waiting for us, it must be a doozy."

Tucker was right. Lucius Dragos wasn't stupid. Far from it, in fact. If Doyle didn't hate the bloodsucker so much, he'd actually respect the hell out of him.

Doyle shot his partner a quick glance. "You're right, and I don't have a clue. Which is why we're going in fast and hard. Pulling out all the stops."

"If I were Dragos, I'd be long gone. Odds are we didn't find all his escape routes." Tucker started climbing into a RAC suit as well. "I bet he's in the wind."

"What the hell do you think you're doing?"

"Going with my partner."

"You think that's a good idea? Your brand of mojo ain't gonna work on a guy like Dragos. And as fucked up as it might be, I've gotten used to having your scrawny human ass at my side. I'd rather not see it get ripped to shreds."

"You go, I go." He smiled broadly, then slipped on the face cover. "Besides, I got my magic duds."

Doyle bit back a curse. "I'm not watching your ass."

Tucker returned an evil grin. "But I've got such a cute one."

Doyle just shook his head, knowing better than to argue with Tucker. Then he turned to Tariq, the mission's RAC team leader. "We ready?"

Tariq's yellow eyes flashed in the glow of the rising sun. "Let's do this thing." The muscular jinn lifted an arm, signaling to the team, and then rushed forward, his touch disintegrating the lock on the store's front door.

"Clear."

"Clear!"

"Over here, too. All clear."

Within moments, the team's calls echoed through the cavernous space as the team split up and searched the premises.

No one.

"Team Two, report," Tariq said into his comm.

"Got nothing," came back the response. "Tunnels all dusty as shit. No sign anyone came through here, at least not touching ground. He coulda moved as mist, but we would have caught him. Had officers at all exit points and hematite nets set up," he added, referring to the nets constructed from the mineral that disabled vampires, even in their mist form.

"He's in the wind," Tariq said. "Came here for something, but didn't stay. We knew going in Dragos would be a hard capture, but this isn't over. You'll find him again." He reached up to activate his comm again, presumably to recall the team.

"No," Doyle said. "He's here. The bastard is here someplace."

"Another crypt?" Tucker asked. "A tunnel to it that we missed?"

"I can get the team searching," Tariq said. "It's a legit possibility."

Doyle nodded slowly, thinking. The cemetery dated from the late 1800s as the resting place of the local rich and powerful. During the silent film heyday, it had become the burial place for many a silver screen celebrity. A tourist destination, the place was modeled after European cemeteries, with crypts and mausoleums instead of the traditional stone lawn markers. It was, Doyle thought, the perfect place for a vampire to hide. Which meant it was where Dragos would expect them to look.

Frowning, he turned and looked thoughtfully around this second sub-basement filled with broken equipment, a bank of security monitors showing the store above them, a corner with a bed and kitchenette, and several panels hidden in the walls that led to various tunnels terminating at crypts in the cemetery. A hidey-hole to be sure.

Or a place staged to look like one.

"He's not in the cemetery. And he hasn't rabbited."

Tariq's angular eyebrows rose. "We've searched everywhere. He's not here."

"Where's Murray?"

Tariq shot him a *what the fuck* look. "In the vehicle, running ops."

"Why the hell isn't he in here?"

Tariq stared him down. "Because he's damn good at coordinating, and when I put together a team, I make it solid."

Doyle nodded, thinking. Wasn't one thing suspicious about Tariq's answer, and yet his bullshit meter was tingling. "You know the suspect?"

"Dragos? Who doesn't?" Tariq answered, which was a fair enough response.

"I mean personally."

"Yeah," Tariq said, and Doyle could practically taste the bitterness in his voice. "Let's just say I won't shed a tear when you slap the hematite cuffs on him."

Doyle had to second the sentiment. And he knew that Tariq and Dragos had gone head to head a half dozen centuries before. And they were both still standing. On most days, the question of why would be an academic one to discuss over a pint. Today, Doyle's gut was telling him that the question was key.

Not that he needed the answer; he simply needed to address the problem.

"Switch," he said, looking Tariq full in the eyes and watching as his diamond-shaped pupils shrank to nothingness.

"Come again?"

"Murray in here. You in the van."

"You wanna tell me why?"

"Not really," Doyle said, stepping closer. "Why don't you tell me why?"

"I don't know what the fuck you're talking about," Tariq said, rage boiling behind his usually calm features.

"And you don't need to," Doyle said. "So long as you go out, and Murray comes in."

Tariq looked from Doyle to Tucker and then back again. "Fuck it," he finally said. "You want to play hot cop in charge, you go for it."

He shot a withering look back toward Doyle, then stormed out of the room.

Tucker looked at Doyle. "What was that about?"

"Gut feeling," Doyle said.

Tucker pondered that, nodded. "And who the fuck's Murray?"

"Werewolf. And I want his nose on the job."

Five minutes later, J. Frank Murray stopped near the far end of the bank of security monitors. "Here," he said, his nose twitching.

"Here?" Tucker repeated. "We know he would have sat here. That's what the monitors are for."

Murray shook his head. "No. There's more."

Doyle signaled the team. "Disassemble it. And do it fast."

The team rushed forward, tools in hand, and Doyle stood back as they removed the bolts from the floor holding the system in place, then rushed forward when Murray held up a hand and called for the team to stop.

"Look," he said, pointing to an almost-hidden lever on the far side of the last monitor station. "Clever." He shot Doyle a significant look that had Doyle rounding up the rest of the team, weapons at the ready.

Then Murray pulled the lever and the entire monitor bank tilted backward, leaving a gap just big enough for a man to slide into. Murray met Doyle's eyes, then did exactly that.

"There's a drop," he called back. "Hold on."

Doyle bent, shining a light into the gap as Murray called back from the void below. "Crawlspace. Get the team down here asap."

With Doyle moving right behind Murray, the entire team inched forward, the height of the crawlspace slowly increasing until they were able to walk upright. Another hundred yards, and they reached a set of stone stairs. The beam of Murray's flashlight followed the stairs to an ornate iron door and the blackness behind it.

Doyle cocked his head, drawing in the scent. He caught Murray's eye. Their prey was in there, playing dead.

"Blow it," he said.

Within seconds, the door exploded, dust and bits of iron scattering as the team rushed in, stakes at the ready. They fanned out, backs to the stone walls for safety, as they quickly laid a hematite perimeter to not only weaken Dragos, but to prevent him from transforming into mist. Someone lit a flare and tossed it on the ground, and the cramped tomb filled with an eerie reddish glow.

And there he was.

Lucius Dragos stood not seven yards away, clad in black jeans, a black T-shirt, and a long black duster, which undoubtedly hid a variety of weapons in its folds. His arms were crossed over his chest, his hands hidden.

The vampire wore wraparound sunglasses, the lenses so opaque that Doyle couldn't even glimpse his eyes. But Doyle didn't need to see the bastard's eyes to know that Lucius was looking straight at him.

And then he turned, his gaze sweeping over the group, examining each face.

"Tariq's not here," Doyle said. Then he smiled. "Psych."

His old friend's face remained hard as stone, his jaw firm. But his right cheek twitched. Fear? Doyle couldn't imagine Lucius Dragos being afraid of anything, no matter how much he should be.

No, Dragos wasn't afraid. The sorry bastard was plotting.

Not that it would do him any good.

"Hands where I can see them," Doyle said. "Now."

One second of insolent hesitation, then Lucius slowly pulled out his hands. He held them up, showing the backs and then the palms as the rest of the team rushed in. Five men surrounded the perp, crossbows at the ready.

Another five fanned out, inspecting the hidden room.

"Over here," one cried. "Tunnel."

"Place is wired," someone else chimed in, bending down to inspect the floor. "Not explosives, though." He followed a lead wire around the room. "Aw, shit. Nerve gas. Gonna put us all to sleep."

"And without any vamps on the strike force, you'd be the only one not affected," Doyle said to Lucius. "Then you slip into your tunnel and go your merry way?"

"Seemed like a good idea at the time," Lucius drawled. "Right now, I'm thinking a few more hours at the drawing board would have served me well."

"Glad you're so amused," Doyle said, "considering we have you dead to rights on a solid murder charge."

"I seem to recall something about a trial," Lucius said. "This isn't over, Ryan."

"Oh, it is. You're done, old friend. Finished. There's nowhere left to run."

"There's always somewhere."

Doyle's hand fisted at his side. He wanted to smash Lucius in the face. Wanted to wipe away that smug grin.

Oh, yeah. Doyle wanted to see the bloodsucker burn.

Lucius turned his head, then the beast reached slowly up and pulled off his sunglasses. The familiar amber eyes stared straight at Doyle. Calm eyes. And too damn arrogant.

"You're going down," Doyle said, stepping forward to slap the binders on his wrists.

"Right now, perhaps," Lucius said. "But there's always a plan B."

TWELVE

Luke paced the hematite-and-glass cell. Or he tried to pace, but as he could take only five strides before colliding with a wall, he gained little satisfaction from the mindless motion. He had never intended to end up caged like an animal, and his own miscalculation frustrated him. Tariq's removal from the active RAC team had been a critical blow, and considering that Luke was now locked in a cell, he took little satisfaction from the fact that Tariq's debt remained unpaid.

He needed another way out.

The possibility of calling upon his usual connections crossed his mind, but Braddock had been a personal matter, and any assistance he requested would come at a heavy price. Since he had no interest in being beholden to anyone, he preferred to keep that possibility dormant until the need was truly great.

Then again, considering that the prosecution intended to remove him from this plane of existence, perhaps the situation called for desperate measures.

Not that this little detour hadn't been useful—Luke had at least been able to confirm firsthand that the evidence gathered with regard to the death of Marcus Braddock was sufficient to condemn him. His hope that a percipient demon would be among the first responders had been satisfied, and both the DNA and the ring had played their intended roles. With such indisputable evidence in its pocket, the prosecution would have no need to look for motive. No need to look closer into Braddock's life and uncover that reprehensible creature's connection to Tasha.

She was safe.

And soon he would figure a way out of this mess and be gone.

Both thoughts gave him some bit of satisfaction. But the latter also gave him sorrow.

Sara.

From this moment forward, she was out of his life forever. The thought left him feeling cold. Empty.

"Sara," he murmured, his body tightening from the mere memory of her touch. He'd craved her for so long, but actually being with her had defied all his expectations. And knowing now that they had been together in the past—that she'd felt the same connection to him that he did to her—made the certainty that he would lose her again that much more devastating.

He closed his eyes, letting his body recall the splendor of her touch. They'd made love with a fierceness born of need, a delicious intensity that was somehow both gentle and rough, giving and accepting. And when they collapsed, sated, in each other's arms, he'd stroked her hair and her dewy skin, relaxing gently against her until they were both calm enough to go again, the next time slow and soft and sensual.

He had gone to her despite the plan he had so intricately worked out, knowing that it was a risk. But how could he have chosen otherwise?

He'd had more than his share of women over the centuries, but she was the first since his wife, now long dead and buried, who had breathed true life into him. He'd wanted to remain by her side. To talk with her, to laugh with her, and not merely to sleep with her. He wanted to watch the stars with her. To take her for long walks on a moonlit beach. To simply be with her.

She'd caught him off guard—both surprising him and fulfilling all his expectations and more. She stilled the writhing of the serpent, making him forget that darkness that was always so dangerously close to the surface.

She was his. He knew it resolutely. Completely. And the knowledge that he would never see her again delivered more punishment than being trapped in this cell ever could.

A high-pitched beep pulled him from his thoughts. That sound was soon followed by the grate of the detention block door opening and the clatter of overlapping footsteps. Luke cocked his head, listening. Three creatures, one surefooted, two oafish, moving in his direction. He returned to his bench, sat, and waited. In a moment, Nicholas Montague's pretty face appeared beyond the glass wall, flanked on either side by the ogres who guarded the detention block.

Despite his angel face, Nick was both vicious and brilliant. And because of his innocent features, he was a far more effective defense advocate than he would be working with his intellect alone, admirable though it might be. They'd been friends for over five centuries, watched each other's backs countless times, and owed each other their lives a dozen times over.

It had been Luke who'd introduced Nick to Tiberius, and as the vampiric liaison to the Shadow Alliance, Tiberius had sponsored Nick's training as an advocate.

As Luke watched, Nick signaled to the ogres, who unenthusiastically began to disengage the series of locks that held the glass door shut. The glass itself was unbreakable and, like an antenna embedded in a car's back window, was infused with a series of thin hematite filaments. The hematite-reinforced glass coupled with the hematite alloy of the walls meant that escape by transfiguration was impossible. Luke knew; he'd tried. As for breaking the glass, that was impossible, too, as the damned mineral sapped his strength considerably.

Escape by less elegant means, however, remained a possibility, and the ogres knew it. The ogre who was not operating the locks raised his weapon, the stake mounted on the crossbow aimed menacingly in Luke's direction.

"Hands," growled the ogre. "Clasp you on head."

Once Luke had complied, the second ogre released the last lock and pulled the door open. He gestured roughly for Nick to step inside, then shut the door and locked the advocate in.

"Twenty minute got you," the first ogre said. The second one grunted and stepped away from the door, then followed his leader out of Luke's line of sight.

Once they were gone, Luke took his hands down and grinned at his friend. "It's not the Plaza, but I've had worse accommodations."

"Goddammit, Luke," Nick snapped, utterly destroying any illusion that the angel face reflected an angel's temperament. "Have you completely lost your mind? You want to tell me when the bloody hell you got so damned sloppy? And how the fuck am I supposed to get the goddamn charges dismissed with that kind of evidence peppering the file?"

Tirade over, Nick collapsed next to Luke onto the cement slab that protruded from the wall and served as a bed. "Dammit," he muttered.

"Good to see you again, too," Luke said, chuckling when Nick shifted sideways, his expression caustic.

"I talked to Tiberius," he said. "Braddock wasn't an authorized kill."

"No," Luke acknowledged. "Braddock was mine."

"This isn't going to go over well," Nick said. "You know that, right? Los Angeles is hot right now, and you, my friend, have just added to his problems."

"The Therians. I know. What's happened?"

"That's the trouble," Nick said. "We don't know. Intelligence has hit walls. All we know is that Gunnolf's planning another play for Los Angeles. Bastard's determined that Los Angeles will be under Therian, not vamp, control. Like he's got a shot in hell of managing to pull that off."

"The Therians have been trying to oust Tiberius from the key territories for years," Luke said. Centuries, really, with the pissing contest played out over different real estate. New York. Constantinople. Prague. Moscow. London. But with the exception of the long-standing Therian control over Paris, Tiberius—and the vampires—had maintained control over the prime territories.

"Talk is this time they've got the golden ticket."

"You believe that?" Luke said. Less than a decade prior, a covert werewolf team had managed to taint the Southern California blood supply. A lot of innocent vamps had died, but the plan hadn't weakened Tiberius's hold over the territory. On the contrary, Tiberius's support within the Alliance had grown, even as Gunnolf's had fallen, despite the fact that the apprehended team members insisted that the head werewolf had no knowledge of the maneuver.

"Hell no, I don't believe it," Nick said. "But as Tiberius's counsel, I can't ignore the risk. The Demon and Earthen liaisons to the Alliance have been making pro-Therian noises recently. If Gunnolf manages to make it look like Tiberius's ironclad control over Los Angeles is slipping, the Alliance members might actually vote to shift the territory away from the vamps and over to the Therians."

In other words, Luke thought, Gunnolf didn't have to succeed at whatever he had planned in order to win. He just had to kick up a shitload of dust.

All in all, a fucking nightmare for Tiberius, and a great big glowing opportunity for Luke. Because if he could figure out a way to help Tiberius with the Therian problem, then perhaps Tiberius would reconsider his decision on the pardon. "I need specifics," he said. "What's the word on the street?"

"Not much chatter, but whatever it is, it's going down soon. Hasik rolled into town a few days ago." An alpha wolf by the light of the full moon and a royal prick all the time, Hasik was one of Gunnolf's top men. If there was a play to shift control of Los Angeles to the Therian, then Hasik would be at the heart of it.

"And Tiberius doesn't have any solid intelligence as to what Gunnolf and Hasik have planned?" Luke asked.

"Not a hint, not an inkling."

"That kind of information would be worth something, don't you think?"

"A price beyond rubies, my friend. So would making the Hasik problem go away. Too bad you're a bit indisposed at the moment." Nick leaned back, looking perfectly at home in the sparse cell despite the tailored Savile Row suit. "Which brings us full circle. And so I ask again," Nick said, his voice now deadly calm. "What kind of crazy shit are you pulling?"

"I assume it's safe to talk?"

"I've got an asset in Monitoring. For the next hour, the observation discs will have unexplained auditory interference."

"You trust him?"

"My asset?" Nick asked, his eyes dancing. "Very much."

A woman, then, Luke thought, and let the subject drop. If Nick said he'd taken care of the problem, Luke believed him. And he should have known Nick's associate would be female. With Nick, that was practically a given.

"Now quit stalling," Nick demanded. "You killed Braddock. Why?"

"The man was a son of a bitch."

"So are you, but you don't see me pulling out a stake."

"And for that, you have my gratitude."

Nick stood, his expression troubled. "Dammit, Luke. You've compromised the Alliance. Hell, you've compromised the secrecy of the kyne."

"I haven't," Luke said, the denial automatic and without conviction. "This mission was outside the Alliance's authority, and the kyne are not involved."

"I'm involved," Nick said.

"You are," he agreed. "And you are no longer active as kyne. Still, that bond remains strong. The bond of friendship, however, is stronger. Or so I would hope."

"God, you're a pain in the ass," Nick growled.

"It is one of my most persistent failings," Luke agreed.

"What about Tasha?" Nick asked, sighing. "Where is she? Do you need me to check in on her? Did you even consider what this would do to her, you being tossed in a cell? She won't understand."

"I considered it," Luke said. "And I weighed everything before acting. About that much, at least, I would think you would give me credit."

"Luke—I didn't mean. I know you wouldn't do anything to put her at risk. I just—It's just that she relies on you."

"A fact of which I am well aware." Frustrated, he moved to the glass and looked out the barrier at the hall beyond. It was because of Tasha that he was in this cell in the first place. Because of her, and because of his own hubris so many years before.

He should have known better, he thought as the memories welled inside him. He should never have brought her over.

He'd found her, alone and injured, fear clinging to her like a blanket, and she'd looked up at him, life fading from eyes so like his own sweet daughter's that he'd been unable to think clearly.

Take, the serpent had whispered, and so help him he'd listened. He took, he drank, and when the change came upon her, he became father, teacher, protector. Most of all, he'd helped her through the Holding, urging her on as she fought her own *Azag Mahru*. It had been a hard battle, but they'd won. They'd brought back the girl within.

A confused, lost innocent who by all rights should have been in heaven with the angels by now instead of walking among demons. Instead of suffering at the hands of bastards like Marcus Braddock, men who took what they wanted and cared little for the consequences.

Whatever particular arrogance Braddock had suffered under, it was stilled now, as was the man himself. And for that, at least, Luke was grateful.

"Tasha's taken care of," he said softly. "I sent her to San Francisco." He turned back to face Nick. "She's with Serge."

"With Serge?"

Something in Nick's voice caught Luke's attention. "What?"

"I called Serge," Nick said. "Not less than an hour ago. I wasn't able to reach him."

Something cold and unfamiliar settled in Luke's stomach. *Fear.* Serge's journey to sanity had been even more dappled than Luke's. Many vampires—most even—were able to control the serpent, to push it back down, and keep it bound.

But if the *Azag Mahru* won the battle—if the vampire could not regain control—the vampire became hunted. A rogue. A threat to society.

And if the vampire was able to keep control despite the serpent's taunt, then that vampire lived on the knife-edge. A difficult existence, as Luke well knew.

So yes, Luke knew the extent to which Serge forced himself to hold on, sometimes by only the thinnest of threads. If that thread unraveled...

"You tried all his numbers? You sent an e-mail?"

"I did." Nick stood and started to pace. "I'll send Ryback over to Serge's condo. He's in Silicon Valley on an assignment. As soon as he wraps, I'll have him go by. I can't imagine Serge would leave Tasha alone, but if he did, Ryback can bring her home."

Luke nodded, unsatisfied. He should be the one going to her, the one bringing her safely back to LA. Since that was impossible at the moment, he reluctantly agreed, and tried damn hard to push the worry out of his head. No easy task.

Nick stopped pacing and looked at Luke, his expression pensive. "You sent her away, which is something I've never been witness to in all these centuries. She could have stayed with me. Even Ryback or Slater would have taken her in, and she'd have been here. Close by you. But you sent her hundreds of miles away. I'm not an idiot, Lucius. You're protecting her. But from what?"

From what indeed.

Slow fury bubbled within Luke as he recalled Tasha's words, her tearful entreaties. The terror on her face when she'd described what Braddock had done to her. And as he thought, the serpent uncoiled.

"He raped her," he said, his voice low and dangerous. He felt his fangs extend, now thick against his lips. "Braddock hurt her. He put his hands on her and he took what he had no right to take."

"And so you took back," Nick said, his voice soft. "From him."

Luke's jaw was set. "Did I have another choice?"

Nick closed his eyes, shook his head. "No," he said. "You didn't."

He moved forward and put his hand on Luke's shoulder. "I would have done the same thing."

Luke nodded. "If I didn't believe that, you wouldn't be the one in here representing me."

"This case could get dirty. Everything you've done, Luke—it could come back down on you."

"I know that." The faces of his victims swam through his memory. Killers themselves, dark creatures that had escaped justice for the murder of their kind and humans. Who had, because of technicalities or corruption or pure cunning, escaped the system that was supposed to lock them up or put them down. They'd slipped free, and even as the filthy rats were congratulating themselves on outrunning the long arm of the law, the Alliance stepped in with soldiers who operated outside the confines of the system, its sticky fingers able to reach where that long arm could not.

The PEC itself answered to the Alliance, and yet in sanctioning its own brand of justice, the Alliance broke the very agreement that had created it. That violation was justified by the need to protect the Shadow society as a whole, to ensure the secrecy of a world that operated on the fringes of and beneath human civilization.

Luke was a player, and expendable. He had always known that. But his ultimate goal was justice. And, yes, he sought penance as well. Redemption for a past that he had managed to escape. A past that crept softly up to him more often than he would like to taunt him, to urge him to sink down under.

He would not.

He had fought long and hard for the control of his soul, and he despised those who willingly succumbed to the darkness, who would not even pitch the battle.

He was kyne for a reason and, acknowledged or not, he would stand true.

"If it comes to that, you know I'll protect the kyne and Tiberius. But I don't expect an investigation that deep. They have my DNA, and Ryan Doyle has already filed an affidavit as to his vision. The case is open and shut. There's no reason to dig."

"The PEC doesn't always need a reason," Nick retorted. "And Ryan Doyle will probably take on your trial as a personal crusade."

That much, Luke thought, was true. "I need out of here, Nick," he said, standing. "I have no intention of staying in this goddamn cell."

Nick didn't even bother to pretend shock or dismay. "I'm assuming you're not intending to wait for my brilliant legal tap dancing to acquit you. So what are you planning, and how is my ass going to be compromised?"

"That is something I've yet to figure out."

"Well, let me suggest seduction."

Luke laughed. "What else would I expect from you?"

"Not me, my friend. You." Nick stood up, then leaned against the glass, looking far more smug than the situation called for. "I was thinking you could turn on the charm with the prosecutor. To be honest, I think you'll enjoy it."

"Oh, and why is that?"

"Remember the woman you pointed out to me about a month ago? Sara Constantine? The one who was prosecuting the Stemmons trial?"

Luke's words tasted bitter as he said, "I remember. Why?"

"Just that you seemed tempted by her."

"And if I was?"

"Well, my friend, the world is a wild and wooly place, full of coincidences and unexpected flights of fancy."

"Dammit, Nick, get to the point. What does my chance at plying the prosecutor for a reduced charge and plea bargain have to do with Sara Constantine?"

"Just everything. She's the newest hire at Division 6 and the lead prosecutor on the case. Under Leviathan's watchful supervision, of course."

Luke sat down hard, the shock of Nick's words settling through him. Sara as the prosecutor.

Sara, who by now knew he was here, in this cell. And she knew what he'd done.

Her involvement would undoubtedly skew his plan. He had seen her tenacity in the pursuit of Xavier Stemmons. She was a woman who demanded answers, and if she went in search of a motive, she might dig deep enough to drag Tasha into this mess.

And that was unacceptable.

He had to see her. Had to assess how much of a risk she was. And he had to explain as much as he could.

It wouldn't matter, though. She'd see only a monster who killed. A beast who'd toyed with her heart.

A vampire.

She'd look at him now, and she'd see her father, dead on the sidewalk.

Her wounds went deep. He hoped her passion did as well.

His plan would likely kill whatever small thing might have begun to grow between them—he knew that, and regret cut him like a knife—but at least he would see her again. Would touch her again. Would see the soft part of her lips as she came and feel the slick brush of her damp skin against his own.

He would use her, but the pleasure he gave her would be real. For Sara, he knew, that would make the betrayal all the worse. That, however, was a reality from which Luke couldn't escape. He had to be free, and he couldn't compromise Tasha's safety because of the whims of his heart.

"I'll make her an asset," he said, hating himself as he spoke the words. He looked up at Nick. "I need you to get me on the street." He needed to see her, needed to put these wheels in motion.

"Do you really think now is the best time? Her first day? They'll be wiring her house with security, placing safety spells and borders. They'll issue her a panic button. You show up, she pushes that button, and the gig is over."

"I have no intention of seeing her tonight," he said, only slightly regretting the lie. He wasn't going to tell Nick about his night with Sara. That much, at least, would remain pure. But without that bit of information, Nick couldn't understand why Luke wanted to go to Sara now. Why, in fact, he believed that she would see him—or why Luke still held on to the tiny sliver of hope that she wouldn't bring the wrath of Division 6 down upon him.

"So, what? You're just interested in taking a stroll around town? See the sights? Catch a movie?"

"Actually, I'm interested in having a little chat with Ural Hasik."

Nick nodded thoughtfully. "Fair enough. Though Hasik might not be in a conversational mood."

"I'm sure we can find something to chat about."

Nick stood. "I'll arrange for a furlough."

"Try Judge Acquila," Luke said. "Remind him of Prague, 1874. That tussle between him and a British diplomat regarding said diplomat's daughter."

"Kind of you to have helped him sort it out," Nick said. He aimed a hard look at Luke. "Hear me well, though. I'll get him to authorize an advocate-escorted furlough for the purpose of reviewing the crime scene with my client. Three hours. And then we walk back into this detention block and they close the cage on you. We'll get you the hell out of here, but you are not escaping on my watch. I want your word."

"You have it."

"I like my privacy, and I'll not have the PEC looking into both of us."

"I'll be outside, Nick, but I won't be free. You know the drill. Escape would be next to impossible. Wasn't it Ferdinand Cristo who broke furlough last summer? His death was not a pretty thing."

"Your promise, Luke," Nick repeated.

"I swear on our friendship and our bond as kyne that I will return to this cell." But before he did, he would have his time with Sara. And though his purpose was dark, his heart still leapt at the thought of touching her again.

THIRTEEN

Sara followed Leviathan into the detention center antechamber, the case file and a profile of Luke held tight in her hand. She'd skimmed the latter in the elevator. The photo —defying the myth that vampires couldn't be captured on film— along with his vital statistics. Height, six foot five. Weight, 220.

Both stats jibed with what she knew of the man. The next statistic, however, had her mouth going suddenly dry: born in Italy in the year 122. Apparently she'd been a few millennia off when she'd guessed that the man she'd invited into her apartment was five years her senior.

And now here she was, about to see him again. Hopefully, she was ready. Hopefully, Leviathan couldn't simply look at her and know that she'd slept with him.

Oh, god. She'd slept with a vampire. A murderer.

She knew he was guilty. She'd seen the evidence, and it was a hell of a lot more compelling than the kind of evidence she usually saw upstairs. But somehow, she still couldn't believe it was true.

Because you're acting like a lovestruck kid. Act like a prosecutor.

With a brisk mental nod, she squared her shoulders and slammed a mental door on her intruding memories.

She could do that, she told herself. She could close it off. Block away the hours in Luke's arms. The way they'd laughed together. All of it.

She could do it, she knew, because in the end, this was the job she lived for. And with that thought, she snapped the folder shut, then went to stand by Leviathan as they waited for the guards to unlock the cellblock door.

A moment later, the red light above the door flashed green, then slid quietly to one side. Sara followed Leviathan into a hall lined with glass-enclosed cells, her head held high as they passed the other prisoners, her heels clicking firmly on the cement floor.

His was the last cell, and he looked up as they approached. She saw it immediately, that spark of recognition. That quick shadow in his eyes that suggested his world was tilting along with hers.

She, at least, wasn't locked up.

The guard—an ogre, Leviathan had told her—unlocked the cell at Leviathan's nod, and she followed him in. And despite knowing what he had done—despite her mind constantly flipping from Braddock's ripped-out throat to her own father's—she couldn't wrap her head around the fact that this man was in this cell on charges of murder.

Not that Luke had the appearance of a prisoner. True, he wore a faded gray T-shirt with "Detention C" stamped across the chest in black letters, but there was nothing about him that seemed bound. On the contrary, walking into that room felt much the same as walking into a conference room, with Luke at the head of the table, slowly surveying those summoned to do his bidding.

Beside her, Leviathan's gaze shifted between the two of them, his eyes dull and unreadable. Then he pressed a hand to her back, easing her forward to one of the two chairs on the opposite side of Luke. If her boss knew that anything other than that a murder investigation was taking place in that room, he didn't show it.

Sara was determined not to show it, either.

She pulled out the chair and sat, then took a yellow pad from her briefcase and placed it on her lap. The investigator's report was tucked underneath, just enough of the page revealed under the pad to signal to Luke that she'd read the report and she knew what he'd done. She kept her pen in her hand, idly twirling it in her fingers as she watched Luke's face. Other than that first flicker of recognition, however, he revealed nothing.

"Lucius Dragos," Leviathan said, taking the chair beside Sara. "It's not often I have the chance to sit across from a man with such a notorious reputation."

"Notorious?" Luke repeated, his mouth curving down into a frown. "I didn't know you listened to gossip, Nikko."

The easy use of Leviathan's first name surprised Sara, and she glanced at her new boss, anticipating his reaction. None, however, was forthcoming. Instead, he merely flipped through the papers in his hand. "Belfast, last month," Leviathan said. "A werewolf dead in Glencairn Park. Nasty business."

"Wasn't it, though?" Luke leaned back in his chair, utterly calm in the face of Leviathan's accusation. "Turns out Division 3 suspected that same werewolf in the killing of a human politician not three days after being released from PEC custody." He shook his head. "I had a pint with the lead investigator. Not only was I not charged, but the bloke picked up the tab for my Guinness."

"And Talijax Feaureaux? Dallas, Texas."

"Apparently I was in the wrong place at the wrong time. The charges against me were dismissed."

"And Milton Craymore?" Leviathan pressed, as Sara sat more stiffly in her chair. This intel was new to her, and the accusations seemed to fly at her like blows.

"I believe Milton was responsible for planning that deadly werewolf raid on the Oslo vampire community center." A slow smile crossed his face as he looked straight at Leviathan, never flinching. "I can't say I mourn the death of one such as him, but I don't know who to congratulate for ridding us of that swine."

It didn't matter what he said. She knew, and Leviathan knew. It was in his eyes. He'd killed. He'd gotten away with it. And he was proud of what he'd done. Proud of the blows he'd struck. She'd bet her new job that no one had gone to trial for any of those crimes. They'd had the right defendant; they just hadn't found the evidence to prove it.

Beside her, Leviathan pushed back his chair. Sara took a deep breath and made sure she had her game face on before looking over at her boss. He was standing, forcing Luke to tilt his head back to look at him. It was, Sara knew, a simple trick that had the effect of creating at least an illusion of power. In this case, however, the maneuver didn't work.

Despite Leviathan's cool confidence, Lucius Dragos lost none of his cool. Instead, he rocked back slightly so that his chair balanced on the two rear legs. He shook his head, ruffling the perfect mane of silky black hair. He could not, Sara realized, run his fingers through his hair, as both hands were currently manacled to the arms of the chair, apparently brought in for this interview. Yet despite that disadvantage and despite the fact that Leviathan now towered above him, Luke was in no way diminished. If anything, the two men now seemed equally pitted against each other.

It was, Sara thought, fascinating.

Leviathan moved closer, getting into Luke's space. Getting into his face. This time, when Leviathan spoke, his words were low and controlled without the earlier suggestion of civility. "Let us understand each other, Dragos. You are here because we brought you in. We trapped you. We caught you. We shackled you. And once we dispense with the formality of a trial, we will execute you."

Luke's eyes flicked up, the heat in them banked by a tight control. "You don't win the game until the executioner's stake slams through my heart. Until then, I think the wise money is on me."

The scent of cinnamon filled the air. "Do not for a moment think that this is a game, Dragos."

"I don't play games. I would have thought you knew that much about me." He turned his attention to Sara, and she forced herself to remain steady, to keep her expression bland as those deadly eyes looked into hers. "Perhaps you speak for your companion's benefit?" His eyes lingered on her, and for a moment, one fleeting, dancing moment, she thought she saw a glimmer of regret in his face. Then it cleared, and all she saw was ice. "I doubt she is as familiar with my file as you are, Nikko."

Leviathan nodded toward her, his expression filled with something akin to fatherly pride. "I would suggest, Lucius, that you work hard not to antagonize Ms. Constantine. She may not yet know all there is to know about you, but I assure you that she is a quick study. She'll learn, Luke," he said, leaning slightly forward. "She'll learn all about you."

"I look forward to being thoroughly examined," Luke said. He turned toward her, the heat from his gaze curling through her.

She tamped it down, angry at herself for letting that heat warm her for even a millisecond.

"You'd be wise not to underestimate me," she snapped, and left it at that. She wasn't going to get into a verbal sparring match with him. Not now. Not ever.

For a moment, she thought he would answer. Then she felt the press of Leviathan's hand on her shoulder. The simple weight of it calmed her, and she drew in a breath, furious with herself for lashing out.

"You are entitled to a representative, Luke," Leviathan said, almost kindly.

"I have retained Nicholas Montague," he said, then shrugged. "Neither of us saw a need for him to be here for this interview."

Leviathan looked as though he would argue. But in the end, he merely nodded. "Very well. Then let us dispense with the pleasantries and move straight to business. Record on. In cell interview with suspect Lucius Dragos, vampire. Present are Division 6 representatives, Director Nikko Leviathan and prosecutor Sara Constantine. Mr. Dragos, you have declined to have a representative present?"

"I have."

"Very well. Mr. Dragos, you are a vampire?"

"I am."

"You are the sire of the Dragos clan?"

"I am the last and only acknowledged Dragos, as you well know."

"Of course," Leviathan said. "Your ward cannot claim the clan name." He flipped through his notes. "In light of her precarious mental state as a human, Tasha was subject to termination. She received special dispensation in 1490, sparing her life, but forbidding her to propagate or inherit, and requiring you to stand as guardian."

"I'm aware of the circumstances," Luke said, his voice hard.

"A hard-fought battle, if I recall," Leviathan said. "I believe there was significant testimony both for and against termination."

"We were both there, Nikko," Luke said. "I'm sure you recall the testimony as well as I do."

"And while you are here, she is under the care of..."

"She is well-watched after now," Luke said, "and successfully survived the Holding all those years ago. Her serpent is bound, and those who fought for her termination can all go to hell." A muscle in his jaw twitched, his hands tightening on the arms of his chair in a visible effort to calm himself. "If you wish to question me about the death of Marcus Braddock, I would suggest you get on with it."

Leviathan hesitated, then nodded. "Very well. Let's cut to the chase. Where were you last night?"

"Isn't that what you intend to prove?"

"Fair enough," Leviathan said, glancing at a message that had popped up on his phone. "Then let me tell you, and you can stop me if I get anything wrong."

Smart, Sara thought. Lead him through the evidence. Let him know how bad it is for him—and with a witness like Doyle, it was very, very bad—and then present the offer for a plea bargain again at the end of the interview.

In the calm, unemotional voice of an experienced prosecutor, Leviathan began a rundown of the evidence against Luke, including Doyle's vision.

"Agent Doyle's conclusions have just been confirmed by the PEC's medical examiner."

"Is that a fact?"

"Division 6 has a record of seven hundred and eighty-six vampires permanently residing in the greater Los Angeles area," Leviathan said softly. "And yet yours was the DNA we discovered on the victim."

Sara lifted her head, startled by the mention of DNA evidence. Luke, however, remained impassive. Unreadable. If anything, he seemed amused. And though she didn't know Nikko Leviathan well at all, she could see that he'd noted the amusement, too. And that it was pissing him off.

"I suppose, though, that some of the thanks must go to you," Leviathan continued. "Until your arrest, we didn't have your DNA on file. And yet you provided a sample to the agents without a court order. I have to wonder why."

Sara worked to keep her features bland, but the truth was that she wondered, too. If Division didn't already have his DNA, why on earth would Luke provide it unless it would prove his innocence? In this case, though, it proved his guilt.

"Would you have been able to obtain a court order?" Luke asked.

"Undoubtedly."

"Then why put everyone to the trouble?"

"That's only one of many questions that we'll be addressing throughout this investigation. We will find all our answers, Lucius. I give you my word."

He stood then, his posture suggesting the interview was over. Sara pushed to her feet as well, accidentally dropping her pad and file. She bent over to pick up the papers and photos and found herself looking into Braddock's cold, dead eyes. Luke had done this. A vampire. A killer.

He'd torn Braddock's neck out, drained his blood. And now he sat there, calm and cool despite having committed such a heinous crime. A crime as personal to her as his hands upon her naked body had been. She fought the memory back, unwilling to think about the intimate things they'd done together only hours after he'd gone out and murdered Judge Braddock.

The thought sickened her, her reaction all the more intense because the man had gotten under her skin.

"Record off," Leviathan said. He turned to Sara, ignoring Luke. "We'll talk in my office."

He headed for the door and she followed.

"I won't say it's been a pleasure, Nikko," Luke said, his voice controlled and confident. "But I will say that I look forward to seeing Ms. Constantine again. I'm sure our future interviews will be illuminating."

Slowly and deliberately, she turned in his direction. "I look forward to it, too, Mr. Dragos. This case is mine now, and I promise you that I won't rest until the dead have justice."

"I believe you," he said, his expression bland although she hoped her words had kicked him in the gut. "And may I be among the first to congratulate you on your new position."

She started to reply, but Leviathan laid a hand upon her arm. "Advise your advocate to be present at interviews. Trust me when I say that you're going to need him." He keyed in the code and pulled open the door. "Constantine, with me."

Sara sat behind her desk, trying to focus on the papers scattered there. She failed.

She couldn't focus on anything. She felt numb and furious and betrayed all at the same time. Annoyed with herself, she opened the laptop that Blair had set up for her, then navigated to the live feed of the cell block. She selected the feed of Luke's cell, and watched as he sat there, as still as death, and wondered what the hell he was plotting. Because there was something going on with him. Something not right.

She might be new to the PEC, but she wasn't new to defendants. She'd tried cases from misdemeanors all the way up to capital murder. And over the years, she'd come to know how defendants thought. Luke, she was certain, was weaving a plan.

But what?

She sighed, her eyes on the screen. She'd never expected this. Never even had a hint that he was the kind of man who could commit murder. On the contrary, he had a giving soul. She thought about the apartment for Melanie and frowned.

He was a protector, not a killer.

Was he that good a liar? Or was she missing something important?

She glanced at the screen again, only to find him looking straight at the camera, and it felt as though he was looking at her, sliding deep into her thoughts. Urging her to trust him even now.

Bastard.

She slammed the laptop shut, then sighed. He'd used her, and she didn't like being used. And now that she was opposing him, he'd try to manipulate her, and she definitely didn't like being manipulated.

Well, he'd picked the wrong woman. Their night together had been exceptional, but if he thought that would push her toward leniency, he was very mistaken.

He was a vampire.

The thought kept returning, as if she was likely to forget.

She wasn't, and yet she still couldn't wrap her head about the reality.

She'd truly slept with a vampire. Worse, with a murderer.

And yet none of those facts lined up with the Luke she knew. With the man who'd touched her so tenderly.

Stop it.

Almost without realizing she was doing it, she pulled her wallet out of her purse, then withdrew the small photograph she kept behind her driver's license. A picture of her and her father. He looked undeniably professorial in a tweed jacket and holding a pipe, and she'd been trussed up in a dress with an itchy petticoat. They'd come —she and her mother—to watch her father receive an award. Sara didn't know for what, only that a lot of people were applauding for her daddy. She'd made it a point to clap the loudest.

Four days later, her father was dead. His neck ripped open. His blood drained. And her own screams echoing through the neighborhood.

She squeezed her eyes shut, willing her mind to replace the horror of that night with happier memories. The smell of tobacco and mint that always laced his jacket. The way he'd stroke her hair when he'd tell her bedtime stories.

And it had been a vampire who had taken him from this world. From Sara.

Full circle, she thought, drying her tears with the back of her hand. Today, everything circled around to vampires.

Vampires.

A vampire had murdered her father, leaving his daughter with only memories and a legacy of nightmares.

A vampire had seduced her, leaving her sweaty and satisfied and clinging to the illusion that she had met a man who was worth something. A man whose kiss had brought her to her knees. A man who'd left flowers along with a silent promise that he would be back.

What a crock.

She pulled the ribbon out of her pocket and twisted it around her finger, cutting off the circulation to the end of the digit. Her naïveté disgusted her. Even if Leviathan was right and she was insusceptible to a vampire's mental tricks, she'd still fallen under Luke's spell. The potent allure of a confident man who takes what he wants; the decadent pleasure of being the woman he desires.

Enough of that.

She released her tight hold on the ribbon, letting it fall to the desktop. Then she flipped open the laptop once again. Now, he stood at the glass wall, his hands pressed to the barrier. Even on the small screen, his presence was compelling, a man who didn't merely occupy a space, but commanded it. Now he was quiet, pensive. And though his expression was no more revealing than it had been in the interview, Sara thought she detected a hint of sadness, of worry.

A bubble of concern rose within her, and she immediately quashed it. Of course he was sad and worried. He damn well should be considering the weight of the murder charge against him.

He moved across the cell to sit on the concrete bench that served as a bed, thighs straining against the thin material of the PEC-issued pants. She told herself she was unaffected by the view, insisting that the lazy curl of desire that eased through her was nothing more than residual lust. She couldn't want him, this murderer, this beast. She was better than that. Had more control over her emotions. Over her damn hormones.

Yet she'd picked up the ribbon again, and now her fingers were tying themselves into knots. And when he tilted his head and once again looked straight at her—at the camera—she felt the heat swirl through her. It shamed her. Infuriated her. Not because of what she'd done with him that night, but because the memory of his hands on her skin still fired her senses, making her nipples peak and her sex tingle.

Even knowing what he'd done—what he was—her body still craved him. His hands. His lips. Even the scrape of danger as his teeth dragged over her bare skin.

She wanted it—a vampire's touch—and she despised that weakness in herself. Despised him for being the cause of her folly. Slowly, purposefully, she looked down and opened the file in Division v. Dragos. She flipped to the crime scene photo and stared hard at the image of Braddock's neck wound, so similar to the wound she saw night after night in her dreams.

The ripped flesh. The dried blood.

There was no room for lust here. No room for desire or longing or fancy wishes of different circumstances.

This was murder.

Luke had killed. She was a prosecutor.

It really didn't get much simpler than that.

She stood up, then dropped the red ribbon into her office trash can. Time to get to work.

FOURTEEN

Ural Hasik slammed through the double glass doors into the Quik-Stop Mart on South Figueroa, his nose twitching. He stopped, then looked around, silently daring anyone to give him grief. A human in a black leather skullcap and an oversized jersey kept his nosy ass looking in Hasik's direction a second too long. Hasik growled, the sound starting low in his throat as he bared his teeth.

The human backed away, almost knocking down a display of breakfast cereals.

Fuck, yeah, you better run away, you worthless piece of human garbage.

He shoved his hands into his pockets and prowled toward the counter, where an ancient wraith of a man was working the cash register.

"Can I help you?" he asked, a definite tremor in his voice.

"You can point me toward the self-service section."

The elderly cashier's eyes went wide. "I—I don't think you want to go down there."

"You're telling me what I want, old man?"

"I just mean ... your kind. Down there. It's not—"

"I'm expected," Hasik said, slapping a C-note onto the counter. Then he twisted his mouth into some version of a polite smile, his white canines gleaming under the fluorescents.

"I—Yes. Of course. This way." He stepped out from behind the counter, then shuffled to the back of the store. He paused in front of the door to the walk-in refrigerator through which the glass display cases of soda, beer, milk, and snacks were stocked. "Through there. All the way back. There's a door. Just past the empty milk crates. Code's O-NEG."

Hasik curled his lip in a snarl, just because he didn't like the bastard. He tugged open the door, then stepped into the cold, the fine hairs that covered his body standing on end. When he reached the keypad box, he punched in the code, then slipped inside as the steel door opened. The corridor was long and damp and twisted down in a spiral pattern until it reached a small stone-hewn room three stories beneath the Quik-Stop. The walls were lined with benches, and on the benches sat at least a dozen pasty-faced blood-suckers drinking blood through long tubes extending through the stone walls. Hasik bit back a snort of disgust. He might not have their life span, but at least he didn't have to put up with that bullshit.

Two young-looking vampires stepped into the room from the underground entrance that fed into the LA subway system and allowed the vamps to come in and feed during the day. They eyeballed him, but he ignored their questioning glances. Not surprisingly, few werewolves ventured into vampire feeding arenas, but these two paid him little heed, moving instead to a kiosk at the far end of the room. As Hasik watched, one slid several coins in, then punched a few keys on a brightly lit pad.

The kid leaned in, studying the display, then turned to his buddy. "Gotta wait. All the stations are full."

"Damn, I'm hungry. We shoulda come yesterday. Told you I was getting in a bad way."

"Almost time. You'll be fine."

"Way I feel right now, I could suck down a human."

The first kid's eyebrows rose. "Whoa now, man. Don't even think about that. That's some seriously illegal shit."

The hungry kid shrugged. "I didn't say I would. I said I could. What, you think I faked the Holding? I got some serious control, dude. But, damn, it would be nice to taste something not through a goddamn straw."

"You hear about that Division judge? Throat completely ripped out."

"I know. Bad mojo, huh?"

"Worst. You ever lose control? Let the dark part rise?"

"No way, man. You?"

A shadow passed over the kid's face, and he shrugged. "Fuck no. I'm solid."

"You'd tell me, right? I mean, you wouldn't try to work that down on your own."

"Shit, man, I told you. I'm good." The kid turned back to the kiosk, now beeping with a seat number, and their conversation died away.

Hasik sneered. *Pussies.* That's what vamps were. All that power flowing through them, and what did they do? They bottled it up.

Idiots. Working so hard to tamp down on something that would raise them to the level of gods. Didn't make any damn sense.

Not werewolves. With the rise of the full moon, the beast within burst free, and man and beast were one. It was glorious, and no way would the wolven Therians—the weren—ever subject themselves to some bullshit ritual. Confinement, maybe. The damn Concordat required confinement of any weren who wasn't cognizant during the change. Young ones. A few others who lost themselves completely to the wolf. All for the protection of the fucking humans. Something else Hasik considered bullshit, but at least he wasn't in that sorry group.

And at least he wasn't a sorry ass bloodsucker.

Damn, but the vamps gave him the willies, and now they were all looking at him, catching his scent, knowing he wasn't one of them.

He bared his teeth, staring them down. He'd killed his share of vamps. Watched the surprise on their supposedly immortal faces as he whacked their heads off. No, they weren't any better than he was. Not by a long shot.

But damn if they wouldn't stop staring.

He shouldn't have come. Should have insisted she meet him someplace else, especially since he'd scanned the whole room and didn't see her. *Caris.* The female vamp. Gunnolf's new squeeze.

Hasik's lip curled automatically. Gunnolf, one of the key Alliance members. Gunnolf, head of the entire Therian community. Gunnolf, Hasik's friend and mentor, and the horny bastard went and hooked himself up with a female vampire. Fucking unbelievable.

Then again, Hasik wouldn't turn down a fine piece of ass like Caris, either.

"You look stupid just standing there." The female voice came from behind, and he whipped around to face her, taking in the short-cropped hair and blood-red lips. She wore a white tank top that hugged her breasts and a diaphanous white skirt that brushed the ground and revealed the curve of her thighs. The outfit of an innocent, but he knew damn well this woman was anything but.

His nostrils flared—he could smell the wolf upon her, the filthy whore. "Mind your manners, bitch," he sneered.

She ignored his menace. "Hard to believe Gunnolf actually trusts you to advise him." Her green eyes narrowed. "Then again, maybe that's why he's not controlling the City of Angels. Yet."

She pressed a hand onto his arm, and he growled, low and dangerous, the sound not fazing her in the least. "You think that's it, wolf-boy? You think you're the reason Tiberius's constantly making your buddy Gunnolf take it up the ass?"

"You watch yourself."

"No," she said, her voice as low and dangerous. "You watch it. You think you have Gunnolf's ear, and maybe you do. But I've got the rest of him, and you damn well know it."

"Meeting here was a mistake."

"I have to feed."

"Stories I've heard about you, I'm surprised you don't find a human. One nobody'd miss much."

The corner of her mouth curved with a secret pleasure, and he wondered if he'd hit the mark. But all she said was, "I'm law-abiding. You got any proof to the contrary?"

"I don't give a shit what you do, so long as you don't screw Gunnolf."

She laughed, the sound light and flirtatious, and right then she didn't seem like a warrior but like a woman. "Too late for that."

Hasik looked around. The other vamps were staring at them. All except one. A white-haired vampire with red eyes who was shifting in his seat, the tube going into his mouth flowing red. Whitey looked up, met Hasik's eyes, then flashed a bloody grin. Hasik turned away. "I don't like it down here."

"Scared?"

"Fuck you."

"Such language," she said, raising an eyebrow and sounding bored. She headed to the kiosk.

He tugged at her elbow. "We talk, I leave, you feed. I'm not sitting here while you do the suck-fest ritual."

For a moment he thought she'd argue, then she nodded. "Whatever you say. I came to this beautiful city to work for you, right?"

"Damn straight. Gunnolf tell you the plan?"

"The basics. Said you'd run me through the full briefing. When do we start?"

"Soon," Hasik said. The plan was beautiful, if he did say so himself. He'd pitched the idea to Gunnolf, and the pack leader had bitten right in. Sabotage that prick Tiberius, sitting all smug and happy in his London headquarters. Make it look like he couldn't control the vamps in the LA territory. Make it look like they were running wild, feeding off humans instead of skulking around in pussified feeding stations like this goddamn place. "This ain't gonna come out well for your kind, you know?"

Her face hardened. "I never said I claimed them as my kind."

"What the fuck? You're a vamp. So what's that supposed to mean?"

She waved the question away. "Give me the deets, and let's get on with this. I need to feed."

"You know Feris Tinsley? Gunnolf's lieutenant in Los Angeles?"

"I've met him."

"He keeps an office in the Slaughtered Goat, a pub in Van Nuys." She nodded. "I know it."

"Meet me there later. I'll brief you."

"Screw that. You tell me now. That's why you came here."

"I came to meet you," Hasik said, standing a little straighter. "I came to make sure I could work with a female." His lip curled. "Ain't ideal, but you'll do. But I don't take orders from you, bitch. You want in on this, you come to the Goat."

He could see the storm clouds brewing in her eyes, a rising fury that had Hasik taking a step backward.

"We're talking now," she said, but no way was he giving in to a woman. Not even Gunnolf's woman.

"No we ain't. You come to the—"

"Noooooooooooo!"

The cry echoed off the stone walls, and Hasik shoved past Caris, searching for the source. He found it in Whitey, the vamp with the red eyes who'd been sucking on a flowing red tube. Apparently Whitey wasn't enjoying his lunch. The albino bastard jerked out of his chair, ripping the tube from the wall.

"Fuck this shit! Fuck this goddamn plastic shit. They got humans back there. Bleeding for us. I want to taste them, dammit. I want to taste the life. This is bullshit. Fucking bullshit!"

He lashed out, knocking the girl next to him to the ground, then crouching over her as the two kids Hasik had noticed earlier looked on with horror. "You full up, bitch? You full up with blood? How do you stand it? How the fuck do you stand it?"

Something light and fast whipped past Hasik, and it wasn't until she had Whitey down on the ground seconds later, a lethal-looking blade to his neck, that Hasik realized the something was Caris, moving faster than he'd ever seen a vamp move. Whitey struggled beneath her, but she held him with ease. "Back off," she said. "Back off right now."

"I can't take it." His face contorted with pain. "How do you take it?"

Caris kept her knife on his neck, then leaned in close. She turned her head slightly, so that she was speaking to Whitey, but looking at Hasik. "You do," she said. "You just do."

"You can go in now," Martella told Sara, who had been hovering around the director's door, waiting for him to end a call.

"Thanks," she said, then drew in a breath and pushed open the door.

"Sara. How was your first day?"

"Wonderful. Strange. Eye-opening."

"That sounds about right." He gestured to a chair. "What did you want to see me about?"

"The Shadow Alliance, sir. You mentioned it in the interview with Dragos. But it's not something I'm familiar with. It sounded like a vigilante organization, and if that's the case—"

"It's not. Well, not exactly."

She shook her head, not understanding.

"The Shadow Alliance is a governing body populated by the leaders of the most powerful groups of Shadow creatures," Leviathan began. "Vampires, Therians, Demons, and the like. A parallel in your world might be the various countries and their governments, each overseeing a specific population."

"Okay," she said. "And Dragos works for the Alliance?"

His smile was almost amused. "Lucius Dragos works only for himself."

She thought of all those cases Leviathan had rattled off and could come to only one reasonable conclusion: Luke was a hired killer. An assassin. And from what she'd seen and read, he was damn good at his work. "No one has ever been able to make a charge stick?"

"Luke is extremely clever," Leviathan said, with an admiration that seemed almost affectionate. "He has powerful friends, both in and out of the Alliance. And as we both know, that kind of power can all too often result in a backroom deal, especially when the evidence is weak or nonexistent."

"Those victims," she began, recalling Luke's responses in the interrogation room. "The way Dragos described them and their crimes—was it accurate?"

"Every one of those men could have easily been found guilty within these walls and staked in front of a gallery of witnesses," Leviathan said. "Does that make what Dragos did right? Or, excuse me, does that make what we suspect that Dragos did right?"

"Absolutely not," she said. She might not have been close to her mother, but Deborah Constantine had worked in the DA's office just as Sara had, and Sara had been weaned on the idea that the courts meted out justice, not civilians. But though she meant her words—truly meant them—she couldn't stop the tiny trill of relief that fluttered in her chest. Relief that maybe, just maybe, the man she'd slept with wasn't as much of a monster as she'd thought.

Still, those crimes were not on her docket, and there was no point analyzing either them or the man who may have committed them.

"The evidence isn't weak in this case," she said.

"No," Leviathan agreed. "It's not." His brow furrowed, his gray eyes going dark with inquiry. "Is there something else on your mind, Constantine?"

She hesitated, knowing that what she was about to say could result in her losing this job altogether. She didn't want that; she wanted to work down here, and not just so that she'd have access to her father's file. And yet she couldn't move forward knowing that she should recuse herself from the case.

"Sara?"

"Sir, I—well, there's something you should know." She reached into her pocket for the red ribbon, only to remember she'd thrown it away. "I, um, okay." She drew a breath. "After the Stemmons trial I was celebrating with friends. I met Luke—Dragos, I mean. And, well, the truth is we slept together. I—I didn't want to say anything because I was afraid you'd kick me back upstairs and I'd lose this opportunity and forget everything I've seen today. But I can't be like

Dragos and just make up my own rules. It's a conflict of interest, and so I should be taken off the case."

She sat back, her body finally relaxed, the relief of having told the truth palpable.

"I see." He steepled his fingers on his desk. "And does this—encounter—in any way impact your ability to prosecute this case?"

She hesitated before answering because the question deserved an honest appraisal. She'd been handed the chance to put a murderous vampire into a cage. A vampire, she now knew, who committed heinous crimes, then abused his connections to the Alliance to wriggle free from the law.

Maybe she had slept with him—and maybe she'd enjoyed it. But that didn't change the facts. She had to be true to herself, and she was not a woman who could let a killer go free simply because he had powerful friends.

"No, sir," she said firmly. "It doesn't impact me at all."

He leaned back. "Very well."

She forced herself not to frown. "Sir?"

"The case remains yours."

"But—"

"As I've already mentioned, you're going to find that we do things differently here. Comparatively speaking, the community is small. And when you factor in the life spans of the various Shadow creatures, odds are high that prosecutor and defendant, investigator and suspect have crossed paths before. Such inter-weavings do not demand an immediate recusal. Not without additional extenuating factors."

"Oh. Well, good. I'm relieved."

"As am I. You're an asset, Sara. And your conscience does you credit."

"Thank you," she said, standing. She'd meant what she said. She would prosecute the hell out of Luke in the courtroom. But outside those walls, she would cry, knowing that he was the opposite of everything she'd believed him to be and mourning the loss of that intense connection that she'd only ever felt with him.

"This is bullshit," Doyle raged as he stalked the length of the antechamber. "Fucking bullshit." He was on edge, his demon half still too close to the surface after his feeding. Couple that with the total fucked-up nature of the situation, and Doyle found himself in a fury that he considered completely fucking legitimate.

At that very moment, behind the thick metal door, Security Section was fitting that murdering fuckwad with mobile detention devices, and as far as Doyle could tell, he was the only one who saw a problem with that little scenario. He lashed out, kicking the door but failing to make even a dent in the metal.

At the far end of the room, Dragos's advocate puppet stood expressionless against the wall, calmly tapping something into his phone. Doyle took a step closer, his fists itching to bloody up Montague's all-too-pretty face, but was held back by a firm hand closing on his shoulder.

He turned and snarled at his partner. "What?"

"Chill," Tucker said. "Push it under."

"Chill? Whose side are you on? That animal's gonna be out walking the streets, breathing my air. And this asshole's standing over there playing the calm cool counselor, when we all know some serious shit's gone down." He tried to take another step toward Montague and once again felt Tucker's hand hold him back.

This time, however, Montague looked up, his face impassive. "Are you talking to me?"

"Don't play games with me, you useless worm. This ain't right and you know it."

"An accused is entitled to an on-site review of the evidence against him with his advocate of choice," Montague said, spouting a load of legalese crap. "Three hours, fair and square."

"My ass," Doyle retorted. "That ain't a guarantee. Dangerous suspect, risk of flight. All those things have to be taken into account."

"As the judge surely did."

"You pulled strings, cut corners." He jerked his shoulder out from under Tucker's hand and shot his partner a warning look. The hand didn't return, and Doyle took a step forward. "What have you got on Judge Acquila? What threat did you make?"

Something dark and dangerous flashed across Montague's pretty face. "I would suggest, Agent Doyle, that you keep your accusations to yourself. Since I'm aware of the enmity you feel for my client, I'm willing to ignore that outburst. But if you once again even hint that I have crossed any ethical lines in representing my client, I assure you that I will make your life miserable."

"Hint? I'll do more than hint, you filthy bloodsucker." A comfortable rage flooded him, and he lunged forward at the same time Montague did, the two men coming nose to nose before Tucker grabbed Doyle by the shoulder and yanked him forcibly back.

Doyle whirled, hissing, and saw Tucker leap back, hands up in defense, fear flickering in those human brown eyes.

Doyle sagged. "Goddammit." He fired another sneer Montague's way. "You didn't even give the prosecution a chance to argue."

"Nor was I required to do so. I wonder, in fact, how you came to be here."

"I keep my ears open," Doyle said. "Especially where defendants like Dragos are concerned."

"I'm gratified to know our civil servants are looking out for the public's best interest," Montague said silkily.

"Underhanded game playing," Doyle muttered. "But you've forgotten who you're dealing with, and it'll be on your head when the bastard skips out on you. How much credibility do you think you'll have in court after that?"

"My client will be returning to custody within parameters. Or are you suggesting that you are aware of a way to disable the mobile detention devices? If so, I suggest you inform Security Section. The failure to disclose such information is, I believe, a Class A violation of the Concordat."

"Fuck you."

Before the advocate had a chance to respond to Doyle's brilliant comeback, the light above the metal door switched from red to green, and it swung open, the hydraulic mechanism hissing. A beefy demon with a thick, armor-like skin stepped out, followed by Dragos, now clad in the black jeans, T-shirt, and duster he'd worn when Doyle and the RAC team had taken him down.

"Uh-uh. No way." He looked Dragos in the eye. "Strip."

The corner of Dragos's mouth twitched. "Truly, Ryan, you're not my type."

"I'm serious. Take it off. No way are you walking out of this room without me seeing the countermeasures."

"Are you suggesting Wrait is untrustworthy?" Montague asked, stepping in beside his scumbag client. Doyle sneered. What he wouldn't give to take both of those sons of bitches down...

"Bartok alesian rhyngot!"

Doyle rounded on the demon, got right in his face. "Damn straight I don't trust you. And the next time you've got something to say to me, you say it in English. You understand me, demon?"

"He doesn't speak English," Dragos said. "Just transferred from Division 18 in Paris."

"Yeah? Then how'd he know what I was saying?"

Dragos shot him a bored look. "Subtlety's not your strong suit, Ryan. It never has been. But if you want to ensure you are understood, speak French. Or demonic," he added with a thin smile.

"Strip," Doyle said, ignoring both the taunt and the demon who was still glowering at him. "Right now, or I'm calling Leviathan."

"You have no authority to—" Montague began, stopping short when Dragos held up a hand.

"Let the little boy throw his temper tantrum. I have nothing to hide." He shrugged out of the duster and handed it to Montague, then thrust out his arms to Doyle. A band of polished silver-gray metal had been cuffed tightly around each wrist. Doyle grabbed Dragos's arm and twisted, looking at the cuff from all sides. A muscle flickered in Dragos's cheek, but the bastard didn't protest. Satisfied, Doyle finally dropped his arm.

He eyed Tucker. "They're solid. No seams. No visible breach points." The hematite bracelets, Doyle knew, prevented Dragos from shifting into sentient mist. He still had strength and speed, albeit lessened, but wherever he was going, he was getting there like a human.

Tucker crossed his arms over his chest, eyed Dragos up and down. "Guy like this wouldn't cut off his own hands to get free of the bands, either. How would he jerk off if he did?"

Doyle barked out a laugh. "True enough, but that ain't a real risk. Any attempts to alter the body in order to remove the bands, and the stake is activated. So let's see it," he added, turning his attention from Tucker to Dragos. "Show me the stake."

Pure hate burned in Dragos's eyes, and it gave Doyle a nice warm feeling of satisfaction to know that he was getting under the murderous bastard's skin. Dragos's eyes cut toward the pretty-boy advocate, who shrugged. "The agent wants to pretend he's got a big dick, I'm not going to stand here and prove to him how shriveled and tiny it is. Just show him, Luke, and let's get the fuck out of here."

Dragos set his jaw, then reached up to the neck of his T-shirt. Doyle expected him to yank it over his head, but instead, Dragos clenched his fists and pulled, ripping the shirt down the center to just over his heart. He peeled back the raw edges of black cotton to reveal a thick metal band strapped tight around his chest. Over his heart, a circular-shaped portion of the metal protruded slightly from the skin. Underneath the protrusion, Doyle knew, was a piece of wood, cut so that it would, upon being triggered, expand and lock into the shape of a stake. A stake that would instantaneously be thrust into the wearer's heart.

Doyle took a step closer, wanting to see the actual mechanism that had the power to end Lucius Dragos, then stopped as he heard the low growl in Dragos's throat.

"It's set," Montague said firmly. "He tries anything, he goes outside of the jurisdictional area, he in any way blows the terms of the deal, and the stake deploys. And I don't care if you're satisfied or not at this point. We're leaving." He looked at the demon then spoke smoothly in French.

Wrait grunted. "Trois heures. Oui."

And then, as if Doyle and Tucker weren't even standing there, Montague and Dragos stepped out the door, and Dragos began the short walk toward freedom.

Doyle waited until the door shut behind them, then he turned to Tucker. "Let's go. And the gods help that bastard if he tries anything. Because I will hammer that stake myself."

FIFTEEN

Sara sat cross-legged on her bed in yoga pants and a tee, eyes closed, taking one deep breath after another. She'd been going a hundred miles an hour since six that morning, and now she felt ripped apart from the inside. Excited, yes. But completely exhausted as well.

She wanted sleep, but Leviathan had insisted that the security system in her condo be updated immediately, so she had to wait up for the installation team. Considering what she now knew was out there in the world, she didn't really have a serious objection.

Without thinking about what she was doing, she scooted to the side of the bed, then bent to open the bedside table's drawer. She hesitated only briefly, then reached in and pulled out the Glock 9mm that she'd bought the day her concealed carry permit had been issued. In truth, she hadn't wanted the thing, but she'd been a green prosecutor working a high-profile drug trafficking case, and Porter had insisted that everyone on the team license up and carry a weapon whenever they were away from the criminal justice center.

Sara had dutifully followed instructions, but the moment the case had wrapped, she'd transferred the gun from her purse to the drawer, and it hadn't emerged since.

Now, she studied it, wondering if it would offer any protection in this new world. A world of different dangers, and one she still didn't understand.

The doorbell buzzed, and she shut the drawer, leaving the gun where it had been for years. At the door, she peered through the peephole and found herself facing a man with a sagging basset-hound face and eerie yellow eyes.

"Security Officer Roland, night shift leader and domicile protection specialist," he said, flashing his Division identification. She led him and the team inside, showed them around, then parked herself on the sofa with a stack of files. She turned first to her copy of the initial report, once again skimming Ryan Doyle's summary. Though he was thorough, she wanted to go over the details with him in person at their next meeting.

According to the report, Braddock had been a shapeshifter, on the bench for two decades, an advocate before that. He'd been born in the late thirties, but Sara didn't know if that meant he'd died young, or if a shapeshifter's life span tended to be about that of a human's. Several years before he'd retired, he'd been sanctioned for accepting bribes, and there'd been murmurs that he'd engaged in blackmail. He'd made restitution, appeared before a review board, and had been allowed to keep his seat on the bench. She made a note. The crime was old and apparently resolved, but she knew damn well that bribery and blackmail could be a solid motive for murder. More than that, those crimes were often only part of the story, and she intended to have Doyle and Tucker dig, and dig deep.

She was about to move on to the medical examiner's report when she caught Roland's eye. "How's it going? This place is tiny, it can't be much longer, right?"

"Like wine and aged cheese, fine security work takes time."

"Oh. How much time?" Sleep was beginning to look like a far-away fantasy.

"Can't rush perfection," he said, leaning against the wall as he hooked his thumbs in the loops of his jeans. For the first time, she noticed the long tufts of hair that grew on the back of his wrists and poked out from underneath the cuffs of his sleeves. "But we're in the final stretch."

"Fair enough." She started to turn back to her papers, then paused, peering at him. "How long have you worked at Division?"

She watched his face run through the calculations. "Eh, three decades? Four?"

"You know Judge Braddock?"

"Sure. Retired what, three years ago?"

"Impressions?"

The hangdog face went flat.

"I'm new, Roland. I'm just trying to get a feel for the victim."

"Yeah, well, the victim was pretty much an asshole."

She shifted, interested. "How so?"

"Oh, he was good with the law and all that. But wouldn't give what he called a lesser being the time of day. Snapped at support staff. Had himself one supreme holier-than-thou attitude. Heard he got into some trouble awhile back. Bribes, I think. Wouldn't wish him dead though."

"Somebody did."

"Dragos, wasn't it?"

"So it seems," she said, working to keep her voice flat, even though the thought that the man who'd touched her so intimately could have done that horrible thing was still twisting her up inside. "Any ideas why Lucius Dragos would want Braddock dead?"

"Well, I..." He paused, as if truly considering the question. "Actually, I can't think why Braddock would even be on a vamp like Dragos's radar. Kinda makes you think, doesn't it? All sorts of stuff going on under the surface all the time. May not see it," he added, "but it's there."

Yeah, she thought. But what exactly was "it"?

"Thanks," she said to him, then looked around the room. "What exactly are you doing here?"

"Ah, this. Now this is interesting stuff. We got you covered for magical entrance—that's Chiarra," he added, waving in the direction of a woman with glowing purple hands. "No creature's gonna be porting right into your apartment after we're done."

"Porting?"

He grinned. "Beam me up, Scotty," he said, then waggled his overgrown eyebrows.

"Oh. Right."

"Not a common trait, but gotta cross the T's." He pointed to the far wall. "Got the seams around your windows and under your doors sealed up nice and tight against mist, too. Don't want any two-cent vamps or their passengers getting in, do we? Especially not when you've got such a high-profile vampire case on your first go out the gate."

"I'm sorry? Two cents?"

"Huh? Oh, no. Two centuries. That's about the earliest age when a vamp develops the ability to mist. Gotta grow into it, you know. You hear about a vamp getting prosecuted by the humans, you know he was a youngster. No older vamp's gonna sit still for steel handcuffs and cages, that's for damn sure."

"And what were you saying about passengers?"

"An older vamp can transform into mist—that's a fact that's crossed over into your human lore. But most humans don't know that they can clutch another person—vamp or human or whatever—and transform them into mist as well."

"Oh." Sara trembled, an image of Luke, his arms tight around her as they both dissolved into mist, suddenly filling her mind. There was something erotic about the thought of being so entwined with him, and she cursed her own inability to move Luke firmly and finally to the "defendant" slot in her brain.

"We'll be leaving an ax and some stakes for you, too. Not high tech, but both do the job."

"An ax?"

Roland's brows lifted. "Well, sure. You chop off a vamp's head, you got a dead vamp. Stake 'em, you got dust."

"Right. Thank you,"

"Glad you're asking questions. Some humans, they're too over-whelmed their first day to do anything but sit back and let the day wash over them," Roland continued. "Don't even ask what anybody is. Think it's impolite or something."

"Is it?"

He shrugged. "Yeah, probably so. But I never was a big fan of Emily Post, you know? Figure if you don't ask, you don't learn."

"So what are you?" she asked, taking him at his word.

"Hellhound," he said. "On my mother's side. Never was too clear on what my dad was. Left when I was a pup. But don't you worry. I ain't one of them wild ones."

"Oh." She considered it, not at all sure what to say next.

Roland didn't notice the conversational lag. "So let me go do a round, and as soon as it's set to go hot, I'll give you a better overview and a run-through of how it works. Okay?"

"Sure," she said brightly, still a little hung up on the hellhound announcement. "No problem."

She watched the team work for another few minutes, then real-ized the rhythm of their movements was rocking her to sleep. She considered making a cup of coffee, but as soon as she did, they'd leave and she'd be up all night, exhausted but jittery.

With no better option and no way to rush the team along, she dove back into work. She studied the crime scene photos, trying to picture how it went down. A dark night, and a man in a dark suit crossing a muddy park.

She closed her eyes, imagining a mist forming into a vampire, and the vampire bending over Braddock. Knocking him down, kicking him hard in the gut, and then swooping over him. While she watched, the creature bit down, then lifted his face to look directly into her eyes.

Luke.

Her heart pounded, but her body had turned to lead and she couldn't move, couldn't cry out, not even when the image shifted, and it wasn't Braddock that Luke was leaning over, but her.

His amber eyes never left hers as he slid inside her, her hips rising to meet him, wanting to take more of him, all of him. Needing him. Craving him.

His mouth curved with male satisfaction.

You're beautiful.

Don't stop.

He hadn't stopped. He'd touched her, played her, his skin smooth against hers, his lips soft, his words and body nothing but need and passion, lust and longing, and all of it focused on her as he moved in and out, taking and giving, flesh against flesh. He was poised above her, his strong arms supporting his weight as he looked at her with pure, sensual hunger.

A hunger she understood, for it burned within her, too.

Take me. Luke, please, please!

He smiled then, and for an instant, her heart skipped from pure joy. Then the smile widened to reveal the bloody tips of his fangs. And when he drew his head down toward her neck, she screamed.

"Ms. Constantine! Sara!"

She opened her eyes to find Roland shaking her shoulder, and she sat up, damp with sweat and completely mortified. "Sorry. Sorry. I fell asleep. I'm okay. Sorry."

He smiled good-naturedly. "It's normal."

"Sleep?"

"The nightmares. I do this for all the humans on staff. Gives me special insight, you know?" He grinned, yellow eyes flashing. "Consider it a breaking-in period."

"Right." She rubbed her hands over her face, then started when he shoved her phone in her face. "When you didn't wake up, I answered it. Says she's Petra. Says it's important."

She fumbled for the phone, clicked it over from mute to talk, and had barely managed a hello when Petra laid into her.

"Who the hell was that?"

"Security," she said. "Division 6 takes security very seriously." She ran her fingers through her hair and stood up, hoping that the movement would shake the image of Luke from her mind. She no longer had to worry about falling asleep. The nightmare had at least taken care of that.

"Wow," said Petra. "Guess Homeland Security really does begin at home. Manny told me about your reassignment. I'm so proud of you. Insanely jealous, but also proud. And I miss you already."

"Listen, Pet, I would say I miss you, too, but I saw you this morning. If you want me to give you a rundown of my first day, we could meet for a quick lunch tomorrow. Right now I'm totally wiped, and—"

"No, no," Petra said. "I mean, lunch is fine, I'd love to. But I'm not calling to congratulate you or gossip. I have news from a source in the LAPD."

"News?" Maybe her brain was still sloshy, but Petra wasn't making sense. "What's going on?"

She heard Petra suck in a breath, felt the hairs on the back of her neck prickle. "Petra," she prodded.

"He escaped," Petra said, her voice flat. Dull.

"What?" Sara asked, her mind automatically flashing to Luke. "What are you—"

"Stemmons," Petra said.

Sara's knees went weak and she sank back onto the bed. "Don't be absurd. They transferred him this evening. He's in solitary by now, and good riddance to him."

"You're not listening," Petra said. "He got out."

"That's not possible."

"He had help, apparently. His transfer guards are dead."

Sara closed her eyes, imagining those poor guards riddled with bullets. "There was nothing in his profile to suggest he worked with anyone," Sara said. "Did he have a shiv? Hire a gunman?"

"No gun," Petra said. "Their throats were ripped out."

Sara's head swam. "Wait. Their throats?"

"Massive blood loss," Petra said. "Only get this—"

"No blood at the scene," Sara finished. "Has anyone contacted Nikko Leviathan?"

"Who?"

"My new boss."

"Oh." Petra paused. "I'm not sure."

"Ask your source to let Division 6 know, okay?" For that matter,

Sara thought, she'd do the same. Because from what little she'd heard, they'd either completely missed the fact that Stemmons was a vampire, or he had help from the fang gang.

"Sure," Petra said. "You wanna tell me why?"

"The MO matches a Division matter," she said. "That's all I'm allowed to say."

"I'd tease you for that if this wasn't so serious."

"Did you hear anything about a task force?" Sara asked.

"Already in place. Do you think Porter will ask you to be part of the team?"

"Probably. And I'm in the second Leviathan okays it," Sara said. "We know Stemmons has at least two hidey-holes we never found. He'll rabbit to one of them."

"Yeah. My contact said they're notifying all the nearby school districts. All the principals in the LA basin have already been contacted, and the police are set to do extra patrols around schools and public parks."

Sara nodded, wishing there was more they could do, but gratified to see how quickly the wheels had been put into motion. Over the course of four months, Stemmons had abducted, raped, and brutally killed seven girls between the ages of nine and fifteen. The girls were all blondes or redheads, with blue or green eyes and tall, lanky builds.

Stemmons was smart and hungry, and Sara knew damn well he wouldn't stop. He'd kill again, and soon.

"Hopefully our intelligence on the locations is correct," Sara said. "It's going to be like looking for a needle in a haystack."

"We know who he is now," Petra said. "That's huge. He can't move around like he used to. His picture's everywhere. They'll get him, Sara. He can't hide forever."

"Thanks," Sara said, then felt stupid for saying it.

"You're okay?" Petra asked.

"I'm fine," she said, trying to decide if she really was. "No, I'm not. He'll kill again. It's what he does."

"I know," Petra said. "We'll catch him."

"We better."

After she hung up, Sara frowned. All those dead girls, and now more little girls were out there, big red targets painted on their backs, and they didn't even know it.

With a sigh, she moved to the balcony and pressed her hands to the glass. Porter had been right. Before today, she hadn't known that vampires and demons and shapeshifters existed. The creatures that lived in the dark, Porter had said. The things that crept out of nightmares.

Maybe so, but Stemmons was more of a monster than any she'd met in Division.

And what did it say about her that she'd gone to bed with a man she should have seen as a beast? That even once she knew of his crimes, she still couldn't keep him out of her head? Could still imagine the soft caress of his hand upon her skin?

He'd stood right there on this balcony and held her, looking out across the night with her, his arms engulfing her, his touch completing her.

He'd filled her, and that night—now locked tight in her memory —he'd been a man, not a monster.

The Slaughtered Goat in Van Nuys was the kind of pub you went to if you didn't care about food poisoning, knife wounds, gunshots, or just general bad service.

In other words, the perfect place to kill, quickly, thoroughly, and without too much fuss.

Luke watched the door from the driver's seat of Nick's BMW. The information that Nick had received from Tiberius indicated that Gunnolf's man in LA, a vile little were-cat named Feris Tinsley, kept an office in the back section, which he habitually visited every evening at twelve-fifteen. Before that, Tinsley spent an hour or two in the main section of the pub, drinking bourbon, eating corned beef sandwiches, and copping a feel off a waitress named Alinda.

Since Alinda was neither appreciative of such affection nor fond of shapeshifters, the elfin female had been more than happy to provide information and assistance when a gorgeous man like Nick had come around asking questions.

Not only had she told Nick that Hasik was due to meet with Tinsley that evening, but she'd agreed to enter the access code on the back door to allow Luke to slip into the back of the pub through the alley. In exchange, Nick would arrange new employment in a new city.

A fresh start for an elf who'd come to the wrong town and fallen in with the wrong people. Luke considered it a fair trade.

As for the job for which he'd come—killing Ural Hasik—he considered that a fair deal, too.

Luke paged through the electronic file on his phone, the images of beheaded vampires burning his eyes and boiling his blood. Ural Hasik had used no stake, but had instead left his victims degraded in death, spread out over the ground to molder and rot.

The darkness within hissed and tensed, tightening and twisting, alive with fury. Alive within Luke.

"Soon," Luke said. Soon the serpent would have satisfaction.

He checked the clock on the dashboard, put the car into gear, then eased around the block and into the dark alley. He left the car near the street and walked the short distance to the pub's rear entrance.

He saw her immediately. A wisp of a girl standing by the back door, holding a sack of garbage. She wore tight red leggings and a transparent shirt, her small breasts pressing against the gauzy material. Fear tightened her features as she looked up at him. A small pink tongue darted out, and she tossed the sack into a nearby trash bin, then turned back to the door and keyed in the access code.

She opened it, slipped inside, and Luke caught the door before it slammed shut. Smooth as silk.

He waited a moment, giving her time to move from the back section to the front of the pub. Then he pulled open the door and slid inside, easily finding the door to Tinsley's office. Normally, he would have already changed into mist, foregoing altogether the risk of being seen by witnesses or by the target as he materialized silently behind him, knife in hand. There weren't many percipient demons walking the earth, but one of the most prominent was determined to see Lucius staked, and he was not inclined to give Ryan Doyle more ammunition.

Now, though, with the detention device, transformation wasn't an option. Not only that, he needed to make the bastard talk. Capture. Interrogate. Kill. Which meant his voice would register in Hasik's mind, even if he were able to take the pup from behind. He'd have to remove the body and hide it someplace where it wouldn't be found until the window for Doyle to look into the werewolf's mind had passed. That would shave off time from his furlough, but he had no other option.

Within, the serpent stirred and Luke's skin tingled in anticipation as he moved quietly toward the open doorway. He paused outside the door, his back to the wall, then eased slowly around until he could peer inside.

Hasik sat at a desk, his hulking form dwarfing even the huge stainless-steel monstrosity. "Don't like the bitch," he said, as Luke searched the room for Feris Tinsley. He found the black cat perched on a bookcase opposite Hasik. The cat leaped, transforming mid-jump into Gunnolf's LA minion. The mangy were-cat's crimes against the vamp community were at least as wicked as Hasik's, and Luke eased back against the wall, his mind humming, the darkness within boiling in anticipation.

"You just spent a half hour laying out the score for her, and I didn't see her flinch once. She's in," Tinsley said.

"She ain't one of us."

"Gunnolf trusts her."

"Gunnolf's fucking her," Hasik said. "Wouldn't mind that myself, but that doesn't mean I'm gonna trust the bitch. She's got Gunnolf whipped. She shouldn't be involved. Not with this. We're already getting closer to the humans than I want. Now we're adding her kind to the mix? It's too dangerous."

"You're second-guessing Gunnolf? Do you have a fucking death wish?"

"I came up with the plan," Hasik growled.

"And a damn good one," Tinsley conceded. "Stage a few vampire attacks. Bloody human deaths. The kind that make the news. Humans won't have a clue, but it'll look to the Alliance like Tiberius can't control the vamps."

At the door, Luke squeezed his hands into tight fists, fighting back an eruption of fury. At least now, no interrogation was necessary.

"Got to hand it to you, Hasik, it just might work. But you listen to me. Gunnolf knows what he's doing. She may be a fucking bitch vampire, but she's also a powerful ally to the Therians, and you damn well know it. Caris is as tied in to the vamps as you can get. Hell, she used to bang Tiberius."

Caris.

Immediately, Luke pictured the chestnut-haired female with cat's eyes and a tiger's temperament. He tilted his head back, finding the fresh scent of a female vampire. Sharp and woody, like a forest after a rain. She'd been here, in this room, and not so very long ago. Once he had thought her an ally. A good match for his leader and mentor. But then she'd rallied the charge against Tasha, arguing for termination rather than salvation. Now her defection from the vampiric community and alignment with the Therians was proof that she had only grown more despicable with time.

A slow burn rose within him, and he had to tamp down hard on the serpent, now screaming for release. He wished that she were there, in that room. Because right then he'd happily add her to the butcher's bill, and return to Tiberius with news of not only his enemy's death, but a traitor's as well.

Since she'd already left, it was time to take what he could get.

It was, he thought, time to kill.

He slipped his hand into his pocket and pulled out the key to Nick's car. He tossed it to the far corner of Tinsley's office, where it landed on the concrete floor with a sharp ping. As he'd hoped, both Hasik and Tinsley turned in that direction, away from him. When they did, Luke snipped the last thread of his control and let the serpent rage. Then Lucius Dragos burst over the threshold, his knife out and flying.

It arced hilt over blade to land deep in Tinsley's back, and the were-cat fell face forward onto the ground as Luke tackled the burly werewolf. He drew an arm tight around Hasik's neck, and the beast snarled and snapped and tried to turn to see its attacker, but to no avail. Even as it twisted, Lucius tightened his grip, his entire being juiced for the kill, satisfaction running high when he shifted, twisted, and heard the sharp pop of Ural Hasik's neck.

He jumped back, letting the body sink to the ground, careful to stay out of the beast's line of sight until he was certain the last light of life had faded from the creature. One moment, then another, then safety. No need to move the bodies now. He'd managed a clean kill after all.

He moved swiftly to Tinsley's body, caught the scent of remaining life, and cursed as he saw the limbs twitching and heard the beast's labored breathing.

Careful once again to stay out of the beast's line of sight, Lucius pulled his knife free, then grabbed a chunk of the were-cat's hair. He pulled the head up off the floor and reached around to draw his knife hard across Tinsley's neck. Blood gushed, and Lucius let the head fall back in its own puddle of blood.

Done.

He gathered up Nick's key, took one last look at the bodies, and then Lucius Dragos slid out the door and disappeared back into the night.

"Holy shit," Nick said, after Luke told him about the plot and about Caris's involvement. They were holed up in one of the Forest Lawn tombs that Luke had purchased over a century before, realizing that the types of tombs celebrities had built for their egos served Luke's purposes well. He'd bought several, then connected them with a series of tunnels in the same way that he had connected several tombs at the Hollywood Forever cemetery to the security shop.

"Caris," Nick said, still mulling over the news. "I never would have believed. Tiberius will be on the warpath."

"He will," Luke agreed. "But Hasik and Tinsley are out of the picture, and unless they've already set their troops out onto the city, their plan is trashed. So you tell Tiberius I want a practical token of appreciation."

"That I will. This is one time I think he'll be happy to pull strings."

Luke nodded, almost tasting the freedom.

"I have good news for you, too," Nick said. "Tasha called."

Luke's head jerked up. "She called you?"

"She called you," Nick corrected. "I had your calls forwarded to my cell while yours is stored at Division. She's fine. She's still in San Francisco. Says she wants to come home."

"Thank the gods." The relief that swept through Luke almost drove him to his knees. "And Serge?"

At that, Nick's expression grew hard. "She doesn't know where he is."

"Goddammit." He drew in a deep breath, forcing himself to remain calm.

"It's worse, Luke," Nick said. "The things she said ... Would he touch her? Would Serge break your trust?"

Bile rose in Luke's throat as he thought of his friend's hands on Tasha's innocent flesh. He wouldn't, Luke knew. Not if he were in his right mind. He feared his friend was not. He clenched his fists as fury rose within him. Serge was his oldest friend, and his dearest. But if he'd touched Tasha, he would pay dearly when they next met.

He closed his eyes, forcing himself to be calm. "Tell Ryback to get to the apartment as soon as he can. Tell him that he's to bring Tasha back now. No side trips, no hesitation. I want her back yesterday, Nick. Are we clear?"

"Crystal. I'll tell him." Nick nodded toward the entrance to the tunnel that would lead them back to a house Luke owned in the hills, their supposed destination during the furlough. "Let's get back to Division and get you out of that contraption before Doyle bursts in here and spoils our party."

"You saw him, too?" Luke asked.

"Hard to miss that baby-shit-yellow car." The tomb they were in was a marker to one of Luke's previous lives, a man now dead on paper two generations ago, his fortune now in the hands of Lucas Drake, Luke's current identity when walking in the mortal world.

"He knows you well," Nick said. "And he's not an idiot. Considering the hard-on he has for you, odds are he's been paying attention to this network of tunnels for decades, just waiting for a chance. He'll have men at your exit points."

"Known exit points," Luke corrected.

"This is Doyle, Luke. He knows the way you think."

"A fact that I know well. Which ultimately gives me the advantage. Not him."

"You're that confident?"

"I am."

"Probably expects you to cold cock me and make a break for it," Nick said.

"Undoubtedly he does," Luke agreed.

"So what do you actually have in mind? You didn't drag me here just because it's a cozy place to chat. And we still have over an hour before your furlough expires."

"Indeed. Why waste the opportunity?"

Nick's eyes narrowed. "Well?"

"Sara Constantine," Luke said, the possibility of seeing her again too tempting to postpone.

Nick shook his head. "Luke, no. I know I suggested making her an asset, but you've got Tiberius in your court now. It's not worth the risk. You're a vampire. You're the prime suspect in a murder. And you slept with her without telling her any of that. She's not going to be inclined to be lenient and breaking the terms of the furlough to go see her won't help."

Luke rubbed his temples, then slowly nodded, not inclined to argue with his friend. "Perhaps you're right."

"I usually am."

Luke chuckled. "I did have some other thoughts. Come with me. I have some information you should see."

As he spoke, he moved to one of the two stone coffins in the tomb and began to shove aside the lid, releasing the thick stench of death.

"And we have to get there by crawling into a tunnel accessed by an empty grave?"

"You can dry clean the damn suit. Just hurry."

"Fine," Nick said, coming to Luke's side and looking down with distaste at the contents of the coffin. But he saw no way into a tunnel.

"Where—" he asked looking up to see the apology on Luke's face, even as his friend's hand moved as fast as lightning.

He had time for only the merest flash of understanding before the hand connected, and black, liquid pain flooded his nose and face.

His knees went weak. The world swam in front of him. And the last thing Nick heard as he dropped into Luke's arms was his friend's murmured apology for doing exactly what Doyle had expected he'd do.

Nick lay motionless at the bottom of the sarcophagus, remarkably at peace for a man who would soon wake in a fury. For that, Luke was sorry, but there was no other way. What he intended must be done alone.

He reached inside the coffin and removed Nick's watch, which had already been set to count down the remaining furlough time. For a moment, he considered also taking Nick's phone. After all, he needed to be careful, and Nick's reaction to Luke's betrayal was an unknown—a potential risk to not only his life, but to Tasha's life and the lives of his friends as well. One call, and Nick could report Luke's treachery. One call, and the stake poised over Luke's heart would be triggered.

No.

He turned away, shamed that he could even consider the possibility of such perfidy. He left the phone in the pocket of the friend he trusted with his life, and never doubted that he'd made the right decision.

And then, with one last look at the man in the coffin, Luke slid the stone lid back into place. Then he pulled up one of the tiles on the floor to reveal the tunnel. He slipped inside and began to crawl, the putrid stench of death that surrounded him reminding him that he had once been human, too, his life marked by the minutes counting down to the day he lived no more, but instead lay in stasis and began to rot. Such a cruel trick was birth, he'd thought, inescapably tainting that gift of life with the horror of death.

And to him, a young man who had seen his mother and baby sister die in childbirth, who had watched his father fall from another man's sword, death truly was a horror. A cruel taskmaster that came without warning, trying daily to cheat the living out of the gift bestowed at birth.

He had been eighteen when he heard rumors of a dark woman of timeless beauty whose kiss could grant eternal life. He had become obsessed, determined to find her and convince her to bestow her prize upon him. For seven long years he searched, but to no avail. As a soldier in the Roman army, he was afforded very little freedom, which limited his investigation to listening to the tales of travelers and interrogating other soldiers returning from duty in the far reaches of the empire.

So futile seemed his efforts, that in time he almost forgot his obsession, his thoughts turning more toward the lusty Claudia, a merchant's daughter with whom he had fallen in love. He had taken her as his bride in the spring, and by the fall harvest she was heavy with child. When, months later, the midwife had placed the tiny Livia in his arms, Luke was deaf to those who urged that she was flawed. To him, she was perfect. He was the one who was weak. For he could never be strong enough or wise enough to fully protect this child, to make her healthy.

She grew slower than other children, each passing year seeming to drain her body of life. Though careful not to let the child see his fears, he nightly succumbed to the crippling horror that death would snatch her from him. He turned not to his wife for comfort, though, as his own impotence shamed him. Instead, he wandered the wheat fields after dark, the baleful sound of his anguish drowned out by the whisper of the grain in the wind.

Livia knew nothing of her parents' fears, and though often confined to bed, her mind grew sharp and quick. By the time she was ten, sweet Livia had her doting father entirely under her control. Still, the joy that stole his breath when he looked upon the child was snuffed out by the fear that he and Claudia would be forced to bury her before the year was out. Her body, the physicians told them, was breaking down, and despite regular entreaties to the gods, her condition worsened daily. Fate, it seemed, had contrived to allow Luke only a taste of true happiness before ripping it brutally from his hands.

He recalled with perfect clarity the day his life had changed forever. Livia had been confined to bed, and both Luke and Claudia were sitting vigil at her side when they'd heard the thunder of hooves approaching. Luke had stiffened, imagining the rider was Death, come to bear his daughter away.

He need not have worried. Death was not coming then. Would not, in fact, come until Lucius himself invited it in.

The rider was Sergius, who had ridden his horse hard to deliver the news that the streets were filled with rumors that the dark lady had come to Londinium. And though Luke had not thought of his obsession since the months before Livia's birth, to him it seemed as though Serge had arrived on the wings of destiny. For how better to save his daughter than to bar Death from the door?

It had broken his heart to part from her and from Claudia, who had wept and clung to him as he'd mounted his horse. He had held fast, though, promising his wife that he would return presently, bearing Livia's salvation.

The trip was grueling, and he'd arrived at the city gates sore and hungry, his horse ridden almost to the point of collapse. He had cared not, his thoughts only on Livia, on finding the dark lady who could return his daughter to him. For three days he and Serge had scoured the city's underbelly, following any rumor, any hint of news, but never finding the lady herself.

He'd been on the verge of giving up when he'd located her in a tavern and pleaded his case. She had declined at first, unconcerned, she'd said, about the welfare of his child. He'd persisted, though, determined that he would have what he came for. That he would win the lady's gift and deliver it triumphantly to his home.

His tenacity persuaded her, and in the end, he won his heart's desire. He would like to say that he hadn't fully understood the terms as she relayed them to him, but that would be a lie. He'd understood. There had been no failure to disclose. No dark trick.

The soul, she told him, is not alone in man. There is evil as well. And the evil has a name and a face: *Azag Mahru*. A living darkness. A presence that slithers inside like a serpent. In some, it is mild. Calm. Controllable. In others, it rages. Burns. Writhes. But in all humanity, it is there, hidden well in most by the power of their soul to suppress it. To quell and control.

But the dark gift releases the serpent, and only the strongest have the strength to battle it back.

He listened. He understood. And he had taken the gift with eyes wide open, arrogant enough to believe that the terms did not apply to him. He was a good man, after all. Kind. He loved his family deeply, and they him. He took the gift not selfishly, but with his child's well-being at the forefront of his mind.

Surely, with motives so pure the gods would exempt him from the gift's dark effects or bestow upon him the strength to control the writhing, keening darkness.

Of course, he'd been wrong. The dark gift had freed the serpent, just as the lady had told him it would. It did not, as human mythology sometimes suggests, allow evil to enter. The evil was already within him, had been there all along. And once he became nosferatu, that evil ran free.

He'd become a killer, a monster, and were he given the chance, he would gladly return to that fateful day and sacrifice himself to the normal course of nature, if only to save those he had hurt.

The innocent. The strangers.

And, yes, his Livia.

Even now, all these centuries later, his stomach roiled and his blood ran cold when he remembered what he'd done, the torment he'd wrought upon the child he'd adored, the woman he'd loved.

With the demon riding high, he'd left Londinium for home, intending to fulfill his original purpose and draw his wife and child into his shiny new world. Claudia, however, had been horrified and had thrown herself on him as she tried to keep him from his Livia.

He'd shaken her off violently, having no patience for the foolish woman who would sentence their daughter to a mortal death. With a newfound strength, he'd thrown her against the stone hearth, and she'd slipped into unconsciousness, her body sagging to the floor.

He'd felt no regret, only a renewed purpose as he'd stalked through the house toward his child. He could smell her, the scent of her teasing his senses. Death waited in the room for her, but Lucius refused to give the vile beast satisfaction. He would snatch Livia from Death's clutches. He would, finally, save her.

She'd smiled as he'd approached her bed, but the expression had faded as he'd moved closer. "Pater?" she'd murmured. "Quis es?"

He'd told her to hush, then drawn her tiny body into his arms. She'd snuggled close at first, reassured, then pulled away, confused, and complained that his skin didn't feel right. "I will soothe you," he'd whispered, and with her scream echoing in his ears, he'd sunk his fangs deep into the tender, young flesh of her neck.

She'd writhed and struggled, but the serpent had swirled unrelenting within him, and he'd drunk and drunk, the taste of her fear causing him no hesitation but instead enticing the darkness within even more. He drank deep, telling himself that he could stop in time —that he could turn her. That he could save her.

And though he felt the whisper of death touch her—though he knew that he was on the verge of taking her too far—the serpent would not stop. *He* would not stop.

He drank his fill and drew the last spark of life from her.

There would be no renewal for his Livia. No life.

He had stolen it from her, thrusting death upon her even as he'd tried to give her unending life.

He had failed, and as he looked up, confused and sated, her body limp in his arms, he'd seen Claudia silhouetted in the doorway, a knife tight in her hand. She held the blade out toward him, her face a mask of fear and fury and grief.

The *Azag Mahru* had whipped into a frenzy from which Lucius had been unable to emerge. Grief, rage, confusion, loss. All pounding inside him. All driving him down, down into the mire. Lost in the call of the blood, Lucius had leaped toward his wife, a part of him wanting to share his grief, another part wanting to snuff out her life because of the harsh way that she now looked at him.

She hurled the knife and ran even before its hilt collided harmlessly against his chest.

He let her go, then turned back and cradled the lifeless body of his daughter. And as grief warred with hunger, he surrendered, fully and completely, to the darkness within.

Xavier Stemmons stood in the dark, the swing set behind him casting eerie shadows in the light of the moon.

Now the playground was empty. Soon, though, the sun would rise, and they would come. The young girls with their soft bodies and beguiling eyes. They were youth; they were life. And he'd taken what they offered, drawing their essence in, capturing their light.

He realized now what a fool he had been.

It was their blood that was key. He should have consumed it, not merely drained it. Taking their life gave satisfaction, but only by taking their blood would he rise up. Would he become. Would he be freed of earthly bonds.

A god.

Without the blood, he couldn't rise like the Dark Angel who had swooped in to rescue him. Who had delivered him from the fools who had sought to confine him, to constrain his gifts.

He breathed in deep of the chill night air, remembering the way she had burst into the van as the second guard had been about to lock the door. She'd moved with inhuman speed, so fast that the guard never even had time to reach for his weapon. With one bold stroke, she'd tumbled him to the ground, moving so fast Xavier hadn't even seen her fall upon him. Hadn't seen her sink her teeth into the guard's neck.

He'd seen only the result—the guard, dead on the van's floorboard, and the blood on her mouth as she'd smiled at him over the body, her eyes soft and sultry, her grin wicked.

The first guard—the driver—never came, and Xavier assumed she'd taken care of him first. Left him collapsed over the steering wheel, his neck gaping open, his life now in her belly.

She'd crawled toward him, a lioness hunting her prey, and for a moment he'd felt the cold pangs of fear. For a moment, he'd understood why the girls had cried out. They hadn't understood what he'd wanted from them, and they'd been afraid. Afraid as he was, even then.

Like his little girls, though, his fear was misplaced. She sought not to take his life, but to raise him to a higher level. She saw the depths of him, she said. Saw his great potential, and promised him not death, but everlasting life. Life, power, light.

Draw the light, draw the blood, and feed the angel.

She'd explained it all so beautifully. And now he knew what he had to do.

Now he knew the true nature of his work.

Satisfy the angel—do her bidding—and she would render upon him the glory of the world.

He spread his arms, embracing the night and imagining the satisfaction of the coming days.

He had freedom. He had life.

And he had purpose.

Xavier Stemmons was a man with renewed vision.

Free, and ready to drink deep of the light of youth.

Luke steered the BMW with his knee as he rummaged futilely in the glove box, cursing Nick for not keeping even a pint of goddamn synthetic in the car.

Frustrated, he sat upright, his stomach clenching with the hunger, his blood burning with need. The fight with Hasik and Tinsley had sapped his strength, and he was cursing his lack of foresight. The serpent stirred more when the hunger was upon him, and without the strength to fight, it would rise and stretch and come out to play.

No.

With a low growl, he clutched the steering wheel and concentrated on driving. The more focused he kept his mind, the less his physical needs would intrude.

He saw the exit for downtown in the distance and crossed neatly over three lanes of traffic. Even at midnight, the traffic was dense, especially on a Friday, when the humans who lived mostly during the day came out to join all the creatures of the night.

He parked on the street across from Sara's building, then looked up, easily finding her balcony on the twenty-fifth floor. Were it not for the bands on his arm, he could have transformed, then arrived at her balcony door on windswept wings. Quick, simple, clean—and utterly impossible given his present circumstances.

Which left him to more mundane, human-oriented methods. Like the elevator. He would be revealed on the building's security footage, but that was a risk he would have to take. If all went as planned, Sara would be firmly aligned with him, and there would never be a need to pull the footage.

He moved toward the entrance, then stopped as the elevator doors within the lobby slid open. With a small hiss, he stepped back, his eyes fixed not on the faces of the pair now leaving the elevator, but on the badges clipped to their shirts.

Division 6—Security Section.

Damn.

He melted into the shadows, waiting until they exited the building, and as they passed by, Luke slipped in. A woman was on the elevator now, the doors beginning to slide closed. He called out, flashed a smile, and she leaned forward to hold the doors open.

He slid in, smelled the slow rise of desire as her eyes dragged over him. Inside him, the serpent stirred, awakened again by the burn of hunger in his blood and the need radiating off the woman beside him.

So easy, he thought, his head pounding and his fangs tingling. So easy to take. To feed.

The hunger pushed at him, growing stronger with the serpent's urgings, and resistance was hard-fought and painful. He kept his mouth shut and took in a breath through his nose, the simple act of drawing in air reminding him of the humanity he'd worked so hard to restore.

He did not harm the innocent. Not anymore.

And no matter how hard and how fast the hunger came upon him—no matter what danger he could pose to Sara should he meet her when the hunger was at its most keen—still, he could not partake.

Not even a morsel.

Not even one tiny, delicious taste.

He couldn't.

He wouldn't.

"Twenty-four," he growled, ignoring the fear that now flashed in the woman's eyes. The way she backed away. "Punch the button for twenty-four."

She did, then pressed herself into the corner as Luke fisted his hands, willing the demon back down, down, down.

Letting the hunger pass. Fighting not to lose himself.

The doors opened and he burst into the hall, slamming his fist through the drywall, trying to wrest control. Behind him, the woman jumped forward, her hand slapping hard at the button to close the elevator doors.

Good.

The sooner she was gone, the sooner he could see Sara.

Even her name calmed him, and he conjured her image, the mere thought of her soothing him, pushing down the last remnants of the darkness.

He stood there, breathing deep. Once he was certain that control had returned, he moved through the halls until he reached the condo directly beneath Sara's, 2419. He moved to 2420, and rapped sharply on the door. After a moment, he heard the low grumble of a human awakened from a deep sleep. The man who opened the door was tall and lanky and clad only in boxer shorts and a ratty flannel robe. "What the fuck?"

"Inspection," Luke said, mentally reaching in to twist the man's thoughts. "Nothing to be concerned about."

"Oh, well, if that's all."

The man stepped aside, and Luke moved through the condo toward the small balcony, even as the man rubbed his fingers through his hair and stumbled back into his bedroom.

On the balcony, he took his bearings. Sara's apartment was up one floor and over one unit. Easy enough to access. He climbed onto the railing. Even weakened from the hematite bands, it was a simple matter to leap up and over.

He landed with a soft thud on her ridiculously small balcony, then pressed himself up against the wall, out of sight of anyone who might be looking toward the door that, he was delighted to see, was slid open.

A male voice drifted toward him—"That pretty much wraps it up"—followed by Sara's rich, "Thank you for doing this. I feel safer already."

Concentrating on remaining in the shadows, he eased forward until he had a view into the room. A group of security techs were filing out, and he caught the distinct whiff of hellhound coming from the creature talking to Sara.

As the hound pressed a small black control box into Sara's hand, Luke knew that he had no time to spare. He took one step closer to the open patio door and slipped inside, unseen.

SEVENTEEN

"So what is this gadget?" Sara asked.

"This here's your standard portable control box," Roland said, tapping the black box that was about the size of a garage door opener. "Exactly like what we've installed by the front door, but it's portable."

"I figured that out just from the name," she said, unable to resist.

"You got a wit, kid. A genuine laugh riot. Now you wanna pay attention?"

Her lips twitched, but she nodded and focused on the box.

He indicated a row of buttons along the top labeled with the numbers zero through nine. "You use these buttons to key in your code when you set or deactivate the alarm. Pretty easy," he said, "so long as you don't forget your code."

She tapped her temple. "Got it."

"Good. And this little baby," he said, pointing to the red button situated right in the middle of the box, "is your good old panic button. Anything hinky goes down, you give it a push and you got the calvary at your side in seconds."

"How?"

"Whassat?"

"How would they get here in seconds? All that stuff you were doing to my apartment, wasn't that to make it so that folks couldn't get in like that?" she asked, adding a snap at the end of the question for emphasis.

"I like you, kid. I really like you. Good question. Shows you were listening. Remember how I said no one can port or mist into your apartment when you've got the system active? Well, you punch that button and all bets are off. Total deactivation, and at the same time, the cavalry comes running."

"Wow," she said. "That's impressive."

"We aim to please."

He crossed the room to close her balcony door, then returned to the front door. "You arm the system the second I'm gone," he said.

"Promise."

He gave her one last grin, then pulled the door shut behind him. She keyed in her code, saw the light on the panel switch to green, and smiled. Her own little fortress. Who would have thought?

And now, finally, she could go to bed.

She killed the overhead light so that the city lights were the only illumination as she moved across the room with the control box. She felt a tiny bit foolish carting it around, but Roland had told her to. And she truly was antsy. Stemmons's escape, the truth about her father's murder, Luke in a cage. It all came together to make her edgy and out of sorts.

She hooked the box onto the waistband of her yoga pants, then reached inside her T-shirt to unfasten her bra. She did a Houdini move and pulled it out through her sleeve, then tossed it on the bench at the foot of her bed. Next, she headed toward her dresser, tugging off her earrings as she moved.

She'd put the tulips from Luke in a vase, and now she set the earrings in a crystal dish next to the flowers, forcing herself not to reach out and stroke the soft petals. She remembered the romantic thrill she'd felt when she'd discovered the flowers on her doorstep, the care she'd taken in arranging them just so. She'd fallen asleep that night gazing at them, feeling warm and cherished.

Even now, her body tingled when she looked at the vase, her skin recalling the feel of his hands, her mouth recalling the taste of his skin.

She told herself she didn't want those feelings, those memories.

And that meant she didn't want the damn flowers.

Determined, she grabbed the bundle with both hands and yanked the stems straight up out of the vase. She dripped water over her dresser and floor before dumping the lot of them in the wastebasket beside her bed.

She looked down at the flowers, still vibrant, and told herself she'd done the absolute right thing.

With exhaustion dogging her every step, she unclipped the panic box and put it on the bedside table, then wriggled out of her pants. She let them fall into a careless heap on the floor. She needed sleep desperately, and neatness was the last thing on her mind.

Clad only in her T-shirt, she slipped under the covers, sank deep into the overstuffed down pillow, and finally—*finally*—drifted off to sleep.

The night surrounded her, caressed her, and, yes, taunted her. *The dream was coming.*

Except she wasn't asleep, so how could she dream? She was awake. Very awake, and aware of everything around her. The crunch of the gravel walking path beneath her shoes. The warm pressure of her daddy's hand engulfing hers. The moon that shone high in the sky.

And the faint but terrifying way that the trees seemed to be laughing as the two of them walked.

"Daddy?"

"It's nothing," he said. "Just the wind."

It wasn't the wind, though. It was Death. And Death swooped down on her father, fangs bared, face twisted with malice.

"Nothing you can do little girl. Nothing at all."

She wanted to fight, to pound, to kill, but all she could do was stand there, feet planted, body cold. Death rippled and changed. First Stemmons. Then something faceless and formless. Something that latched onto her father's neck, releasing a fountain of blood. Warm and sticky, the liquid poured over her, and Sara did the only thing she could do—

She screamed and screamed and screamed and—

"Sara!"

Gentle hands. Holding her close. Murmuring her name.

"Wake up, Sara. It's a nightmare. A dream. You're safe. I've got you."

Luke?

She knew that voice. Knew that touch, and without thinking, she clung to him, pressing her face into his solid chest, losing herself in the strength he offered.

Luke was there.

She was safe.

"Sara, hush. Hush, it's safe. You're safe." Her hands fisted in the thin cotton of his shirt, her body heaving as she sucked in air, growing calmer as he whispered soft words, even as he wanted to lash out in impotent fury at whatever horrible thing inhabited her dreams.

Remnants of sleep clung to her as he stroked her back, her hair, every touch sweet torture. The scent of fear that had engulfed her was fading, replaced now with comfort and faint tendrils of desire, and he knew it would be easy—so easy—to take exactly what he desired most. *Sara.*

His body thrummed with the knowledge that he could have her, the allure all the more powerful because he knew that she still wanted him. Wanted his touch, his caress. Wanted to forget the nightmare from which she'd awakened and lose herself instead in pure sensual pleasure.

So easy.

He couldn't have planned it any better if he'd tried. Yet he hesitated, wanting to savor this moment, this one snapshot in time where she was once again with him, without guile or pretense, but because in his arms was where she wanted to be.

Her hands relaxed, her palms splaying out across his chest, her fingertips brushing bare skin where he'd ripped the shirt down the middle in his cell. The shock of her touch sent ripples of pleasure through him, and he tensed, fighting the urge to thrust her back onto the mattress and claim her mouth with his, not because that was what he had planned to do, but because right then he would go utterly mad if he couldn't touch her. Couldn't taste her. Couldn't lose himself inside her and pretend that nothing else existed and it was simply Luke and Sara, and screw all the rest of it.

"Luke ..." Her voice, soft and dreamy, teased his senses. She nuzzled close, sighing, and something he identified as happiness bubbled up inside him, only to burst as she pulled back, the sweet fragrance of desire drowned out by the bitter stench of fear.

Her fingers, once soft, hardened as they shoved him away, and she scrambled backward until she was crouched on her pillow, the panic box from her bedside table now tight in her hand. The hem of her T-shirt barely covered her, and he could see her bare thighs, muscles tense and ready to leap.

She was breathing hard, her chest rising and falling in an effort to control her fear, and he held up a steadying hand, hoping to calm her down.

"Sara."

"No," she whispered, and right then he knew that he would have preferred that she scream at him. A scream was anger and rage. But this soft whisper held disappointment. And fear.

This time, the fear was directed at him, and the knowledge that he was the thing that now made her cower was almost enough to make him forget his mission and leave.

Except Luke never walked away from a mission.

More than that, though, he couldn't bear the thought that she was afraid of him. Whatever else there was between them, he didn't want it to be that.

"Why are you here?"

He needed to move closer, to try to calm her. Needed to do all those things he'd planned before he'd stepped into her apartment.

He stood up, determined to do exactly that, yet somehow unable to find the will to take the first step. In front of him, he caught a glimpse of red and looked down to see a dozen tulips dumped carelessly into her wastebasket.

In his long life, he'd suffered many an injury, and yet none cut so deep as the knife that Sara had just thrust into his heart. He bent to pull out a flower, then caressed the soft petal with his thumb.

When he looked up, she was eyeing him warily. "You don't have to fear me."

"I think I do." Her finger shifted, covering the panic button. Luke stiffened, waiting, knowing he should leave, should run. But he stayed, subjugated to her will, his life in her hands.

Slowly, she moved her finger away.

Slowly, he relaxed.

"What are you doing here?" she asked again. "You're in jail. In that cracker box they call a cell."

"I'm here to talk to you."

"To talk to me?" Her voice rose with incredulity. "About what? The weather? No, wait. Maybe we can talk about local bars. Bars where badass vampires go to pick up prosecutors. Seems to me that would make one hell of a conversation opener." She snapped off her words, as if embarrassed that she'd shown her hand.

"No," he said, determined that she know the truth. "There was no ulterior motive between us. I wanted you. Hungered for you even as I do now. I took only what you were willing to give."

Guilt washed over him, because though his intentions that night had been innocent, now they were anything but.

"Don't," she said, shaking her head, her eyes sad. "Don't come here with sweet words and try to twist me up in knots. It won't work."

"Do you want me to go?" The words were out before he had considered them, and he froze, waiting for and fearing her answer.

"How did you even get here?" she asked, and he relaxed ever so slightly and took a single step toward her even as he reached up and opened his shirt, revealing the detention device.

"Advocate-escorted furlough," he said. "And this band ensures that I do not run. I did not break out of jail, Sara, but I did abandon my escort."

She licked her lips, a simple motion he found unbelievably sensual. "Why?"

"To see you."

She shook her head. "You shouldn't be here."

"And yet who would have comforted you had I not come?" He moved to sit on the edge of the bed, the tulip still in his hand, and felt a flood of relief when she didn't protest. "What were you dreaming?"

She met his eyes, hers defiant, yet still wary. "Of monsters."

"What kind of monsters fill your dreams, Sara?" He would slay them if he could. Kill the monsters and free her from the horrors of the night.

"Vampires," she snapped. "What do you think, Luke?"

The words were like a blow, and he inclined his head. "Yes. Of course."

She closed her eyes, sighing, then whispered, "Dammit." He tilted his head, his nostrils flaring, and was relieved to find that the scent of fear was fading.

"Sara?"

"It was a vampire in my dream. The one that killed my father. But that wasn't—" She ran her fingers through her hair. "I'm not afraid of you, though I probably should be. You didn't trigger my dream. Stemmons did."

"Stemmons?"

"He escaped," she said, and a wave of fury crashed through him. "More than that, he had help. The kind of help that walks at night and sucks blood—maybe you're familiar with the breed? And now he's gone and by now he probably has the next girl picked out. And it's pissing me off," she said, voice rising and tears welling. "Really pissing me off that I did everything right. Everything. And still he's free. He's evil, and he's out there, and he's going to kill again."

She pressed her fingers to her cheeks and wiped away tears.

Luke tensed. "Are you in danger?" It was a foolish question. No matter how she answered, he would consider her in need of protection until Stemmons was caught.

"I'm okay," she said. She still held the security box with one hand, but with her other, she reached out, as if to take his, before she quickly jerked it back. Even so, the brief movement eased him. Her actions did not match her words, and for that reason he was still in the room. Still basking in the pleasure of simply being near her.

"I almost wish I were in danger," she added, the sentiment making him grow cold. "I can defend myself against the things that creep in the night. But the victims, the girls, they don't know what he is."

"I would destroy him," Luke said, the thought of a man who preyed as Stemmons did on young girls sickening him. "If I could find him for you, I would gladly destroy the beast."

"You'd kill him," she said, her voice flat.

"I would," he admitted. "With no hesitation, and no regrets. Does that offend you?"

Once again, she licked her lips. "It offends the law," she said simply.

"Your system isn't a panacea, Sara. Sometimes the law is insufficient to render justice."

She tilted her head, looking at him with grave intensity. "Is that why you killed Braddock?"

"What? Have I so quickly been tried and convicted?"

"Luke." Her voice was hard.

He looked pointedly at the security box in her hand. "I would not deny you the pleasure of doing your job."

She met his eyes. "I heard that laundry list of kills Leviathan rattled off today. Do you think I don't know the truth?"

"The truth," he repeated. "Shall I tell you the truth? Yes," he said, as her eyes widened with shock, "those men died by my hand."

"You shouldn't tell me that. You can't expect me to just stay silent."

"You are not naive, Sara. You know how governments work, how intelligence systems work."

Her brows rose. "Now you're James Bond? License to Kill for this Shadow Alliance?"

"Something like that."

Her expression was flat. "I want to believe you," she said. "I want to believe it more than I should. But even if you're some secret agent guy who does sanctioned kills for the vampire leader—Tiberius, right?—that has nothing to do with Braddock."

"Doesn't it?"

"Is that why you came? To tell me that Braddock was a player in Alliance intelligence games? I may be new to this world, but I'm not stupid."

"You most definitely are not. Am I?"

She blinked. "Excuse me?"

"I am not a fool, Sara. If I killed Judge Braddock, there must have been a reason."

"That doesn't matter in the eyes of the law."

"Perhaps it should."

"That's not our call to make. There are lines, Luke. And someone has to draw those lines. The courts do that. Not me. Not you."

On the contrary, he had drawn that line on many occasions, and still believed himself justified in doing so. That wasn't a debate for tonight. He came here to gain her support. To make her an ally in his case and an asset for his continued work as kyne. And, yes, to undermine her case if need be in order to allow him to go free.

That had been his plan.

And now he found that he could not do it. He wanted no such duplicity between him and Sara. She deserved the truth.

"Luke?" Her brow furrowed as she studied his face. "What is it?"

"There are things I must tell you, Sara. I don't have much time. Will you let me speak?" He nodded at the security box. "Will you put that down?"

She eyed him warily, but put the box on the bedside table. "Talk."

"Do you remember saying to me in this room how my touch seemed familiar? That it felt to you as if your fingers knew the lines of my face? And do you remember that I told you the same?"

"Yes. Of course, I do."

"It is true."

She scooted back, pulling the comforter onto her lap. "What are you talking about?"

"About three years ago you went to a coffee shop to meet a witness," he began, "do you remember?"

"Yeah. A Starbucks. He knew about some murders—vamps, I realize now—and I thought he might give me a clue as to what happened to my father."

"And did he?"

"He didn't show. I was pissed. Went home and went to bed. Ended up catching the flu and was out of it for a few days."

"No."

"No?" she repeated.

"He showed," Luke said. "And he would have killed you. I was there, Sara. That was the first night we spoke. You went home, and I followed, along with my friend Sergius. We feared for your safety, and we were right to. You were attacked again."

"By vampires?"

He nodded. "There was a battle. Serge and I defeated them. We—"

"You fought them." Her eyes widened. "He had blond hair. And that night you and I...."

"Yes," he said, fighting a smile. "You and I."

She licked her lips. "The next morning, vampires attacked us at my house, and you fought them, too. You and Serge. You told me that they were young, so the daylight didn't affect them. And you told me that vampires don't really need an invitation."

"Yes."

She reached out, tentatively touching his chest, her palm against his skin exposed by the ripping of his shirt. "And you said that your skin is usually cold because your blood moves slowly. But that it is warm when you're aroused." She met his eyes. "It's warm now."

It was everything he could do not to pull her close and claim her right then. "When I am with you, my blood always burns."

"I remember," she whispered, withdrawing her hand and making him want to cry out in protest. "I think I remember all of it. It's all flooding back."

"It did for me as well. There was nothing, and then I remembered everything. Every kiss, every touch. Sara, by the gods, you were mine. And then we were lost to each other."

"When? When did you remember?"

"Not long before they captured me."

"You didn't know that first night? When we kissed in Probation? When you came here?"

"I didn't. I only knew that I wanted you. That I'd been in love with you for years."

"You told me that, too. How you'd been assigned to protect me after my father died." She licked her lips and a tear streaked down her cheek as she reached for his hand. "I remember seeing you change. I was terrified. I sent you away, and then I didn't know how to find you. But you came back." Her voice was shaky. "I wanted you desperately, and you came back."

"I couldn't stay away then any more than I can now."

"Luke, I—I loved you."

"You did," he said, wishing that her use of the past tense didn't torment him so. "And I, you."

"They stole my memories?"

He clutched her hands. "I couldn't protect you. Sara, forgive me. I couldn't protect you."

"Three years," she whispered once he finished. She extended her wrist with the tattoo. "That's when I got this. I never understood why I wanted it. Just that something seemed missing." She lifted her head to meet his eyes. "You," she whispered, her voice full of wonder and love. "Luke," she said, making him want to weep with joy. "It was you all along."

A tear snaked down her cheek, and her voice shook as she whispered. "And my father..." She squeezed her eyes shut. "I remember that, too. He worked for the PEC, but he thought that the Shadow creatures should make themselves known to the humans. I can see why he believed that. He was so fascinated with this world. Your world."

"Yours too, now."

She nodded, tears sparkling in her eyes. "I miss him," she whispered, the pain in her voice breaking his heart. "Serge," she whispered. "I remember Serge confessing that he killed him."

Luke swallowed. "I remember that, too."

"He was a traitor," she said, a single tear escaping. "My father, I mean. He was going to leak the truth about the Shadow world, with no plan and no authority. There would be a war, of course. And to silence him, Tiberius ordered him killed."

"He issued the order, yes. But all Alliance leaders sanctioned the decision."

"Do you think it was the right call?"

Luke's entire body went tense. He would answer, but he needed to tell her all of it. But how could he when she was in his arms again? How could he after she'd said that she had loved him? When he desperately wanted her to love him again?

"Yes," he finally said. "It was the right call. The world is not ready for the truth, but your father was a good man who believed that people could get along. That their better natures would always win out."

"But that's not how the world works, is it?"

"No," he said.

"He always did see the good," she said. "He was always so kind."

"Tell me about him," Luke said gently, both because he wanted to soothe her and because he wanted to know everything about her.

"He used to tell me stories when I got scared," she said. Her expression remained flat, fixed. And just when he was about to give up hope, a soft smile touched her lips. "He'd hold me and spin tales about anything that came to mind." She relaxed as she spoke. "And what came to mind was usually something paranormal. He'd talk about creatures living among humans. About the world changing and being full of power and magic. When I was little, the stories lulled me back to sleep. When I was older, I'd pretend to have bad dreams just so I could stay up late and listen to him."

"I had a daughter once," Luke said. "I would do the same for her. Soothe her with stories until she fell asleep in my arms." Automatically, he reached into his pocket, his fingers seeking the tiny gold serpent ring he'd given Livia on her fifth birthday. Even through his dark haze, he'd thought to keep it all those centuries ago, a reminder of the family he'd once had and a talisman from which he could draw strength to soothe the writhing serpent. He had not been without it since that fateful day, but it was gone now, wrenched from him and put into an envelope with his other personal effects in the detention area.

The softness in Sara's eyes worked like a balm against the sadness that had welled in his heart. "I bet she was very pretty."

"That she was," he said. "And with the sweetest disposition."

She started to ease toward him, then stopped, carefully planting herself on the far side of the bed from him. "Luke—"

He lifted the tulip, wanting to silence her, not wanting to hear that he needed to leave, especially since all he wanted to do was stay. "I'm sorry you didn't like the flowers."

Her cheeks bloomed pink. "I liked them."

He glanced at the wastebasket.

She lifted an eyebrow, amused. "That? That's because I didn't much like you."

"And now?"

She swallowed, hesitated. "Don't press your luck," she said, but he saw the smile in her eyes, and there was no way she could hide the scent of her arousal or the way her nipples peaked beneath the thin T-shirt.

He inched closer to her, the comforter the only barrier between them.

"You can't be here," she said, but she didn't retreat. "I can't make peace with what you did to Braddock."

"But I am here," he said. "And I have not been found guilty yet."

"Luke, we can't." But she didn't ask him to leave.

He reached out, wanting to touch her. Knowing this was why he'd come, this sweet seduction. This wasn't about plans or plots or exit strategies. It was about Sara. The woman looking at him with enough longing to fill his heart with hope.

"You touch me, Sara, in ways that it would be better that you did not. I know I should leave—know even that you should push me away. And yet I cannot stop."

He reached out, brushing a hand to her cheek. The tempo of her heartbeat increased beneath his fingers, and he thought of the blood that flowed in her veins. Sweet, delicious, like the woman herself. He thought, and he wanted, and the hunger that he had been fighting for hours surged within, the serpent crying for release.

He beat both back down, subordinating them to his desire, now a living, breathing thing. "Sara," he said, voicing the only words that mattered. "I love you."

He saw the glow of pleasure on her face, then felt the warmth of her lips on his. A wild, claiming kiss that spoke more than words ever could.

She was his. By the gods, she was truly his.

He pulled her closer, his hands sliding over her bare thighs, then higher still until he groaned against her mouth when he realized she wore no panties. She writhed against his fingers, her hands cupping his head as she deepened their kiss.

She was giving him all of her, and the knowledge humbled him. Even with everything she knew about him—with Braddock lying dead in the morgue—Sara was giving herself to him.

She loved him.

The knowledge was both arousing and humbling.

And yet it wasn't real. It couldn't be real. How could it, when she didn't truly know everything?

He froze, and she pulled back, her brow furrowed in question.

"Luke?"

"There is something I must tell you. I cannot keep it from you, though I wish I could. I fear I will lose you, my love. And yet you must know."

"You're scaring me."

"Then we are even." He closed his eyes. "It wasn't Sergius," he said, his words tasting like chalk in his mouth. "It was me."

For a moment, she said nothing. Then she scrambled off the bed, her eyes wide and her arms crossed over her chest. "You? You're the one who killed my father?"

"I'm so sorry. The rest is true. I was ordered—"

"You need to leave." Her words held the chill of ice.

"My love, please. You know the circumstances. You said you understood."

She shook her head, her face pale. "Please. I need you to go."

"Sara, I—"

"*Go!*" she screamed, and in that moment, the serpent burst free, the hunger taking over as his fangs extended and he pulled her close, lost in the craving for her touch and her blood.

Sara screamed, yanking out of his grasp to lunge forward, grab the control box, and jam her finger hard onto the panic button.

EIGHTEEN

She shivered, couldn't stop shaking, the cold threatening to consume her.

He'd killed her father.

He'd confessed, and then he'd changed right before her eyes, his fangs bared, his dark eyes full of hunger as he'd yanked her toward him.

Then he'd run, ripping open the patio door, leaping from the balcony into the thick, black Los Angeles night.

A gray mist filled the room, and even as her foggy brain registered that the mist must be the security team, Sara scrambled to her feet and stumbled toward the patio. Hands on the railing, she breathed deep and looked out over the dark, empty night, her eyes searching futilely for Luke. He deserved it. Whatever happened to him, he deserved it.

And if he was dead, well, she told herself that was absolutely fine with her.

She told herself that, but she didn't entirely believe it. Not when she remembered the way he'd held her and calmed her. The closeness they'd shared in those recovered memories. The shock on his face when he'd bared his fangs. The horror and self-loathing in his eyes.

And yet he'd killed her father. The man she loved was the vampire she'd been hunting all these years.

Loved.

Did she love him? Once, yes, she had. She could feel it inside her.

Could curl up, warm and comfortable with her recovered memories. But she hadn't known the truth then. She did now.

"Constantine." The deep voice spoke with an accent she didn't recognize, and she cringed as someone draped her favorite afghan over her shoulders. She pulled it tight around her, suddenly realizing she was clad only in the tee, then turned to face a creature with a mangled face, his body hidden beneath a filthy gray cloak. She looked into the dark pits that served as eyes and knew that nothing Luke ever did could spook her as much as this being, whatever it was.

"The dwelling is clean," it said, in a voice that chilled her to the bone. Behind it, three similar creatures, all clad in the same cloaks with the same twisted faces, moved through her apartment. "There is no quarry. For what purpose did you summon the Phonoi?"

If she'd known what she was summoning, she certainly wouldn't have. As it was, all she could do was shake her head. The creature studied her, the inspection leaving her so cold she was certain she would never feel warm again. Then it turned its head toward the balcony.

"It fled," the creature said. "That which scared you. It slipped back into the night."

"I—" She licked her lips, then swallowed. Wanting to answer, but not knowing what to say.

The truth? That was certainly her usual MO. But then why weren't the words tumbling out?

He'd killed her father. He'd been about to bite her, too. So why wasn't she pointing in the direction he'd jumped and screaming for these creatures to find him and drag him back to hell where he belonged?

Because when he broke away, Luke had been in hell already. She'd seen the horror and self-loathing on his face. And the regret.

"Sara Constantine." The creature's deep voice thrummed within her, like a heavy bass beat. "I ask again. For what purpose did you summon us?"

She didn't answer. Couldn't answer. Couldn't condemn Luke with the truth. And yet despite the pain in her heart, she knew that she couldn't completely trust him, either.

Something was prodding him.

Luke blinked, then sputtered, surprised to find himself floating in inky black waters. Surprised even more to find himself looking into two concerned brown eyes.

"Oh, wow. Holy crap. Hold on. Hold on." The woman couldn't be more than twenty-three, her wild mass of blond curls pushed back with a headband, the panic coming off her in waves. She wore bright blue workout clothes and held a pool skimmer on a long handle. *The pool.* He remembered the elevator panel: Fitness Center/Pool Deck. Fifth Floor.

He'd jumped. Twenty stories down to the pool.

No wonder his head was throbbing.

"Can you grab it? Come on. Grab it, okay?"

He did, his fingers screaming with pain as they closed around the cool metal of the pole. She tugged, and he tried to move his limbs, tried to help, but there was no help to be had. His limbs were utterly unwilling to function.

His mind, however, was firing back to life, the lingering scent of Sara's hair dancing on the edge of his memory, along with the fear and horror he'd seen in her eyes. A fear that had done more damage to him than any stake ever could.

"Did you jump? Did you fall? God, how high were you? Damn you landed hard! I heard it from all the way in the gym, and then there you were." She was crouched down, her arms under his as she tugged him toward the steps. "God, oh God. You're a mess. I gotta get my phone. Gotta call someone. You need a hospital. Your leg, you know, it really shouldn't look like that."

She shifted to leave, but he managed a small sound, and she stopped. "Huh?"

"Stay." Blood. He needed to heal, and the hunger was on him like a living thing, the intensity of the rising serpent only quelled by the shock of the fall.

"I'm not gonna leave you. Honest. But I gotta call someone. You need help, and there's no one else here. Never is in the middle of the night."

"Time," he said, his voice little more than a whispered croak.

"Huh? Oh." She twisted around to look at a distant clock, revealing a long, taut neck, and he trembled, knowing what he had to do and hating himself for it. She turned back and told him the time, her own words sealing her fate. Because time was running out.

He had no other choice. No other options.

He could feed. Or, he could die.

"Look," he whispered.

She leaned closer, her brow furrowed. "What?"

"Look," he repeated, then turned his head to meet her eyes. He was tired, weak. But his will was strong. And this girl had no barriers, no natural defenses. He slid inside—the hunger firing even more as he did—and made her mind his own.

"Closer," he said. She whispered the word in response, then leaned toward him, turning her head to expose her neck.

His body tensed, anticipating. His fangs extended as the hunger rose up inside him, sniffing. Marking territory. Moving in for the kill.

Come to me.

There was no longer a need to speak. Their minds were one, and she slid into the water, curved herself against him. He could smell her skin, could see her blood pumping in her veins, and though he told himself he did not want this—that he'd forsworn what he was about to take—his senses were primed. Ready. Keening with need.

He shut off his mind. Shut off the recriminations.

Instinct took over. The pure, clean instincts of a predator. The desperate, dark instincts of the beast.

Her skin was firm and tasted vaguely of salt and chlorine. Then his fangs pierced the dermis and the arterial wall, and the blood began to flow, warm and sweet and full of life.

He wanted this, this sharing. This connection. Praise the gods, he wanted this desperately—but not with this woman. *Sara.* He wanted her in his arms, intimately enfolded in them. Their bodies pressed together, his mouth on her neck.

He groaned, drinking deep, his cock hardening with need, responding to the woman in Luke's head and not the woman pressed close against him.

He'd been so long, so very long, without the intimacy of a true feeding, and as he drank—as he healed—he let his mind linger where it should not. On fantasy and fiction. On Sara, warm and alive beneath him, her blood calling to him, her breath on his skin, her lips whispering his name.

She healed him. Her blood, making him whole. Bones knitting, bruises fading, strength returning.

Sara.

His mind called to her. Sought her—

Annie.

—and then slammed back when he found not the woman he craved, but the woman he'd taken into his arms.

Annie.

The thought was weak. Fading. Her strength dissipating even as his own grew.

My name is Annie.

With a jolt, he broke the mental connection, then gasped as he drew away and saw the damage to her neck. To her.

Her body was fading along with her mind, and he blocked the images. Of Annie. Of Livia. Of Sara.

He had to act quickly, had to stay in control.

She looked up at him, eyes wide in her pale, gaunt face. He needed to leave. It was nearly time. He had to get back, for Tasha, for the kyne. He had to leave.

And yet, he could not.

"Annie," he said, shaking her shoulders. "Look at me. Look at me."

"Sara?" she whispered, the word like air through dry lips that barely moved. "Who is Sara?"

"Only you," he said, meeting her eyes. "Right now, it's only you."

He brought his own wrist up to his mouth, then bit down, opening a vein. He pressed the wound to her mouth. "Drink," he said, then held her head as she suckled him, stroked her hair as one might a child nursing from its mother. "That's the way. Not too much, you must be careful."

Too much blood, and she would not simply heal, but would fall in tune with him, giving him access to her fears, her hopes, her desires. Even more, and the dark gift would embrace her. He would have neither for her, so he watched her carefully, and the moment a hint of strength returned—the moment he was certain she would last at least as long as it took for help to arrive—he pulled his wrist away.

"More," she said.

He didn't answer. Instead, he rose up out of the water, the girl in his arms, and carried her to a deck chair. He took a towel from a nearby trunk and spread it over her, gratified by the steady, strong beat of her heart. He brushed his fingertips over her cheek. "Sleep now. Sleep, and heal."

She drifted off, and he stood, saw the time, and swore.

Think, dammit, think.

He tilted his head, looking up toward Sara's balcony.

Perhaps, he thought, there was hope after all.

Nick woke in the dark with a raging headache and a boiling anger. It had been one hell of a long time since he'd been clocked—longer still since he'd been taken by surprise—and he wasn't sure who he was angrier with, himself or Luke.

His head pounded and he amended that thought. *Luke.* He was most definitely angrier with Luke.

He shifted, trying to get his bearings, his vampiric eyes adjusting to the pitch black of the tight receptacle into which he'd been dumped.

"Damn the bastard," he murmured as he kicked up, using the strength in his legs to push the top off the sarcophagus. It fell to the floor, the reverberating crash of stone against stone cathartic.

His friend had put him in one hell of a sticky situation. "God-damn arrogant fool."

"I'm guessing you're referring to Dragos, and not whoever you're sharing that sarcophagus with." Ryan Doyle's gritty voice greeted Nick as he grabbed the sides of the coffin and pulled himself up. He tightened his grip, forcing himself not to leap out and close his hands around Doyle's neck.

"Get the fuck out of here," he said, with admirable calm. "You've got no right to intrude on an advocate-escorted furlough."

"Got a point," Doyle said, then made a show of looking around. "'Cept I don't see you escorting anyone. You see anybody else in here, Sev?"

"Not unless dem bones gonna rise again." Agent Tucker took a step toward Nick, then flashed a smug smile as he peered down into the coffin. He looked back at Doyle. "Nah. They don't look the type."

"Nice job, Counselor," Doyle said. "Lost your client, and now the sorry SOB's going down." He punctuated the remark with a shit-eating smile that had Nick leaping from the coffin to land a rock-solid punch on Doyle's smug, sorry-ass face.

"Motherfucker!" Doyle said, flying right back on Nick, eyes red, veins bulging, skin shifting to a slightly greenish hue.

And every ounce of that famous temper pumping right beneath the surface.

"Whoa, whoa, whoa!" Strong arms grabbed Nick's from behind, tugging him away from Doyle, who looked about to explode. "Let's settle down, boys."

"Let. Me. Go." Nick could break away, no question about that. Tucker was strong, but he was only human.

"Don't even think about it," Doyle growled, those red eyes tight on Nick's face. "Maybe you can take my boy, and maybe you can't, but I know you can't take me. Think you learned that lesson years ago."

Nick shook his arms free from Tucker's grip and stood tall, his hands fisted at his sides. "Things can change over the centuries, Doyle."

"Things, maybe. Not people. Not vampires." He flipped open his phone, pressed a speed-dial number. "And certainly not Dragos. Learned that centuries ago, too." The phone was set on speaker, and Nick heard the electronic buzz as it rang at the other end, then the computerized voice requesting identification.

"This is Agent Ryan Doyle, badge number 1026C, reporting violation of furlough by defendant Lucius Dragos. Requesting activation of mobile detention measures and immediate termination of subject Dragos."

"Goddammit, no!" Nick yelled, leaping forward again.

"Acknowledged and analyzing. Please hold for verification of subject termination."

Sara raced through the halls of Division, part of her wondering what the hell she was doing, and another part fearing she was going to be too damn late.

"No," she yelled into the phone at the Security Section desk drone. "Constantine. With a C, dammit, and I'm prosecuting this case with Nikko Leviathan supervising. You engage that security device, and I will have your ass in a sling."

"A termination request has been input," the drone said.

"And I'm overriding it, dammit." She didn't have a clue whether she had authority to do that, but she damn well intended to make the argument. She hurried onto the elevator and stabbed the button for the detention level. "Just wait for me. Don't do anything until I get there."

No answer.

She pulled the phone away from her ear and stared at it. Call failed. No signal.

Dammit, dammit, dammit.

She jabbed again at the elevator button, as if that would make the thing move faster, but she couldn't simply stand and do nothing. What if they did it? What if they killed Luke?

And why the hell do you care?

The voice in her head was sharp. Dangerous.

But she did care. Maybe she shouldn't, but that didn't change the facts. She cared, and no way in hell was he going to die tonight.

She closed her eyes and forced herself to breathe, remembering the way his voice had sounded when she'd answered the phone in her apartment only minutes earlier, so desperate when he'd called her for help.

She'd already dismissed the Phonoi—claiming a nightmare and a foolish impulse to push the panic button—and she'd been sitting on the floor, her back to the glass, trying to process everything he'd told her. Trying to get even the tiniest bit of a handle on how she felt.

Luke was a vampire. A defendant in a murder trial with exceptionally compelling evidence. A man who'd blindly followed orders and killed her father. A creature who'd changed before her and almost attacked her.

She'd been trying to convince herself that she hated him. That she didn't trust him. That he could rot in hell for all she cared.

But the words weren't getting through.

She'd forgiven Serge for killing her father, hadn't she? That's what she remembered, anyway. He'd been acting under orders, and though she'd been shocked and heartbroken, she hadn't ordered him out of her home. On the contrary, she'd thanked him for fighting alongside Luke. For saving her from the horde of vampires who'd burst into the house.

She'd told herself that Luke was nothing more than a hired assassin. He'd essentially admitted to as much. And yet she knew there was so much more to him than that. He cared about justice. He saw the evil in Stemmons just as she did. And he'd cared for and protected his ward for centuries.

She banged on the wall, both to make the elevator go faster, and in frustration with herself. She was like one of those simpering girls in every bad horror movie out there. So into the guy that she did something stupid and wound up dead from a lunatic axe murderer.

She was smarter than that. Wasn't she?

All of those thoughts and more had been roiling in her head when he'd called. "Sara," he'd said the moment she answered the phone. "I need help."

She'd remembered the way his face had hardened, the way he'd bared his fangs, and she'd almost hung up.

"Wait," he'd demanded, and so help her, she had.

"What is it, Luke? What could possibly make you think you have the right to call me now? That I would *ever* want to help you?"

"No right," he'd said. "No expectation. Just hope, Sara." He needed intervention, he'd said. The fall to her pool deck had injured him, and there was no way he could return to where he'd left his advocate before Security Section activated the stake around his heart.

"I'm going back to Division," he'd said, "but even that's no guarantee. I need help, Sara. Will you speak for me?"

She hadn't answered, her mind too filled with the remnants of both fear and longing, but she'd hung up and was already dialing Division and racing toward work before he had a chance to ask twice.

She told herself that she was stepping in because she wouldn't see a man condemned without a trial, but she knew it was a lie. He'd touched something within her, and right or wrong, she couldn't let him die. Not like this.

The elevator doors slid open and she raced through, pounding the redial button even as her eyes scoured the hall for someone with authority. But down here, where Security and Detention were accessed through long concrete halls, there was no one but her. "Is he there?" she demanded the moment the drone answered the call. "Is Dragos there?"

"He arrived," the drone said.

"Then you damn well better make sure he's not ash by the time I get there," she said, and when she finally burst through the door, there he was. Standing right in front of her, dark and dangerous and smolderingly sexy. She gasped, not only because of the heat she saw in his eyes, but because he was looking at her with a combination of gratitude and longing so intense it weakened her knees.

"Ms. Constantine," he said, his voice a caress. "You came."

"I—" She swallowed, the sensual maelstrom building within her almost overwhelming her. She turned away, afraid he'd see too much on her face. Instead, she focused on her nemesis the security drone, a tiny creature with bulbous eyes and a high-tech headset.

"Ms. Constantine," the drone said with a small nod.

"Call Leviathan if you have to, but if Dragos is here, termination serves no purpose."

His lips pursed as he tapped something onto his computer, then leaned in close to a monitor. "Director Leviathan concurs," he said, and Sara had to grab onto the table to not sag in relief. "Termination denied."

She allowed herself one deep breath, then squared her shoulders and looked at the officer standing with Luke, Officer Quai according to his name tag. "Get him out of that contraption," she said. "And then give us a minute. I need to talk to him before you take him back to his cell."

As she watched, Quai went about his work, unfastening the clasp that was now between the two binder cuffs at Luke's wrists and securing one to the wall before instructing Luke to pull his now-free arm out of his coat. Then he had Luke shift before repeating the process with the second arm.

Now, Luke stood in shirtsleeves, his biceps straining under black cotton.

He was powerful.

He was dangerous.

And tonight, he'd held her close, comforting her, protecting her even in her dreams.

"Keep looking," he said, making her jump. "Perhaps you'll see something in me you didn't see before."

"I was thinking," she said. "Not looking."

"About me?" That generous mouth barely moved, but even so, she had the impression that he was smiling at her. Once again, she had to push back a wave of surprise at the utter incongruity of it all. He was in prison, for Christ's sake. His shirt pulled apart to reveal an achingly familiar chest, over which was strapped a device that could have killed him only moments prior. Yet he was standing tall and commanding, the room filled with the essence, the power, of Lucius Dragos.

"Ah, then," he said, knowingly. "It was about me."

To her utter mortification, Quai took that moment to swivel his slightly orange head around. His large eyes narrowed as he looked at her, and she transferred to him the glare she'd earlier aimed at Luke. He immediately turned back and concentrated on removing the metal band from Luke's chest.

"As a matter of fact, I was thinking about you," she said, delighted to see surprise flicker in his eyes. Well, why not? Two could play the one-upmanship game. "I was thinking that I should avoid talking to you."

"Is that so? Any particular reason?"

"Me prosecutor. You defendant. And a defendant with an advocate." She upped the sugar value of her smile. "I'm afraid I can't talk to you without your advocate present."

"So far, I'd say you're failing miserably at that task." She had the impression that his lips quivered, but his expression hadn't changed.

She wanted to laugh, but bit back the urge. "I guess I'll have to put more effort into it. Probably easier once you're gone. Out of sight, out of mind."

"I sincerely hope that is not the case," he said, with such heat in his voice it made her knees go weak.

Quai stepped back, having released Luke from his binds, though one ankle was now bound to the thick concrete by a short length of heavy metal chain. "Give us a moment," she said, in a voice that broached no argument. Quai nodded, then stepped out, the security drone following behind.

"Sara," Luke said the moment the door closed behind them. "Thank you."

"No problem," she said, keeping her face bland and hoping he couldn't see beneath the mask. "I wasn't going to have my first big trial at Division ripped away from me just because the defendant went and got himself staked."

"I can see how that would be an inconvenience to you."

She stifled a smile, then almost immediately turned serious. "Luke, you jumped from the twenty-fifth floor. I've read up, and there's no way you could just walk away from a fall like that. Not when you couldn't transform."

A muscle twitched in his cheek. "Do you have a question for me, Counselor, or are you merely stating facts?"

"I want to know how you survived. Look at you." Lord knew she was looking hard enough at him. "You're perfect. Not a scrape, not a bruise." She moved closer. "How, Luke? How can that be?"

"You know what I am, Sara."

"You fed." She closed her eyes. "Oh, God ..."

"Sara." His hand clutched her wrist.

"Tell me." She looked up, saw the pain and regret on his face. "Tell me now before I find out some other way."

"I fell to your pool deck," he said. "And, yes, I was injured." He looked hard at her. "The damage could have healed with time. But I did not have time."

"The furlough," she said, and he nodded.

"Do you know what heals a vampire, Sara?"

"Blood," she said, then closed her eyes.

"There was a girl."

"Oh, God."

"Sara."

She shook her head. "Give me a second. Give me a second to get my head around this." She forced herself not to close her eyes. Not to imagine him, mangled and broken beside the pool. And, God help her, she forced herself not to wish that it had been her at his side to help him heal. "Is she alive? This girl?"

"Yes. She will be fine."

Something in his voice caught her attention. "Tell me."

"The hunger was upon me," he said, and she recalled the raw need she'd seen on his face before she'd punched the panic button. "I had ... lost control, was still in the throes of that need, that hunger, when I drank from the girl. Annie." He drew in a breath. "I took too much," he said. "Took her close to death."

"What did you do?"

"A vampire's blood heals," he said. "I gave. She drank."

He closed his eyes, and for one single, shame-filled moment, Sara despised the woman, this girl who had shared something so horribly intimate with Luke.

Disturbed and embarrassed, she looked away, not wanting to picture him cradling the girl, helping her, keeping death at bay. She tried to focus on his file, on all the people he was suspected of killing. The list was long and colorful, yet it was this girl who filled her thoughts.

"You were almost out of time," she said. "Why save her?" Why save one girl when he'd so boldly killed so many others?

"Because she was innocent," Luke said, and for a moment, a brief, fleeting moment, Sara had a fresh glimpse into the heart of the man.

"Will she ..." She tried to imagine the horror of being thrust into that world, feeling the dark serpent rise. Of becoming the very thing that had killed her father. "I mean, will she be a vampire, too?"

"No." The word was quick and sharp and said with such force that she took a step back. "I gave her only enough to keep her safe until help arrived. I would not turn her. I—" He broke off, and though his voice remained steady she saw the pain on his face, and she wondered.

"Luke," she said, stepping forward, wanting to comfort even though she didn't understand. Her fingers brushed his, the contact enough to fire her senses, and then the door burst open.

She jumped back, guilty, as the most gorgeous man she'd ever seen in her life got right in her face.

"What the fuck are you doing with my client?"

"Nicholas ..." Sara didn't miss the warning in Luke's voice. Neither, apparently, did his advocate.

"Dammit, Luke—"

"No," Luke said. "I chose to speak to her on my own. I'll not have my judgment questioned."

The advocate stood stock-still, clearly not liking the situation. "We'll talk about this later."

"I have no doubt," Luke said. To Sara, he added, "My advocate, Nicholas Montague."

"So I gathered."

Nicholas turned his attention to her. "Whatever you talked about—whatever he told you—it was said without his advocate, and it's out of bounds. Are we clear on that?"

She stiffened, her arms crossed across her chest. "Thank you for the lesson, Mr. Montague. But I assure you I know the law."

"In that case, you know that I'm entitled to a moment alone with my client."

She nodded, agreeing with Montague's words, but her eyes were on Luke.

"We will speak again," Luke said to her. She nodded again, then stepped from the room, and realized her lips were curved with anticipation.

"Are you not afraid of the dark?"

Xavier shivered, the Dark Angel's breath on the back of his neck like the whisper of a goddess.

"My Angel," he said, bending his head low to show his submission. "The dark gives me strength."

She laughed, as if delighted with his answer, then moved around the swing set to face him. Her beauty stunned him, her eyes compelling. Radiant eyes that he would follow forever.

But it was her fangs that he desired. He would become as she was—she'd promised him so. He had only to prove himself worthy, and then he would be able to take the little girls' light with a kiss. A special kiss to the neck, and their light would be his.

He trembled with anticipation.

She lifted her wrist to her mouth then tore her flesh. "Drink," she said, thrusting her arm toward him.

"My Angel," he said, his heart leaping. "You would change me?"

"I would make you strong," she said. "The change you must earn. Now drink."

She didn't have to ask again. His mouth closed over her wrist and he drew in the sweet, tangy taste of her blood. He drew it in and felt the power thrum through him. So much power in her, and soon, when he'd proved his worth, that power would be his, too. His to control. To wield.

He would be invincible. A true creature of the night.

And they could never again stop him from taking what he desired.

"If the dark is your strength," she asked, swaying slightly as he drank from her, "then why do you hunt during the day?"

He drew away, his mouth tingling, his head bowed deferentially. "The females," he said, trying to explain. "The ones who fill me up. They don't come out at night." He laughed, suddenly amused by his words and the situation. "There are monsters at night, you know."

She smiled, showing her fangs as she laughed. "Where do they live? The young ones. The ones afraid of the scary, scary dark?"

"All around," he said, his finger pointing to the darkened houses. "There is a ripe one lives there," he added, pointing to a pretty house on the corner. A pretty house for a pretty girl.

"Then watch," she said. "Watch and see."

Before his eyes, she dissolved, her body fading into a pale white mist that matched the color of her gown. It moved over the park as fog then disappeared into the house, creeping through cracks and crevices. Only moments later, it returned, riding low over the ground, then rising as a whirlwind in front of him.

The whirlwind slowed, the mist took form, and Xavier found himself looking again at his Dark Angel, a sleeping girl clutched tight in her arms.

"She's for you, Xavier."

He couldn't speak, so deep was his craving, and she laughed, understanding. Then she bent her head to the child's neck, and the girl's eyes opened in terror, her gaze fixed right on him. Seeing him. Knowing him.

He pressed his hand over her mouth as she began to scream, but with that moment of clarity, reason abandoned him. He knew only the craving. The hunger. The need.

"Mine," he said. And like a thing possessed, he took her and fell to the ground with her, closing his mouth over the wound the Angel had made for him, then drawing in the life. The light.

His light.

"I came here planning to punch you in the face," Nick said, his perfect face twisted in anger. "Now I'm postponing my assault, however much you may deserve it, as I've got something more pressing to talk with you about."

"My relief knows no bounds," Luke said.

"Oh, what the hell." And then, before Luke could anticipate it, Nick's fist shot out and slammed into his nose. Bone and cartilage shattered. Blood oozed down the back of his throat.

And somewhere deep within Luke, the serpent bared its fangs and hissed.

Luke forced himself to be calm. Forcing the anger back down where it belonged, taking hold of the chains and twisting, trying to choke the life from the beast. And only when he was certain that he could control it did he look up at his friend.

Nick took a step forward. "You locked me in a coffin. And I had to wake up to Ryan Doyle's ugly face."

"About that, I truly am sorry. No one should have to suffer that way."

"Dammit, Luke, after everything we've been through, and you pull this shit? Play anyone else you like, line up your pieces however they make sense to you. But you do not play me. Not me. Not ever. We clear?"

"We are." Luke understood Nick perfectly, which wasn't the same as acquiescing, but he didn't feel compelled to point that out. "Now tell me what's gotten under your skin." He needed to speak to Nick about the escaped serial killer and the vampire who had helped him, but that conversation would have to wait. Something was up, and Luke quelled a growing sense of unease as he waited for his friend to speak.

"Ryback called," Nick said, as dread latched its claws into Luke. "Tasha wasn't in the apartment."

"There's more," Luke said, a slow, boiling fury replacing the dread. "Tell me."

"He found goblin blood."

Dear gods, Tasha. "You tried her cell?"

"I did. No answer."

"You go there," Luke said, his voice tight with fury. "Use my jet so you can travel by day, but go there, find Serge, and find out what the fuck has happened to my ward. And get my bail hearing moved up. I cannot be in here with Tasha lost in the world. She's a child, Nick, trapped in the body of a woman. She needs protection. She needs me." He looked hard at his friend. "Do whatever you must to make it so."

"I will," Nick said, "though your actions tonight might make that more difficult." Luke lifted his brow in question. "Constantine's pool deck," he continued. "Caught the news as I was coming here. The human cops have swarmed the place. Apparently some girl had the blood sucked out of her. She'll live, but dammit, Luke, you had to go and feed?"

"As a matter of fact, I did."

"It's a crime to suck the life from a human," Nick said mildly. "Or hadn't you heard?"

Luke shot him a look that had his friend recoiling, but all he said was, "The girl is alive."

"If the prosecution connects the dots, that's not going to help your case on bail."

"The prosecution already knows," Luke said, then waited for Nick to connect *those* dots.

It didn't take long. "Dammit, Luke. You told her? A gung ho prosecutor with something to prove? She might make a fine asset, Luke, but don't let the game turn into something more." He cocked his head, as if rearranging a puzzle in his mind. "Oh, no. *No.* Don't go there. She's the prosecutor. *Your* prosecutor. That's all she is, and all she ever can be. Whatever fantasy you're clinging to, you need to let it go."

Ironic, thought Luke, that his friend could find that one sliver of hope despite all Luke's efforts to hide it. "Don't worry," Luke said. "I know who and what she is." What she was, he thought, was dangerous. A woman who would imprison him. Who must surely hate him for what he'd taken from her, and yet he couldn't regret telling her the truth.

She was also the woman who saved him from certain death. And she was the only woman who had ever calmed the darkness within.

He did not know if he could have a future with Sara, but he knew that he had no chance if their path was paved with lies.

Nick eyed him warily. "You know who she is," he repeated. "But don't forget who you are, too. Who you are, and what you do."

"I have not," Luke said, and the knife in his voice drew Nick up short. He drew a breath, calming his temper. "She will say nothing."

"True," Nick agreed. "She can't. Thank the gods your moment of idiocy was between you and her alone. She can't use any of your conversation in court, so I guess that's something."

Nick checked his watch. "I've got a call in to Tiberius, and I'll see what I can do about moving the bail hearing up before I go."

"Good," Luke said, his mind on Tasha. On the goblin's blood. "I need to know what happened to Tasha. My enemies? Serge's?" He met Nick's eyes. "Most of all, I must know that she's okay."

TWENTY

The ground shivered beneath Serge's feet, as if the dead were trying to rise, beating their way through the dirt and the mud, flesh clinging to their moldering bones as they clawed their way up, up, up to the sunshine.

And wasn't that the surprise? You claw your way out of hell, only to get burned in the end. What a world. What a goddamn, depressing, fucked-up world.

All around him, the walls shook, and while Serge rather liked the fantasy that his own personal walls of Jericho were tumbling down, in fact he could blame the noise and the dust only on the Bay Area Rapid Transit system. But since BART had donated the abandoned train tunnel in which he currently resided, he couldn't quite work up the enthusiasm to curse the blasted subway that ran only a few feet from his barren, concrete walls.

Not that BART was aware of its magnanimity. As he had done for a similar home in Manhattan, Serge had acquired this property in a decidedly nontraditional manner, and had thus far enforced his claim by bending the will of weak-minded humans. Granted, there were a few flaws in his overall plan, and one day he fully expected to meet a human who was not amenable to his particular methods of persuasion.

But until that unfortunate day, he was quite content to hold on to this charming address. A small pied-à-terre to complement his hilltop high-rise.

A place where he could go when he began to see the world

through the eyes of the serpent. Where he could recover after a mission as kyne. Where he could call upon the Numen to release the flames and the blood that would once more bind the *Azag Mahru* through the ritual of the Holding. Because no matter how sophisticated he might look in a three-piece silk suit, the condo board had a tendency to frown when you invited hell into your living room. San Francisco was funny that way.

Dear gods, he was losing it.

He pressed his hands to the sides of his head and pushed, letting the pressure build. He'd killed men with those same hands in that same method. Could he press hard enough to end his own life? To end this now? All of this? And most of all—goddammit—the urge to claw his way back up to street level, get his ass back to his condo, and fuck the brains out of the girl whom his best friend had entrusted into his care?

No, no, no, cried the man.

Ah, yes, whispered the serpent.

And, fearing the darkness would win, Serge had left. He'd brought in a goblin to stay with her, and then he'd left.

At least he'd had the presence of mind to call for Graylach. The creature was a fat, lazy slob, but he'd watch the girl. Keep her company. And as goblins found the human form utterly unattractive, he'd be immune to Tasha's allure.

A damn good thing, because she was certainly trying Serge's patience. He wanted. Wanted. And the serpent wouldn't be denied.

The steady jangle of the signal bell came just in time to save Serge from pacing another lap. He hurried to the door—thick wood with ornate carvings he'd acquired from a nearby church two decades prior—and pulled it open. The woman standing in the dank tunnel looked sickly in the grim yellow light that barely illuminated the subway engineering tunnel. But when he pulled her inside, he couldn't say that the incandescent lighting of his hallway favored her much better.

She had fuchsia hair that had been coated with so much gel it stood out from her head like railroad spikes, and most likely with as much strength. Her skin was so pale her freckles appeared to float in front of her, as if leading the way. Dark shadows rimmed her eyes, accentuated by the thick line of kohl. She wore a white tank top with no bra, through which he could see quarter-sized brown nipples on breasts that would have been more appropriate on a thirteen-year-old. Hip-hugger-style jeans shifted on her body as she moved, as if trying to find a hip to actually hug.

The girl was so utterly emaciated that she could have passed as a runway model, a breed of women Serge found uniquely unattractive. He couldn't recall the specific date when women had collectively begun to despise their natural curves, but he rued that day nonetheless.

"I'm here," she said, and took another step into his foyer. "God, what a nightmare that was. Least you tossed out some good directions. But I gotta say, this place is pretty damn frosty."

"I'm thrilled you approve." He had once spent an entire week acquiring and installing the flagstones that led from the entrance into the living area. He had done it because it pleased him, though no one else would see the stones. To know that this creature was sharing even an iota of the pleasure he'd felt seemed almost more obscene than the reason he'd called her to him in the first place.

An army surplus-style backpack dangled from one anorexic arm. The inside of her left elbow was bruised from fresh puncture wounds. If it was sore, she showed no sign.

"So, anyway, like, here we are," she said, swinging the bag off her shoulder. She reached inside and pulled out a long coil of plastic tubing, along with a needle and an empty IV bag. "You into suck or puncture?" she asked. "Oh, and I guess John-O told you my rates, right? And I don't do more than two pints. Makes me too damn woozy, you know?"

Considering that he doubted she had two pints of blood in her entire tiny body, he certainly did know.

"I suck," he said, making her smile. "And we can set up in the backroom." He waved a hand, pointing her toward the heavy steel door.

"Whoa, Nellie," she said, as she stepped inside, and he knew that she was looking at the manacles chained to the walls. "You can really get the kink on in here, huh?"

"I can indeed," he said, following her more slowly, letting the anticipation build. "I've found it's safer this way. You don't mind if I am bound?"

"Hey, you jump all over that safety thing. That's fine with me. I just do what the client wants. But let's be straight here, ya know? I make my living selling this," she said, gesturing to her body. "Pretty much any way you want it. I don't do drugs, and if you want a fuck, you gotta put some jammies on your hammie. But that's about as safe as I get, you know? I mean, hell, if I wanted to play it safe, I coulda got a job waiting tables. Let some wanker grab your tits, and he'll double the tip, too."

"You don't have any tits."

She snorted, then slapped her thigh. "Aren't you a funny dude? Funny bloodsucker. Heh. Maybe you oughta do stand-up or something?"

"I'll look into it right away."

"So what's your deal, anyway? This some sort of religious thing for you? I mean, I know the whole vampire cult thing's all the rage, but I mean, gross me out on the drinking human blood."

"It's extremely nutritious, I assure you. And no, it's not a religious thing." He tilted his head, examining her even as she examined her nails. "Has John-O never told you about your clients?"

"What? Other than you guys are all freaks?"

"Yes," he said dryly. He suppressed a shiver of pleasure at the thought of tasting her, the feel of her blood flowing over his tongue. His cock twitched in anticipation and he couldn't understand his need to engage in this pointless conversation. But if he didn't, the serpent would be harder to restrain, harder to control, and he was barely hanging on as it was. "Other than that."

"Nah. He just says it's more interesting than selling plasma. Pays better, too." She glanced once more at the wall, at the manacles that dangled there.

He smiled. "Perhaps you would like the honors? I could be persuaded to remain unbound."

For a moment, she looked intrigued. Then she shook her head. "Better not. Wouldn't want you to lose your natural rhythm, what-o?"

"What-o, indeed."

With her rather eager assistance, he was soon stripped naked and manacled to the walls. Steel cuffs, and strong. But not too strong. He wanted to be bound—to keep the faunt who came so trusting to his door safe.

And yet there was a part of him...

Well, that part insisted on steel and not hematite. Less sport, perhaps. But the potential for so much more satisfaction.

"So, like, you got no free arms. How you going to hold the tube?"

"The tube?" He was spread-eagled on the wall, arms and ankles bound tight. Certainly no threat to anyone at the moment. And still the girl licked her lips, took a tiny, apprehensive step backward.

"Yeah." She held up the plastic tubing, the bag, and the needle. "Whatcha gonna do? Just clench it between your teeth?"

"I'm sure the experience would be delightful, but that is not where I find my pleasure." No, he found it in the flesh. The skin beneath his mouth. And that sweet moment of hesitation before the flesh was punctured and the blood ran free.

It was forbidden, of course. What he wanted. To puncture a human ... it was a crime, and yet he wanted it still.

"So what you thinking about?" she asked, looking at his crotch, where his cock had sprung to attention, quite in anticipation of the main event. "What's getting you all hot and bothered?"

"You are, of course," he said.

"Yeah?" She strutted toward him, then pressed her finger to his lip and drew it down, down, down, then flicked the end of it hard on his cock. He winced, with both surprise and pleasure—and knew then that he would have this one.

She laughed, satisfied, and danced back away from him, her expression teasing.

He could tease as well. "Let us play a little game."

"Yeah?"

"Drop the bag. Drop the tube. Drop the needle."

She did.

"Now come to me."

She took one step, then hesitated, her eyes narrowed. "John-O said I shouldn't—"

"Am I not strapped to a wall? What harm can come from indulging a bound man?"

"Well ..."

He met her eyes, looked deep ... and let his will be done.

"No harm," she said, easing closer, the seductive smile ridiculous on her pixie face and brightly colored hair.

"No harm," he agreed. "Come closer."

She did, pressing herself to him, one hand closing around his shaft. She stroked him in a slow, practiced motion that had him groaning, fighting the urge to let her finish. But no. He had other plans for her, and in a low voice, he told her.

She looked at him, and for a moment he thought the hold would snap. Thought he would have to change into mist, transform to chase her down. He didn't want to. The shackles, though illusory, kept the serpent at bay. A reminder, he supposed, that he'd once won. Once upon a time, he'd beaten the serpent back fiercely.

Besides, he got off on it. On being exposed to them. Vulnerable to them.

Because he *so* wasn't vulnerable.

This one, though. This one wasn't cooperating. Instead, she was squirming against him, fear in her eyes. The fear that came with understanding. In finally realizing what he meant to do.

He'd told her, of course. But until this moment, she hadn't believed.

Concede.

She sighed, long and languid, as the suggestion filled her mind. Then she tilted her head to the side, exposing her neck for him. So white, so smooth. Like marble, and yet not. Pliant and delicious and living. Pumping with life. Pumping with blood.

He breathed deep, letting her scent envelop him, letting the pressure build within until he was certain he would come when the first drop of her blood touched his tongue. And then, when he could stand it no longer, he sank his fangs deep into her throat, his entire body convulsing with pleasure as the blood began to flow.

Ecstasy.

This was it. What he needed. What he'd been craving.

But it still wasn't enough.

He needed to taste the tang of fear in her blood. Needed it to bring him out, to pull him through.

Had to have it.

Now.

The bond between them snapped, and the instant it did, she screamed. And inside Serge, the wakening serpent stretched and uncoiled and slithered that much closer to freedom.

Sara flipped through the pages of one of her father's journals that she'd brought with her to work that day. The entries were cryptic, but now that she was looking at them with the perspective of someone inside Division 6, she was able to make some things out. *Tiber & D*, for example. Dragos, maybe? And the notes about the Shadow creatures walking among the humans—he didn't mean as they did now. He meant with full knowledge of everyone in the world.

It was a terrible idea.

Even from her perspective of only a few days in this world, she knew that it would overwhelm. The Shadow world would be too tempted by the possibility of power. The human world would lose its shit and fight back even without an actionable threat. There would be violence and chaos, and war between the Shadow factions. A war in which the humans would become casualties.

Her father was an idealist, but he was not practical. And as much as she hated to admit it, she agreed with the decision to silence him.

But no one would ever convince her that the method had been just.

With a deep breath, she sighed as she wiped away tears before continuing to flip pages, looking for familiar words and names. The one she saw the most was Dragos.

Luke.

The entries were cryptic, but it was clear her father knew something about him. Loyal to the vampiric leader. A warrior. An honorable man.

All terms that described the man she knew.

And yet he'd taken her father from her.

Under orders.

And yet he'd murdered a judge.

But why?

With a sharp snap of fury, she hurled the book at the far wall. Was she really fighting herself now? Her brain telling her heart the reasons she should hate Luke? The justifications for never again being in his arms?

Was it truly Luke she hated, or was it Tiberius? After all, Luke had shown the courage to tell her the truth even knowing that she would condemn him. He laid the facts at her feet, leaving her to decide if she loved him.

She closed her eyes.

Damn her, she did.

She didn't want to, but she did.

It wasn't Luke she hated, but Tiberius. She only hoped that someday she'd have the chance to get her revenge.

She closed her eyes, then jumped at the sharp rap on her office door, which then flew open without waiting for her invitation.

"You banging him?" Doyle demanded, bursting into the room with Tucker at his side. "Oh, wait," Doyle continued, putting his hands on her desk and leaning in close. "You're a human. Not really his type. So maybe you just like his pretty face. Or maybe you're just stupid enough to do the bastard favors."

Because his insult skirted very near the truth, she took the time to consider her response. "I'm tired, Agent. I've barely slept. And in case you didn't get the memo, Dragos's bail hearing's been moved to tonight. So I'd appreciate it very much if you'd back the fuck off."

She still couldn't believe that bit of news. Apparently Luke really did have connections, because the word had come down all the way from Nostramo Bosch, the Director of all of the North American Divisions, that the hearing was being bumped up. *Lovely.* Maybe she'd sleep next month. Right now, she had work to do if she wanted to keep him incarcerated until the Braddock trial. And she did. No matter what she might feel for him, the evidence was clear that he murdered Braddock. No way should he get out on bail. Lucius Dragos was a dangerous man, though she couldn't help but wonder if he was anywhere near as dangerous to the public as he was to her heart.

Doyle took a step forward, clearly upping the intimidation factor. She stood her ground.

"Why don't you tell us what you were doing sprinting to Division in the middle of the night?" he demanded. "Especially after what he did to that girl at your pool?"

"I didn't know he'd fed when I arrived," she admitted. "How did you find out?"

Doyle moved away, then leaned casually against the wall, giving off the appearance of a benign man having a simple conversation with a colleague. But there was nothing benign about Ryan Doyle. She could see the danger bubbling beneath the surface. She imagined that edge made him an exceptional investigator—not to mention a tireless opponent.

"Human police band. The address popped as yours."

"All right," she said, because so far he was making perfect sense. "But there's still no straight line that connects me and Annie and Lucius Dragos."

"The hell there isn't." He reached out his hand, and Tucker passed Sara his phone. She peered at the small screen, then let out a small gasp at the image of Luke, battered on the steps of the pool, and Annie moving in close to him.

"Smile," Doyle said. "That fuckwad's on candid camera."

"Got him dead to rights on this," Tucker said, retrieving his phone. "Drawing from a human. Feeding a human. Big no-nos for vamps. Brings the darkness too close to the surface."

"And don't be so naive as to think a vamp's ever really got that snake under control," Doyle said, his color rising. "That may be the politically correct party line, but it's a bunch of bullshit, and everyone in the Shadow world damn well knows it. The darkness can't be controlled—won't be controlled. And when it comes out, it's like a visitation straight from hell."

Sara shivered, then realized she'd been hugging herself. Tucker, she saw, had moved closer to his partner, who shook his head violently, then turned away. Personal, she thought. The darkness in vampires was real, but it was also damn personal to Doyle.

"So how did you get this? There aren't security cameras on the pool deck."

Tucker snorted. "Two vamps live in your building. You think the PEC doesn't have some surveillance of its own?"

She frowned, her gaze dipping back down to that image. An image of Luke, with his mouth on Annie's neck.

She tore her eyes away, ignoring the fresh burst of absurd jealousy, the same that she'd felt when he'd told her the story. Dear God, he was feeding on the girl. Sara didn't want that. How could she want that?

"So you'll use this, right?" Tucker asked. "At the hearing?"

"Of course she will," Doyle said, looking at her hard. "I'd say this is some pretty solid proof that Dragos is a danger to the community. Wouldn't you, Counselor?"

She hesitated, weighing her options.

"It is," she finally said. "And yes, if we need it, we'll use it." She told herself that she wasn't crossing any lines by doing so. After all, Doyle had learned about Annie and Luke all on his own.

Still, she felt a twinge of guilt. With a great deal of mental force, she quashed it. She needed to remember who she was—the new human prosecutor on a high-profile case. Her boss was expecting a seasoned advocate. One who knew how to play the game, and didn't let her personal feelings get in the way.

And she was that girl. She hadn't made it to the top of her law school class without a competitive edge. Wouldn't have landed Stemmons behind bars if she didn't have skills. And she wouldn't have been selected to work at Division if Leviathan wasn't fully confident in her abilities.

If Montague wanted to argue that Luke had fed off Annie to save himself, then Montague could damn well raise that as an affirmative defense.

She ran her fingers through her hair and nodded toward Tucker's phone. "Okay. Good. This goes a long way toward establishing the element of danger to the community. But risk of flight's harder. He came back to Division of his own accord."

"With a stake strapped to his chest."

"True," Sara acknowledged. "But it'll be there during his bail term as well."

"So we put on evidence suggesting that given more time he would have found a way to remove it. Three hours wasn't enough. But three days? Three weeks? A guy like Dragos, he must have connections that could pull that off."

Sara nodded. "Right. So we suggest to the court that he's looking to shake loose of the countermeasures. Couple that with the evidence about Annie, not to mention the silver signet ring, the DNA, and your vision. With all that, I think the court will surely deny bail."

Doyle leaned back, his hands shoved deep into his pockets. "Huh."

"What? You disagree?"

"Nope. We're good. Just surprised is all."

"By?"

"You. Didn't figure you had the balls to go after him."

She lifted her brows. "And I didn't figure you had the balls to admit you were wrong, so maybe we're even. But speaking of balls, you ever come at me in attack mode again, Doyle, and I will nail yours to the wall." She smiled, wide and flirty. "We're clear?"

He let out a guffaw, just as she'd expected he would. She'd spent years with hard-ass detectives, and she knew a thing or two about the care and feeding of same.

"You're not a pushover," he said. "That's good. You last a month in the basement, I'll buy you lunch." He stuck out his hand.

She closed her hand over his. "You're on."

"My eyes are going to fall right out of my head soon," Sara said, looking up from the papers spread across her desk as Blair entered.

"I know a demon who did that," Blair said. "The eye thing, I mean. Big hit at parties. Huge," she added as Sara gawked. "What? It was a hoot."

"Remind me not to go to a party with you."

Blair smirked. "Not even a worry. You're growing on me. But we're not besties yet."

"The day's looking up already."

They shared a grin, then Blair settled back in one of the guest chairs. "So what do we still need to pull together?"

Sara skimmed the piles that Blair had organized. "Honestly, I think we're in good shape." After finishing the interview with Doyle, she'd had a meeting with Leviathan, followed by another with the preternatural version of Human Resources. When she'd reached her office, she'd been greeted by two stacks of paper on her desk. On the left, the rough draft of a brief in support of Division's Opposition to Defendant's Motion to Set Bail. On the right, all the case law relevant to both the motion and the opposition.

All in all, a huge help, and she'd dug right in, the rhythm of the law helping her find her center and cling to the familiar in a decidedly new world.

"You'll take care of filing our briefs and making sure the evidence is labeled and organized?"

"Sure," Blair said, tapping out a note to herself. "Now we just need—"

A sharp knock interrupted them, and Sara looked up to see Leviathan standing in the doorway. "A human child was discovered in Echo Park a few minutes ago."

"Stemmons?" she asked, her chest tight with dread.

"Apparently so," Leviathan said. "The rapid response team has already confirmed his scent."

She was already up and at the door, Blair right behind her. "A Division team at a human crime scene? Is that usual?"

"It's not," he said. "But this is a Division matter because of the evidence that vampires assisted Stemmons's breakout. You've been assigned to the joint task force because of your history with him. But be careful. The cover story is still Homeland Security."

"Yes, sir." Her mind was already spinning. "If vampires helped him escape, they're probably still with him, and the victim may have seen one of them. I'd like Doyle to come along, too. With any luck, his visions can help."

"Make the call," he said to Blair as he and Sara stepped into the elevator. "Have Agent Doyle meet us at the scene."

"Yes, sir," Blair said as the doors closed and the elevator whisked them to the parking level. On the drive, Leviathan gave her the relevant details: ten-year-old female abducted from her home. No witnesses.

The news, and the dry recitation, about broke Sara's heart. But it was the sight of the little girl herself, pale as paper, eyes open in terror, that had sharp tears stinging Sara's eyes, and a flood of pure rage boiling through her head.

Her neck had been ripped open, which wasn't Stemmons' traditional MO, but since his scent had been confirmed, Sara had to assume that the vamps were teaching him a thing or two.

Her hand ached suddenly, and she realized she'd been clutching her fist. She forced herself to relax, to let go of the wave of disgust that was keeping her rooted to the spot.

Goddammit.

"Sir." A tall man with dark skin, a shaved head, and a neatly trimmed beard approached Leviathan. He wore a T-shirt, jeans, and cowboy boots along with a blue windbreaker that had *Division 6* stenciled on the back and *Forensics* on the front. "I have a preliminary report."

"Sara Constantine, this is Dr. Orion, head of forensics and our chief medical examiner."

"Ms. Constantine," Orion said, extending his hand. "Nice to meet a kindred spirit."

"I'm sorry?"

"Orion is human, too," Leviathan told her. "At the moment, you two and Agent Tucker are the only humans working within Division 6."

"Oh. Wow. Well, it's great to meet you."

"We'll have coffee," he said. "I'll tell you tales. But before that pleasant interlude, we have a little girl to attend to."

"We do," Sara said. "What can you tell us so far?"

"We've analyzed the residual essence from Stemmons' escape, and there's no question that Stemmons was assisted by a single vampire, but the signature isn't reading clearly and we can't even determine if the vampire was male or female."

"Can you tell if that same vampire was here?" Sara asked.

"You beat me to it," Orion said. "I was just about to say yes. We're picking up the same signature."

"We need Doyle," Sara said. "If the girl saw the vampire…"

"Has Agent Doyle reported to the scene?" Leviathan asked. The question, however, was mooted by Doyle's appearance across the playground. He scanned the scene, slipped under the county crime tape, then crossed quickly, with Tucker at his side.

"What the fuck?"

"A task force matter," Leviathan said. "Constantine thinks your skills would be useful."

His eyes cut to the child's body, now surrounded by the human police. "Too crowded."

"We'll clear the crowd," Leviathan said.

"It's bullshit," Doyle said. "She's human."

"She's a little girl," Sara countered.

Doyle's face tightened. "You got any idea how fucking hard it is to do what I do? How much it drains me when I do it often? What seeps in around the edges when I'm weak?" His lip curled up in a snarl. "You ask me to do this thing, but you don't know the cost, Constantine. You don't fucking live in my world."

"What about the cost to that little girl?" Sara asked, refusing to be intimidated.

"She's human. Killed by a human. It's not my world. Not my problem."

"A vampire helped Stemmons kill her, Doyle," Sara said, getting right into his face, because if it hadn't been for that damn vampire, then Stemmons wouldn't be out preying on little girls. "That's your world."

He kicked the ground. "Fine. Fuck. Clear the goddamn scene."

Leviathan and Tucker took charge, with Leviathan urging all extraneous personnel to leave the scene, and Tucker using his unique skill set to move the process along.

When the crowd had dwindled and only a few humans remained nearby—their minds ready to be wiped by Tucker—Doyle bent over the body and placed his hands on the little girl, one over her head and one over her heart. His body went slack, his eyes glassy.

"How long?" she whispered to Tucker.

"Depends," he said. "I've seen a hundred of these things, and they're all different. It's the curse of being partnered with a Percipient. They ship him all over the damn globe when they got a fresh one."

"You, too?"

Tucker's expression was grave. "We're partners. Don't always make it to the scene in time, though," Tucker added, looking at his partner. "Doyle's got a thing about wormholes. Won't go that way. Says they lead straight through hell. Doesn't matter how hot the case, he'll only travel by PEC transport. So sometimes the aura fades." His expression turned wry. "This one looks fresh, though."

Sara hoped it was. She wanted answers, and right then, Doyle seemed like the best bet. Small convulsions wracked his body until, finally, Tucker grabbed Doyle's shoulders and yanked him free of the girl.

Doyle looked up, his face pale, his eyes glassy, and Sara realized her hands were clenched at her sides. "Female," he said. "The vamp bitch is female." He eased backward, shaking his head. "All I could get. Hem of a dress. Impressions from the kid."

"Shit," Sara said, realizing how much she'd been hoping for Doyle to ID the vampire, give them some lead, some clue, something. Because she knew time was running out for the next little girl, and if they didn't hurry, she'd soon be standing over another pale, sweet face.

"Constantine!" Manny called to her from across the crime scene. "We got a lock of hair."

She hurried over, peered into the evidence bag at the curl of auburn hair held together by a golden ribbon. "Under the body, just like before."

She swallowed. "Hell of a way to see each other again," she told him.

"We'll get a drink and catch up one day. Office doesn't feel the same without you in it."

She looked up as Leviathan approached, then indicated the evidence bag. "He kept them," she told him. "The girls. Took two or three at a time and kept them in cages. Then when he'd kill one, he'd leave a little clue as to the one he was going to do next. Hair. A favorite toy." She closed her eyes, swallowed hard. "One girl, he left her tongue."

"Son of a bitch," Leviathan said.

"He's got the next one in a cage already," she said, her stomach in knots. "And unless he's changed the way he operates, he's already got the one after that picked out."

CHAPTER
TWENTY-ONE

"Tasha!" The elevator doors opened directly into Serge's San Francisco condo, and Nick's voice echoed over the polished marble. The foyer led into an extravagant living room, a semicircle with walls of specially manufactured tinted glass from which Serge could look out over the night, then flip the finger at the rising sun through the impervious glass.

According to Serge, the chemistry upon which the glass was made was sound, but Nick couldn't help but wonder if Serge was secretly longing for the day it failed, leaving the troubled vampire as nothing more than a pile of ash by the windows, the deadly sunlight having accomplished its purpose.

Thankfully, today was not that day.

In fact, Nick found nothing at all and wondered if perhaps that was even more disturbing.

"Come on, Tasha," he called. "It's Nick. Come on out for me."

He waited for her reply. A soft whimper, a terrified yell, even an irritated wail that she'd been left all alone. But the apartment remained quiet, and the fear in Nick's gut bloomed red.

Determined, he stalked through the place, peering into all the rooms, looking into all the closets, under the beds. Any place a scared girl would hide.

He didn't find her. More telling, he didn't find any of her dolls.

The goblin blood, however, was exactly where Ryback had said, its vinegar scent still pungent.

"By the gods," he whispered. "What the hell happened here?"

He feared the answer, but also knew he had to find Serge. More, he knew where he had to look.

He'd been to Serge's subterranean abode only twice, the first time accessing the underground corridors through the basement of the high-rise, and the second through a descent into a subway tunnel. They'd hopped the tracks, then entered the maze of tunnels through a maintenance door. With the sun now shining brightly, Nick had no choice but to take option one and hope that he could find his way through the putrid tunnels to the oasis that was Serge's hideaway.

With luck, Serge would be there when he found it.

The basement had not been designed to connect to the city's labyrinth of tunnels. And, indeed, it was not Serge who had forged the way. That task had fallen upon the misbegotten of the city, the destitute and homeless who searched for a place other than the street to sleep. How they had discovered the thin stone wall behind the industrial washing machines in the basement laundry room, Nick didn't know. Someone had, though, then chipped away to create a narrow passage that could be accessed by shifting one of the machines slightly to the left.

Someone, possibly Serge, had finally become frustrated with the frequent movement of the appliance and had pushed it permanently aside, then situated a draped table in front of the access point. Ostensibly a place for residents to fold clothes, the table provided a permanent doorway for anyone who crawled beneath and pushed aside the drape.

It was, thought Nick, the kind of portal to hell that populated children's nightmares. The place where they would disappear. Where the monsters would grab them.

He moved quickly inside the tunnels, passing these humans, these people who would look upon him either as monster or as savior. Had Serge turned any of them, he wondered? Had he made these gutter rats into their kind?

The possibility disgusted Nick. Serge would say he was a snob and, in fact, he would be right. Because there was a beauty to what they were. Nosferatu. Creatures born of night and filled with night.

They suffered, yes. And those who lost the battle within could spend eternity lost in torment. But if the battle could be won—if the beast could be tamed—then the world seemed to exist for their delight, the most powerful and feared of all the Shadow creatures. With strength and grace and abilities like none other.

It was intoxicating.

It was, he thought, divine.

And had it not been divinity that he had searched for, all those years ago in Venice? Had he not sought the face of God through his studies? Through examination of the stars? In the very art of his ancestors?

He shook his head to clear his meandering thoughts. He did not often think on his nature, as he did not want to tempt fate. Become too complacent—too arrogant—and the darkness would rise up and try to wrest control.

That had happened with Serge, he was certain.

The serpent had burst forth. The only questions now were how many had it killed, and how much of Serge was left.

Rats scurried around his feet, and he trod carefully on the metal flooring. The way was narrow in places, but when the tunnel widened, he could see people huddled together over Sterno cans, their eyes white behind filthy faces.

One foolish man stepped into Nick's path, a metal shiv held at the ready. "Whacha doin' down hae?"

"I'm out for a stroll," Nick said. "You'd be wise to go your own way."

"Smart man. Fancy man."

"Deadly man," Nick said, and bared his fangs.

That was all it took, and the man scurried away like the rats Nick had passed earlier. He didn't stare in awe and wonder. Didn't snarl and claim Nick was a monster. He turned and ran.

And that, Nick thought, was telling. These people had seen a vampire. Knew what one was, and what one was capable of.

He stopped, for the first time really looking at the people huddled together, their eyes fixed on him. He lifted his chin, sniffing the air, finding their scent. Heroin and sex. Blood and vomit. But they would know, and they would tell.

He took a step toward the closest one, and she scooted backward, her halter top falling open to expose a flaccid breast. "Get away, get away, get away."

"You know me?"

"I know like you," she said, then spat at his feet. "Evil inside."

He cocked his head. "What do you know of it?"

"Tossed her out. Out of his big house. Hell house, underground, just like the way to hell. Find her, and she's all broken and can't fix her, just like that egg boy."

"Egg boy?"

"Humpty," she said. "Egg boy."

"Ah, yes."

"Just wanted to get her groove on, that's all she wanted. Just trying to get by, get high."

He stepped closer. "Move."

She hesitated, and he curled his lips. That sufficed, and she scuttled sideways, revealing a mound under a tattered, filthy blanket. He bent closer, saw bugs scatter as he reached to draw the cloth away, then found himself staring at an emaciated young woman with a mass of dark, curly ringlets. She was pale and motionless, and the scent of death was upon her.

"Where?" Nick asked. "Where does he live? The one who did this thing?"

The woman stuck out a thin arm and pointed to the left fork of the tunnel. "He's evil. He'll rip your heart out as soon as look at you. And he just tosses them away, all the pretty girls. Just trying to get by. Just trying to get a fix."

He left her prattling on, her words echoing eerily in the tunnel.

He found Serge's door easily enough. There was no mistaking it. The polished, ornate oak, completely devoid of graffiti. Because who in the tunnels would be fool enough to deface the monster's doorway?

"Serge! Open up!" Nick pounded, ignoring the eyes that peered out from the dark. "Dammit, Serge, open the fucking door."

Nothing. No sound. No noise. Nothing.

"Fuck." This time, the curse was whispered, more to himself and the door than to anyone inside. "Too bad. It's a damn nice door." And with that, he reared back, kicked, and sent the heavy oak door flying across the flagstone-paved entrance hall.

His eyes told him the place was empty. His nose told him otherwise. The pungent, enticing scent of blood hung in the air, laced with fear and a little piss and shit just to give it that nice round edge.

"Bloody hell, Serge," Nick whispered, moving slowly through the place. "What the fuck are you into?"

He heard it then—a single, low growl that had him racing to the far door that led into Serge's private playroom.

Serge was there, naked and prostrate over a huge broken mirror. Deep gashes marred his arms and legs. Fresh, Nick knew, as they hadn't yet begun to heal.

"Serge."

His friend twitched, but didn't look up.

"Serge, look at me."

He turned, and Nick saw the serpent in his eyes warring for control. And the horror of what he'd done—what he would do— etched on Serge's face.

"Can't bring the Holding. Can't call forth the Numen," Serge said, taking a shard of glass and digging it deep into his arm.

The blood ritual. The spirit guide.

Even now, Nick felt the cold, hollow grip of fear. The terror he'd experienced when he'd slid into the netherworld for that ultimate battle. And the sinking knowledge that he could still lose the battle despite the Numen at his side. And if he did, he would be forever trapped, the serpent Nick evolving, while the other Nick dissolved into nothing.

In front of him, Serge howled with pain, but didn't stop mutilating his skin. "Come, you bitch! Get it the fuck out of me. Push it back!"

"Serge. Serge!" Nick knelt beside him, grabbed his shoulders with one hand, and with the other took the bloody glass. "You're you. You're still you. It's working. You're fighting. You don't need her yet. You're pushing it back. I can see it. You're pushing it back."

"No, no, no." With a terrible, heart-wrenching squall, Serge looked up, met Nick's gaze with drunken eyes. "I lost it. It killed her."

Nick stiffened, a cold terror racing through him. "Who?" he asked carefully, afraid that Serge had spilled Tasha's blood. That he had staked her, and that she was no more. "Focus," he said, shaking his friend. "Tell me. Who? Who did you kill?"

"The girl with kaleidoscope eyes," he said, his smile crooked and his voice singsong. "Came here selling herself. A faunt," he said, referring to the humans who sold their blood to feed vampires. The word sent relief coursing through Nick. Not Tasha. Thank the gods it wasn't Tasha.

"Wild hair," Serge was saying, which meant that this girl wasn't the one Nick had seen in the tunnel. "Practically pink. Chatty. Liked her, too. Killed her anyway. Didn't like the rest. Didn't even know them."

Nick closed his eyes, trying not to imagine the damage a powerful vampire like Serge could cause. "How many?"

Pain flashed in the haunted red eyes. "Don't know. Just killed them. Found them, and had them."

"Fight it back," Nick said, his body tensed for battle, his words wary. "Kick it back to hell where it belongs."

"I am in hell," Serge said.

"There you go," Nick said, and earned a slow smile from his friend. "That's it. Come on back. Fight, dammit. Fight."

"Want to," he said. "Getting harder every day." He reached behind him, and from the mess of blood and glass managed to produce a wooden stake. He thrust it at Nick. "Take it. Use it."

"The hell I will."

"Dammit, end me."

"No." Nick snapped the stake in two. "Listen to me."

"Son of a bitch. You goddamn, fuck-faced fool." The serpent was coming out, riding the crest of Serge's anger. Well, fine, Nick thought. After all of this, he was gunning for a fight anyway.

"Listen to me," Nick repeated, but he knew Serge wasn't listening anymore. He was sinking inside himself, and something else was coming up.

Nick wasn't going to let it get there.

Without warning, he hauled back and punched Serge hard in the gut. His startled friend howled, then pounced, but Nick was ready, leaning back so that he had leverage, and then kicking out and catching Serge hard across the throat with the sole of his foot. Serge staggered back, blood in his eye, and came forward again.

"Enough," Nick growled, as Serge barreled into him, knocking them both to the ground. "I won't kill you, no matter how damn much you provoke me."

"Fuck you, Nicholas."

"No, fuck you." And he reached down, grabbed his friend's naked balls, and twisted.

The effect was pretty much what he'd anticipated. Serge dropped like a stone and clutched his crotch, which gave Nick the opportunity to get back to him, crouch down, and place half the broken stake right at his buddy's temple. "It won't kill you," he said, "but you won't be the same."

"Knock my brains out, and at least I won't know what I'm doing." The pain that colored Serge's voice had Nick lowering the weapon.

"You're back."

"You twisted my nuts into a knot, damn you. You think the serpent's gonna hang around for that kind of torture?"

"You clear? Good and clear?"

Serge looked up, met Nick's eyes, then shook his head no. "But I'm steady. I can fight. I can," he added, in response to Nick's doubtful expression. "Dammit all, it's been building. Growing in me. Taking over. Fucking nightmare. Fucking goddamn life."

"You should have told us."

"What? Hey, dudes. Losing myself here. If I fall, don't piss too hard on me?"

"You should have told us," Nick repeated.

Serge sighed. "I know." He ran his fingers through his hair, standing it on end. "Dammit, I know."

"Where's Tasha?"

"You think I'd let her see me like this? I got Graylach to stay with her."

"The goblin's dead, Serge. It's dead, and Tasha's gone."

He could see the shock flash in Serge's eyes. More, he could see the flash of opportunity—the serpent taking a tentative peek out once again.

"Focus for me. Focus, damn you. Where is she? Did someone know she was staying with you? Someone who'd want to hurt Luke?"

"I don't know." He pressed his hands to his skull. "I don't know. I left. Had to keep her safe."

"Safe?" Nick repeated. "Safe from what?"

Pure pain glowed in Serge's eyes. "From me."

He drew in a breath, then clutched his head even tighter. "By the gods," he whispered. "Lucius. He will have my life for this."

"No," said Nick, standing up and looking away from his friend as compassion warred with disgust. "Right now, I don't think your life is worth the debt."

Luke listened as Nick told him the story, forcing himself to bury his rage—and his fear—under an icy calm. If he lost control now, he'd be hard-pressed to ever get it back.

"You cannot feel her at all?" Nick asked. "There is no blood connection between you? Not even the slightest?"

"You know there isn't," Luke said. It was one of the reasons that the Concordat prohibited the turning of those without full capacity. With any other, he would be able to seek them out, discern their feelings, come close to actually reading their mind.

With a mind such as Tasha's, though, that was not possible.

"Dammit." Luke grabbed the edges of the small sink in his cell, fighting once again for control, feeling it slipping away. "The dolls," he said, forcing his mind to think clearly. "You said that her dolls were gone?"

"All of them. Her clothes, too."

He considered the fact, focusing on the scenario, pushing emotion out of the mix so that he could think clearly. Because unless he was clear, he couldn't find her. "A killer would not take such things."

"There'd be no reason," Nick said, agreeing. "Neither would someone holding her to send you a message."

"And where is the message?" Luke asked. "There is none, because it is not my enemies who have her."

"She left on her own," Nick said, nodding. "But that's not a whole hell of a lot better."

"No," Luke agreed. "It isn't." She may have left Serge's of her own free will, but so far she had not contacted Nick again. And to Luke's mind, that meant trouble.

"She would have come to Los Angeles," he said.

"To you," Nick said. "Of course."

"And we know that Caris is in town."

"Fuck," Nick said. "You don't think—"

"I think it's a possibility," Luke said. "Payback for my taking out Hasik and Tinsley. For fucking up Gunnolf's little plot." Nick had briefed Tiberius, who had in turn paid a visit to Gunnolf. For now, Gunnolf's plan was on ice, and as Tiberius had agreed not to inform the rest of the Alliance about Gunnolf's treachery, Tiberius had acquired a powerful political marker. As had Luke.

"You think Caris would know it was you?"

"Tiberius knows it was me, and I'm sure she still has sources within his organization. But even if she doesn't know, I wouldn't be surprised if she'd snatch Tasha simply out of spite. Damned ancient history. And if that traitorous bitch really has laid a hand on Tasha, she'll soon feel the sharp end of a very hard stick."

Nick nodded slowly. "But we have to find her first."

"I know. I want you on the street. Find out where Caris is holed up."

"In case you've forgotten, you have a bail hearing in a few hours. A hearing that I had to do a particularly complicated tap dance to get moved forward."

"Then get Slater," Luke said. "Tell him it's a favor to me."

"Will do," Nick said. "If Caris is still in town, we'll find her."

"Tell him I want a location by the time this hearing is over. I haven't seen Caris in years. I think it's time to renew an old acquaintance."

"What about Serge?"

Luke sagged. "He is more than kyne, Nicholas. Of all of us, Serge is the only one I can truly call brother. But if he did this ... if he touched her..."

He closed his eyes, a barrier against the horror of his friend's betrayal, and incongruously, he thought of Sara. Sara, searching for justice in a world where it was so rarely found. Sara, in whose arms he had forgotten, for just a moment, the sharp edges of the world in which he walked.

TWENTY-TWO

The Los Angeles branch of the International Order of Therians was housed in a refurbished 1940s historic mansion on South Highland Boulevard, two blocks from the local Starbucks. Doyle and Tucker had stopped in for a caffeine hit before heading on to their scheduled interview with Ytalia Leon, the organization's acting president. So far, the coffee had been the best part of their day, as the investigation was turning up a big, fat zero.

Specifically, their inquiries into Braddock had revealed a dozen or so colleagues who thought the shapeshifter was a royal prick, but nobody was spouting specifics other than the bribery and blackmail charges, and at least to Doyle's way of thinking, that was old news.

"Our man's either very good at keeping secrets," Doyle said, "or Constantine's got us running in circles." The prosecutor had latched onto the bribery complaints that peppered Braddock's history and insisted they dig, so they were digging. And while Doyle agreed with her theory that bribery often cloaked a multitude of sins, so far the theory that he was into something else that got him killed wasn't panning out.

Tucker flipped through his notes. "Sanctioned for taking bribes. A few allegations of blackmail. Some undisclosed financial accounts. Yeah, I'd say the guy was a natural on the secret front."

The steady clip-clip of heels on wood echoed down the hall, shutting off further speculation. A moment later, the sound was followed by a petite woman with short red hair, an angular nose, and sharp, small eyes. Following her was a young woman with long straggly hair and a face bent perpetually toward the floor. She shuf-fled to a corner of the room and began to sort a stack of papers into neat piles. Ytalia ignored the girl, but focused exclusively on the agents, her hand extended in a formal greeting.

Doyle took it, gave it a firm shake, then indicated for her to sit. He mentally flipped through her file, remembering that Ytalia was a were-coyote. Yeah, he thought. That fit.

"You wish to discuss Judge Braddock?"

"That's right," Doyle said, noticing that on the far side of the room, the younger woman stiffened.

"I'm happy to help in any way I can."

"You were his secretary when he was on the bench, right?"

"That's right. And after his retirement, he was very active in the Order. In the fight for equal rights for all were-creatures. He was a most vigorous advocate for our cause, and we're all extremely distressed by his unfortunate demise."

"Yeah, murder's a bitch."

She peered down her nose at him. Beside him, Tucker cleared his throat.

"We've talked to quite a few people, ma'am," Tucker said, "and the picture we're getting is interesting, to say the least."

"The man is dead, sir. I'll not have you besmirching his good name."

"Did he have a good name?" Doyle asked. At Ytalia's glare, he spread his hands. "Just asking."

"The judge had some vices, it's true. But he worked very hard to overcome them. He should be honored for his fortitude and determi-nation. Not vilified."

"What vices, exactly?"

"Is this relevant?"

"Everything's relevant in murder."

She sighed, then shifted so that she was speaking more to Tucker than to Doyle. "He was ... proud of his position. He had worked very hard to rise so far, and while he deserved the honor, I think in some ways it went to his head."

"Sure," Tucker said, nailing the role of good cop with such preci-sion that Doyle was sure an Oscar was in the boy's future. "Who wouldn't get a swelled head?"

"Exactly," she said, clearly pleased to have found an ally. "That power ... well, it can be heady."

"He took bribes. He used his position to blackmail," Doyle said.

"He did, he did." She looked positively miserable at the admission. "And he recognized the error of his ways and worked hard to overcome it." She leaned forward, speaking earnestly to Tucker, whom she obviously saw as the more reasonable of the two. "And he did overcome it. He really did."

"All that heady power," Doyle said, "it push him toward anything other than blackmail?"

Her back stiffened. "I don't know what you mean."

"Just thinking aloud," Doyle said, but he was focused more on the girl—who'd become frozen in the act of sorting papers—than on his interviewee.

"Even rumors," Tucker said. "We're looking for a motive here. Maybe his killer got it wrong. Heard something untrue, but acted on it."

"Well, I don't know what," she said, turning back to Tucker. "The judge was a good man at heart, and nobody says otherwise. Certainly not around here. He did some rousting in his youth—packs of were-creatures tearing through the nicer neighborhoods, stirring up the humans. It's ridiculous, and of course it's frowned upon. Frightens the humans something awful, but there's no real harm. Of course he was sanctioned for it. But that was ages ago. Long before he was ever put up for the bench."

"Even whispers," Tucker pressed. "Irate phone calls. Anything."

"Nothing," she said. "Nothing." She shook her head. "I can't believe he's dead. I simply can't."

"Anyone new in his life? Business associates? Girlfriends?"

"He was seeing a nice young woman," she said, and though her voice was level, her hands twisted in her lap.

Doyle leaned back, casual as you please. "You didn't approve?"

"What?" She sat up straighter, her hands now on her knees. "It's not my place to approve or disapprove."

"And yet?" Tucker pressed.

Her shoulders sagged, the bodily equivalent of a sigh. "She was too young for him, if you ask me, an elder statesman such that he was. But he seemed truly smitten."

"Got a name?" Doyle asked.

"Oh, no. I don't. He never brought her here. I heard about her, then saw her in his car once. Just a glimpse. Lovely girl, but young, as I said."

"How about Lucius Dragos?"

"The vampire?" Her nose crinkled, and Doyle's estimation of the woman rose a notch.

"Did Braddock have any business with Dragos? Any of the blackmail or bribery schemes touch on him?"

"Not that I'm aware."

"Did the judge keep any papers here?" Doyle asked. "We'll need to take them back to Division for review."

"Just the file that the Order maintains on all the Therians." She stood up, as if grateful for something to do. "I'll run and get it for you."

She slipped out, and Doyle started walking casually around the room, ending up at the table with the girl. "Got a pile of work there, kid."

She nodded, but kept her eyes down.

"How old are you?"

She lifted her head. "Sixteen."

"And you work here?"

She nodded. "My mother does. I've been coming with her all my life. They gave me a job last year. I do the filing."

"Sounds like a good job. What's your name?"

She blushed ferociously. "Liana."

He pulled out a chair and sat down. "Nice to meet you, Liana. I'm Doyle. Did you know Judge Braddock?"

She swallowed, then nodded once.

"What do you think of him?"

A shrug. "I don't really think of him, you know?"

"Like the guy? He friendly?"

She focused on her papers. "Sure. Yeah. Whatever." She looked up. "He's dead now, right?"

"That he is."

She held his eyes for a moment, then looked back down at the tabletop. She didn't say a word, but Doyle would have sworn the girl smiled. Not that he got a chance to ask, because Ytalia was returning, a file in her hand.

Doyle moved toward her, ignoring the pursed look of disapproval she shot his way as he stepped away from the girl.

"Is that all?" she asked, passing him the file.

"I think that about does it," Doyle said. And if Tucker's open mouth was any indication, the wrap-up was a surprise to him.

"What are we doing?" Tucker asked once they were outside the building, the file in the Catalina's trunk, and the two men leaning against its polished mustard-yellow body.

"Waiting," Doyle said, an activity that took another ninety minutes and included sending Tucker on a Starbucks run. He'd just returned when Doyle saw what he was waiting for—Liana, leaving by the side door and walking away from them down the sidewalk.

He hurried to catch up, leaving Tucker and the coffee behind. "Hold up there, kid."

She slowed, looking back over her shoulder, and frowned. Then she kept right on walking. He fell into step beside her.

"Anything you want to tell me?"

"No."

"The man's dead. He can't hurt you now."

She stopped, facing him with wary eyes. "If he's dead, what does it matter?"

"Goes to motive," he said. "Hard to put a killer away if you don't know why he killed. Even with solid evidence." At the same time, if Doyle's suspicions were correct and Braddock had been abusing little girls, he was going to come off as even more of a son of a bitch and end up making Dragos look better by comparison. *Shit.* That was one hell of a fucked-up trade-off.

"I'm glad he's dead," the girl said.

"Why?" Doyle asked, certain he knew the answer.

"He told me not to tell. He told me I'd get in bad trouble."

"He can't get you into trouble now."

She looked down at the sidewalk. "I was thirteen," she said, her voice so soft that he could barely hear it, even with his preternaturally keen senses. "I kept his dirty secret," she said. "But I don't have to keep it anymore if I don't want to."

"No," Doyle said, fighting to stay level. Now wasn't the time for the rage to rise. He needed to be calm. Needed to not scare the girl. "Tell me what he did, Liana. What did Marcus Braddock do to you?"

"He hurt me," she said, her voice flat. "He raped me."

And then, with Doyle gently prodding the truth from her, Liana told him everything.

The prep meeting for Luke's bail hearing was in thirty minutes, but instead of heading to the conference room, Sara took the elevator to the detention level and found herself urging a foul-smelling ogre to escort her to the prisoner's cell.

"Meeting you set, open we the door."

"Either you let me in now, or I'll get Mr. Leviathan down here. Your choice."

The ogre grumbled, but he stood. He slid a stake into a holster above his beefy hips, then grabbed a battle-ax. "Go we now."

The detention block consisted of a series of glass-walled cells, and Sara kept her eyes straight ahead as they passed cell after cell occupied by a variety of creatures that shouted inventive sexual suggestions at her, alternating with pleas for release. She'd walked this path once before with Leviathan, and the inmates had been quiet then. Apparently she was less intimidating than the Director.

She kept her eyes forward and tried to ignore the catcalls, relaxing only when they reached Luke's cell and the ogre unlocked the door to let her enter, then reset the lock behind her.

"Sara," he said, and the pleasure she heard in his voice was enough to make her tremble.

"Stemmons killed again." She swallowed thickly, thinking of the child's large eyes and bloodless face. "Ten years old. We've identified the body. Betsy Todd," she said, her heart breaking for Betsy, for her parents, and for the next child who Sara feared was already dead.

Immediately, the pleasure on his face turned to pain. "Sara, I'm so sorry. It's not your fault."

"It's not," she agreed. "But it feels like it is. I worked so damn hard to put him away, and now he's starting all over again."

Luke stood for a moment, his body tense, his jaw tight. He clenched his fists at his side, then stalked to the wall of the cell. He pulled back, then punched hard, so hard Sara swore she felt the room shake. When he stepped back, a spiderweb of cracks radiated out from the spot where his fist had landed.

He was anger and energy, but she didn't hesitate. She went to him, pressed her hands on his shoulders and softly whispered his name.

He was silent for a moment, and she could feel the tension in his body, his muscles corded like wires. "My daughter was ten when she died," he said, his back to her. "If I could, I would kill this man for you. Would you keep me from that task?"

She turned away, not willing to answer him, not sure she could answer honestly, because she did want Stemmons dead. So help her, she wanted him dead and rotting and burning in hell. "It's a moot point," she said. "You're in here, and he's out there, some vampire working with him, and time is running out."

Luke turned to her, his body relaxing slightly, and the effort to make it so reflecting in his eyes. "What do you know?"

"Not much. Only that the vamp with Stemmons is female. And that he's already got another victim in a cage."

"Female," he repeated, and something in his voice made her frown.

"Does that mean something to you?" He hesitated, and she stepped closer. "Dammit, Luke, if you know anything—anything— that might help us, you had damn well better tell me."

He met her eyes and then slowly, very slowly, he nodded. "There are things at play that you do not yet fully understand. Rivalries. Political positioning."

She frowned. "And this is relevant how?"

"You already know that the vampire and Therian communities are old enemies," he said. "And I've learned that a Therian plot to paint the vampires in a bad light has been foiled."

"What kind of plot?"

"The Therians intended to kill humans. To make the kills appear to be the work of vampires."

Sara hugged herself, thinking of the bite marks on little Betsy's neck. "Go on."

"The primary instigators have been stopped, but one remains at large. A vampire. A traitor to the race who has aligned herself with the Therians."

"Herself," Sara repeated. "A female."

"Her name is Caris," Luke said. "Take care not to underestimate her."

"And you think she could be involved with Stemmons?"

"I think the pieces add up. Tell me," he said, "how did Stemmons kill Betsy?"

"A neck wound," Sara said slowly.

"Caris has reason to increase the number of vampire attacks around town. Or at least to make it appear that they have increased. And the more offensive, the better. She wants to finish what her team started. And she wants to thumb her nose at the vampire community for foiling the Therians' original plans."

"How can we find her?"

"I don't know," he said. "Yet."

Sara nodded. "Thank you." This was a solid start. She could find this Caris, and with any luck, they would find Stemmons and the next child, too. "I need to go." A humorless smile touched her lips. "I have a hearing to prepare for."

"You'll forgive me if I don't wish you luck."

She smiled and was reaching for the button to summon the ogre when his voice stopped her. "Tasha is missing."

She turned, saw the flash of worry on his face. "I'm so sorry. Can I help?"

He reached for her hand, and she gave it. "You help simply by asking."

"I could speak to Missing Persons," she said, wishing she had a cure, a fix, some way to ease his fear. "I don't know if the PEC has a section like that, but I have friends in the LAPD. They could—"

He pressed his palm to her cheek, the touch affecting her more than it should. "Thank you. All I ask is that you contact Nick. Tell him I need to speak with him before the hearing."

"All right. Of course, I will." She hesitated, thinking about propriety and her position and the whole damned mess. She didn't care. She leaned forward and brushed a quick kiss over his cheek. "I really am sorry," she said. "I'm so terribly sorry."

"Sara," he said, heat flaring behind the pain in his eyes.

She stepped back, her hands shoved into the pockets of her suit jacket, not quite believing she'd just leaped gleefully over that line. "We've been investigating Braddock," she began, thinking of the report she'd just received from Agent Doyle. "Luke, did he harm Tasha?"

He drew in a breath, then slowly released it. "Welcome back, Counselor."

She flinched, but held her ground, staying silent as he moved back to the concrete slab that served as a bed.

"Unless I am mistaken, this subject is forbidden without the presence of my attorney."

He was right, of course. "In that case, you can speak freely without fear of your words coming back to bite you." She tried again. "Is that why you killed him? Revenge for Tasha?"

He smiled thinly. "I have admitted things to you that I never should have spoken of. But Sara, never once have I admitted to killing Marcus Braddock. Though I do not deny an intense joy that the bastard is in fact dead."

"That's hardly a denial."

"As I said, we're only talking in hypotheticals. Unless you want to summon Mr. Montague?"

"I imagined killing Stemmons," she admitted. "I wanted him to suffer the way those girls did, and even with the death penalty, he wouldn't experience their pain and their fear. But I would never do it. Justice is found in the law, not on the streets."

"Always?"

She lifted a shoulder. "There are tradeoffs for living in a civilized world."

"Perhaps those like me fill the gaps between what is just and what is right?"

"Or perhaps you're trying to absolve yourself of guilt."

His brows rose. "Guilt? No."

She studied him, this man who knew her so intimately. Even now, she wanted to go to him. To fold herself in his arms and let him help shoulder the weight of those dead children she longed to avenge.

Avenge.

If it came to that, could she go outside the law to put Stemmons back in a cage? Or in the ground?

She didn't know, but she did understand that urge—that need—to avenge someone you love. "Luke," she began, softly, hesitantly, "what did he do to Tasha?"

He stiffened, silent, and for a moment she feared he wouldn't answer. Then he stood, crossed the room and faced the hard stone wall.

"I witnessed nothing," Luke said, but the sharp edge to his voice told a different story.

"Did he come to her? Seduce her? Take advantage of a girl who didn't understand what was happening to her?"

"Sara—" His voice held both warning and pain.

"Mitigating circumstances, Luke," she said, moving forward and pressing her hands to his shoulders. "If there are circumstances, you need to raise them in court."

"Will you stand now as my defense attorney?"

"Dammit, Luke, let me help you. My goal is not a stake to your heart. I'm looking for the truth."

"Truth is often elusive, and some debts are best paid outside the bounds of the law."

Her chest constricted, knowing that she'd just heard as close to a confession as would ever cross his lips. He'd killed Marcus Braddock. And yet she didn't want him going down. Not if there was a defense, a way to save him. "If he was harming Tasha..." She trailed off, giving him an opportunity to speak, to latch on to the defense. He was silent.

She rubbed her fingers on her temples. "Luke, please. Tell me what happened. Don't go down hard if you don't have to."

"I have nothing to say." He turned to face her. "And anything I have said here today cannot be used against me."

"No," she agreed. "It can't. But if you work with me, maybe we can get the charges reduced, even dismissed. At the very least, we can get you out on bail."

He turned around, and she was surprised to see that he was smiling. "I have the utmost faith in your system," he said. "This evening, I will have bail."

She crossed her arms over her chest. "Don't count on it, Luke. I play to win."

"A wager, then," he said, both heat and amusement lacing his voice. "If I am released, I want you in my bed."

"You won't win," she said, though she couldn't deny that part of her desperately, deeply, hoped he did.

The girl lay on the floor, ripe and ready. Fourteen years old. This one long and lean. An athletic build, with strong hips and breasts that were just beginning to ripen.

Delicious.

The girl stirred slightly in sleep, and Xavier pressed a hand to her forehead. "Calm now," he said, his caress soft. Soothing.

It wouldn't do for her to fear him, not when she was giving him the gift of blood. The gift of becoming.

Across the small basement room, his Dark Angel stood watching, her gaze fixed on the girl's face. "Drain this one, and the light will surely fill you."

He bowed his head in deference. "Will you feed, too, Angel?"

"I feed," she said. "You feed." Her mouth drew into a thin smile. "We will have a feast."

Beneath him, the girl stirred; the drugs were wearing off. Good. It was better when they were awake. Asleep, and they seemed dead. Awake, and he could watch the life flow from the child to him.

He stroked her neck with his fingertip. "Wake up, wake up. It's time for the gift. Time for the light."

He turned his head, looking at his Angel. "This one is all for me?"

She laughed, delighted. "How will you make the wound?"

It was a problem. His teeth were not sharp like hers. Not yet. Not until he proved himself worthy. And though he could rip and tear at her flesh, that would spoil the beauty of the soft, sweet skin.

He moved to the table for his knife. It had served him well so many times before. It would serve him again. Open the wound, and close his mouth over the sweet flow of life.

But it would drain out too quickly. He needed another, and the cages were empty, the hunt not complete.

"We will hunt after?" he asked.

She laughed. "So eager."

"I seek only to please you." He kept his head down, wanting to ask about her plans for him, but not sure that he should. In the end, though, he couldn't keep silent. "Am I worthy? Will you take me with you to your side?" He wanted to be like her; he wanted to feed only on the blood. On the light.

She laughed, then twirled, her skirt flowing outward. "Some of my kind are worthy. Some waste their gift. And some should never have been turned at all."

"And me?" he asked, praying she would find him worthy.

"You are meant for wondrous things. Special. So special." She glided toward him, circled him. "Tell me, Xavier. Do you know the one who bound you? Who called your genius criminal?"

"I know her," he said. "A bitch prosecutor." He looked up, afraid he'd gone too far, but the Angel was only smiling at him.

"She is horrible. Takes things that do not belong to her."

"My life," he said. "My freedom." But he had his freedom back now, and the bitch prosecutor didn't matter. Only the girls mattered, and this one especially. This one who even now stirred at his feet. "It's time to get started," he said.

"Then do not hesitate."

But he did, because the girl was not enough, and he needed to know. Needed to be certain another would come. Another would fill him. "And after?" he asked. "When the light is gone?"

"Then we will hunt again," she said, satisfying him.

And with the greatest anticipation, he pressed the knife to the child's throat, and listened as the scream came, yanking her back from the depths of sleep.

TWENTY-THREE

The hearing was not going well. She'd put on more than enough evidence to show that Luke had connections—serious connections of the type who could wrangle a way to remove the detention device. She'd presented evidence of guilt—the DNA, the silver signet ring from the crime scene, Doyle's testimony. And she'd even been allowed to provide evidence of Luke's notoriety—the kind of evidence that would never have been allowed upstairs—to show that he was a danger to the community.

She'd done everything right, and still she was losing. She could see it in the way the judge shifted and turned on the bench, his beady bird eyes seeming to look past her evidence to a conclusion he'd already established.

"I'm sinking," she said to Leviathan.

"You're putting on the best case you have," he said, which didn't make her feel better. This was her first hearing in her new job, and she was sitting at the counsel table with her new boss. She wanted a win, dammit, and the only way she could think to get it was to play her trump card.

She looked over at the defendant's table—at Nick, sitting there looking smug, and Luke beside him, his manner, his appearance, his very essence both screaming of importance and warning of danger. She told herself this wasn't about him—about them—and then, because her feelings for Luke should never have affected her prosecution of the case, she stood up, finally resolved.

"Your Honor, the prosecution moves to introduce video footage of the pool deck of the Plaza Towers taken late Friday night."

Now Montague surged to his feet. "Objection. Your Honor, may we approach?"

The judge turned one of his beady black eyes on Montague. The gryphon—with an eagle's head and a lion's body—was huge and imposing, and he could maintain order in his courtroom with nothing more than a glance. "Approach? But there is no jury present."

"No, but the gallery is full, and Ms. Constantine is about to lead us into mine-filled waters."

The feathers that covered the judge's face ruffled, but he agreed.

"This is completely unacceptable," Montague continued. "Counsel is addressing an area that must be treated as off the record."

"Your Honor," Sara said, "that isn't exactly accurate. My conversation with Mr. Dragos is off the record. But Agent Doyle acquired the same information entirely independent of me or Mr. Montague or Mr. Dragos."

The judge considered for only a moment, then nodded at Sara. "Proceed."

A little trill of victory shot through her, only to be quashed by Montague's harsh words as they walked back to the counsel table. "There is the letter of the law, and then there is the spirit, Ms. Constantine. I think we both know that what you've done skirts propriety. At the very least you should have given us notice that you intended to piss on the good faith that Mr. Dragos and myself showed to you."

She swallowed a bubble of guilt. "My client is the PEC, Mr. Montague, and I haven't done anything except protect its interest to the fullest extent of the law. Without, I might add, overstepping the bounds of that law."

She sat down calmly enough, but considering the firm hand that Leviathan placed on her shoulder, she had a feeling that her irritation was showing. She hadn't crossed a line. Not really.

Yet she couldn't discount the fact that it felt as if she had.

"Your Honor," she said. "The prosecution calls Agent Ryan Doyle." Doyle would introduce the evidence, and through him, she could turn the court's attention to the fact that Luke fed on Annie.

Before Doyle could approach, though, Montague stood again. "If it please the court, my client will testify to a Directive 27 violation and ask that the court entertain evidence on an affirmative defense at the close of the prosecution's case."

The judge's head bobbed. "Directive 27?" he repeated as a murmur flowed across the gallery.

"Yes, sir. A human woman. Mr. Dragos both fed off the female and fed his blood to her." He turned and flashed a bright white smile at Sara. "A stipulation, Counselor. Just to make sure we're out of here by the dinner hour."

"If you really want to be out by dinner," she said sweetly, "then drop the affirmative defense."

"We shall all dine in a timely fashion," the judge said, "as this court is ready to issue its ruling."

Sara glanced over at the defendant's table, caught Luke's eye, then ripped her gaze away. She stood with Leviathan at her side and waited for the ruling.

"Bail is granted," he said, "in the amount of five million dollars."

A murmur ran through the crowd.

"The defendant will be required to wear the standard mobile detention device," the judge continued. "And in light of the Directive 27 stipulation, the defendant will also be fitted with a bloodletting impediment." He slammed his gavel on the desk. "So ordered."

As soon as the judge had left the courtroom, Sara leaned toward Leviathan. "Bloodletting impediment?"

"A secondary detention device," Leviathan explained. "This one will trigger if Dragos takes blood directly from a human again."

As she gathered up her papers, Leviathan shifted beside her, and Sara thought she caught the subtle scent of cinnamon. "Under the circumstances, the possibility of Lucius staying in jail while the case came up was slim. But you gave them a hard battle, remained firmly on the side of the law, and proved yourself an asset to the team. Good work."

She pasted on a smile, accepting the compliment along with a smattering of "you did good" and "you'll nail his ass in trial" from well-meaning onlookers, some of whom she recognized as other prosecutors in her office.

When she finally did slip through the door and into the hall, she sighed. She may have lost her first hearing, but it was only one battle.

In the grand scheme of things, the battles meant nothing. The only thing that mattered was the war. But since the resolution of that war could see Luke staked, she had to admit, if only to herself, that for the first time in her career, she didn't relish the battles yet to come.

"Batorak metoin shrebat."

"If you're asking me if it's comfortable," Luke said in French, as the weight of the new mobile detention device once again pressed against his flesh, "the answer is a resounding no."

The demon pressed a hand to his shoulder. "Bon chance," the demon said, switching from demonic to a language Luke could understand.

"Merci." Luke inclined his head as his fingers manipulated the tiny white buttons, closing the shirt Nick had brought him to replace the T-shirt that had been shredded in this very room. A black tray sat on the table in front of him, and he retrieved his wallet and cell phone, then carefully picked up the tiny gold serpent ring he habitually kept in his pocket. Were it not so small, he would slip it onto his little finger. But Livia's hands had been tiny, and the ring didn't fit. As was his habit, he slipped it deep into his pocket, then reached in, checking to make sure it was in place.

Now ready, he turned to Nick. "Counselor, shall we depart this place?"

"It would be a pleasure," Nick said. They moved through corridors and down the elevator, ignoring the stares and whispers of those who worked within Division 6.

"About Caris," Nick said as they approached the elevator, "We think we found where she's been holing up. I sent the address to your phone. Standard encryption. Known recent associates included, too. Details in the file."

"Excellent."

"You really think Caris would align herself with a human?"

"If it serves Gunnolf's purpose—or her own—then yes."

"And it does," Nick said. "Tasha even fits Stemmons's profile. Young girls. Red hair, blue eyes. She's older than he took in the past, but she looks young."

"Caris won't care about that," Luke said. "But Stemmons will, and she'll want him cooperative."

"And if she brings Tasha into the mix, she serves Gunnolf's purpose even while cutting you like a knife."

"And Tasha has become both a pawn and a prize." He drew in a hard breath, certain Caris would not hesitate to take the opportunity to destroy Tasha. To use Stemmons and his blade to cut down the innocent child that Caris believed should never have been allowed to live.

"I'll go with you," Nick said as they stepped onto the elevator.

"No. She's mine." After battling back his darkness so hard and so often, letting the serpent uncoil would be a pleasure.

Nick hesitated, his gaze dipping only momentarily to the device strapped to Luke's chest. "All right," he said. "But be careful. Caris isn't one to be trifled with."

"Neither am I," Luke said. "What word do you have from Tiberius? I'm not inclined to return to this place after we leave, and I'm less inclined to keep this device strapped to my chest."

Nick's face shifted, going hard. "About that, we have a little problem."

Luke turned, wary, the serpent starting to writhe within.

"Tiberius said to tell you that you did good work with Hasik, but that his hands remain tied."

"Politics," Luke said, spitting out the word, forcing himself to keep his rage under control. "I need out of this contraption, Nick. And Tiberius needs me on his team."

"He does. But with his control over LA so strained, he's not willing to take chances. I'm sorry, Luke," Nick said. "You're on your own with this one."

Luke gave a sharp nod, clinging to control.

"It's not over, Luke."

"I know." He ground out the words, then drew in a cleansing breath, forcing the rush of wild violence down. He thought of Sara, imagined her beside him, and felt the calm flow through him.

He shoved the serpent under with abrupt finality. "I'll find a way."

"I don't doubt it," Nick said as the doors slid open and he stepped out into the lower-level reception area.

"Mr. Dragos!"

He turned to face the reception desk, where a young woman with a blue braid wrapped into a cylinder upon her head waved frantically at him.

"I'm supposed to ask you to stay."

"I believe the court has spoken otherwise."

"Huh? Oh! No, gosh. Not for permanent. But Ms. Constantine wants a word with you and Mr. Montague before you go."

"I see," Luke said, impressed by the calm in his voice despite the fact that the mere mention of her name made his blood flow warm.

Nick, he saw, was watching him. "Tell Ms. Constantine that my client has enjoyed the PEC's hospitality long enough. If she needs to speak to either of us, she has my contact information."

"Nick."

"I am still your advocate," Nick said. "And if you wish me to remain in that capacity, you will follow my advice." His expression softened along with his voice. "Luke, the path you want to walk leads nowhere."

Luke knew that well enough, yet he refused to accept it. Impossible though it might seem, he would find a way to make Sara his.

"I will speak to her," he said, his tone broaching no argument.

"You need to back away." There was both warning and compassion in Nick's voice. "Leave it. And leave her."

"She compels me," Lucius said. "I cannot shut her out any more than I could willingly harm her." He stood still, trying to conjure the words that would make his friend understand. "She brings light to the dark inside me," he finally said. "Tell me that you do not understand. Tell me honestly that were you in my position you would walk away from her. That you could walk away."

He saw the pain pass over his friend's face. The memories of Elizabeth, the woman who had once soothed Nick beyond all others. Who had hurt him beyond all others, too.

"We will speak about this later," Nick said, but the edge had left his voice.

"I have no doubt," Luke said.

The elevator opened, and Sara stepped out, her cheeks rosy from having rushed. Their eyes locked, and he felt it. A sensual tug he associated only with her. A hard jolt to his senses that had his body firing and his imagination traveling to forbidden destinations.

She held his gaze. One moment. Another. And then she looked away, but not before he saw it on her face—desire.

He saw it, and he cherished it.

Mine, he thought, and knew that no matter what else transpired between them, there was a truth in that one simple word.

She walked with exaggerated purpose toward him, sliding her

palms along her skirt as if they were damp. "Mr. Dragos. Mr. Montague. Thank you for waiting."

"My client is pleased to cooperate with any and all reasonable requests posed by the prosecution, Counselor. We hope, of course, that the favor will be reciprocated this time."

"I ... of course," she said, but her voice was distracted, and her eyes were on Luke. "Oh, hell. I was hoping to speak to you. Privately," she added, glancing pointedly at Nick.

"Of course. Nick," he said. "A moment, please, with Ms. Constantine."

Nick sighed, long and put-upon. "We've had this conversation, Luke. As long as I'm your advocate—"

"You're fired."

Nick's expression couldn't have been more startled if Luke had dropped his pants and mooned him. "What?"

"You're fired," he repeated. "It's a simple concept resulting in the termination of any business relationship between us."

"Don't do this, Luke."

"Don't fight me, Nicholas." He turned to the receptionist. "Do you have access to the relevant databases? Can you make a notation that Lucius Dragos is no longer represented by counsel, but is proceeding in pro per?"

"I ... um ... I..." She glanced frantically toward Sara, who nodded.

"I'll take responsibility," Sara said, the laughter in her voice delighting him. "Go ahead. I expect you'll be adding Mr. Montague back to the database after Mr. Dragos and I conclude our conversation."

Luke chuckled. "I like the way you think, but no. Mr. Montague and I have reached the end of the line. Irreconcilable differences," he said, with a brief nod to his friend.

"This isn't over," Nick said, his voice a taut wire, ready to snap.

"I expect no less from you," Luke said. "But for now, it is."

Nick tossed his car keys into the air, caught them. "Fair enough, my friend. But find your own ride home."

And with that, he slipped through the doors and into the PEC parking garage.

Luke turned his attention to Sara. "I think he's upset," she said.

He fought a smile. "Imagine that."

"I wanted to say thank you. For the information about Caris."

"Have you found her?" He almost feared that Doyle or another detective had—he wanted the sweet pleasure of ending her himself.

"Not yet. The investigators are following a bunch of leads." Her mouth quirked up. "I've been a little busy with a hearing, so I'm not completely up to date."

He glanced over her shoulder, saw that the receptionist was trying to watch them without being obvious. "I must go," he said, fearful that Division would soon have the same information about Caris's whereabouts that he held in his pocket. "But I believe there is the matter of a wager between us. I will collect."

She shook her head. "Luke, please. Don't. Don't press me."

"Why not?" He moved closer, drawn in by the heat of her, the desire that emanated from her. She was denying him, yes. But her heart wasn't in it.

"Because I want to," she admitted, her voice small but her words running through him like a song.

"Sara—"

"No." She shook her head, her voice firm, and he sensed the resolve within her. "This isn't about my father. I want you to know that. I understand that you were following orders, and that my battle isn't with you."

Relief flooded him. "Thank you. That my actions hurt you—Sara, that has been a burden I've carried as long as you have."

"I know."

"Do you?"

She nodded. "I really do."

"And you forgive me?"

"It's not on you, Luke. So there's nothing to forgive."

He saw the truth in her eyes, but also a fire that he feared would spark into revenge. "Be careful, Sara. My allegiance was and is with Tiberius. But the Alliance acted in unison to issue the order. Your father was a threat."

"I know. And I'm not planning to take on the Alliance. I understand why they made the decision. I do. I just wanted you to know that I've been thinking about it. And there is no shadow of my father standing between us."

"And yet?" he said, because he could practically see the words coming.

"And yet, whatever this is, I won't encourage it. I wish—Never mind. But we can't, and please don't push me on it."

"I cannot agree to that," he said, "but neither can I argue about it now."

She tilted her head, her brow crinkling with worry. "Tasha?"

"I must go."

She reached for his hand, and the touch almost did him in. "I remembered what you told me, about having a daughter long ago. That's what Tasha is to you now, isn't she?"

"Sara ..." Her name came out raw, gravelly with need. He wanted to pull her close, to have her soothe his fears. To lose himself in the simple pleasure of having her beside him.

He could do none of that, and he hated the circumstances that had brought them to this impasse.

He reached into his pocket, his fingers finding Livia's gold serpent ring. He wanted to draw comfort from it, but comfort didn't come. He feared that now that he'd met Sara, he would be soothed only by her touch.

"You'll find her," she said gently. "But, Luke," she added, her voice now sharp with warning, "when you do, don't run. It will be worse for you if you run."

Despite his better judgment, he cupped his hand to her cheek, enjoying the shocked expression on the receptionist's face. "My darling Sara," he said. "Considering the PEC would have me dead, I cannot imagine how it could be worse. But I appreciate your warning nonetheless."

He stepped away from her, moving toward the door. "We'll speak again."

"Ms. Constantine?" the receptionist called. "Mr. Leviathan's assistant is on the line." She held the phone out for Sara, and Luke stayed put, listening.

"There's been another child found," a woman said, her smooth voice marred with regret. "The task force requests that you go immediately to the scene."

When Sara hung up, Luke was by her side.

"I'm going with you."

"The hell you are."

But he would broach no argument. "You may work with me or against me, but I am going, and I'm going with you."

"No way," Doyle shouted, his finger stretched out to point at Luke. A finger that was about to be broken if the para-demon didn't get it the hell out of Luke's face. "No fucking way."

Sara stepped between them. "He stays. He helps."

"He's a murderer."

Sara stepped up, getting right in Doyle's face, a sight that warmed Luke's heart. She pointed to her left, toward the adolescent body, now splayed out in death, over which the techs were doing their job.

"Do you have any reason, Agent, to think that Dragos committed this crime or any crime related to this murder? Do you? Because I don't. But I damn sure want to find out who did, and if I think Dragos can help, then he stays. And he stays on my authority."

"You're on thin ice, Constantine."

"Then it's a good thing I know how to swim, isn't it?"

The look Doyle shot Luke was one of pure hatred. Then he stalked away, leaving Sara seething. She looked up at Luke, her face flushed. "Dammit," she said. "All I want to do is find Stemmons before he kills the next victim. I don't need the rest of this bullshit."

"You said he kept all the victims caged? I need to get close to the body." He needed to see if the little girl had Tasha's scent on her. If they'd shared a cage. And he needed to search for the scent of Caris.

"All right," she said, looking at him sideways. "But I'm sticking my neck out on this, Luke. Don't prove Doyle right."

"Never."

By the time they reached the body, the Division staff had cleared out most of the county workers, and Severin Tucker and a few other agents that Luke didn't recognize were adjusting the thoughts of the few who remained. Sara spoke with Leviathan, who turned, stared at Luke, and then gave one quick, curt nod. She cocked her head and Luke joined her. "Two minutes."

"I won't need any more."

He bent over the naked body, focusing only on the smell, forcing himself not to think about the loss, the youth, the horror of this young life ripped away so brutally.

The memory of another time and another place rose within him. Livia laughing, calling his name. He shoved it down. He couldn't go there. Not now. He needed to keep control. Needed to keep the serpent in check. Tasha's life hung in the balance. Lose control, and he could lose her.

He lifted his head, nostrils flaring, breathing in deep the scent of the night. Of raw earth. Of grass. Of the child herself, and the pungent odor of death taking hold.

And just when he was about to give up, he caught it. A familiar fragrance like lavender in the fields. Innocence and beauty.

He turned, finding Sara beside him. "Tasha."

Sara's eyes went wide with understanding, and she grabbed his arm, tugging him back away from the crowd. "Tasha?" she repeated. "You came here because Stemmons has Tasha?"

"I feared that Caris had taken her." He drew his hands through his hair, trying to think. So far he had no scent of Caris, and he began to walk the perimeter of the crime scene, searching the night for her woody scent.

"And you didn't tell me? Dammit, Luke, how long have you suspected this?"

He stopped, stared down at her. "Does it matter now? Your monster has Tasha, and unless I've missed my guess, Caris is with her."

She fell in step beside him. "I went out on a limb for you, and—"

He held up a hand. "There."

"What?"

They were at least twenty yards from the crime scene, but there was no mistaking the scent. She'd been there. The vile bitch had stood on that exact spot, and not very long ago, either. "Caris." He turned to Sara. "I must go."

"Go?" she repeated, looking back toward the body. "Go where?"

"Silver Lake," he said, referring to the information on Caris's whereabouts that Nick sent to his phone.

She hurried to keep up with him as he rushed toward her car. "Why?"

"She's there," he said tightly.

"Tasha?"

"Caris," he said. "And with any luck, Tasha, too."

"Then we need the team. We need—"

He stopped, taking her arm. "I need your car, Sara. I do not need the team. And I can't have you accompanying me."

"I don't care what you need. I'm going with you."

"She is dangerous."

"So are you," Sara countered.

"I'll not argue about this."

"Good. But you're going to be wasting a lot of time if you don't take me with you."

He stopped, his focus utterly on her. "Why?"

It was a question she couldn't answer, because she hadn't been thinking, only reacting. She knew why he was going—what he would do to Caris if he found her. But she couldn't fight him on this. "It's Tasha," she said, simply. "And she's important to you."

As she watched, he closed his eyes, then swallowed. When he looked at her again, he was all steel. "You come," he said. "But you stay in the car."

Even in the middle of the night, it took them twenty minutes to get from North Hollywood to Silver Lake, and Luke was cursing when he ran the car up over the curb and plowed to a stop in front of the house. He aimed a single finger at her. "Stay," he said, and she swore that she would, a promise she immediately found hard to keep.

She knew almost nothing about Caris other than the brief dossier Blair had run for her after Luke had first mentioned the name. There'd been little information. She was a former lover of Tiberius, but they'd had a falling out a few years prior. Rumors were thick, but the most likely suggestion was that she'd hooked up with a were-wolf, which screamed of the political intrigue that Luke had told her about. The bottom line, though, was that Caris was a vampire, and she'd apparently aligned herself with scum like Stemmons. She was killing, and she was dangerous, and she wasn't constrained by hematite bands.

So, yeah, Sara was worried.

She waited, her eyes on the house. The quiet house. The way-too-quiet house.

Hell.

She opened the door, not at all sure what she was going to do. She knew she had to see what was going on in there. And as soon as she did, the front windows shattered, and she saw Luke silhouetted in the void.

"Luke!" She raced toward him, not thinking of the danger until she'd burst through the front door. But there was no danger. There was only Luke in a fury, a chair thrust high over his head as he hurled it through the darkened room at the far wall, where it shattered into pieces. "Luke, stop!"

He turned, eyes wild, his face contorted. She stopped, eyeing him warily, realizing quickly that the house was empty. Tasha wasn't here. Neither was Caris.

He'd run out of hope, and the serpent inside was furious.

"We'll find her," she said, moving toward him, this man who had once held her so tenderly, who now burned with the loss of one he loved. She understood the depth of his rage; she felt it herself every time she thought of the order that had stolen her father from her. Tasha, however, wasn't yet gone. "We'll find her," she repeated, and this time she moved in close, ignoring the prickling of fear to cup his face in her hands, letting him know that she was there, and, yes, that she understood.

Slowly, she felt the tension ease from him, and as he collapsed to his knees on the floor, she went down with him, cradling his head against her chest. "Sara," he whispered. "I thought she would be here."

"We'll find her. I bet Division has a lead. We'll follow it up. Luke," she said, her heart breaking for him, "we'll do whatever it takes."

She tipped his face up to hers and waited until he met her gaze. The beast was there, trembling beneath the surface, but Luke was in control now. Barely. Sara felt a shiver of fear but didn't release him. She stroked her fingers over his cheek.

"We will find her," she promised again. And then, as naturally as breathing, she bent forward and kissed him.

She felt the tension ease from his body. Felt his fingers twine in her hair as he deepened the kiss, wanting more.

She threw herself back, breaking the connection, then sat facing him, her breathing ragged and her heart pounding as if she'd run a marathon. "I'm sorry. I—I wasn't thinking."

For a moment he said nothing. Then the corner of his mouth lifted. "Perhaps not," he said. "Or perhaps you were thinking with your heart."

TWENTY-FOUR

"Someone who works at the Slaughtered Goat might know where Caris is," Luke said to Bael Slater. "Any lead, I want you following it."

"No problem." The huge vampire leaned back, the small chair creaking under the strain. They were in a small bar near the Division 6 offices where Luke had gone after Sara had returned to work with the team. "Division's got nothing, huh?"

"They don't have shit," Luke said, taking a sip of Glenfiddich. "I'm going back to the crime scenes. Try to pick up another scent."

"Didn't Division already tug on that line?"

"The vamps on the team are at least four centuries younger than me," Luke said. "Their senses aren't as well honed."

"Long shot," Slater said.

"At this point, even the long shots are worth following."

His friend stood. "I'll be in touch." Luke started to stand, but was startled by the sharp ring of his phone. He snatched it quickly from the pocket of his duster, hoping to see Tasha's name on the caller ID. Instead, the phone identified the caller as TQ.

"What have you learned?" he asked without preamble. Luke had called the jinn after he'd parted from Sara, demanding satisfaction for Tariq's botched assignment that first night.

"Still Scotch, Luke?" Tariq asked, as Luke lifted his glass. "Still single malt?"

Luke hid his small smile behind the glass as his eyes searched the room. He should have expected the wily creature to be nearby.

He didn't find the jinn, but his blood pounded hot when he saw a lithe woman with cropped dark hair and feline eyes. Caris. He stood, upsetting the table in his haste, but a second later she was gone.

She'd either transformed into mist and left, or his eyes were playing tricks on him. He forced down a wave of discontent and concentrated on finding Tariq, ultimately locating him by the back door.

"Tell me what you know," Luke demanded as he approached.

"That depends. Will this do us square?"

"What does your conscience say, Tariq? It was you who wronged me. Does this balance the scales?"

"It does."

Luke stayed silent, remembering that cold night in Munich many centuries before.

"Dammit, Lucius, it does."

It did not, Luke thought. But that point could be raised at a later date. "Tell me."

"Then we're square?"

"I did not say that."

"Fucking-A. Fine. Got me under your goddamn thumb for the rest of my natural life."

"The countermeasures, my friend. Tell me what you know of the detention device and its countermeasures."

"They'll fry your ass if you get free of them," Tariq said.

"I don't recall saying that was my purpose. I'm a lover of knowledge, Tariq. Knowledge for knowledge's sake."

"Fuck," Tariq said. "It's your ass. Whatever. It's a fail-safe system."

"I expected as much."

"Leviathan. He's got the power to release the device by remote."

"And the judge?" Luke asked, thinking that perhaps Acquila had not yet outlived his usefulness.

"Nada. Once bail's granted, he's out of the loop."

"So Leviathan is my only hope?"

"I didn't say that," Tariq said. "The system's also tied in to the prosecutor and the lead investigator. On their command, Security System disables the device."

Luke tensed, the possibilities dancing in front of him. "Say that again."

"I know," Tariq said almost giddily, and then repeated himself. "Sweet, huh?"

"Together?" Luke asked, ignoring the jinn. "Doyle and the prosecutor must be together?"

"Either one can do it," he said. "Doyle, Constantine. But they can't do it remotely. Gotta be in Division, in Security Section. Key in access to the primary system, then key in the abort code."

"Interesting," Luke said. He would take much pleasure in dragging Doyle's sorry ass back inside Division and making the parademon do that which would set Luke free.

But despite the pleasure he would undoubtedly derive from such an adventure, he had to admit that the risks were legion, as were any attempts to use Leviathan.

He frowned, not pleased by the possibilities. "Are there alternatives?" he asked Tariq. "Who installed the fail-safes?"

"Lucius," Tariq said. "Take the easy route."

"It's none of it easy," Luke answered. "We'll speak again." And then, before Tariq could protest, he turned and walked away, his thoughts on Sara.

At one time, he would have used her without hesitation, but that time was long gone.

He thought of Sara and her sense of rules, of justice. She would never agree to do this thing, and more than that, he knew that he could not ask her to.

There had to be another way, he thought, as he stood to leave, and somehow he would find it.

The security in Lucius's Malibu home rivaled Buckingham Palace, but that was hardly a deterrent to a man like Serge. He slipped through the defenses in mere moments, then stepped inside among the shadows that roamed within his friend's home.

The ocean, he told himself, eyeing the shadows with trepidation. Not the manifestation of nightmares.

The home perched on the beach, the west wall nothing but glass. And tonight, the moon reflected on stormy seas, the shadows cast inside the home were both beautiful and frightening.

He exhaled loudly, scoffing at his own foolishness. A man like him jumping at shadows. A man who could kill with hands or fangs, who had done exactly that many times over. The very thought shamed him.

No more.

First, he had to find Tasha. That much, he owed to Lucius.

He lifted his nose and breathed deep, finding her subtle smell in the air. But how long she had been gone he did not know. Days, perhaps. Or possibly only hours.

A flutter of hope danced in his chest, and he followed the scent, searching for her room, hoping in vain that she had returned to this place.

He found what he was looking for on the second floor. Not the girl herself, but the room that she had made. A child's room, a girl's room. White and pink, with porcelain-faced dolls on shelves that ran along the wall, a foot or so beneath the ceiling.

An innocent's dolls, but she wasn't innocent. Not anymore. He'd seen something new within her. But whether it had been there before, or whether Braddock corrupted her, he didn't know.

All he did know was that he had to find her.

Had to find her for his friend, to satisfy his obligation. To ensure that she was safe.

He told himself that was where his motivation ended.

That, however, was a lie. He *wanted*. Not Serge. Not really. But the dark that was rising within him.

By the gods, how it wanted.

He could feel her, the scent of her enveloping him, caressing him. Soothing him.

He stood beside her bed, not moving, not even breathing. And then, slowly and deliberately, he reached for one of Tasha's porcelain-faced dolls and hurled it against the wall.

Sara woke with a start, jerked awake by a sharp pounding at her door. Not that she minded too much—she'd been teetering on the verge of another nightmare—but at two in the morning, it was quite possible the visitor could be worse than the tormenting dreams.

"Coming," she shouted, sliding into a robe. She hurried to the door, checked the peephole, and found herself looking at Luke's sexy, scowling face. She keyed in the alarm code, opened the door, and soon discovered the reason for his scowl—her across-the-hall neigh-bor, Mrs. Fitzhugh, was standing in the doorway in curlers, her expression both shocked and disapproving.

And why not? With his long, dark coat, his warrior's eyes, and the scar that cut across his brow, Luke looked decidedly formidable. "It's okay, Mrs. Fitzhugh. He's a friend." Which wasn't the least bit accu-rate. Friends didn't make her melt from a single look. And it was only around Luke that she felt like her body was a fire that only he could extinguish.

And, she noticed as she ushered him inside, he'd brought her a flower.

He handed it to her, and she stroked her finger over the soft petals of the bird-of-paradise. "It's beautiful. Thank you." She frowned, looking more closely at the flower, and then at his slightly sheepish expression. "Where did you get it?"

"The garden in front of your building," he admitted. "There aren't many options at 2 A.M."

She bit back a laugh. "No, I guess not." She headed toward the kitchen to find water for the flower.

"You shouldn't be here."

"And yet I came anyway."

"Why? There's no news about Tasha," she added. "You would have told me already."

"I wanted to see you," he said, his voice somehow both strong and vulnerable. "I followed Stemmons's trail tonight. Tracking away from each of his original crime scenes as best I could. I found noth-ing. No hint of Caris or Tasha."

"I'm so sorry."

"Afterward, I came here. You're in my head, Sara. I hear your voice. I smell your scent. I feel your touch." His shoulders lifted. "I had to come."

Her heart tripped in her chest. "Oh." She swallowed, knowing she shouldn't say more, but unable to stay silent. "I'm glad you did."

"Are you?"

"We're probably breaking a lot of rules."

He moved toward her. "Oddly enough, I've never been good at following rules."

"Why do I believe that?"

"But the rules are important to you," he said. He caressed her cheek, making her want to break down and purr. "Do you want me to leave?"

She hesitated, knowing that for the sake of her sanity—and possibly her job—she should lie. Instead, she spoke the truth. "No." She looked at his face, the perfect, classic lines marred by the warrior's scar. A face that had seen death and a man who had surely wrought it a thousand times over. Yet right then he was looking at her with such tenderness it made her breath catch in her throat. "No," she repeated, her voice little more than a whisper. "I want you to stay."

"Good," he said, the simple word conveying a wealth of emotion. "Let me hold you."

She hesitated only a moment, then moved in and pressed her cheek against him.

Luke sighed, his chest rising and falling beneath her, steady and calm.

"Luke," she began, then stopped. She wouldn't tell him that she wished things were different. That they'd met under different circumstances. Instead, she told him the most basic of truths. "No matter how I feel about you, I will do my job."

"Do you think I don't know that?"

She tilted her head up to look at his face. "It doesn't seem to bother you overly much."

"You will do what you must," he said. "As will I."

She swallowed, knowing that as a prosecutor she should push, try to determine if he was intending to run, and if so, how. As a woman, though, she didn't want to know. Didn't even want to think about it. Because if he stayed, he would undoubtedly be executed for murder. And if he left, she would never see him again. Impossible.

"We met at the wrong time," she whispered.

"When would you have preferred?"

She laughed, considering the question. "I don't know. The thirties? Odds are good I wouldn't have been a lawyer back then."

"Except that you would not have been born," he said, his fingers lazily stroking her back. "And as inconvenient as it may be for us, I am fond of the woman you are."

"I am, too," she admitted. "Still, it would have been nice. To be with you, without all of this noise surrounding us." She thought back, enjoying the game, the fantasy. "Then again, maybe not the thirties. Maybe the 1800s, and I could have worn fabulous gowns."

"Ah, but then we would have to work so very hard to free you from the corset."

Her breath hitched as she imagined him undressing her. "If it was your fingers doing the unfastening," she admitted, "I'm not sure I would mind."

"Nor I."

It struck her suddenly that he surely had actual experience with actual corsets, and the realization was both fascinating and overwhelming. "Were you here during the Civil War? The American Revolution?"

His laugh seemed to rumble through her. "If I tell you that I was, will you run?"

"No," she whispered, trying to imagine all that he'd seen, that he'd experienced. It made her expected eighty or so years seem inadequate and puny. "It's overwhelming, you know. Thinking about all that you've seen and done."

"Then we are even," he said, "because you overwhelm me as well."

His words seemed to trip over her skin, a skimming rock on a pool of water, sending little ripples of pleasure outward over her body. She wanted him—there was no point in denying it—and yet she knew damn well that taking this any further would be a bad, bad idea.

"Luke—"

"Hush." He brushed his lips over her hair, then tucked a finger under her chin and tilted her face up to his. She drew in a breath, knowing she should protest, even going so far as to form the words in her head. But they didn't come, and when his mouth brushed hers, she moaned with the pleasure of it.

The kiss was slow and gentle, a promise of future delights, and her body fired in anticipation, her breasts aching and her thighs gathering warmth between them. She clenched her hands, gathering his shirt in her fingers, and opened her mouth to his.

"Sara," he whispered, his lips brushing her ear in a wonderfully arousing manner. "I would have you in bed."

He didn't give her time to answer, simply slanted his mouth over hers even as he drew her close until their bodies pressed together, and she could feel every inch of him, including his growing arousal. She moaned, her lips parting with the sound, and he took full advantage, his mouth sliding greedily over hers. His mouth was both soft and firm, and he slid his tongue over her lips, between them, deepening the kiss as her body warmed under his ministrations.

Every inch of skin tingled, and her panties were damp with need. She shifted, wanting, and pressed harder against him. "Luke."

He stole his name from her lips with a kiss, hot and demanding. His hands were on her shoulders, and he pushed her back, hard, onto the bed, and the slow burn of passion transformed into something desperate and demanding.

She moved beneath him, wanting to feel him, to have more of him, and she heard herself moan, her body overwhelmed by the simple, exquisite touch of his lips upon hers.

When he added his hands to the mix—when he shifted to straddle her and his hands slipped inside her robe and beneath her T-shirt—her mind seemed to snap. There was no way—no possible way—that she could survive the onslaught, this bliss.

"I want to see you." Roughly, he shoved her shirt up. His mouth closed on her, teasing the erect nipple through the thin cotton. Sending delicious shocks through her body, loosening her. Readying her.

"Naked," she whispered. "Why aren't you naked?"

"I think I can remedy that oversight," he said, then eased back to work the buttons of his shirt.

"No," she said, her own nimble fingers taking over, enjoying the rush of touching him. Of being totally lost within him.

She pulled the shirt open and splayed her hands across his chest, the cool metal of the band he wore pressing against her palm. She closed her eyes, wishing it could simply disappear.

"It is not there," he said. "Tonight, there is nothing standing between us." He spoke with force, his hands reaching up to cup her breasts, teasing her and tormenting her as she arched against him until any thought of arguing melted from her brain.

"So beautiful."

Eyes closed, she smiled. She thought the same of him, and she fell greedily upon him, her mouth on his chest, his neck, his cheek and the scar upon it. "How—"

"An altercation with a sword before I was turned," he said with a wry grin. "The sword won."

As she laughed, he took her shoulders, pushing her back and trapping her beneath him, his busy hands and mouth sending all sorts of sensations rocketing through her. His mouth closed again over her nipple, the pleasure of the sensation so acute it was almost painful, certainly almost unbearable. She writhed against him, against her own roiling emotions, her back arching up toward him as she fought down a scream of pleasure. As she fought not to beg him for more, harder, faster.

He seemed to know what she wanted anyway, and his clever fingers dipped down, then ripped her panties off with a low growl. Then his hands were on her, cupping her, his fingers finding her wet and needy, and his moan of satisfaction almost enough to send her over the edge.

When he closed his mouth so intimately upon her, the edge did rise up, engulfing her, sending shocks reverberating through her body, so intense she had no choice but to cling to his shoulders for fear that if she did not, her body would explode with the intensity of it.

Wave after wave, his sensual assault continued, until she couldn't take it anymore and she screamed for satisfaction, for his kiss.

He drew himself up, his lips still warm with the taste of her, finding her mouth, battering it, taking. Claiming.

She struggled to free him from his jeans, and once he was naked, he rose over her, a dark god, a fierce warrior, and she reached for him, wanting to be his spoils, his battleground, and knowing that he would fill her. Her body, her emotions, her deepest desires.

Her body trembled with anticipation, and she whispered one single word. "Now." That was all it took. His eyes darkened with desire, his fingers pushing her thighs apart, and then the sensual, erotic assault as he thrust himself into her.

She groaned, so wet and so ready, her body opening for him, taking him, drawing him in. The pleasure was exquisite, and she bucked against him, matching his thrusts, the need rising within her again as she cried for him to not stop, to never, ever stop.

His touch was a promise, his thrusts a caress, and as she traveled up, up, up, she knew that he was coming with her. "Now," he said. "By the gods, Sara, now."

She exploded. Shattered. Her body—her mind—held together only by the force of her will and his firm hands upon her.

"Luke." The name was soft, like a tribute, and he pulled her close. "Ah, Sara. My Sara."

And right then, with his arms tight around her and her body warm and sated, she could almost believe that she was his. Could almost believe that somehow, someway, they stood a chance.

TWENTY-FIVE

Luke left Sara's house well before dawn, and now the Mercedes's headlights cut a path through the night as he maneuvered the curving Malibu canyons. He would have liked to have stayed—would have liked to have made love to her again and again—but he needed to be home during the daylight hours. He might not be able to hunt or prowl, but he could work the phone and the computer, and by the time night fell again, he would have a lead on Tasha. On Caris.

It was not over yet.

His phone rang, and he hit the button for the speaker, then listened as Slater's deep voice filled the car.

"Nothing yet," Slater said, "but I've got a bead on a few para-demons the staff at the Slaughtered Goat says used to come in there about the time Caris first showed up. I'm going to track them down, see what they know."

"Get back to me as soon as you do."

"You got it. Something else, though, my friend. Some shit went down here the other day. Maybe you heard about it?" Slater asked, his tone making clear that he knew exactly who had killed Hasik.

"I've picked up some rumblings," Luke said. "What of it?"

"Apparently, there was a witness. Division's been called in."

Luke bit back a curse and thought of Sara. Of the disappointed way she would look at him when they met again. "Interesting."

"Thought you might think so. I'll keep you posted," Slater said, then clicked off as Luke considered this new inconvenience. Alinda.

There was no other explanation. Nick's little elf had gone and ratted him out.

It was not, however, a problem that he could address now, so he put it out of his mind, focusing instead on sliding the car into the garage, and then stepping inside. He almost called for Melton, only to remember that he'd sent his butler to the Beverly Hills mansion after Doyle's intrusive visit. The butler much preferred the kitchen in that location, and he tended to bake when he was worried. Apparently, it calmed him.

No lights burned in the house, yet the moment Luke opened the door, he knew that someone had been there. Not Tasha, though. Sergius.

Luke tensed, nostrils flaring, shoulders rolling into a fighting stance as his temper reached the boiling point.

Back it up. Back it up and keep the serpent at bay.

This wasn't the time, he told himself. Not the time to lose control. Not when so much was riding on him remaining calm. On him thinking rather than acting.

"Serge!" he called. "Where the hell are you?"

No answer.

"Dammit, Serge. We do this now or we do it later. Choose."

Silence echoed in return. The house was empty.

The ocean.

The moment the thought entered his head, Luke knew that was where Sergius would be. Like himself, Serge had always had a fondness for the sea. For the sting of salt in the mist, the tug of the currents, and the mystery of black, unplumbed depths.

He stepped onto the back deck, then climbed down the steps to the beach, the sand glowing in the moonlight.

At first, he thought that he was mistaken, for he saw no sign of Serge. Then he looked closer and saw the faint outline of a body prone in the sand, the surf crashing over it. He stalked to the water, then stood over his friend, who lay sprawled in the surf.

"Get up," Luke said, extending his left hand to his friend to draw him up, the slow burn of rage and disgust growing within.

"Fuck you. Fuck me. We're all fucked anyway, aren't we?"

He pulled Serge to his feet. And when the other man had steadied himself, Luke reached back with his right arm and punched his closest friend and fellow kyne hard in the face, knocking him back down into the sand. He fell upon him then, his hand splayed wide over Serge's heart.

"Do you remember?" he whispered. "Do you remember what we did? In the village outside of Prague? How we took over the town? How we killed our competition? How we cut the hearts out one by one, lining them up so that the next victims would know what was coming? And then how we cut off the heads and left them on pikes?"

His eyes met Luke's, the pain evident behind the serpent's steely gaze. "I would die rather than be that monster again."

"I would not give you the satisfaction," Lucius spat as the serpent rose up in fury, preening and roaring and ready for a fight. "You lost her," he hissed, as his fists rained down on his friend. "I trusted you, and you lost her. You touched her. Did you fuck her, Serge? Did you fuck my ward?"

The answer was immaterial. It was only the wrath that mattered. As hot as molten steel, as sharp as any blade, and his serpent fed on it. Tasted it. Sucked it in. And, yes, grew strong.

With clawed fingers, he reached down, his hand over Sergius's heart as he clutched, hard, wanting to rip through flesh, wanting to dig through muscle. Deep within, a voice yelled for him to stop, to wait, but he was too far gone, and soon the man he had once called friend would be gone, too, the serpent having taken action, having gotten rid of traitors and fools.

Hot hands clutched his wrist, and Lucius met Sergius's eyes. Serge may have wanted to die, but the same could not be said of the darkness that raged inside him, and Lucius gave a roar of satisfaction as the beast met him, challenged him in combat. A pretty fight it would be, he thought, as Serge rose up, slamming his forehead into Luke's and knocking him backward.

Sergius did not waste the advantage, springing up and attacking, the serpent not hesitating, not planning or considering.

They'd been changed on the same day, and both men and *Azag* were equally matched. This night, however, Serge held the advantage, as his serpent writhed free. Lucius knew the cost, and held back, determined even within the throes of the rising darkness to cling to the shred of both humanity and sanity.

Serge's heel intersected with Luke's jaw, rattling his teeth, and Lucius considered that sanity was overrated. He rushed, sideswiping Serge's steadying leg before the kick came back to center. Serge lost balance and Luke pressed his advantage, falling hard upon his friend, his enemy, his brother.

He had no stake, but that seemed hardly important at the moment. He crushed his hands against the sides of Serge's skull.

Beheading killed a vampire just as well, and right then, Lucius could rip the bastard's head off.

Deep within, Luke pressed back, trying for control. Trying to surface.

On the beach, Lucius held fast, eyes on Serge's face, relishing the moment when the fiend was ripped apart.

"I didn't," Serge said, his eyes flashing red, but his body going limp.

Lucius hesitated, the serpent wary, looking for some trick. "Speak," Lucius demanded.

"I did not touch her," Serge repeated, the fire fading from his eyes. "I swear."

Within Lucius, the part that was still human battled back, taking advantage of the serpent's surprise, finally beating it under. "Serge," he whispered, releasing his vise grip on his friend's head. "By the gods, Serge."

"We haven't fought like that in over five centuries," Serge said, drawing in deep swaths of air. "Now I remember why." He rolled onto his side. "You always beat me."

"You are yourself?"

"For now," Serge said. "I don't know for how long. It comes," he said. "It stays."

"You're going to have to find the strength to fight," Luke said, fearful that strength was fading within him. It was far too easy for the serpent to come out this night. It needed release if it was to be crushed back, docile, within.

"My serpent is not the problem," Serge said. "Tasha is gone. Graylach was slaughtered. Your enemies, Lucius—"

"I know," he said. "Caris has taken her."

"Caris?" Serge asked, his confusion clear.

Luke kept his voice flat, unemotional, and told his friend all that had happened.

"What can I do?"

Luke unbuttoned his shirt. "Who designed this device?"

He watched as Serge's brows knitted, as he reached out and touched the cold metal. "I've heard of these, but I have never seen one before." He looked up at Luke. "Someone of great power made this."

"Can you find him?"

"Perhaps. If not, I may have another solution. I'll leave word where and when to meet me tonight, and we'll see what can be done."

"Nothing new on Stemmons's location," Sara said, hanging up the call from Porter and turning back to face her team. "So we switch gears for a moment and focus on the Dragos matter. We've got three weeks until trial."

Her attention moved to Doyle and Tucker as Blair flew in, folded back her wings, then sat. "What more have you two got for me on the rape?"

"We've run down five victims," Doyle said. "The judge was a damn prick, and hell on wheels for keeping secrets. But once we tugged on the thread, it all started to unravel."

"And Tasha?"

"Not a word, not a whisper." Doyle narrowed his eyes as he looked at her. "You ever consider that Dragos is blowing smoke up your skirt?"

"What are you talking about?"

"That he knew Braddock was dirty, and he's tossing you this load of crap about his ward figuring you'll do exactly what you're doing."

"Not buying it." She'd seen the pain in Luke's eyes. No way was she going to believe he was bullshitting. "So I want you to keep looking. And I also want you to flag the interviews with the other rape victims. Have Blair make copies and send them to Dragos."

"Are you fucking kidding me?" Doyle said, as beside him, Tucker almost choked on his salt-and-vinegar chips.

She turned to Blair. "That rule plays down here, too, yes? We come across evidence that might clear the defendant, we have to turn it over?"

"Check," Blair said. "Pretty sure humans took that one from us, too. An earlier incarnation of the PEC established that rule in, oh, about 600 B.C." She frowned. "Maybe 1600 B.C. Anyway, before that, it was pretty much anything goes."

"Reading that rule awfully broad, aren't you?" Doyle said, blood rushing to his cheeks, and his eyes flashing red to match. "Dammit, Constantine, do you want the guy to get off?"

"What I want is justice." She pressed her palms flat on the

conference table and leaned over into his face. "And that means, Agent, that we don't try to stake innocent men. So if you find anything that suggests Dragos didn't murder Braddock—or if you find anything that suggests mitigating circumstances—then you flag it, you copy it, and you send it to the defendant. Are we clear?"

"I get you," Doyle said. "But we're not going to find anything. Dragos is a son of a bitch. And for once—finally—he's going to get what he deserves."

His phone buzzed and he answered it with a growl, then looked up at Sara with the kind of bright smile that made her very nervous. "Well, well. Look what we got here," he said. "A double murder in Van Nuys, and an eyewitness who swears it was Dragos."

"That's him," the girl named Alinda said, pointing a bony finger at an image of Luke.

Sara felt her mouth go dry. "You're certain."

"Totally." She turned toward Doyle. "Just like what I said when I called it in. I was in the alley, and I saw him break in."

"Hasik and Tinsley died late Friday. Why are you coming forward now?"

She licked her lips. "I was talking with people. Checking webpages, for the news, you know. Our news, I mean. And I saw his picture. He's the one who killed that judge, right?"

"Lucius Dragos is the defendant in the Braddock matter," Sara said. "Had you seen him before?"

"His kind don't much come into a place like this."

"His kind?"

"Vampire," Doyle said. "This is a Therian bar. Mostly, anyway. Get a few hellhounds, a few demons. Vamps mostly avoid it. The breeds don't really get along."

"But he didn't come in with the public, right?" Sara said. "Didn't you say he went in through the alley?"

Alinda nodded. "There's a keypad. He used it."

"Did he know the code?"

"Sure," the girl said. "He got in, right?"

Sara didn't bother answering.

"Why don't we go in?" Doyle said. "Although I don't know what we're going to find. Can't catch an aura without a body."

"Guess we'll have to rely on old-fashioned detective work," Tucker said, then cringed under Doyle's dark look.

"Hardly a challenge," Doyle said. "We got an eyewitness. This thing is wrapped."

The owner, a burly shifter named Viggo, escorted them to a small office off the back hallway. There was nothing remarkable about the crime scene. The victim's office looked as Sara imagined it always had, slightly unkempt, very lived in. It wasn't until Doyle passed her his phone with the crime scene photos that the full impact of what had happened here—of what Luke had done—hit her.

Two bodies seemed to cover the floor. One, a heavyset man with his neck broken, his head lolling at an obscene angle. The other, a wiry creature that lay in a pool of its own blood originating from the long gash across its neck.

She closed her eyes as bile rose in her throat, the acid taste lingering in her mouth. She'd seen thousands of crime scene photos and dozens of actual crime scenes, many much more brutal and bloody than this.

But she'd never before seen one rendered by Luke's hand. Except maybe Braddock's. And her father's.

She fought a shiver as around her, Doyle and Tucker inspected the room. "Got security cameras?" Doyle asked.

Viggo shrugged. "Tinsley had cameras. Whether he bothered to turn them on—"

"Pull them."

"Don't bother." They all turned toward the doorway and saw Nikko Leviathan stepping into the room. The victory evaporated from Doyle's expression, replaced with cold wariness.

Leviathan turned to Viggo. "Leave us."

"What's going on?" Tucker asked, the moment Viggo closed the door.

"Prosecutorial discretion," Leviathan said. "We'll not be pressing charges against Dragos. Not for this."

"Fuck that!" Tucker said, even more loudly than Doyle.

Even Sara, who had no desire to see Luke charged, couldn't comprehend the insanity of Leviathan's statement. Yes, she'd reviewed the file. And yes, she'd read the list of terrible things that both Hasik and Tinsley had done. But that didn't mean they should be cut down in cold blood. So why the hell would Division decide not to press charges when they had two dead bodies and an eyewitness? Unless...

Doyle took a step forward. "This is bullshit. Goddamn vigilante Alliance bullshit." He shoved a finger in Leviathan's face. "It's not right," he said, and with that, Sara had to completely agree.

The moon hung heavy and bright in the sky, silently watching as Luke moved through the thick clusters of trees. He moved with purpose, despite the lack of a path, his steps never hesitating, his way certain.

And when he reached the clearing, he stood in the shadow of a tree and waited.

Serge had said to meet him there, and now Luke could only wait and hope that Serge's efforts to help him remove the detention device had paid off.

Around them, the forest was quiet, though not silent. The baleful hoot of an owl cut through the night, as if echoing Luke's concerns. Minutes passed, and Serge didn't show.

Restless, Luke paced, irritation building, then shifting into cold, hard dread as minutes shifted into hours.

Serge wasn't coming. Of that, Luke was certain.

He was, however, equally sure that his friend would never betray him. Would never make a promise he did not intend to keep.

And that could mean only one thing: The wildness within Sergius had won the battle, and his friend had disappeared into the dark.

He was on the verge of turning around when he heard footsteps in the brush. He peered into the trees, and watched as Nicholas stepped toward him.

"You fired me," his friend said without preamble.

"I had no choice." Luke turned, pointedly looking around the clearing. "You came all this way to complain about our advocate-client relationship?"

"I came to deliver a message," Nick said, his voice clipped with emotion.

"Serge?"

"The fool approached Tiberius."

Fuck. "In the state he was in? With the *Azag Mahru* so close to the surface? Why the hell would he do that?"

But even as he asked the question, Luke knew the answer. Serge had wanted to make amends for failing in his promise to protect Tasha. Unable to find any other way to free Luke from the detention device, he'd foolishly approached Tiberius, hoping the vampire leader would use his influence and pull the necessary strings. "The goddamn fool."

"Damned is right," Nick said. "Tiberius tried to put him down." A small smile touched Nick's lips. "It didn't go well."

"He's gone rogue."

Nick nodded. "He's gone dark, Luke. Gave in to the monster."

"I understand," Luke said. But at least his friend was free. Had Tiberius captured him, Sergius would be no more.

"Tiberius has assigned me to search for him."

Luke's brow lifted. "What will you do?"

Nick lifted a shoulder. "I'll search. Doesn't necessarily mean I'll find. And in a few months, Tiberius's interest will wane."

Luke nodded. For the time being at least, Serge was safe from Tiberius. From himself, though ... that was a different matter.

"I'm also here with a message. Tiberius sends his regrets about Alinda's betrayal."

Luke almost smiled. "I'm sure he does."

"He said to tell you that he's arranged to make the problem go away. It won't come back to bite you in the ass, Luke. All things considered, that's better than nothing."

TWENTY-SIX

Sara stared at Luke's sprawling Malibu house, formidable and yet alluring. Much like the owner himself. She almost hadn't come. Had, in fact, been driving aimlessly in the night for more than an hour, trying to wrap her head around what she'd learned at the Slaughtered Goat.

The truth was that she didn't know what she was going to say. All she knew was that she had to see him. Had to see the Luke who was in her head, and erase the image of the Luke who had sliced that creature's throat. The Luke who had broken Ural Hasik's neck.

The Luke who had lived up to every horrible thing described in his file. Crimes for which he would never be prosecuted, and for which the dead would never have satisfaction.

A set of wooden steps surrounded by lush greenery led down to a solid steel door beside which she found an intercom panel. She pushed it, then heard a faint click. She tried the knob, found it unlocked, and stepped inside.

"Luke?" she called, tentatively at first, and then with more power. "Luke, are you here?"

There was no answer, so she moved all the way inside, shutting the door behind her.

The house was less ornate than she would have expected for such a ritzy address. Instead, she found it homey, lived in, as if Luke had long ago abandoned pretense for comfort and had been concerned with pleasing only himself. It pleased her, too. The bright colors. The overstuffed pillows. Luke undoubtedly never saw the room in the light of day, but it was bright and cheery nonetheless, with a long glass wall at the back that opened onto a wooden deck and a stunning view of the moonlit Pacific.

She imagined standing there with him and watching the sunset, then felt a pang of regret that they would never in fact see the sun together. A foolish notion, especially considering her purpose in coming here tonight.

Except, of course, that she wasn't certain what her purpose was, other than to see him. Was she expecting him to deny his actions? Or to promise he would never do it again? She wasn't naive enough to believe the first, but she couldn't quell the fear that he would absolutely refuse the second. Fear, because unless he did step away from the blood and death that papered his file, she knew that they would never find a common ground. And a common ground was something she so desperately wanted with him.

"You are a fool," she whispered. At the end of the day, what did it matter if they solved one set of problems? There was another looming—the trial.

After a few minutes of standing alone in his living room she called his name one more time, then debated leaving. She couldn't bring herself to do that, though, and instead moved through the house, determined to see him.

She found him on the third floor in a room filled with pink and white, the walls lined with dolls that stared down at them, their faces full of bland disapproval.

Beneath the porcelain-faced audience, Luke stood at the window, looking out at the white-tipped waves. He knew she was there, of course. Even were her image not reflected in the glass, he would have known simply from the scent of her.

"I came in here to think of her," he said. "To remember the way she would sit on the bed and play with her dolls. To picture her running on the beach in the moonlight, her face lit with a smile. Innocence," he said. "And that bitch and her human cohort have sullied her."

"I'm so sorry. But I still believe you'll get her back."

She watched as his shoulders sagged. "I know."

The silence loomed between them, and still he didn't turn around. He had to know why she'd come, but he didn't say a word about it. This was her issue, her battle. And she was going to have to strike the first blow.

"I've just come from the Slaughtered Goat," she said.

"Are you here to arrest me, Counselor?"

"No. There won't be any arrests in that matter. Prosecutorial discretion. No charges being pressed."

She thought she saw the slightest relieved sag in his shoulders before he lifted his head so that she could see his face in the glass. He was looking straight at her with unmistakable heat, and she felt desire stir inside her, her body responding to nothing more than the intensity of his gaze. She drew in a breath and stood still, determined not to show it—at the same time certain that those damn vampiric senses could hear the increased tempo of her heart and find the scent of her desire.

"Then why are you here, Sara?" he asked, his tone both an invitation and a challenge.

"Because of you. Because of me. Because there can't be a you and me if you do that."

"Do what?" he asked. "You're a prosecutor, Sara. Aren't you trained to be precise? The word you're looking for is kill."

"Yes, dammit, it is. And you can't just go out and decide who lives and who dies."

He turned away from the window to face her. "We've had this conversation already."

"No, we haven't. This isn't one of your James Bond kills, and you can't—" She stopped, remembering how the plug had been pulled on the investigation into the murders at the Slaughtered Goat. That must have been Tiberius's doing. She tilted her head and sighed. "Well, hello, 007."

"This is who I am, Sara. It's what I do. I thought you understood that."

"I thought I did," she admitted. "But you have to accept me as I am, too."

"I do." He moved closer to take her hands. "The world isn't black-and-white. Especially not this world. It is painted in shades of gray, an infinite number all blending together to make a pattern. I think we understand that better than most."

"Maybe you do. I'm still trying."

"Then keep trying, my love. I need you to truly see me. To under-stand that I do what I do to keep the serpent at bay."

"Surely there's another way," she said, hating that he had to fight and kill to keep that darkness from overwhelming him.

"Perhaps. But I'm not going to seek it out. There are some rules in this world of ours, and one is to move through it with the serpent harnessed. There are those who don't subscribe to that rule. Who kill humans with glee and torment their own kind. Those who haven't tried to subdue the darkness within. I hunt them down, Sara. I hunt them, and I kill them. Which is no more than they would do to me."

"I get that, Luke. I do. But it still doesn't make it right."

"And that's the fundamental difference between us. You see right and wrong while I see an evil that must be stopped." He took a step toward her, his body tense, his expression dark. "I was once the very thing I now hunt. And make no mistake, that darkness lives in me still, and one day I may not always be strong enough to contain it."

"You are," she said, her voice weak, her mouth dry. "You will be."

He caught her wrist and pulled her close, then bent down to whisper in her ear. "Are you certain?"

There was danger in his voice, along with a warning. She didn't heed it. Instead, she embraced it, her pulse quickening, her skin suddenly so very sensitive. "I am," she whispered.

His hand went around her back, and he pulled her toward him until their bodies ground together. "You play with fire, Sara, and yet when I'm around you, the serpent sleeps. You soothe me. But right now I don't want to be soothed."

His mouth crushed hers like an invader, vanquishing whatever remnants of hesitation remained within her. His tongue plundered her mouth, and she met him stroke for stroke savoring the taste of him. Scotch and heat and pungent desire.

His hands gripped her rear, drawing her closer, fitting her tight against the erection that strained beneath his jeans. She whimpered, her hands clutching the material of his shirt, holding tight against the rising sensations that filled her, claiming her and leaving her begging for more.

She broke the kiss, tilting her head back to look into eyes that reflected the depths of her own desire. "Luke." It was a plea, a prayer, and an invitation, and he accepted, scooping her into his arms and carrying her into the hall and down the stairs as if she weighed no more than a feather.

"My room," he growled. "My bed."

A huge bed dominated the room, lit by moonlight streaming in through the window. She still had enough of her sanity left to look for the shutters and found the metal blinds tucked in at the sides, ready to close as dawn threatened the sky.

"I've missed the feel of you," he said, laying her gently on the bed, his large hands struggling with the tiny buttons of her blouse.

"Screw it," he said, then grabbed the material and tugged, sending buttons flying and making her laugh as the cool air brushed over her naked skin.

His finger caressed the lace of her bra, tracing the swell of her breast against it. "So beautiful."

"Touch me," she begged, longing to feel his hands on her breasts and the weight of him pressing down upon her. "Touch me now."

He wasted no time fulfilling her command. His hands grazed down her belly, finding the button on her linen slacks. He tugged them off, taking her underwear at the same time, until she found herself naked from the waist down, clad only in her bra and her open blouse.

"Beautiful," he whispered, his hands caressing her thighs, stroking the soft skin and sending ribbons of white-hot heat curling throughout her body. "Clothes," she said. "Off."

He took care of that quickly, stripping naked as she watched, his body as magnificent as she imagined any god's could ever be. "Better?" he asked, sliding once more to brush his fingers up her legs.

She couldn't answer. Could only moan, the ache growing between her legs forcing her silence. She craved his touch, the velvet stroke of his fingertips, his breath against her clit, his cock filling her. She wanted everything—all of him—and she was absolutely certain that she would die of frustration if she didn't have it all right then, right there.

"Here," she said, taking his hand from her thigh and pressing his palm against her sex. "Now, please, now."

A low growl rose from his throat as his finger slid inside her. "You're wet for me, Sara. Tell me how wet you are for me. How much you want me."

"I am," she said, spreading her legs, giving herself to him. "I do."

He moved up her body, exploring her with his mouth as he went. With deft fingers he unfastened the front clasp of her bra and released her breasts. His mouth closed over her nipple, laving it with such intensity she thought she might come right then.

He pulled away, leaving her mourning the distance, then twined his fingers in her hair. "Kiss me," he murmured even as he descended hungrily upon her. She matched him, their mouths meeting, warring, claiming.

Between her legs, his erection twitched, hard and ready. She reached down, lifting her hips, her hand finding him. He was velvet steel beneath her fingers, and she guided him to her core, straining up, silently urging him to take her. To fill her.

He didn't disappoint. With a low groan of pleasure, he pushed slowly inside, giving her body time to adjust, to take him. But when she was ready, when she'd clasped her legs tight around him, all pretense of ease evaporated as he thrust inside, their hips pistoning in perfect time as the deep, carnal pleasure crescendoed.

He took her right to the edge, then slowed—the torment enough to have her crying out. He wasn't finished with her, though, and as he entered her in long, measured thrusts, his hand slipped between them, the pad of his thumb stroking her until it was pleasure—and not frustration—that had her pressing her lips tight together to try to keep from screaming as she came, the world bursting into a million particles of light.

Her fingers clawed at his back as he thrust harder and faster, finding his own release even as the last starbursts of her orgasm fizzled and popped around her. "Oh, wow," she said, as he collapsed beside her, pulling her tight against him, their bodies as connected now as they'd been during sex.

"I think that sums it up nicely," he murmured, the grin on his face reflected in his voice. He shifted, propping himself up on his elbow, his massive body shadowing hers. He traced his finger lazily over her stomach and up near her breast, the effect anything but relaxing.

"Your body is like a treasure," he whispered. "More beautiful than the statues carved by the masters themselves."

"You're very sweet. Insane," she added with a laugh, "but sweet."

"Insane, am I? How can you doubt a man who watched the masters themselves? Who knew the models personally?" There was a tease in his voice, and she fought not to laugh. "I assure you that I know what I'm talking about."

"That must have been amazing."

"At the time," he said, "it was only my life. Looking back now—seeing the way the world has changed—yes, it is amazing." He sat up, pulling her into his lap and tucking her close to his chest. "I would love to show you my past. To walk you through Rome, through Britain. To tell you the stories of what I saw on the streets and the people I once knew."

A deep longing filled her. "I'd like that. I'd like to hear your stories." She eased close, head tucked against his chest, suddenly melancholy.

"Sara? What is it?"

"Foolishness," she said. "It's just that for you, I'm not much more than a blip on the calendar."

"Never," he said, with conviction so warm and strong that she was sure nothing would ever shake it. "I will walk through history with you, and we will make these years our own."

She laughed, forcing herself not to think of the looming trial, the very real possibility of his demise. "Even if we did, it would be a short history. I'm longevity challenged, after all."

He stroked her hair. "To me, a single moment with you is more precious than a century with someone else."

The sentiment delighted and flattered her, and she snuggled closer, then lifted her face for a kiss before pressing her palm over the strap around his chest. "I'm sorry about this."

"You don't need to be."

She sighed, feeling perfectly at ease. "It was like this before, too. I remember."

"Me wearing a stake and us on opposite sides of a trial?"

She propped herself up on an elbow and scowled at him. "Us," she said firmly. "It felt like I knew you the moment I saw you. Like we were fated."

"No," he said. "Not Fate. I love you for who you are. What you stand for. The battles you fight. You're fearless, Sara. Even as a child. And you always stood up for what was right. Always took care of yourself."

"Somebody had to. My mom sure didn't step up."

"No," he said. "She didn't."

Sara scooted back so she could sit up and look at him. "You know that? How closely did you watch me?"

"Not every second, I assure you. But I made sure someone I trusted always watched over you. And when you were older, I watched you less and less," he said, his voice soft, "because I wanted to watch you more and more."

The warmth in his voice was like a caress. "Is it odd that's one of the things I love about you? I didn't even know you were my protector, and yet you've always made me feel safe. Even when I caught you on the street watching me from the shadows, I was never afraid of you. Just the opposite."

"I'm glad."

"Oh, I'm not done," she told him, fighting a grin. "I also love that it's not just me you protect. You could have simply left Annie on the pool deck. And I see how deeply you care about Tasha." She pressed her palm against his bare chest. "I don't agree with some of what you do. I never will, but I understand your code. And I know that you are honorable."

"Such praise. I would think you were fond of me."

"I love you, Luke." It felt so good to say the words. To match out loud what was in her heart.

He pressed his hand over hers. "I've loved you for so long, my Sara, but I never dreamed that I would hear those three sweet words."

"Then I'll say them again. I love you. And I don't want you to go."

"Am I?"

"You'll find a way out of this," she said, tapping the band around his chest. "And when you find Tasha, you'll take her and run."

"I will. I'm sorry, but I have no wish to live my life in a cell, and we both know the prosecutor is excellent."

"Luke, don't joke."

"Then come with me."

"You know I can't."

"Star-crossed," he said, cupping her cheek. "Our first love was stolen from us. This time, we'll be yanked apart."

"But we always find each other."

He brushed a tear off her cheek. "Yes, my love, we do."

Sara spent the next day at the office dealing with the mundane, which, after viewing the dead so often, had been a welcome change.

Afterwards, she forced herself not to go straight to Luke's, and to instead join Petra for a drink at Probation. "It seems like you've disappeared on me," her friend said when Sara slid into her chair, then gratefully took a sip of the whiskey that was waiting for her at the table. "Did Division 6 swallow you up?"

"You could say that," she admitted. "I wish I could talk more about it, but—"

"Covert division, big secrets, yada yada. I get it."

"Trust me, you don't."

Petra shrugged. "Maybe. Maybe not." She hesitated, then leaned forward. "Listen, Sara, there's something—oh, never mind."

Sara frowned. "What's going on?"

Petra shook her head. "Nothing. Really. It's just that I worry about you. That's all. And," she added, pointing a French fry at her, "I miss you."

"I miss you, too," Sara said, then shook her head. "Honestly, I *would* miss you, but I haven't had time. I'm working pretty much twenty-four/seven."

"Don't you dare burn out. Work in some chill time at least." She paused, then grinned as she studied Sara's face. "Oh. My. God. You are such a liar."

"Excuse me?"

"You're not working around the clock." Petra leaned in and lowered her voice. "Not unless wild sex is part of your job description."

"Petra!"

"You're going to deny it?"

She felt her cheeks burn, and Petra laughed so loud the guy reading the paper two tables away turned and gaped at them. "It's Luke. The guy from the night of the Stemmons' verdict. We've gotten, well, serious."

"Ha. I knew it." She popped two more fries in her mouth. "Tell me everything."

Sara didn't fully comply with that request, but she told Petra as much as she could, egged on by Petra's claim that she needed to live vicariously.

They'd stayed out until almost ten, laughing and talking, and by the time she got to her condo, Sara knew that she had to do better. She couldn't lose herself entirely in her work; not if it meant sacrificing her friendships.

She called Luke, then shared the details of her evening, making him laugh when she described Petra's reaction to her PG version of a date with Luke. "We've never been on a real date, so I had to make that part up."

"I suppose we'll have to remedy that," he said, his voice full of heat.

"I look forward to it, Mr. Dragos. And how was your day? Anything new on Caris or Tasha?"

There wasn't, and the frustration in his voice made her heart ache.

"Will you come tonight?"

She almost said yes, but she'd brought home a briefcase full of files on other pending matters. "Tomorrow? I should be caught up then."

"The anticipation will make seeing you then that much sweeter. Sleep well, my love."

She got into bed with the files, but had only managed to review one when her vision started to blur. She closed her eyes—just for a minute—and woke to the sun streaming in through the balcony door.

With a groan, she sat up and stretched, working out the kinks from falling asleep in such an uncomfortable position. She used the remote to click on the television, then froze when she saw a grave-faced reporter describe Stemmons's two victims and announce that the police assumed this was the work of escaped killer, Xavier Stemmons, but that authorities had no leads as to the escaped killer's location.

As the report ended, she heard a tap at her door.

Luke.

But, no. It was daylight.

Frowning, she hurried to the door, only to find that there was no one standing there when she peered through the peephole. She disarmed the system, then opened the door, and found herself looking down at a familiar porcelain-faced doll with red lips and a pink dress. A small sheet of paper was pinned to the doll's apron, one word scribbled across it: *next.*

With her blood pounding in her ears, she grabbed a pencil from the table beside the door, then used the eraser end to carefully turn the doll over. Still using the pencil, she lifted up the back of the dress to reveal the doll's cotton body—and the name written in black marker along the seam. *Tasha.*

Sara cringed as Luke hurled what had to be a thousand-year-old piece of pottery against the perfectly painted wall of his Malibu living room, then watched as it shattered into a million pieces. He reached for the companion piece, and she jumped forward.

"Luke! No."

"Goddammit," he raged. "He will not hurt her ... He will not touch her..."

"They're doing everything they can. A half-dozen agents are scouring my front hall right now hoping to pick up a trail."

"I need to go there."

"It's morning, Luke. You can't."

He stalked across the room, hands fisted, his entire body tense with rage and grief. She watched him, her heart aching. "You have nothing else on Caris's location?"

"Nothing," he said.

"Can I do anything? Can I be your eyes and ears during the day?"

He turned, and the raw emotion she saw on his face made her tremble. "There is one thing," he said.

"Anything."

"I will not lose you, too."

She shook her head, not understanding.

"I want you to stay here," he said. "With me."

"In case you forgot, you're the defendant and I'm the prosecutor."

"I think we've already destroyed whatever walls are supposed to exist between our two roles."

She couldn't argue with that.

"Stemmons or Caris left that doll on your doorstep," he continued. "They know where you live. And I will not see you harmed."

She opened her mouth to protest that her apartment was oozing with security, but closed it when she saw his face. His concern was real, as was his determination. And she knew damn well this was not a battle she would win, even if she wanted to. "All right," she said. "I'm not entirely sure how I'm going to make that fly at work, but I'll figure it out."

"Thank you," he said simply. "There is another thing." Though he spoke firmly, there was a catch in his voice. A hint of reservation.

"Luke? What is it?"

"My blood. I want you to drink from me."

His words surprised her, but what surprised her even more was that his words didn't repulse her. Slowly, she tilted her head, looking at him from this new angle. "Why? Why would I do that?"

"With enough of my blood in you, I can find you. I can reach out in my mind and locate you through your thoughts and sensations." He brushed her cheek. "You would be safe, and I would rest easier when you were out of my sight."

She bit her bottom lip, unable to deny that what he proposed was appealing. Erotic, even. The promise of a forbidden intimacy and the excitement of dancing on the edge but not slipping over. What would it taste like? Feel like? And would such an intimate encounter change her?

"No," he said, his words sharp in answer to the question she voiced. "I would not change you even if you wished for me to. I would not risk that with you, Sara. Not ever."

"Risk? You mean the *Azag Mahru*?"

"That is part of it." He stood and moved to the wall of windows, now covered by metal shutters. "I told you before I would have you know everything. That there would be no secrets and you would understand who and what I am."

"Yes," she said, a hint of worry rising within.

"Then it's time for you to hear the rest of it." He turned to face her. "I killed my Livia," he said, his voice deceptively impassive.

She sat on the couch, her knees suddenly weak.

"She was so young, and death was upon her, a weakness that she was born with and only got worse as the years went on. I was newly turned and arrogant. I thought I could save her. But I had never gone through the Holding, and the serpent was not bound. It rose up, and I surrendered to it. Instead of saving her, I took life from her, and lost myself utterly to the darkness. It was centuries before I went through the Holding. Centuries during which I did unspeakable things."

"It wasn't you," she said, feeling cold. Feeling sad. "It was the serpent."

"It was me," he said firmly. "The serpent is within me, and though I have more control now, that darkness lives just under the surface within me always." He sighed, looking back toward the shuttered window.

She pressed her lips together, willing herself not to cry. "Leviathan told me that vampires who haven't controlled the dark are rogue. Are hunted." She winced, thinking of him like that. "He told me you weren't rogue."

"I'm not," he said. "But at one time, I was. And there were those who lost their lives trying to put me down. My serpent is powerful, Sara, and it was not until I met Tiberius that I was forced to succumb to the Holding. For six months, I endured the torment of that ritual, and when I emerged, I had control, and I had regret. Tiberius stood for me, arranged a pardon for my actions, and in the centuries that have passed since then, I have battled to keep my will dominant. To control and use the serpent rather than it using me. Most often I have won that battle. But not always, Sara. Not always."

He reached into his pocket and pulled out a small gold ring, a coiled snake, so tiny it seemed to disappear into his palm. A child's ring. "Livia's," he said. "I keep it as a reminder of what I did. Of what I am capable of."

"Luke—"

He held up a hand, cutting her off. "No." She watched as he collected himself, then focused again on her. "When you drink from me, you will not be changed—you will not be able to seek me out, to feel my emotions. It works only one way without the change. There will be some increased strength, your senses sharpened. But no ill effects. But I will be able to find you."

"It sounds intimate."

"It is." He took her hands. "Very."

She pressed a soft kiss to his cheek. "Then my answer is yes. But I don't get it. Didn't Tasha have to drink your blood when she changed? Why can't you find her? The same way you'd be able to find me."

"With Tasha it is different. I cannot feel her, nor she me. I cannot close my eyes and find her in the world. I cannot look at her," he added, moving to her side, "and sense her fears or her joys."

"Why not?"

He considered his answer. "Her injury," he said. "Her mind allowed the change, but resists the connection. It is one of the reasons for the prohibition against turning those who are addled."

She heard the sadness in his voice and took his hand. "We will find her."

His fingertips brushed her cheek with all the intimacy of a kiss. "You are sure? You will drink from me?"

Her heart skittered, and she knew that what he asked of her was even more intimate than sex. But she wanted it—despite everything that still loomed between them, she wanted him. "I will."

"Thank you."

"Luke, about your blood—you said it strengthens me. Will I live longer, too?" she asked, teased by the allure of more time with him.

He shook his head. "No, Sara. I am sorry. If I could have you with me forever, I would."

"But you can," she said, her mouth dry, her words surprising her. Surprising her more because she only then realized how much the idea tempted her.

"No." The word came out so harsh she cringed. "Do you think I would wish that horror upon you? To see you succumb to the tumult of the serpent? Do you think I can bear to think about your body, bloodied and battered, as you fought? And if you died before you were even given the chance to fight?" He stood and paced between the couch and the wall of shuttered windows, his fears and memories driving him. "For you to survive the bloodletting, I must control my own serpent, and that I cannot promise."

He saw understanding in her eyes. Compassion. "You were young then. You have control now. You drank from Annie and she survived. And you turned Tasha, right?"

He bit back a bitter laugh. "Control?" He recalled the way he'd been lost when Annie's blood had flowed. The serpent had burst free, reveling in the blood, dancing in the power. He'd almost lost control. Taken too much, and Annie had nearly died because of it.

And he'd done so because he had imagined that it was Sara in his arms.

"I did not know Tasha," he said, trying to make her understand. "I did not love her. Not as I loved Livia. Not as I love you." He cupped her face, wishing he could have her always, but knowing he couldn't risk it. Nor would he want her to suffer the horror of the change and the Holding. "The serpent latches on. It wants what it desires, and it would take all. It is strong, and I cannot guarantee that I am stronger. Not then. Not with my mouth on your vein.

"No," he continued, taking her hand. "The change is not for you. Never for you. But my blood. Sara, I would share my blood with you, and I will swear to protect you always."

She nodded, overwhelmed.

"Then drink," he said, and sank his fangs deep into his wrist. She hesitated only a moment, then she looked up at him, her eyes locking with his as she lifted his wrist to her mouth, pressed her lips down upon him, and drew in his blood.

The tug of pleasure that went through him was instantaneous, and he drew his head back, his body already hard, his need for her desperate. He reached for her, his hand clasping the back of her neck. He held her tight as she drew him in, as he met and merged with her, and gave of his strength.

Mine.

Hunger rose in him, but not the vicious hunger of the beast. Not the serpent. On the contrary, she soothed the darkness, brought him under control even as he lost himself utterly in the sweet pleasure of Sara's lips upon his skin.

"Enough," he said, pulling away. Her skin glowed from the power of his blood, and he could feel her desire, her arousal, the connection between them vivid and sharp.

"I need you," she whispered.

"I cannot wait," he said as he pulled her shirt up, desperate to feel her skin against his, to plunge inside her. To ravage.

"Don't," she said, the passion in that single word bringing him close to losing it.

He needed no further encouragement, and he made quick work of the rest of their clothes, then thrust inside her, his palms pressed on either side of her, his eyes on her face, watching as passion rose within her. Within Sara.

Mine.

Yes, he thought, as the world exploded around him, she was well and truly his.

And he was hers, as well.

The creak of the automatic shutters opening startled Luke, so intent had he been on the computer screen in front of him.

He and Sara had spent the day in front of the computer and on the telephone, searching for a lead, a clue, anything that would lead him to Caris, to Stemmons, to Tasha.

"This," he said, tapping the screen. "I think I may have something."

Sara came over, her hand casually on his shoulder as she leaned in to read the screen. "What is it?"

"Property records for the house that I thought was Caris's. I've been following a paper trail and found an interesting deed from the 1920s." He pulled up the image, then showed Sara the name on the deed—CV Enterprises.

"Caris Vampire?"

"Could be. She always had an interesting sense of humor."

"And you found other properties owned by the same company?"

"I did," he said, pushing back from the computer. "Two commercial buildings and one house. I'm going to investigate the house now."

He saw the worry on her face. "Be careful," she said.

"Always."

She grabbed her purse, which made him frown. "You're leaving? Sara, you promised to stay here."

Confusion brushed her features. "Well, yes. But not every second of every day. I still need to work. And I need to go to my apartment and get some things."

He nodded. She was right, of course. "Be careful. And let the security team at Division know about the doll. Have them assign you protection."

"I will."

"And cry out in your mind if you need me." He stroked her hair. "I will come for you."

"I know."

He kissed her forehead, felt his body firing, and stepped away. "Later," he said, brushing his fingers over her lips. "We shall continue this later."

"We certainly will," she said.

His phone buzzed, and he reluctantly answered it, frowning at the unfamiliar number.

"Lucius?" Tasha's voice, and his heart tightened at the sound of it.

"Tasha? Where are you?" He held out his hand and found that Sara was already beside him, holding him tight, keeping him steady.

"They hurt me. Said I'm broken. But I'm not broken, am I, Lucius? I'm a good girl."

"You are," he said. "Of course you are."

"I did a bad thing, though," she whispered.

Fear rippled through him. "What did you do?"

"The thing inside me. I let it out. I let it out even though you told me never, ever to do that. But I couldn't help it. I needed to get away. They were going to hurt me, Lucius. They were going to cut off my head."

His body tensed, the serpent rising, ready to fight. Ready to kill. "Are you safe?" he asked, grinding the words out past clenched teeth.

"Yes. But I'm scared. Will you come?"

"I will," he said, clutching Sara's hand. "I'll come right now."

TWENTY-SEVEN

The serpent was snapping at the edges of his control by the time he found his ward, curled up in the single-stall bathroom of the gas station on Santa Monica Boulevard. The attendant was pounding on the door, screaming that customers were complaining. Lucius grabbed him by the shoulders and tossed him the length of the building, where he crashed into a row of newspaper machines, knocking them over and spilling quarters out over the sidewalk.

He didn't bother with the door handle—he simply ripped it off its hinges. Inside, Tasha screamed, then scrabbled to him on all fours, her now-gray dress dragging in the filth and muck on the bathroom floor.

"I'm here, I'm here," he said, holding her close to his chest and soothing her. "Are you hurt? Do you know where the son of a bitch is?"

"He drank from me," she said after several false starts. "The human. From me and from all those little girls."

"Was he alone?"

She shook her head. "A female. A vampire. She promised to change him. Promised to bring him over if he killed me. Said I was wrong. That I shouldn't even exist. Scared me, Lucius. Wanted to hurt me. Wanted to kill me." She pressed her face against his shoulder, and he held her as shivers wracked her body. "I let it out. The monster inside. And I got away. But they wanted to hurt me, Lucius. They wanted me to be ash."

"Nobody will hurt you," he said, calling upon all of his strength to keep his voice calm. Soothing. "No one will ever hurt you again."

"You'll protect me," she said, lifting her head to look at him, the pain in her eyes almost enough to bring the serpent back to the surface. "You love me."

He breathed deep, willing the beast back down. "You are mine," he said, holding her tight. "And I will protect you to the death."

Since Blair had called while Sara was in her car with the news that the medical examiner wanted to see her, Sara skipped her floor altogether and headed straight for the forensic section of Division. She found Richard Erasmus Orion IV eating a peanut butter sandwich in the break room. He was leaning back in his chair, his eyes closed as classical music blared, his cowboy boots perched on the shiny clean Formica tables.

She cleared her throat and he jumped, then immediately shut the music off and held out a sticky hand for her to shake.

"Sorry! Sorry! Hard to find fifteen minutes around here. I was just taking five."

"What have you got for me?"

"DNA," he said, cocking his head and leading her across the hall and into one of the labs. The lab lights gleamed on his bald head, and he wore a long white lab coat that flowed when he moved, revealing a hint of the Hawaiian-print shirt he wore beneath.

"I've already read the report on the DNA evidence," she said. "Was there an error?" She had the absurd fantasy that he would tell her that Luke was no longer implicated.

"More of an oversight," he said as he poured coffee into a mug that said The Dead Do It Stiffer, then took a sip.

"An oversight," she repeated. "What kind of oversight?"

"The kind where we find more DNA."

She paused while reaching for the second mug he offered her. "Would you mind repeating that?"

"Happenstance, really," he said. "I was taking another look at the wound, and that's when I noticed that the bite radius was a little hinky."

"How?"

"I'll show you." He punched a few buttons on a computer terminal and the familiar image of Braddock's neck appeared on a wall screen. "Ripped up a bit," he said, "but you can see the contact points of the fangs here and here," he said, indicating with a laser pointer. "But this was what caught my attention. See this? Another fang impression, right? But at a slightly off angle." He tilted his head to demonstrate. "Like our perp wasn't happy with his initial grip on the victim's neck."

"All right," Sara said, wondering what this had to do with DNA. She knew better than to try to rush him, though. She'd learned long ago that when an ME had a point to make it was best to be patient; eventually they'd get there.

"So I thought I'd check the bite radius. Just make sure it was our perp. And there you go."

"It wasn't?" She couldn't keep the surprise from her voice. "There was another biter? A first biter?"

"A cookie for the little lady," he said, tapping the side of his nose.

"And DNA confirmed that?"

"Did indeed," Orion said. "Not enough markers to make a match, but enough to definitively conclude that there was another biter."

"I need your report," Sara said, her mind churning.

"Not a problem." He went to a terminal, tapped a few keys. When he turned back, he held a ceramic candy dish shaped like a human hand. "Tootsie Roll?"

"No thanks."

"So how much damage does this do to your case against Dragos?" he asked.

"A lot," she admitted, unable to keep the smile off her face as she considered all the possibilities. "It messes it up a lot."

With Orion gaping at her, she raced back toward her office, her phone plastered to her ear, and Blair at the other end of the line.

"Question for you: What if Tasha attacked Braddock? Took him just to the point of death. Self-defense because he was raping her. Where does that put us legally? If the DNA proves my theory, then that would knock Dragos down from a capital crime to a lesser charge, right?"

"Well, yeah," she said. "You seriously think that's the way it went down?"

"Just go with me on this. Okay, so Dragos gets charged with a lesser crime—gets to avoid execution. But what about Tasha? If that's really how it happened, then what happens to her special dispensation?"

"Hang on. Hang on." She heard Blair typing. "Nope. No leeway. It's clear. She takes steps—she lets the darkness take control—she's terminated."

Sara leaned back, incredulous. "Even with evidence of rape?"

"Regular vampire wouldn't have such a raw deal, but, hey, she wasn't supposed to be allowed to live in the first place."

"Shit. Okay. Thanks." She clicked off the call and tried to sort through her thoughts, because she was positive she knew what had happened. Braddock raped Tasha. And Tasha, terrified, lashed out against him, her own serpent probably coming out for revenge. She went after Braddock, wanting to end the torment, and somehow Luke realized what she was doing.

He followed, found Braddock on the brink of death, and realized what would happen to Tasha if the PEC tied her to the murder. So he did what Sara had come to expect of Luke: He protected the girl. He put himself out there as a target to draw the fire away from Tasha. He staged the scene, leaving his ring, leaving his DNA. All of it, every bit, designed to lead the PEC to him.

He'd intended to run; of that she was certain. Draw them in, make sure he said enough to be determined guilty in absentia, and then escape. That had been the point of the nerve gas in the tomb when the team had rushed to capture him.

Something had gone wrong, though, and he'd been incarcerated. And unless she introduced the evidence about Tasha, he would most likely die for a crime he didn't commit. Implicate Tasha, though, and Luke's ward would be staked.

There had to be a way to protect Luke without putting Tasha's head on the block.

And as she passed under the Judicare Maleficum archway, she realized that she knew exactly to whom she could go to for the answer.

"You're asking me to consider dropping a capital murder charge down to manslaughter?" Nikko Leviathan peered at Sara from behind his desk, the hint of gray in his temples glinting in the overhead light. She stood her ground, back straight, shoulders square.

"Yes, sir. I think the evidence will show that Dragos was protecting his ward. She was being subjected to repeated abuse by the defendant."

"You have proof of the abuse?"

"Working on it."

He stood up, began pacing behind his desk. "When you were first assigned this case, you told me your relationship with the defendant would not affect your judgment."

She bristled. "And it hasn't."

"Hasn't it?"

She lifted her chin. "Sir, I've learned that it was Dragos who killed my father under Alliance orders, the crime pardoned, of course." She made an effort to look as if she was holding back a wild fury. "I'm the very picture of objectivity."

He leaned back. "I see."

"Sir, I'm only asking you to consider this if it's supported by the evidence. Whatever my feelings may or may not be, they can't change the facts."

He stared at her, the scent of cinnamon filling the air. "What exactly are you looking for here, Constantine?"

"Reduced charges and house arrest. He wears the detention device until time served."

"This is a high-profile matter, and you're suggesting that we should forego incarceration?"

"Sir, he was protecting a woman who couldn't protect herself. How is justice served by locking him up?"

Leviathan exhaled loudly, then drummed his fingers on the desk. After a moment, he nodded. "You prove the rape, I'll authorize the deal."

She forced herself not to sag with relief. Not yet. "Thank you, sir. I'll get the proof."

"And then we'll talk again," he said, but he was smiling. "And, Constantine? You can go easy on calling me sir."

In the hall, she tried to walk without an added little hop in her step, but didn't quite manage it, and when she caught sight of Doyle and Tucker in the hall near her office, she hurried to meet both of them.

"What have you got?" she demanded. "I need solid evidence that Braddock raped Tasha."

"We've got shit on the girl. Rape, yeah. Tasha, not a thing. We can't even prove he knew her."

They followed her into her tiny office, then flopped into the two guest chairs as Sara paced. "Would there be physical evidence left on her?" she asked. In a human, she knew the answer would be no. For a vampire, though ... She just didn't know.

"Hit or miss," Doyle said. "But if we can get her to agree to a session with a Truth Teller, that's pretty weighty shit. I thought she was missing, though."

"Apparently she's back."

"All right, then. We'll bring her in." Doyle started to push out of the chair.

"No," she said. "I'll arrange it."

He glanced at her, eyes narrowed, nostrils flaring. "You have his blood in you."

"The hell I do," she said, not willing to discuss her personal affairs with the likes of Ryan Doyle.

"Hope not," he said, his nostrils flaring. "Because I like you, Constantine. Not entirely sure why I like you, but I do. And I'll be damned if I'll stand by and watch that bastard hurt you."

"Then you don't have a thing to worry about."

CHAPTER
TWENTY-EIGHT

Lucius sat on the edge of Tasha's bed and held her hands in his. She was showered and changed, now in pink pajamas and a flowing pink robe. "You are centered now? The serpent well under?"

"I am." She licked her lips, her eyes wide and scared. "I was so afraid I wouldn't see you again. They wished to keep me away. Far away. And then they wished to kill."

He stroked her hair, then pressed his hands against her shoulders, willing her to understand. "You are here. You are safe. And they will never threaten you again." *Never.* As soon as she was steady Luke was going after Caris. He'd kill her. He'd kill Stemmons. And he'd do it in the most painful way he could devise.

On the bed, Tasha pulled a rag doll to her and hugged it tight. She tilted her head back, her nostrils flaring. "Girl," she said. "The scent of a girl fills my room." She lowered her head and stared at him with wide, guileless eyes. "Why, Lucius?"

"You have caught the scent of a friend of mine."

"I saw," she said, making him wonder. "Pretty girl. The way she touched you in that bar."

"What bar?"

"Before," she said. "Before you killed for me." She tilted her face up to him. "That's what he did to me. The judge. He did to me what you did to the pretty girl."

"It's different," Luke said, an unwelcome chill in his bones as he remembered a similar comment she'd made when she was in San

Francisco with Serge. "How long have you been watching me, Tasha?"

"I always watch you." She rocked on the bed, and he knew that he was losing her again.

"Tasha, focus. The woman is important to me. And she will be staying with me for a while. Can you understand that? Can you be nice to her?"

Her eyes widened. "I'm always nice," she said, then her forehead creased. "Except when I'm not. I wasn't nice to them tonight, Lucius. The ones who kept me. The ones who wanted to hurt me."

"And to them you never need to be," he said, taking her hand and cursing his earlier fears, cursing himself for seeing cunning and contrivance even in innocence.

"Have to be nice to the girl, though. Your woman. Your Sara."

"Sara," he repeated. "You heard her name?"

"You love her."

His heart twisted. "Tasha, you know that no one will ever replace you."

"You do things with her," she said. "Naughty things. You've never done naughty things with me."

"And I never will." He leaned forward and pressed a chaste kiss to her forehead. "Rest," he said. "I must go take care of something. I'll be back soon."

She said nothing, and he left the room, his thoughts turning to Caris and the thousand ways he would hurt her.

The phone buzzed and he snatched it up without looking at the display, expecting Slater. "What have you got?"

"Your balls in a sling, you son of a bitch." Ryan Doyle's gruff voice filtered through the phone. "What kind of games are you playing with her?"

The fury that had been aimed at Caris took a sharp turn, as the image of Luke's fist intersecting with Doyle's face filled his mind in a most satisfying way. "I don't know what parasite is infecting your brain, Doyle, but if you have something to say to me, you can damn well say it to my face. Or are you too much of a coward?"

"You couldn't keep me away."

Luke clenched his fists at his side, forcing calm. "After so many insults between us, what the hell has happened now sufficient to have you ringing me up to chat?"

"Sara."

"What's happened to her?" Luke demanded, his voice tight with fear.

"You did, you shit. She drank your goddamn blood."

"She did," Luke admitted, "though it's no business of yours."

"It's my business when you mess with the prosecutor's head."

"I offered her protection."

Doyle barked out a laugh. "The fuck you say. Whatever game you're playing, Dragos, it isn't going to work. You're not sliding out from this murder charge, and you're sure as hell not hurting that girl. I won't see you destroy her the way you destroyed my life, my woman." Pain filled his voice, the words bringing to the forefront the events that had shredded the bonds between them. Luke clenched his fists. Now was not the time.

"I should have killed you then," Doyle continued.

"We all have to live with regret."

"I'm warning you," Doyle spat.

"And yet your words mean nothing. You want to finish this, then get your ass here and we will. But don't come unless you mean it, because if you land the first blow, I will kill you. With no thought to our past friendship or the debt that I may owe you. I will kill you. So if it's death you seek, then bring it on now."

"I'll be there in an hour," Doyle said, and before Luke could respond, he clicked off and the phone went dead.

Sara had nicknamed her assigned guard Guido. Not only because he looked the part, but also because she couldn't for the life of her pronounce his real name.

"I'm not going to be long," she said, opening the door. She'd reported the doll incident to Leviathan, Doyle, and the team, and they'd all agreed that Stemmons was taunting her. And that he could turn dangerous at any moment.

"You stay," Guido said, grabbing her by the shoulders and lifting her over the threshold. He plunked her down by the door, closed it, then pointed a warning finger. "No move." And then he disappeared for a rundown of the entire apartment. Since it was a studio, that didn't take long, and he was back with an efficient nod before her arms had even stopped aching from his clutch.

"Right," she said as he stationed himself in front of her door, as immobile as a Buckingham Palace guard.

She hurried to her dresser and shoved some yoga pants and a few T-shirts into a duffel bag. She added a few work outfits, an extra pair of shoes, and the last of her father's journals. She paused for a moment at the bedside, then reached for the gun. After a second's hesitation, she chambered a round, then put it into her purse. If she was worried enough to have Guido following her around, then she was worried enough to be armed.

Out of habit, she hooked the portable panic button onto her waistband, then ran into the bathroom for essentials. Once she had everything she needed, she headed back into the living room to meet up with Guido, still standing perfectly still at her door.

She checked her watch and smiled—ten minutes past midnight. She'd managed to pack for a trip to a man's house in less than fifteen minutes. That had to be a female record. "Ready," she said.

He nodded and stepped aside, allowing her to punch the exit code into the control box. As Roland had taught her, she held the portable panic button in one hand and entered the code with the other. "Gotta protect you in those few seconds when you don't know what's outside the door," he'd said.

The system disengaged, she peered through the peephole, and since nothing was there, moved to open the door. Guido got there first, edging in front of her with a stern wag of his finger. He opened the door and took one step forward—just far enough for the sword that slashed downward to lop off his head.

Sara screamed, her finger fumbling for the panic button even as her mind registered the attacker—a teenage girl with auburn hair and an expression of grim satisfaction. And right by her side was Xavier Stemmons.

Sara pressed the button hard as she stumbled backward, tripping over the bag she'd dropped. Even as the gray mist of the security force filled her apartment, she grappled in her purse, her fingers closing around the butt of the gun. She yanked it out, and as Stemmons leaped upon her, she fired.

His body jerked from the impact, but he held tight, the woman holding on to him as well so that the three of them were locked in an unwelcome embrace.

And as Stemmons's blood spilled out upon her, Sara succumbed to the odd sensation of her body disintegrating.

The last thing she saw before her mind turned to mist was the dark form of the Phonoi materializing in her living room.

And the last thing she heard was the girl's singsong voice whispering, "Lucius is mine. Mine, mine, mine."

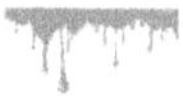

Luke hadn't bothered to wait for Doyle. If the para-demon had a death wish, he could damn well wait at Luke's house for him to return home.

Luke had a more pressing engagement: Caris.

He raced down the Coast Highway, then maneuvered the busy streets until he careened to a stop in front of the private drive that led to the house his research had revealed was owned by CV Enterprises.

He hoped to hell she lived there. If not, he was all out of leads.

He killed the car's engine then sat in the dark, weighing his options. He ruled out approaching by car, as that would eliminate the element of surprise. As for climbing the fence and approaching on foot, the security cameras that dotted the landscape would similarly alert her to his presence, something he would rather not do. He wanted her weak. He wanted her vulnerable. And that meant that he needed the advantage of surprise.

His wants, however, weren't aligning with the physical reality of her home. As he was cursing that fact, he heard the low, strong purr of a motor. A Jaguar, unless his ears deceived him.

He smiled and stepped out of the car. The element of surprise had just been tossed back into the mix.

He eased back, out of sight, but still close to where her car would emerge. He stood still in the dark, waiting and watching, listening as the hum of the engine drew his quarry closer and closer. The first hint of headlights cut through the dark, and he tensed, his body ready to pounce. And then, as the gate opened and the car eased through, that's exactly what he did.

Caris turned as he leaped, slamming the car into park even as she began the slide toward the opposite door. It did her no good. He'd yanked the driver's door open before she was even half out of the car.

He lunged, snarling, his hand grabbing her shoulders as they both slid through the car and out the passenger door to land, hard, on the rough asphalt. Whatever surprise she'd felt, she'd recovered, and now she kicked back, trying to free herself from him.

"Nowhere to go, Caris. Nowhere to run."

She spat in his face, then froze, her expression one he knew well. Transformation. He clung tight to her, the hematite bands at his wrists seeming less of a burden now that their proximity was screwing with her abilities.

Confusion flashed in her eyes, and he closed one hand around her neck. With the other, he pressed a stake to her heart. "The truth," he said, "or you will die. Are you prepared for that, Caris?"

"What do you want, Dragos?"

"Tasha," he said. "I want revenge."

There was a pause, then her brow furrowed. "What the hell are you talking about?"

He reached down and ripped open the white linen shirt she wore, then pressed down on the stake, hard enough to draw blood, the serpent itching to press harder. To kill. "Do not fuck with me. I should end you this instant for the things you've done, but first I need you to tell me where Stemmons is." He leaned in close and lowered his voice. "Go ahead and resist. Trust me when I say I'll enjoy getting the information from you."

Not a hint of fear rolled off her. "Stemmons? That human worm? Like I'd associate with that kind of garbage. And you know damn well I'm not inviting little Tasha over for tea." Her eyes flashed. "So tell me what the hell you're talking about, or stake me. The asphalt's cutting into my ass, and I want to get up."

"Don't tempt me," he said, increasing the pressure on the stake. "And do not even think about lying to me. I caught your scent, Caris. At the Slaughtered Goat, and then at the scene of Stemmons's last victim."

"Well, color you clever," she said. "I had my reasons for being there."

"Share," he said, twisting the stake like a drill.

"Dammit, Lucius, I—"

"Tell."

"I'm in town for a project," she said. "But it doesn't have a damn thing to do with your precious little ward. So why don't you get the hell out of my face?"

He opened his mouth to retort, but the words never came. Instead, his head seemed to explode, bursting apart from the force of Sara's scream all the way on the other side of the city. A scream and then the sharp snap of an image forced into his mind—the bastard Stemmons, and beside him, Tasha.

TWENTY-NINE

Luke backed away from Caris, his head pounding with pain and the image still sharp in his mind as the truth hit him with the intensity of a punch to the face. *Tasha had played him.* The girl he loved like a daughter. The child he'd saved.

The woman he should never have turned.

She'd hidden her growing abilities—abilities that he'd given her by turning her in the first place. And now she was

playing a game of revenge to punish him for wanting another woman, and to punish Sara for being the woman he desired.

He ran.

Blood pounding and terror racing through him, Luke raced back to his car, terror raging through him as he raced down the street. She was trapped. She was scared.

He saw snatches of her hand. Felt the pressure of fear coiling inside her. The smooth grip of the gun in her hand.

And then the connection popped.

Gone. Nothing.

The lock he'd had upon her thoughts had snapped like a rubber band. They'd taken her, and in him, the serpent raged, screaming to kill, to find, to rend.

Calm, he told himself as he pulled the car over, trying to find a center, a place where he could think and plan. Sara needed that. Needed him sharp. Needed him calm so he could find her.

He lifted his head, nostrils flaring, as if he could catch the scent of her on the wind. There was nothing, of course, but the motion, the effort, seemed to sharpen his mind. Allowed him to hone in, bring him closer.

To see what she saw and feel what she felt.

Except there was nothing but the faintest hint of her essence. Panic rose within him, and he fought it back. But he knew now what had happened. They'd taken her. Transformed her into mist. That was why he couldn't find her with his mind.

He needed help. And right then, he could think of only one person who could offer the help he needed.

He pulled out his phone and called Doyle. "They've taken her," he said without preamble. "Goddammit Doyle, Stemmons has Sara."

He heard the sharp intake of breath, then Doyle's gruff and steady response. "Where was she?"

He released a breath. "Her apartment. They took her. Stemmons and Tasha. Transfigured and got her the hell out of there."

"Materialized yet?"

"No." He said the word forcefully, because he had to believe that the connection between him and Sara would remain strong. Once she was solid again, he'd find her in his mind.

Once she was solid again, he would save her.

"Tucker's on the phone beside me contacting Security Section. We'll meet Roland at her apartment. See if we can learn anything."

"I'm in my car," Luke said. "Call me the moment you know anything." He had to keep moving. Had to keep *doing*. If he didn't, he was certain he would go mad. Goddamn the detention device. It kept him solid. Kept him there. Kept him from moving fast and striking hard.

Dammit, dammit, dammit.

With no other way to unleash his fury, he took it out on the streets, once again flooring the Mercedes and careening around curves as he drove. Ignoring Tasha's betrayal. Ignoring his own blindness against the vile serpent that had been preening within all these years.

Ignoring everything except the singular task of getting to the woman he loved, and getting there as fast as he could despite the shackles on his body.

He moved through traffic like a wild man, running lights, cutting off the late-night, barhopping crowd crawling along the road at a fucking snail's pace. He was exiting I-10 for Wilshire Boulevard when Sara ripped into his head once again, her terror and pain enough to stab a thousand holes in his heart, the pain counterbalanced only by his relief in finding her once again.

He punched the redial button on his cell phone to connect with Doyle and focused on locating her, on pulling thoughts from her head. Thoughts that would give him help. A clue. Anything.

Fear.

Fear, and death.

Death all around her.

But no scent of it. Only the trappings.

Stone.

Bars.

And something familiar. Not to her—her thoughts were confused, ragged. But to him. He knew this place. The small flashes in her mind adding up to a picture of—

Luke!

I'm coming, he said uselessly. She wasn't like him. She couldn't hear him. Even so, he had to call out to her. Had to let her know. *I'm coming,* he repeated. *I swear that I am coming.*

"Where?" Doyle demanded, his voice sounding hard and fast over the speaker.

"Hollywood," Luke said. "My crypt. He took her to my own fucking crypt."

"Steady," Doyle said, his gruff voice surprisingly gentle. "We'll get her back. I promise you. We're going to get her back."

"Please, no." Sara knew it wouldn't matter. Knew he couldn't be reasoned with, yet she begged anyway. Begged for the life he was about to steal from her. A life she now desperately wanted to share with Luke. "Please. Don't do this."

"But I have to." He looked at her with glassy eyes. "You were very naughty."

"I was. Absolutely." Her head pounded, and she wanted to reach up and clutch her skull in her hands, but her wrists were bound. She was naked, her pants and shirt in tatters on the ground.

As if in a dream, she realized where she was. A crypt, cold and dank. And she herself strapped down to the lid of a hard stone coffin.

"The blood is the light," he said. "My Dark Angel feeds on the light."

In her mind, she screamed for Luke and prayed that he would hear. But there was nothing there. Nothing but the pounding in her head and the shivers that wouldn't stop. Bone-deep trembling that shook her so much her teeth were chattering.

"You'll be warm soon," Stemmons said. "The dead don't feel the cold."

"I don't want to die."

"You won't at first," he said, and then he actually smiled at her. "First you have to give the light. To me and to my Angel. The light nurtures. The light heals. I have drunk my Angel's light, and it has healed. Soon, it will make me divine."

He'd fed off Tasha, Sara realized, and the gunshot wound now looked like nothing more than a scratch. All her fantasies about blowing him away, only to learn that it wasn't a gun she needed. Because he was truly a monster.

He stepped closer, and for the first time she saw the knife in his hand, glinting in the hint of moonlight that crept in through the bars of the crypt.

"I would say that this will only hurt a little, but I'm afraid that would be a lie." He smiled wide. "And I don't lie. That's very, very naughty."

She wanted to cry, wanted to scream, but no sound came out.

No sound that is until he dragged the tip of the knife across her belly. Until he rent flesh and muscle.

When he did that, the scream burst from her, a desperate cry. A piercing plea for Luke to come, to please come, to save her.

And as the world started to turn gray around her—as Stemmons sliced his knife into her breast, her thigh, her neck—she imagined that she saw him there, her dark warrior, her life, her love.

He would come.

He would come for her and end this nightmare.

But as the world slipped away from her, she knew the nightmare was real, and this time, she wouldn't wake up.

Blood.

Sara's blood.

He could smell it, could practically taste it, and the scent of it drove the serpent wild.

Lucius let it. He needed the beast now. The serpent's speed, the *Azag's* rage.

Needed to use the darkness he tried so hard to keep buried to destroy the bastard who had dared to hurt his Sara. And as for Tasha...

His heart twisted with the pain of it even as he raced forward, feet pounding over the soft earth, Sara's scent drawing him, her thoughts—incoherent, terrified, pain-filled, but alive, still alive— calling to him.

She was close. So very close.

Luke...

The tiniest of echoes, but the beast within him unfurled, fangs bared, rage boiling.

He'd traveled by land, the route swifter than the tunnels beneath the store. And now he raced toward the familiar structure. Moving swiftly. Moving silently.

And then felt the shock of seeing her like a punch in the gut when he peered through the bars at the horror that lay within.

Stemmons was there, and he stood over Sara with a blade tipped in blood. Lucius tilted his head back and drew in the scent. Tasha. But not present. Not there.

Instead, her blood was within the human.

She'd not turned him, but she'd made him strong.

Deep within Lucius, the serpent hissed. *Not strong enough.* Not fucking strong enough.

Sara was naked, her breath coming in stops and starts, and he could hear the shallow, weak beat of her heart. He could smell the blood that had been spilled on the stone. The life that was draining out of her.

No time, the serpent cried. *No time.*

With a guttural roar, Lucius ripped the door off the crypt, then tossed it aside. Stemmons turned, his eyes so wide it was almost comical, and found the beast barreling down on him.

"Die," Lucius said, and took the blade the human wielded. Then swiftly, purposefully, Lucius drew it across the man's own throat.

Blood gushed like a faucet, but its scent did not entice. The human was putrid. Rotten.

And only Sara mattered.

He rushed to her side, his every cell screaming out in denial and fear as he felt the life draining from her.

Back it up, he thought, trying to gather himself. He had to think, and he couldn't do that with the primal beast raging in pain and fury within.

He felt the beast withdraw, as if understanding that the life of the woman depended on its departure.

"Sara." He stroked her forehead. "Sara, my love."

Her eyelids fluttered, and when he again caught the scent of her pain, a new swell of fury rose within him.

"Knew ... you'd come. Had ... to say ... good-bye."

"No." He stroked her face, held her hand. "No, you cannot leave me."

"No ... choice." Her voice was so weak, but still she smiled at him, even as a vise tightened around his heart.

"I'll heal you. I can make you well." With grim determination, he bit his wrist, then pressed it to her lips. "Drink."

She did, but her eyes did not spark. The life did not return. She was too far gone, and he was losing her, his blood barely prolonging the inevitable.

He pulled his wrist away and brushed her hair off her face. Lost, so terribly, terribly lost.

Footsteps behind him, then Doyle's voice. "Oh, God. Oh, damn. That son of a bitch. That goddamn fuckwad."

"Your coat," Tucker said. "Doyle, put your coat over her."

"Getting ... darker," Sara said as Doyle draped her. "No time." Her lips twitched, as if she was trying to smile. She looked straight at Lucius. "I love you."

His heart twisted, and he felt his eyes well with tears. He had not, he thought vaguely, cried in centuries. Now it felt as though if he started he would never stop. "You cannot go."

Another flash of pain crossed her face, and her fingers twitched as she tried to grip his fingers.

"Do something," Doyle said.

"My blood is not healing her. She is too far gone."

"Dammit, Lucius, she's not there yet. You can save her. You can change her. Don't let her go. Not like this."

"I cannot." He thought of Livia. Of the serpent within. Sara was too weak, and he felt too much. He would go too far. He would fail.

And even if he succeeded, it was not what he wanted for her. The serpent. The horror. The never-ending battle within.

And yet...

He drew in a breath, felt a tear trickle down his cheek.

And yet he could not see her gone.

"What the fuck?" Doyle spat. "Cannot? The hell you can't. You're a goddamn bloodsucker."

"I cannot," Lucius said again, this time standing up and pressing a hand to his chest. "Countermeasures. One taste of human blood and the stake is triggered, and I must feed to turn her."

Doyle sagged. "*Fuck*. Goddamn fucking hell."

"There is a way," Lucius said, turning back to Sara and holding her hand. Her eyes were glassy, her grip weak. But her fingers moved beneath his. "Hold on," he said. "Hold on, my love."

"What way?" Doyle asked, and Lucius told him about the fail-safe, the mechanism by which the detention device could be released by either the prosecutor or Doyle inputting their authorization code back at Division. "Right. Of course."

"You will go?"

"Hell, yeah, I'll go."

He headed for the door.

"Ryan," Lucius said. "There is no time to drive."

He saw Doyle hesitate, and he saw the sharp jab of fear. Then Doyle glanced at Sara. He swallowed, then nodded. "Right," he said. "No time."

He turned then and faced the wall, his hands thrust out in concentration. The bones in his face seemed to shift, rolling beneath his skin, even as his eyes grew beady and red. His skin turned a pale orange, the color seeming to gather at his fingertips. He drew in a breath, then another, then whipped his arm in a circle, as if drawing upon the air.

In the wake of his hands, a hole opened, dark and black. He stepped inside, and the air mended itself, the hole disappearing.

"How long?" Lucius asked Tucker, who was staring slack-jawed at the place where his partner had disappeared.

"I have no idea."

Lucius bit back a curse and knelt again at Sara's side.

"Luke," she whispered.

He clenched his teeth together, determined that she would not see the tears threatening his eyes or the fear that coursed through his veins. The memory of Livia was so close to the surface, his failure with her as fresh as if it were yesterday. And even if he did not fail again, he could not protect Sara from the darkness that would be released. That, she had to battle on her own.

"Safe," she said. "With you ... I'm safe."

Her trust humbled him, and he thrust one hand into his pocket and pulled out Livia's ring. The reminder of how he'd lost control. The talisman that had soothed him before he'd found Sara. It would, he hoped, protect them both now. He slipped it onto her little finger, then clasped his hand over it as Sara struggled to breathe.

"Not long now," he said. "Not long, and you will be healed."

"Dark." A hint of panic tinged her weak voice. "It's getting ... so dark."

Fear stabbed at him. Where the fuck was Doyle? "Hold on, Sara. Don't leave me."

Behind him, Tucker paced, his phone plastered to his ear. "Where the hell are you?" Tucker shouted. He turned to Luke. "Now. He's doing it now."

Even as Tucker spoke, the band around Lucius's heart popped open. And as it dropped to the ground, Lucius leaned forward and sank his fangs deep into Sara's throat.

THIRTY

She was his.

Sara. Her blood filled him. Primed him. *Surprised him.*

It gave him life and strength even as he drew the same from her. He had to take her to the edge—right to the edge, and no further. Too far, and she would slip away, unable to be turned. But pull back too quickly, and she would never recover, alive but damaged from the loss of blood, the loss of this sweet, tangy life that he now drew from her veins.

This was the connection he'd craved. That the *Azag Mahru* had begged for, yearned for. The sharing. The connection. The blood. The serpent uncoiled as he fed, crowing with joy and need.

It wanted to consume her, to feel her life within him, to draw her to the surreal point of death and take and take and take some more.

"Luke," Tucker yelled. "That's enough. Luke! Pull back!"

Something tight and firm closed on his shoulder, but he ignored it, instead clutching Sara against him, her body trembling next to his, his mouth curved to her neck, the sweet smell of her skin filling him, arousing him. And the blood. By the gods, the taste of it, such sweet nectar that he would lose himself forever in the sweet, decadent delight.

"Luke! Stop!"

He could hear her heartbeat, its steady rhythm now spotty. Somewhere within, he realized he needed to stop, to pull back, and though he knew that, he couldn't do it. Couldn't push past the serpent. The lure of the blood was too intense, the pull of the darkness too strong. And then it was Sara inside his head, telling him to drink. To drink it all. To consume and live and glory in the allure of the blood.

Pater!

Pater, stop!

He froze. That voice—that cry of *father*—it belonged to Livia. His Livia. And the moment he realized that, his senses rushed back.

Sara.

By the gods, Sara. What had he done?

She was curled up in his arms, the beat of her heart almost indiscernible even to his ears. Her eyes glassy, her skin deathly pale. He'd almost taken her too far, but there was no time for self-recrimination. He bit down hard on his wrist, then pressed the wound to her mouth.

"Drink," he ordered. "Drink, Sara."

Despite his worst fears and premonitions, her lips closed over his flesh and she drank, her thirst strong and deep as life flooded back into her. As his blood warmed and changed her.

He held her tight as she suckled and said a silent thank-you to the gods and to the sweet voice of the child he'd once failed.

This time, he'd beaten the darkness—and Sara still lived.

She woke to pain and light dappled across a velvet darkness. Her body, sore and weak, was covered with beads of blood rising off long, slim cuts.

Concrete walls surrounded her. Above her, a ceiling with drilled holes.

And in the distance, she heard the low, harsh growl of a monster.

A sharp blade of fear cut through her as she realized that she remembered nothing. And the fear grew steadily stronger as slowly, ever so slowly, memory returned.

Stemmons.

Tasha.

Blood.

And Luke. Always Luke.

She shivered, remembering suddenly the way he'd thrust his fangs into her neck. The way her body had arched in response, the pull of blood strangely enticing, all the more so when she took from him, drinking and drinking until she'd collapsed beside him. Until she writhed in the agony of death, then stretched with the strength of rebirth.

She'd wanted this. Despite the fear, despite the unknown, she'd wanted it because it meant that she would be with Luke. That they would be together, forever.

Now, though, the fear was rising. She was trapped. Alone with a beast. Her beast. The *Azag Mahru*. The serpent. The darkness.

Dear God, what had she done?

Time to feed, Sara. Time to come out and play, play, play.

All around her, the room seemed to whisper. A soft female voice urging her to feed, to kill. Her whisper. Her voice. And as it spoke, the hunger rose within her.

She explored her mouth with her tongue, felt the tips of her fangs —and reveled in the burst of power that seemed to explode within her.

It's what you are now. It's who you are.

Nosferatu!

Vampyre!

Monster!

Kill! Feed! Live!

Each word struck as a blow, knocking her back, pummeling her flesh. "No!" She screamed the word, slammed her hands over her ears to shut out the voices and thrust her head between her knees to ward off the blows. But they were in her head—the words, the blows —and nothing she did would stop them.

That's the way. Hide, Sara. Hide and let me take over. Let me live. Release, release, release me and you will be free.

She tried to stand, dizzy from the voices battering her, her mind still fuzzy.

But she understood now. Understood that she couldn't push the voices away because they were within her. They were the evil—the serpent—and she was lost inside the Holding, with no way out.

She heard a whimper and realized it came from her. She didn't want to succumb. Didn't want to stay hidden down here. Didn't want the beast to feed while she cowered below.

But she didn't know how to stop it.

He hadn't told her how to fight.

"Luke!" she cried. "Luke, help me!"

This is all his fault. Stay away. Stay here. Stay down here and punish him for what he did to you. Easier, so much easier, to stay.

"No," she said, and then with more force. "No."

Coward.

Bitch.

Liar.

The words came at her like blows, knocking her off her feet. She fell, confused, then found a hand reaching down to help her up. "Luke?" She was safe. He was there. "Is it really you?"

He smiled at her. "I'm here to help you."

The Numen. It had to be. She nodded and let him draw her up. "Your *Azag Mahru* is blood and fear," he said. "Do not give that to her."

"But I'm so scared. And my body bleeds."

"Come," he said, and she melted into his arms. "Do not think about the pain." He laid her gently on the ground. From his fingertip, he drew blood, then traced it over her wounds. The skin knitted in his wake, leaving her tingling, her body suddenly awake and alive.

She realized with a start that she was naked.

"Pleasure," the Luke-Numen said, as his hand slipped down to cup her between her thighs. "Take pleasure from me. Take strength from me. And we will fight the serpent together."

His fingers had found her core, his mouth her breast, and she gasped, focusing only on Luke as the whispers around her grew louder, bolder. "Are you real?"

"I am as real as you need me to be." He flicked his tongue over her nipple, and a hot thread of desire shot through her, finding the finger that teased her clit.

"Please," she said, her hips bucking shamelessly. "Please take me."

"You need to go over," he said. "Do you see the walls?"

She turned her head, saw the walls of the room and realized that the ceiling had disappeared, replaced by a black sky, twinkling with stars. "Just get over the wall, and you'll be fine."

"How?" The walls were steep and slick and seemed to stretch up forever.

"I'll take you there," he said, and as he did, he thrust inside her, filling her.

She moaned, her hips rising up to meet him, wanting to take more and more of him in. It was a dream. A fantasy. She knew that.

She *knew* it. But it didn't matter. He was there with her. And with him, she could find that place, that path up to the top.

"That's it. Yes, yes, that's it."

She looked at him above her, the love in his eyes urging her on.

"Please," she said. "More. Harder."

"Dear gods, yes," he said, and took her, slamming into her, battering them both. She arched against him, eyes squeezed shut, desperate, so desperate to climb, to take all of him. To consume him, to be with him, wholly and completely.

She was climbing. So close. So close to the top.

And then over, over, over, over.

It came upon her fast, her body's surrender, and when she opened her eyes, she was warm and soft and curled up within his arms.

His arms. Not a dream.

Luke.

It was over.

And then she wept, his soft murmurs caressing her as the tears spilled out.

"How long?" she asked when she could speak again. "How long was I in that place?"

"A week," he said, wiping her tears. "But you're free now. And you're in control."

She closed her eyes and looked within, where the serpent was bound up deep. "Yes," she said. "I won."

She smiled up at this man she loved, and who loved her. "I knew you'd be there. I knew you'd help me through it."

"I was terrified that I'd lost you. That I'd failed you."

"Never," she said, pressing a hand to his cheek. "You saved me."

"You're spoiling me," Sara said, setting aside the biography of Augustus Caesar that Luke had brought her the previous afternoon.

"And I will continue to spoil you," Luke said, stepping into the room with a breakfast tray. "So I suggest you get used to it." He settled the tray over her lap. An English muffin, sausage, coffee, and a thermal mug filled with warm blood. Looking at it, she realized how hungry she was, even for the blood, which she'd discovered was surprisingly tasty. Or, perhaps, her taste buds had simply changed. So far, she'd sucked down liters of the stuff, with Luke assuring her that the thirst would wane as time passed, and she would not feel the need to feed at such regular intervals.

She took a sip, then turned her attention to the muffin as he sat on the edge of the bed beside her. "I'm not an invalid, you know."

His mouth twitched. "Have I been treating you as such?"

She recalled the vigorous sex they'd had the previous night, and had to concede that he hadn't. "It's been more than two days, though. Leviathan is going to think I skipped out on him."

"Two weeks off," Luke said. "And if my memory is correct, he instructed you to take it, or else."

That much was true. After the ordeal at the crypt, Ryan Doyle had apparently gone to Leviathan and explained what had happened. Following a brief review of Sara's notes and a short interview with Luke, the charges in *PEC v. Dragos* were dropped. In support of the dismissal, the PEC entered a stipulation formally outlining the facts as known. That Dragos's ward had not entirely prevailed during her Holding. That her *Azag Mahru* had broken free and was, as Ryan Doyle had once commented, clever enough to wait, silently watching the workings of their world even as the serpent became more and more entwined with the girl who'd become obsessed with having Luke all to herself.

She'd concocted a plan to force Luke to go on the run with her, and although no one knew for sure if Braddock had actually raped the girl, everyone was certain that Tasha had taken advantage of Braddock's past history. She'd gone to Luke hysterical, swearing she would kill the judge for what he'd done to her.

When she knew that Luke was going after the judge, she went first, attacking him and leaving him injured in the park. Luke found him like that, and if he'd had any hesitation about killing the judge, Tasha's actions had resolved that. Luke would not allow Tasha to risk punishment, and had stepped in to protect her, hiding her attack under his own DNA and going so far as to drain the last drops of blood from the already critically injured victim in order to frame himself.

"A decadent plot," the judge had said. "Maybe someday we'll know all the pieces to the puzzle." And Sara, who heard about the judge's words after the fact, had to agree.

The judge had signed the dismissal of the charges against Luke at the same time that he'd issued the warrant for Tasha's arrest. It was not a case Sara looked forward to prosecuting, because every day that Tasha was on trial would be another twist of the knife in Luke's heart. Another reminder of the depths of her betrayal.

"Has there been any word?" she asked.

"None," he said.

"There may never be any," she said gently. "She could be on another continent by now. And you can't keep me hidden in here forever."

His smile was small and sad. "You see too much now."

"I see you," she said. The bond between them had grown stronger since the change, but even without the new connection, she would have known what he was thinking. What he feared.

And known that there was something he wasn't telling her.

"Luke, what is it?"

He shook his head, then kissed her forehead. "We cannot close our eyes to the possibility that she'll try to harm you again."

That wasn't what was troubling him, but for now, she let it pass, instead offering him a smile. "Well, the price isn't too bad. I get to sit here in this incredible house and read books and be totally pampered. I've never really taken a vacation before," she said. "I honestly don't know what to do with myself."

She was gratified by his quick smile. "You're not vacationing," he said, stroking his fingers lightly up her arm. "You're recovering. And if you're at a loss for ideas, I'm sure I can think of one or two things to keep you entertained."

"Yeah? You want to show me?"

"Very much," he said. "But I'm afraid we'll have to wait. Right now you have a visitor."

"Really?" She wanted to ask who it was, but he'd already crossed the room and stepped out. A moment later, he returned with Ryan Doyle in tow.

"Well, look at you," Doyle said, a grin lighting his usually sour face. "You look a damn sight better than you did the last time I saw you. You doing okay?"

"I'm great," she said, happy to see the investigator. "Thanks for coming. And thanks for handling the wrap-up. Blair told me you talked Leviathan through everything. Smoothed out getting Luke's charges dropped.

He shrugged. "Least I could do, what with you almost dying." She noticed that he didn't look at Luke. Whatever trouble had brewed between them was still there. Perhaps, though, it had faded a little.

He was turning as if to go when Luke's phone rang. He held it to his ear, but with her newly sharpened hearing, Sara could easily hear both sides of the conversation.

"Pain, Lucius," Tasha said, her voice thick with tears. "And blood, so much blood! The serpent. It came out, Lucius, and I tried to fight it. Tried to do what you told me. Tried to be good, but it wouldn't let me." She sobbed. "It kept me under for so long. It kept me buried. It made me lie and hurt people. Hurt children! And it wouldn't let me find you."

"Tasha," he said, and Sara bristled at his low, calming tone. "Hush. Hush. It's okay. Everything's going to be okay. Where are you?"

"South. La Jolla. You'll come get me? You're not mad at me? I did bad things, Lucius. Naughty things. But it wasn't me. I wouldn't. I didn't, and I'm so scared now. Scared of me, and what's inside. We need to push it back again, Lucius. Please, please help me. Help me push the monster back under."

"I'll come get you," he said in that low, toneless voice. "I'll help you. You know that I will."

"Because Lucius Dragos takes care of what's his." Her voice was calmer, the relief palpable. "I'm yours, Lucius. I'm yours, yours, yours."

"That's right, Tasha," he said, with a hard look toward Sara. "Lucius Dragos takes care of his own."

The moment he hung up, Doyle rounded on him. "What the fuck are you doing?" he asked, voicing Sara's exact thoughts.

"Exactly what I have to," Luke said, his face hard and his eyes sad. "I'm doing exactly what I have to."

Tasha stood on the roof of the house across the street from Luke's Malibu mansion, miles away from the Los Angeles subway tunnels where she'd been hiding in grime and filth. A dark place, not right for someone like her. Someone precious. Someone extraordinary.

She tossed her arms out at her sides and let the breeze blow over her, causing the white gown to billow around her ankles. So soft. So pretty.

He should have wanted her. Should have taken her. And yet he'd never touched her. Never bit her lip and drew sweet, sweet blood. Never thrust himself inside her.

She'd played, though. She'd played with other boys' toys, and there'd been blood and teeth and glorious pain and their thick bodies filling her up, making her spread her legs and draw them in, and it was good and nice and she wanted it more and more and more.

But Lucius never saw it. Never saw her.

So now she had to show him. Had to make him see.

Needed him to prove he loved her. Prove he'd be with her always. That he'd take care of her.

That he truly did love her. Did, did, did.

Wasn't that why he killed that pasty-faced Braddock? Hadn't she planned everything just so?

Except she hadn't planned for the bitch. And the bitch had swooped in.

And now the bitch had Lucius.

He was *hers*. Not the bitch prosecutor's.

Tasha had tried to get rid of her. She'd learned about the murderous human the bitch had trapped in a cell. Formed her plan. Played the rescuing angel for the human, the one who was almost worthy. It was a good plan. A smart one. And she'd even gotten lucky when the vampire Caris had swooped into town, drawing Luke's attention away from the truth.

But still her plan hadn't worked. The worthy human was dead, and the bitch was in *her* house. *Her* bed. With *her* Lucius.

Not for much longer.

From where she stood, she couldn't see into Lucius's bedroom. But she could see the garage, and she felt a trill of satisfaction when the door swung open and Lucius's Mercedes purred down the drive-way, cleared the gate, and took off down the street. La Jolla was nearly two hours away. Plenty of time for a little talk with the bitch. Just girl to girl.

Getting in wasn't a problem. Lucius had changed the access code, of course, but she'd known his override code for a decade. Never bothered to mention that to him. Some secrets a girl had to keep.

The code worked as she knew it would, and Tasha was soon inside, the marble floor cool against her bare feet.

The bitch would be in the master bedroom. She'd be thinking that was where she belonged. There, in the bed, with Lucius.

She was wrong. Tasha would have to explain that to her. And as she climbed the stairs, she let the anger rise in her, the power that it gave calming her, making her strong, making her confident.

The bitch had changed, Tasha knew that, but a new vampire was weak after the Holding. Weak, that is, unless it emerged in harmony with the serpent. Then there was strength and power. So sweet. So strong. So very, very clever. Had to be clever. Let the serpent show, and bad things happened. Stakes. Blades. Had to hide inside. Had to be smart.

She climbed the stairs slowly, quietly, then padded down the hall to the doorway that stood open to Lucius's room. The bitch was there, sitting pretty in the bed, and she looked up, eyes wide with surprise at Tasha's presence.

"Tasha? I—are you okay? Luke just went—I thought he went to get you in La Jolla."

"Changed my mind. Allowed to do that, aren't I? Change my mind?"

"Sure." She shifted on the bed, one hand holding a book, the other under the sheet. "Ah, um, do you want to call him? Tell him you're here?"

"No, no, no." She took a step toward the bitch. Easy. Was going to be so easy.

"You know I'm prosecuting the Braddock murder, right?" The bitch's tone was chatty, and Tasha wanted to giggle. Death was in the room, and she didn't even know it. "I was wondering if I could ask you something. The detectives have some questions and—"

"Ask me no questions and I'll tell you no lies."

"Will you tell me the truth?"

"Maybe, maybe, if I like the question."

"What did Braddock do to you?"

"Bad man. Naughty man. Said things to me. Mean things."

"What did he say?"

"He insulted us."

"Us?"

"Me and I. I and me. We are we."

She almost laughed as the bitch frowned, trying to figure that out.

"Insulted the serpent you mean?"

She touched the side of her nose. "Clever, clever girl. But no prize for you. Clever girl's been bad. Took what didn't belong to her."

"Did Braddock touch you?" the bitch persisted.

"Wouldn't. Not at first. Told him to. Lucius wouldn't, so I told the judge to. He wouldn't, either. Said he was being good now, and no touching allowed." She smiled, thin and cold. "But I changed his mind. Told him what I wanted. All the naughty things in my mind. Told him, and touched him, and then he did them. Naughty and nice, and all for me. Do you want me to tell you, too?"

"No." The bitch frowned, as if she didn't like the story. "Luke went after him to protect you."

"Sweet, sweet Lucius," she said. "I got there first."

"Because you knew that Luke would cover for you. Knew that he'd put himself at risk for you."

"He loves me. Had to show me. I had to know." She took a step toward the bed. "So you see, he can't be yours. He's already mine. He always will be."

Tasha smiled, and drew a stake from the folds of her gown. "I think it's time to say good-bye now."

"I don't," the bitch said, and suddenly she didn't seem so small and vulnerable. Suddenly, she was up in the bed, a stake in her hand, too, and she had it aimed right at Tasha.

Tasha laughed. "You think you're a match for me? For us? Newly made against one so strong with the *Azag Mahru* inside?"

"No," the bitch said. "I don't."

"But I am."

Lucius!

He spoke from behind Tasha, having moved to her with lightning speed, the edge of his sword now pressed hard against her neck. She turned slowly, eyes wide. "Lucius ... Where—"

"Closet," he said, flicking his head only slightly to where he'd waited and watched and listened.

"But you went away. You drove off to get me. I saw you. I saw you leave."

Luke thought of the Mercedes with its tinted windows, and Ryan Doyle in the driver's seat. "Psych," he said.

She closed her eyes in concentration—then opened them again, surprised.

"Hematite sword," he said. "You're not transforming, Tasha. You're staying right here."

Fear colored her face, and he steeled himself. Remembering what she was. What she'd done. To Sara. To those murdered young girls.

"Lucius, no. Please. It's me. It's Tasha. You love me. You protect me. You watch over me. I'm yours, yours, yours."

"You are," he said, remembering the snowy night when he'd

succumbed to the horror of what he was—a night when he'd tried to find redemption for the death of his daughter in the immortality of this injured, traumatized young woman. His hubris had been dwarfed only by his pain, and he'd made a foolish choice, then compounded it by arguing so vigorously for special dispensation.

He'd looked at Tasha and seen Livia. He'd looked at her and seen life and love and the promise of a future without the pain of his errors hanging over his head.

He'd been a fool, and now they were both paying the price. And though it tortured him, he knew that now it was time to step up and do what he had not had the strength to do so many centuries before.

"You are mine," he repeated. "My child. My ward. My responsibility." And with preternatural speed, he swung the sword out and around, the razor-sharp blade slicing through the skin and tendon and bone of her neck. "You are," he repeated as the body collapsed to the ground. "And I do now what I must."

He closed his eyes, steadying himself, letting go of regret and loss and sadness. And then he looked at Sara through tear-filled eyes. "There will be no trial," he said. "No court. This is your justice, right here, rendered by my hand." He looked at her, saw the anguish in her face, and knew they'd reached a line across which Sara might not follow. "Can you stand for that?"

She looked from him to the lifeless body of Tasha, the child who'd been his surrogate daughter. The vampire who had betrayed him.

Then she moved across the room and pressed her hand into his. "I stand with you," she said, and relief poured through him. "And I always will."

Moonlight cascaded through the leaves, casting long shadows across the graveyard as Tasha's casket stood closed, ready to be moved into Luke's crypt. Sara stood by Luke's side as he looked down at the simple steel box, her fingers twined with his, so overwhelmed with love it took her breath away. She wished she could make this night easier for him, and at the same time, she knew that he had to do this. Had to say good-bye to the young woman he'd once thought to save, the young woman he'd once loved and protected.

"Not all of her was vile," he said, looking not at Sara, but at their reflection on the polished metal lid. "There were moments when it was truly Tasha under my protection." He shifted, then met her eyes. "I have to believe that."

"And you should." She thought of the girl he'd once described to her. A girl who'd danced on the beach and played with her dolls, and in her heart she knew that he was right. The real Tasha, that poor tortured child, was hidden somewhere beneath the serpent. "You freed her, Luke," she said, then blinked back tears. "No matter what else happened in that room, the Tasha you once loved is free now."

He pressed a hand to the casket, closed his eyes, then nodded. "I'm ready," he said after a moment, then stepped back from the casket.

She nodded to the men standing near the crypt door, and they came slowly—Nick, Doyle, and Tucker.

The four men lifted the casket, then carried it into the crypt, settling it into one of the stone sarcophagi. Nick stepped back, then pressed his hand to Luke's shoulder. "Shall we slide the stone into place?"

"Not yet," Luke said.

Sara started to follow the men out, but Luke held her back with a hand to the arm. "Don't leave."

"Never," she promised.

He reached over and lifted the lid on the coffin, and when he looked in on the girl, she could see the pain on his face, and tightened her hand in his.

"Luke?"

As she watched, he pulled Livia's ring from his pocket, then gently placed it on Tasha's little finger.

He turned to her, and she forced herself to speak through a throat clogged with tears. "You're certain?" He'd carried it with him for so long that she feared he would miss not having it in his pocket.

"I am," he said. "It's time."

Gently, she lifted her hand and placed a palm to his face, a warrior's face, strong and scarred, yet soft with love.

He had buried two children tonight—Tasha and Livia—and the pain he felt burned through her. Yet he stood tall and strong beside her. He would heal, she knew. They both would.

"Come," he said, taking her hand. And together they left the crypt and stepped back into the night.

EPILOGUE

"Are you nervous?"

Luke's soft words from behind made Sara jump, and she twisted around to smack his hand away with her pen. "No. Of course not." Hell, yes, she was nervous. "Now go sit down. You're supposed to be in the gallery, not at the bar."

"I believe, Counselor, that court is not currently in session."

No, it most definitely wasn't. She knew because she'd been stalking the halls of Division 6 for the past five hours, waiting for the jury on her first trial to come back. A demon who'd set up shop on the Internet, luring in aspiring actresses for screen tests, then using a specially manufactured camera to suck the life out of the human females as they read their lines. She'd been prepping the case for more than a month. The facts and the law were solid.

Now all that was left was for the jury to do its job.

According to Blair, the jury had finished, and the parties had been asked to return to the courtroom for the verdict.

Sara had been the first to arrive.

"There is very little more nerve-racking than waiting in a court-room for a jury's verdict," Luke said.

She lifted a brow. "And how would you know? You've avoided the courtroom in at least as many cases as I've tried."

He pressed a hand over his heart, his overly innocent expression making her laugh. "Counselor, I'm shocked. I don't know what you're talking about."

"I only wish that were so." But she was teasing as well. Over the

305

past several weeks they'd reached a tentative sort of truce. Luke stayed out of her courtroom—well, out of the defendant's chair, at least—and she wouldn't question what he did for the Alliance. What he did, she knew, to keep his own *Azag Mahru* at bay.

Nikko Leviathan pushed through the gate with a curt nod toward Luke. Sara shooed him away, then watched, exasperated, as he took his time moving out into the gallery to sit directly behind her.

Slowly, the courtroom filled, and when all the parties had returned, the bailiff—a skinny gremlin—announced the judge with a shrill, "All rise!"

The judge, a wizened old vampire who sipped blood during testimony from a plastic travel mug, took his seat, then asked the defendant to stand as the foreman read the verdict.

Sara held her breath, certain she could feel Luke's support wafting from behind her.

"Guilty."

Sara sagged with relief. Beside her, Leviathan offered a hand in congratulations, along with a hearty, "Good work, Constantine."

At the opposite table, the defendant snarled as the bailiff came forth with the shackles.

In the gallery, the applause was deafening, as all the prosecutors and staff from Sara's section celebrated her first trial—and victory—within Division 6.

She saw Blair flash a thumbs-up. She returned the gesture, but the man she was really looking for had already pushed through the crowd and was standing beside her at the table.

"You did good, Counselor," Luke said, laughing after she drew back from the kiss that she swore she wouldn't give him, not while she was at work. "Perhaps we should hit Probation before we go home to celebrate?"

She grinned, thinking back to that previous celebration that had led her into this world, and into Luke's arms. "I can't think of a better idea," she said, hooking her hand in his and tugging him toward the door, following the path her boss had taken.

She clung tight to Luke's hand as they walked back to her office. "You can't keep it from me forever, you know."

"What?"

She cocked her head. "Whatever it is you've been debating telling me ever since the night I was changed."

He closed his eyes, then shut her office door.

"Your blood, Sara. It's not entirely human."

She frowned, completely lost. "What are you talking about?"

"Vampire," he said, squeezing her hand. "Sara, my love, that is why they called you Abomination those years ago. Not because your father was marked a traitor. But because you were a vampire's child without a vampire's power. Thousands of years ago, before the PEC, the vampire community outlawed such unions. There were stories that such creatures had access to witchcraft. To magic that was mostly lost. But that was only a tale to cover the true reason."

"Which was?"

"They feared that the need to protect a child with no defenses would weaken the vampire even as he was needed to fight the Therian threat. It's a foolish prejudice, but it hung on."

She stared at him, wondering if this was some kind of a joke. But she could feel the truth inside him. "That's all very interesting, but my father wasn't a vampire."

"I saw the truth in your blood, my love. You're a dhampir. That is why you weren't susceptible to Tucker's mind games."

"I have powers?"

"None other than that. At least not that I'm aware of. Most dhampirs don't even have that."

She nodded slowly. "Except this doesn't make any sense. You're the one who drained him. If my dad was a vampire, you would have known back then."

"I know," he said, taking her hand. "And he wasn't. But your true father was."

"Oh." Her stomach twisted. "Do you know who..."

He inclined his head. "I do."

She started to ask, then realized she didn't have to. "Tiberius." She closed her eyes. "My mother was in London before she married my dad. And after the Alliance issued the order to kill Frank, he ordered you to watch over me. He wanted to make sure his daughter was safe." She closed her eyes. "My mother never told me."

"She probably only knew that she came home from a trip to London pregnant."

Luke was right. Tiberius would have sent her back without any memory of him.

"It might not be him. Maybe someone close to him. One of the kyne."

Luke shook his head. "No. All the kyne drink from their leader when taking the oath. I know his blood, Sara. Tiberius is your father.

Do you wish me to take you to London? Do you want to confront him? To hear his explanation? To tell him that you know the truth?"

She shook her head. "Not yet. He brought us together, and for that, I will always be grateful. But he never sought me out, and I already have a father. So, no. I have no use for him. Someday, perhaps, but not now." She met his eyes. "You will keep my secret? You won't tell him you know? Or that I do?"

"You know I will keep your counsel."

She drew in a deep breath, relieved.

"I am sorry that Frank wasn't your father. I know you loved him."

Her smile was thin. "He was my father. Blood can't change that."

"No," Luke agreed. "It can't."

"You were right, you know. Sometimes things really are gray. Especially in this world."

"They are considerably less gray with you in the world with me," he said. "Now, I live in the sunshine again."

She laughed, delighted, as she took his hand, this man she'd come to love beyond all reason. "But don't ever let me see you in the defendant's chair again."

His mouth curved up, his smile reaching his eyes even as his arms pulled her in. "Ah, Sara," he said, then brushed his lips softly over hers. "I promise, I'll never let them catch me. You, though," he added, his tone tugging at her heart, "you, darling Sara, have captured me completely."

THE END

I hope you enjoyed EMBRACE ME DARKLY. I would very much appreciate if you would spread the word and post a review at Amazon and Goodreads, along with sharing on your social media! As you know, reviews help authors tremendously!

Be sure to keep reading for an excerpt from Book Two, Torture Me Gently, followed by the entirety of Crave Me Roughly, Luke and Sara's prequel novella!

TORTURE ME GENTLY

Keep reading for an excerpt from Book 2 of the Dark Alliance series.

CHAPTER

ONE

The shadowed moon hung low in the Parisian sky, thin fingers of dark clouds obscuring its feeble glow.

Only seventy-two percent waxing gibbous. Not enough to wrench the wolf within free, but more than sufficient to wake it.

A dozen years ago, Rand wouldn't have known a lunar phase from a lunatic fringe. Now those phases burned in his blood, his power and strength growing with the moon.

Within, the animal writhed, ready to hunt. Ready to end this thing.

He made no noise as he followed the Avenue des Peupliers toward the Avenue Neigre in the Cimetière du Père Lachaise. On either side of him, the houses of the dead rose in the moonlight, their smooth stone surfaces gleaming.

He slid into the shadows and closed his eyes, letting the sounds of the night surround him, the scents find him. He'd been a soldier before the change, first on the streets of Los Angeles, later on foreign soil. A kid who'd protected his turf. A soldier who'd targeted enemies of the state.

He remained a hunter now. A wolf stalking its prey.

The change had intensified his senses and augmented his strength. Even in the dark, he could see with his own eyes instead of the night optics he'd trained with so many years ago. But this enemy could do the same, so the darkness gave him no advantage. But the moon remained his ally, and even at only seventy-two percent, he could hear the softest whisper, could catch the faintest scent. The brush of wind over wood. The scurrying of insects. The scent of rotting corpses.

There.

He opened his eyes, twisting his head as he caught the demon's earthen scent, like decaying leaves mixed with shit. He followed it, the excitement of the hunt burning in his gut as he stole down the cobbled street and then onto the narrow gravel lane that was the Champs Bertolie.

His muscles were tight and ready to pound the bastard, but he'd brought weapons with him, too. The Ka-Bar sheathed at his thigh. The switchblade in his hand. The length of wire he'd habitually kept in his pocket since the week before his ninth birthday. They were as much a part of him as the wolf that writhed within.

He'd dressed in black, his dark skin smeared with camo paint and his shaved scalp covered by black knit, rendering him nothing more than a shadow in the darkness. He heard the sharp snap of a grate creaking open and realized his target had entered one of the tombs. Rand sniffed the air—he'd lost Zor's scent. In its place, he smelled only fear.

Fear?

A hint of foreboding twisted in his gut. Even if the demon knew he was being tracked, he was too arrogant to fear Rand. Yet the scent was unmistakable. He tensed, realizing with sickening surety the source of the fear.

A female.

The fucker had abducted another female.

He hadn't heard that any more Parisian Therians had gone missing, but that was the only explanation. Zor had taken another, and now the female werewolf was trapped and terrified and possibly dying.

A cold rage sliced through him, so intense it threatened to overcome reason. He pushed it back, calling up his training to use the fury rather than be used by it. The scent led him north, and he moved silently, curving around the monument until he stood, back pressed to the stone, near a wrought-iron gate that acted as a door to where the dead rested within.

Another step, along with a slight tilt of his head as he peered around the corner, and he could see inside, his hyped-up vision making it easy to see the kenneled woman. Her eyes were rimmed in red, her lips pressed tight together as if she refused to give Zor the satisfaction of seeing her cry.

She was naked, and even from a distance, Rand could see the red welts on her back from where the demon had removed long strips of skin. Zor would pull off every inch, feeding on her pain until the flesh was gone and it was time to kill the woman and find a new one.

Five females. Six counting this one.

A muscle in his jaw twitched. There would be no more.

He checked his perimeter, finding no sign of Zor, then approached the cage.

"Non." The woman scrambled backward, eyes as wide as quarters.

"I'm not going to hurt you," Rand said in the woman's language. He studied her face but didn't recognize her. "Je suis un ami."

She remained in the corner, as far away as possible.

He crouched down and inspected the cage. Straw littered the floor, along with a tattered blanket and a dish filled with kibble next to a bowl of stale water. One lone water bug moved across the surface, disturbing a thin layer of grime.

After a moment of searching, he found the hidden hinges as well as the lock that kept the cage sealed. He tugged at the door, but it didn't give.

Apparently, he should have brought C-4 and a det cord, and left the Ka-Bar behind. He peered at the woman. "La clef?"

A hint of hope fluttered across her shell-shocked features. "Je ne sais pas."

Fuck. Most likely Zor kept the key on his person. Still, he scanned the small room, just in case.

Nothing.

Two ancient swords hung on the wall, forming a cross above a stone coffin. As Rand considered the blades' usefulness for freeing the woman, a new sound caught his attention. The rough scrape of stone against stone.

The woman's cry of "Monsieur!" filled the chamber as Rand spun toward his attacker, the switchblade extended and tight in his hand, as comfortable as an extension of his own body.

He sliced through the demon's shirt and knocked the bastard backward, but not before the demon grabbed the hilt of the Ka-Bar sheathed at Rand's thigh, taking the knife with him as he tumbled away. Zor's reflexes were sharp, honed from his recent feeding, and the monster sprang back to action almost immediately. Greasy strands of pure white hair hid his face as he crouched near the opening to the tunnel he'd come through.

"Running, Zor? Go ahead. You won't last long."

"Against you?" The voice was low and gravelly. "I'll barely have to strain myself."

"I wouldn't bet the bank." He was being arrogant, and he knew it. Unlike older weren, Rand couldn't intentionally summon the change that merged wolf and man, elongating his features, stretching his muscles, and turning him into a wolf-man that resembled the creatures from childhood horror flicks.

He changed only with the full moon, and when he did, he lost himself entirely, his body shifting into the form of a preternaturally strong gray wolf, his human mind lost inside the mind of the animal.

But even though he couldn't change at will, the wolf lived within him always, drawing power from the pull of the moon, and tonight seventy-two percent would do just fine.

Arrogant or not, Rand knew he wouldn't lose. The beast within wouldn't allow it.

Zor would die tonight, and Rand would savor the killing blow.

The demon seemed to hesitate, and for a second, Rand thought that Zor would bolt. He didn't. Instead, he attacked, leading with Rand's own knife.

Rand cut to the side as the beast lunged, the blade slicing through the back of Rand's shirt and the flesh of his shoulder blade. The wound was hot and deep and stung like a mother, but Rand ignored it. Not the time; not the problem. Instead, he rolled over, taking his weight on the wound as he kicked up and out, his heel intersecting Zor's wrist, forcing the son of a bitch to drop the knife, which skidded across the stone floor until it was lost in the shadows.

His own blood stained the blade now, and Rand could smell it—covering the steel, seeping into the floor, soaking his shirt.

He breathed in deeply, the scent and the pain rousing him, thrusting him into the warm, familiar black where nothing mattered but the kill.

He sprang up, determined to kill the demon right then. The demon might be older and stronger, but Rand was certain Zor underestimated him. In the ancient demon's mind, a werewolf barely twelve years into the change hardly posed a threat.

Sure enough, the creature leaped forward, wiry muscles propelling him high into the air. He lashed out on descent, his kick soundly intersecting Rand's chin. The blow sent Rand's neck snapping back, but he didn't falter, managing to snag the beast around the ankle and sending him to the ground.

Rand pressed the advantage. He lunged forward and slammed his knife through the demon's gut, releasing a gush of snot-yellow liquid through which ran thin strands of crimson blood, together but separated, like oil and water.

The scent of blood rose, and the wolf within Rand snapped and growled. But it wasn't the wolf who would take Zor. It was the man —and the animal inside him.

He leaned in close, hot breath on Zor's ear. "If I could destroy you six times over, I would, you twisted motherfucker." He gripped Zor tightly around the neck as he straddled him, his knees crushing into the beast's sides as he kept him pinned to the ground. "Six long, slow deaths for each of the females you tortured. Six trips to hell and back. Six times you would look into my eyes and know that I'm the one who brought you down."

"Destroying the mortal shell will not destroy me, you foolish animal." Zor's eyes filled with loathing. "You, however, will stay dead."

His body seemed to explode from within, the force of the assault tossing Rand backward and knocking the blade from his hand. Zor leaped to his feet, larger now, all sinew and muscles and taut, tight skin, his body as good as new. His eyes glowed a savage orange, and when he spat at Rand, the spittle ate a hole in his shirt. Acid.

Well, shit.

"Playtime is over, wolf cub. Time to die."

He charged, and Rand didn't even have time to wonder how he'd so quickly lost the advantage. He could only react. Could only trust his training and his strength and the cunning of the wolf inside. He spun out of the way, slamming his chest against the side of the tomb under the crossed swords. He reached up and grabbed them.

Rand couldn't see the demon behind him, but he could smell him, could feel the shift in the air, and without thinking, he extended the sabers at his sides, then whipped around, scissoring his arms as he did so. It worked. The steel sank into Zor's gut, too dull to cut all the way through, but it didn't matter. Rand had him now, and he used the force of the blow to knock the bastard backward.

Zor fell, his eyes wide with surprise, and he only had time to haul back and spit before Rand pressed his foot on the creature's forehead, held him still, and used the sword as an ax to chop off the creature's head.

"Told you not to bet against me, you worthless piece of shit."

Only after the head rolled to the side, eyes staring blankly, did he realize that a bit of the spittle's spray had landed on his face. Rand reached up and wiped it away, ignoring the acrid scent of burning flesh as he bent to pick up his switchblade. Then he turned to the woman, whose wide eyes contemplated Rand with an expression usually reserved for quarterbacks and MVPs.

"I'll get you out," Rand said. When a search of the demon failed to turn up a key, he lifted the head, jammed the blade of his knife into the back of the beast's throat, and then used the acid that spilled from the ripped salivary gland to eat through the lock.

The door swung open, and he took off his shirt and tossed it gently at her feet. She bent slowly, then put it on, the hem hanging down almost to her knees. She stood in the doorway of the cage, looking at him as if waiting for a signal.

Rand rolled the head across the tomb, out of sight. Then he retracted the blade. "Il est fini." He turned toward the door, then back to her when he realized she hadn't moved. "Allons-y. Vous êtes sûre."

Slowly, very slowly, she walked toward him, pausing a few feet away. "Mon mari?"

"We'll find your husband," Rand promised. "We'll go right now."

Her eyes flickered, as if trying to smile, and she reached for him, wanting comfort, but he wasn't the one to give it. He'd given her life; that would have to be enough.

Slowly, she lowered the hand.

"Let's go," he said, then saw her eyes widen with fear. In one motion, he turned, shielding her petite frame as he flipped open his blade. He let it fly toward the tomb's doorway, only to have it knocked aside by the strong arm of the man standing there.

"Have I been so poor a leader that you would seek to take me out with a blade to the heart?" Gunnolf asked. He reached down to pick up the knife, then slid his fingers along the blade's edge, drawing a thin line of blood. "A steel blade will render no permanent harm to a werewolf, lad. You know that, aye?"

"That was a warning," Rand said, inclining his head both in respect to his leader and to hide his amused grin. "But next time maybe you shouldn't sneak up after a fight."

"Aye. You have me there." He crossed to Rand in three long strides, his wild mane of fiery red hair more suited to a Viking than to a political leader. Not that the Alliance was a typical political entity. Nothing within the Shadow world was typical.

It had been Gunnolf who'd found him, confused and angry and changed. Gunnolf who'd fed him and sheltered him. Gunnolf who'd taught him what he now was—as much animal on the inside as he'd always been on the outside.

And it had been Gunnolf who'd given Rand a killing role in this new world, a role he understood and a part he could play with ease.

Gunnolf glanced down at the woman, who now stood behind Rand, clinging to his shoulders. "Do you know who I am, lass?" Gunnolf asked, compassion softening his sharp features.

The woman nodded, stepping close, finding the comfort with Gunnolf she hadn't found with Rand. "Oui."

"She needs to find her mate," Rand said briskly. "And she needs a medic."

"It will be done." Gunnolf pressed a hand to the woman's shoulder, then glanced down at Zor's body. He shot Rand an ironic smile. "You found the bastard, then?"

"I did."

The alpha turned slowly, taking in the tomb, the cage, the rank smell of death and decay with casual acceptance. "You took a hand to the matter yourself, I see," Gunnolf said, his meaning clear. Rand had gone after Zor without official sanction. Without Gunnolf's okay and without involving the Preternatural Enforcement Coalition, the organization with jurisdiction over all the Shadow creatures.

"Yes, sir. You wanted the problem solved, and I solved it."

"Aye," Gunnolf said slowly. "You did right." He paused, stroking his chin. "There is another matter. A delicate one."

Rand stood at parade rest, his hands at the small of his back in a long-practiced show of respect.

"There are not many I can put on this task," he said, shooting the woman a quick glance. Rand understood his alpha's shorthand. He was referring to the kyne, a secret group of warriors who did the bidding of their particular Alliance leader. "Of those I can ask, you are the one I want."

"Sure. Whatever you need." Gunnolf said nothing, and the heavy weight of dread settled on Rand's shoulders. He shook his head. "Oh, shit, no. Not that."

"I haven't asked."

But he had. Even in silence, Gunnolf was asking him to do the impossible. "The answer is no."

Gunnolf looked pointedly at the female. "Let us return the woman to her pack, and then we can discuss this."

Rand squared his shoulders. "Now."

Gunnolf's shoulders dropped, and for a moment Rand thought he'd pushed too far. Then Gunnolf lifted his chin, and though Rand saw compassion in his alpha's eyes, what he saw most was determination. This wasn't a request; it was an order.

"I have another job for you, Rand. I need you to return home."

TWO

Rand killed the Ducati's engine and leaned back, his feet planted on the asphalt as he balanced the bike and looked across the street at the puke-green apartment complex in the heart of Panorama City. Jacob Yannew was in there. Apartment 212, shared with five other Therians. A pack-dweller, unlike Rand, who chose to live alone, roam alone, hunt alone.

Right then, Rand needed Jacob alone.

The little shit was the reason Rand had come back to Los Angeles, the place to which he'd sworn never to return. "The wee devil's kept a low profile," Gunnolf had said, "but it's him who's telling lies behind me back. Stirring up old accusations."

Rand intended to find out why.

He pulled out his phone and opened the file on Jacob that Gunnolf's assistant had transmitted en route. He'd already memorized his target's stats, but he reviewed the information anyway, the rote action part of a familiar routine. Five foot two. Mouse-brown hair. One eye scarred shut, the result of a knife fight two years before he'd been changed.

Jacob Yannew had lived in the gutter before the change, and he lived there still, his days spent panhandling on the city's busy corners, and his nights spent roving the town, sucking down hard liquor at the various Shadow hangouts. He was a known snitch, willing to share any information he'd learned about his fellow Therians—hell, about any of the Shadow creatures—with anyone willing to pay his price.

Unfortunately, his snitch status went hand in hand with a reputation for being in the know. Recently, he'd started spreading rumors that Gunnolf was looking to wrest control of the LA territory away from Tiberius, his vampire counterpart in the Alliance. Specifically, that Gunnolf had ordered his men to kill humans, but to make sure the kills looked like the doings of a vampire.

Since the exact same rumors had been flying a few short months ago—and the issue was never fully resolved back then—this new amped-up rumor was getting serious play within the Therian community. So much so that some were starting to wonder if maybe it wasn't time for Gunnolf to step down as the Therian representative to the Alliance.

Someone was pulling Jacob Yannew's chain. Tonight, Rand would find out who. Find out, deal with the problem, and get the fuck out of LA.

Another fifteen minutes passed before Jacob emerged from the apartment building's main door. He slid into a battered Honda Civic that looked to be last millennium's model, then took off. Rand followed, easily tracking him as he maneuvered his way to the freeway, then over to the West side before pulling into the parking lot of a drab, gray concrete building tucked away on Pico. The sign gave him no information, the flicking neon flashing only *Or do*.

It was a Shadow bar, of course. The uninviting exterior meant to discourage anyone who wasn't already aware of the nature of the bar's most frequent clientele.

He parked, waited for Jacob to enter, then followed, pushing open the scuffed and filthy metal door onto which was stenciled *Orlando's*, the lettering surprisingly neat considering the rest of the establishment.

When he stepped inside, he realized that the inside of the place was clean and contemporary. And he knew immediately from the scent and the scenery that the place served two things—alcohol and sex.

Interesting.

He took another step inside and was stopped by a tall Black man with shoulders almost as wide as his own. Hell, they could have passed for brothers. Except that this man—in his red tee stamped with SECURITY—was clearly there to keep the peace. And Rand had a much different mission in mind.

"Help you?"

Rand glanced around, letting his eyes stop at the U-shaped stage atop which several scantily-clad women were dancing for the pleasure of the customers seated on the stools. The open portion of the U was blocked by a bar behind which a scantily-clad bartender mixed drinks with expert speed.

Slowly, Rand turned his attention back to Security. "Just stopped in to take the edge off. A drink. Maybe more. Depends on my mood. And what's on the menu."

Security looked him up and down, clearly assessing. "Don't get a lot of your kind here. How'd you find out about us?"

"I hear things. And I'm not here to cause trouble." *Not to the establishment, anyway.* He held his hands out at his sides, glad he'd made the decision to leave his Ka-bar in the car. "We good?"

Security studied him a moment longer, then nodded. "No cover tonight, but there's a two drink minimum."

"Not a problem," he said, then circled the stage. He'd already found his prey on the far side, sipping a drink and staring up the very short skirt of the dancer who was shimmying in front of him.

Rand slid into the seat next to him, his contempt for his prey rising when Jacob didn't note his presence. A fucking werewolf and he didn't catch the scent of a tail? Useless bastard.

He leaned over, then grabbed the area just above Jacob's knee, squeezing hard. "Jacob Yannew," he said easily. "I think we need to have a talk."

The little weren stiffened, and Rand worried he might summon the change. But this wasn't a Therian bar, and a few of the patrons were human. Which meant changing would not only be reckless and stupid, but also illegal. And Rand didn't think a weasel like Jacob had the balls to flaunt the system.

He stood, pulling Jacob off the stool and shoving him into one of the dark booths that lined the walls. "Sit."

"I want a whiskey," Jacob said, and Rand had to smile. It wasn't exactly backbone, but it was something.

"I want to be out of this hellhole," Rand said, sliding easily into the seat opposite. "But I'm learning to live with disappointment."

The bastard hawked up a wad of phlegm and spat at Rand. It missed his face—which was good for Jacob's overall life span—and landed with a wet splat on his collar. Rand wiped it away, his eyes never leaving his prey's.

"You know who I am?"

"I know you're in my face."

"I'm Gunnolf's," he said, and watched as the face crumpled. And then, almost as quickly, shifted back into snarling indifference.

"Good for you," Jacob said. "Now get the fuck out of my face."

"Not just yet." He leaned back in the booth, all cool and casual. "Word on the street is you've got a big mouth."

Jacob said nothing.

Rand frowned at the irony. "Maybe word on the street was wrong."

"Fuck you."

Rand leaned forward, his eyes never leaving Jacob's. "You've been spreading rumors about Gunnolf and dead humans. I want to know why."

"I don't know what you're talking about."

Fast as lightning, Rand lifted his foot under the table, then jammed it forward, closing the distance between them. His heel intersected Jacob's crotch, but he didn't slow, not until there was nowhere to go, and Jacob's puny balls were crushed beneath his heel.

He maintained the pressure and smiled congenially, the other bar patrons oblivious. "Talk," he said.

"You'll pay for this."

Rand ground his heel, saw pain rise in Jacob's eyes. "Maybe," he admitted. "But not today. Talk. Or never get it up again. Your choice."

Jacob spat on the table, but that was just posturing. As soon as Rand increased the pressure at Jacob's crotch, those malice-filled eyes lifted to meet Rand's. "You're howling at shadows, boy."

"Am I?"

"I'm not the one you want."

"Then who is?"

"Don't know."

Rand bore down with his heel, and Jacob's fingernails dug into the hard wood of the booth.

"Goddamn you, I don't. Older. Weren. Smelled like damp and moss. Only saw him the one time. Figured him for an Outcast," he said, referring to shunned Therians who betrayed their pack and were forced to live outside the formal shape-shifter community, their privileges stripped along with their money and even their identities. Known only as Outcast, the creatures were forbidden to interact in either human or shadow society, and any Therian caught interacting with an Outcast could be shunned himself.

Apparently that possibility didn't bother Jacob, who merely shrugged. "Old bastard paid damn good."

"When did you see him?"

"Weeks ago. He tossed a C-note into my can when I was working down on Hollywood. I noticed 'cause that kind of scratch makes an impression, and he was the only Therian I'd seen that day. I caught his scent, you know."

"He hung around? Talked to you?"

"Shit no. Was a message scrawled across Ben's face. Big black numbers all graffiti-like on that hundred-dollar bill."

"What numbers?"

"Phone number." Jacob rattled it off. "Said it was a pay phone. Found out later it's here. Back by the bathrooms." He lifted his scrawny shoulders in a shrug. "Was curious, you know? That's how I found this place. Sourced the call, then decided to come check it out. Not bad, right?" He held out his arms, as if to encompass the entire establishment, then nodded at a passing waitress, clad only in a filmy skirt and G-string. "And you can't beat the view."

"Tell me about the weren. He picked up when you called?"

"Sure did. Said he'd left instructions taped under a trashcan near where I'd been working the street. Found it. Did the job. Spread a few rumors. Never saw or heard from him after that."

"And the instructions?"

"Ripped up and flushed, just like he told me to."

"Name?"

"Not a clue."

Rand considered him, nostrils flaring as he took in the scent. There was fear and sweat, but nothing to suggest Jacob was lying. Considering the little weren valued his testicles, Rand figured he wouldn't risk a lie.

"Why?"

Jacob rolled one bony shoulder. "Figured he wanted to fuck with Gunnolf."

That about summed it up. Rand leaned back but didn't move his foot. "And did he have the scent of blood on him? When he dropped Ben Franklin into your can?"

"You mean is he killing the humans? Don't know; don't think so."

Rand cocked his head. "Why not?"

Jacob looked him hard in the eyes. "Wasn't the scent of blood I caught on him. Was the scent of vampire."

It was the most interesting revelation that Rand was able to extract, despite ten more minutes of ball-crushing interrogation. Interesting because vampires and weren tended not to mingle—at least not unless the mingling was laced with fighting.

"Go," Rand finally said, moving his boot down to the ground.

Jacob's face twisted, and Rand was certain the little weren was biting back a burning desire to fire off a stream of insults. Wisely, Jacob kept his mouth shut, then left through the front door.

Rand waited a moment, then rose, too, Jacob's scent still plenty strong to track. He tossed back the rest of his drink, then slid out of the booth. He moved casually, once again letting his gaze drift over the place, wondering if the Outcast was there right now.

He glanced around the space, then looked up toward the offices. The moment he did, he took an involuntary step back, overwhelmed by the sensual punch to the gut that hit him the moment his eyes met hers.

She was exquisite, her body held straight with an attitude of command, in charge of the very air that filled the place. He knew that because she took his breath away.

The golden waves of her hair seemed to absorb the light, and he could easily get lost in her pale blue eyes, the same color as his Aunt Estelle's favorite curtains. His entire life had been asphalt and camouflage, not blues and golds, and right then, he wanted nothing more than to stand there and simply watch her.

She was looking out from the huge office window, and her eyes had held his only for an instant. And yet it had been enough to cause all of his cells to sing.

He wanted to go to her. To feel her voice wrap around him. To lose himself in her touch. The desire disturbed him. One glance at a beautiful woman didn't usually make him hard, and yet this woman had undeniably gotten under his skin.

That wouldn't do.

Regretfully, he turned his attention to the nearest dancer on the bar, a beautiful girl who was nothing compared to the woman in the window. With a low growl of frustration, he slipped a twenty into the dancer's g-string. Then he moved with purpose to the exit. He needed to get away from the woman.

He needed to do his job.

He felt clearer once the night air hit him, and he paused to find Jacob's scent, then increased his pace, coming up behind the clueless little worm on the next block. He rushed forward, and in one swift motion, he clasped his left hand over his prey's mouth, then yanked the disloyal, backstabbing asshole back into the shadows.

Jacob tensed in his arms, trying to summon the change.

But there wasn't time. Rand's knife was already at his temple, and with one quick thrust, he drove it home.

Jacob crumpled to the ground, and Rand turned and walked away, letting the darkness swallow him.

Lissa stood behind the the glass that made up an entire wall of her private office and looked down over the successful club she'd built over so many years.

But it wasn't the dancers or the Art Deco bar stools or the efficient movements of her security team that she was looking at.

It was a man. Or, more accurately, it was the memory of a man.

Only minutes ago she'd seen him. He'd been standing by the stage, his head turning as he looked around the space. She'd watched, noticing the hard angles that dominated his face, the only softness around his mouth. His smile was probably dazzling, but the harshness in his eyes suggested that he didn't smile often.

His scalp was shaved, and except where the light touched his dark skin, he seemed to melt into the shadows. He radiated mystery and power, and considering the types of creatures who frequented her club, Lissa had to admit that was saying something.

She knew immediately that he was weren. There was no mistaking the wolf inside him. It was there in the deliberate way he watched the room and the muscular grace with which he moved.

As if he'd felt her watching him, he'd lifted his head. His eyes had met hers, and she'd seen the restrained beast staring back with animalistic hunger. She'd actually gasped aloud, fighting a tug of sensual pleasure so intense and unexpected that she'd had to look away, then wipe her damp palms on her linen slacks before stepping away from the window.

Her reaction confused her. Anger that he could create such a weakness inside her warred with a secret excitement. It was the nature of a succubus to entice, and with each rebirth, succubi were trained not to feel lust. A succubus desired the soul—it was her life, her nourishment, and her most intense pleasure.

It was the soul, not the man, that enticed.

That, at least, was usually true. Tonight though, it had been the man himself who'd pushed Lissa's buttons. And that made the weren male both intriguing and dangerous.

But Lissa had never shied from danger. Now, she lifted her chin as she returned to the window, intending to meet his look with one of her own. The kind backed with all the power of her nature and targeted to bring a man to his knees.

He was gone.

She'd frowned, his unexpected absence troubling her as much as his presence had.

Intellectually, she knew that some males were immune to the sheen of the succubi, but she had never met such a man, at least not that she remembered. For that matter, there was no reason to think that this man was impervious. She wasn't close enough to him to have any sort of real effect, and she hadn't even tried to ramp up her charms.

But he'd looked at her as though she'd turned it on full throttle— and then he'd walked away.

Just as well. She didn't want to know a man who could walk away from her despite that heat. A man like that was danger. A man like that could wrest control right out of her hands.

She tapped a finger on the back of a chair, undone by a sudden desire for a cigarette, not to mention the urge to go downstairs and look for him.

Instead, she focused on Anya, the fragile, dark-haired beauty who was strutting her stuff with confidence, her allure cranked up high and working its magic on the slack-jawed men at the table, who wanted nothing more than to hand Anya both their money and their souls.

The girl was the newest addition to the club, and Lissa had risked more than usual to get her here. Still, she'd do it all over again if she had to.

As Anya danced, Lissa surveyed the five males closest to the stage —two demons, a jinn, a Therian, and a vampire. She ruled out the vampire and the demons immediately. Their souls were buried too deep. Anya's week had been stressful enough. Tonight she needed an easy hit. The shape-shifter, she decided.

"Marco," she said, speaking into the microphone that led into her security chief's ear. "When the set is over, tell Anya that Customer Three is hers. The taking room's available whenever he's ready." She cast another glance toward the girl. Despite Anya's smile, Lissa couldn't help but notice the worried way her eyes kept darting to the front door.

Fear. Anya was afraid he'd come after her.

Lissa shivered, understanding the girl's concern. Hell, the thought made her tremble, too, and once again she cursed herself for not being more careful. She'd let her temper and her concern for Anya fuel her actions. But there were better ways. More subtle ways.

Ways that wouldn't potentially return to bite her in the ass.

Still, what was done was done, and now Anya was one of her girls, deeded to Lissa fair and square. But her former master hadn't done it happily, and now the girl was afraid of reprisals. That wouldn't do. Lissa was willing to shoulder the fear for both of them. Anya deserved to finally have peace.

She spoke again into the microphone. "Tell the E Team to fully credit Three's account, but not to perform the extraction."

On the floor, she saw Marco tap his earpiece, then tilt his head up to look at her. "Say again, Sparrow."

"I want Anya to keep as much soul as she takes," she clarified, knowing firsthand the sense of peace that came from absorbing and retaining a decent-sized piece of soul.

Confusion flickered over Marco's face, and Lissa understood why. Normally a girl would entertain the client in the taking room, pulling bits of his soul into her while the male enjoyed the pleasure of her company.

Later she would slip away to the basement, where the E Team would carefully withdraw the fragments of the client's soul, leaving the girl only the nourishment that kept her strong and very nearly immortal. The client paid for the privilege of lying with one of the girls, but also got house credit for the amount of soul tendered.

Then Orlando's would sell the souls on the open market, usually at a nice profit.

So for Lissa to tell Marco not to perform the extraction went entirely against her business model. But to his credit, he didn't ask for an explanation. Orlando's was hers, after all.

She'd sure as hell earned it.

As far as she knew, no other succubus had managed to buy her way out of the cortegery, the court of succubi owned by a particular trader. And certainly no other succubus had managed to scrape and claw her way to becoming a trader herself. One who owned a licensed, bonded, and sweetly profitable soul-trading enterprise.

Then again, as far as she knew, no other succubus had Lissa's particular skill set—a dangerous gift, and one she guarded closely, but used when she had to. When it was important. When it tilted the balance in favor of her girls.

Like it had with Anya.

As she watched Anya work, Rhiana—Lissa's closest friend and the senior girl working the floor—cocked her head toward the shadowy area in the front of the club where people tended to pause or mingle before making up their minds to head to the booths or to the bar stools by the stage.

Lissa peered into the dark and saw immediately what had troubled Rhiana—two clusters of bristling males, standing too close together to be friends, the tension between them so thick she could feel it even from her office. Even behind the glass.

Three vampires about to face off against three werewolves.

Not in her club they weren't.

She grabbed her jacket from the brass-and-ivory rack and slid it on as she crossed to the door, her heels clicking on the polished wood floor. Given the gang wars that frequently sprouted up between the fangs and the furs, vampires getting in the face of werewolves was not a good thing.

By the time she reached the club level, Marco had shifted his post to a few feet in front of the males. He wouldn't interfere—he knew better than to ever interfere without her specific signal—but his presence was sufficient to cause the two clusters to break apart. Good.

She glanced around the club, ensuring that the tension that had sparked in that corner hadn't tainted the overall mood of the place. As far as she could tell, though, none of the patrons had noticed the brewing trouble.

None, that is, except one.

Him.

He was standing next to the stage, but if he was interested in the dancers, he showed no sign. Instead, his attention was entirely on her, and she felt the sensual pull all the way down to her core, a raw, delicious feeling that she rarely experienced, mostly because she never let herself relinquish control.

She hadn't relinquished it today, either. He'd taken it. And that reality tempted her almost as much as it scared her.

He was walking toward her, moving with slow, easy steps as if he had all the time in the world, and every right to take it. When he reached her, his expression was flat, but she thought she saw just the hint of a smile in his eyes.

"Nice place," he said, looking only at her.

"We strive to keep the customers satisfied."

He took a step closer, and she caught his scent, dark and woody and utterly male. "Do we?"

Her breath hitched as he tilted his head to the side, the angle enhancing the feral quality that clung to him. He was watching her like prey. Like a conquest. But she wasn't a prize to be won. Not anymore. Not ever again.

"Your guard handled that situation well."

For a moment, she didn't understand, then realized he was talking about Marco deflecting a potential vamp/weren scuffle. "Friends of yours?"

"No."

She lifted a brow. "So you didn't come to babysit the young pups like Yannew?"

He tilted his head, his eyes narrowing. "You've been watching me."

"I watch everyone."

His eyes skimmed over her as he spoke, and damned if she didn't feel that sizzle up her spine. That arousal that signaled a loss of control. And Lissa had no intention of losing control. Not with this man. Not with anybody.

She flashed her hostess smile. "Perhaps you're here for happy hour?"

"That depends on how happy you're going to make me."

She ignored the way his words worked on her, easing over her like warm honey, overflowing with sweet promises. Instead, she forced herself to take them at face value. He was a client and he was in her club and what he wanted was perfectly clear. They were negotiating now, and that she could handle.

With a broad gesture, she laid the club out at her fingertips. "Let me take you around. I'm sure we can find a girl that pleases you."

She took a step, but he stopped her, his hand closing over her forearm. The shock of his touch ricocheted through her, and she took a second to adjust her expression before she turned back to him.

"I'm already pleased." Once again, his eyes took her in. This time, though, they traveled slowly, his inspection as intimate as a caress.

The hot gaze moved over her breasts, then slowly, so slowly, down to her thighs.

Lissa forced her voice to stay steady, determined to keep a businesslike demeanor. "I'm flattered, but I'm the owner."

"And?"

"I have a very limited clientele."

"Really?"

He wasn't making it easy. For that matter, she wasn't making it easy. Her thighs tingled in anticipation of something that was not going to happen, and she felt a bead of sweat drip down the back of her neck. She reached up to wipe it away, her fingers brushing over the quarter-sized scar just beneath her hairline, a reminder that in Orlando's, she was the one in charge.

She straightened her shoulders. "We have policies, Mr...?"

"Rand. Vincent Rand. And policies can change. It's your club. That's a perk of being the boss. You can do what you want."

He had a point. But no. Absolutely no. And not because it was bad precedent, and not because she had another client engagement lined up; she didn't.

No, she was turning him down because of the way he made her feel. Just being near him was like approaching a charged fence, as if her body could sense the hum of power even before she touched it. He was as dangerous as that fence, too. Touch him, and she wouldn't be able to let go. Grab on to him, and his heat would burn her straight through.

This was lust, plain and simple, and that wasn't acceptable. So what if he looked at her with heat in his eyes? What man didn't? Of course he wanted her—her nature, her raison d'être, was to be an object of desires. But that didn't mean she had to fulfill those desires, not when another one of her girls would serve that purpose just fine.

"I am doing what I want, Mr. Rand," she said firmly. "Let's go find you another woman."

Surprise crossed his features, and she felt the thrill of a minor victory. Apparently, he was a man used to getting what he asked for.

"I want you," he said, and she fought an unexpected rush of pleasure.

"And if I don't want you?"

He pressed a hand to his chest. "I think that would break my heart."

With her most seductive smile playing on her lips, she leaned forward and caressed his cheek. "I guess you'll have to learn to live with disappointment."

Visit Amazon to grab your copy of Torture Me Gently in digital format, or your favorite vendor to order it in print!

And keep reading for Crave Me Roughly, the prequel novella to Luke and Sara's romance!

KIRA JAMES

CRAVE ME ROUGHLY

A DARK ALLIANCE NOVELLA

CHAPTER

ONE

"I hate you," Petra Tsang said, her always-gloved hand tucking a long strand of dark hair behind her ear before lifting her martini glass. "I mean, just look at you. Career taking off while I'm trapped in my little office."

"You love your job," Sara countered. "And you're good at it."

"Hell yeah, I am," Petra retorted. "But you deserve some serious accolades. Co-counsel on a trial with the District Attorney himself? I am so freaking proud of you. Hate-proud, don't get me wrong. But still proud."

Sara Constantine bit back a laugh and lifted her own drink—two shots of Maker's Mark with one oversized ice cube. She clinked glasses with her bestie, then took a sip. "Hate-proud. Got it. I can live with that." She sighed happily. Alexander Porter was one of the best District Attorneys in the country, and he'd hand-picked Sara to second chair the high-profile murder trial of one of LA's most notorious drug dealers.

Petra reached for the last street taco from the plate they'd been picking at for the last hour. She paused long enough for Sara to nod consent, then took the thing. "I could live off these," she said.

"You practically do."

"I'm a woman of simple needs," she said, which made Sara laugh again. Petra was about as high maintenance as an A-List actress on Oscar night, and not just because she was such a germaphobe. "Incoming," Petra said, nodding across the dimly-lit bar.

Sara turned so that she could see the front door of Probation, the slightly divey bar in downtown Los Angeles that was a regular gathering place for the local legal crowd. "Don't call him over," she said as Dan Cummings stepped over the threshold.

"No? I thought there might be a thing brewing between you two. Or are you saving yourself for your stalker?"

Sara lifted one eyebrow, a trick her father had taught her before he'd died, then gave her friend a long, cool stare.

"Oh, don't even," Petra said, totally unintimidated. "We both know you're intrigued."

"Curious, maybe." That was as close to an admission of interest as she was willing to make about the tall, gorgeous man with dark hair and broad shoulders. She'd seen him watching her on four different occasions. Most recently last Thursday when she was walking to a friend's downtown condo to crash after staying at work well-past midnight. Then two different times within the last few months after leaving Probation alone at closing time.

The first time had been just over a year ago when she'd gone home with a corporate attorney after a shitty day where the jury had come back with a not-guilty verdict for an obviously guilty drug dealer. She'd only been a few months into her job as an Assistant District Attorney, and the corporate lawyer had sat by her at the bar and listened to her run the case over and over, trying to pick out where it had gone wrong. She'd been second chair to a more senior prosecutor, so she knew it wasn't her burden to shoulder. But damned if it hadn't felt that way.

Corporate had let her vent, and she'd returned the favor. He'd had a crap day, too—some decision had come down that cost his client millions. Then he'd invited her to his place, and she went because they'd wanted the exact same thing: one night, no strings, and minimal conversation.

She'd noticed the dark-haired god of a man in a shadowy doorway, his eyes following her. After that, she hadn't seen him again for almost a year, but his face had remained etched in her memory.

As for Corporate ... well, she couldn't even remember his name.

"It really doesn't freak you out?" Petra asked. "This guy watching you?"

"A little," Sara said, not meeting Petra's eyes.

Her friend frowned, seeing through the lie. "You need to stop," Petra said, her voice firm.

"I don't know what you're talking about," Sara said, knowing *exactly* what Petra was talking about.

"Bullshit. You're a brilliant attorney, but you do stupid things. Going to bed with guys you pick up. Not calling this stalker out. You think I don't get it? It's me, remember? I've known you since college. And we both know that you get a little thrill thinking about the possibility that Mr. Shadow Stalker might be dangerous. Because then every time he doesn't slit your throat—every time some random guy you fuck doesn't hurt you— means you beat the bad guy who killed your father."

Sara's entire body had gone tense, but she kept her voice level. "And you've been a shrink how long?"

"What? Now you're mad at me? I'm just saying it out loud. You know it's true." She tilted her head. "If you get a pic or point him out sometime when we're together, I can check him out."

Sara stayed silent, considering it. As a private investigator, Petra could do exactly that. But for some reason, that just didn't sit right. "He probably just lives around here," she finally said. "It's probably not even about me. Coincidental sightings. Totally random."

For a moment, Petra just stirred her drink, and Sara steeled herself for another lecture. Then her friend sighed and shrugged. "Or, who knows, maybe he just wants to ask you out."

Sara drew a breath, the tension easing out of her body. Of everyone in her life, Petra was the only one who seemed to truly understood what haunted her. Who, for the most part, didn't judge when Sara lashed back at the darkness that had hung over her since she was eight years old.

"Yeah, maybe he just wants a date," Sara said. "Maybe he's outside right now, trying to see me through Probation's etched glass windows." The possibility was undeniably enticing.

"There's always Dan," Petra said. She flashed a wicked smile. "I mean, I can totally see inviting him home to help take the edge off."

"Right?" Sara said, even though she knew Petra was just posturing. Her friend had a skin condition that bothered her so much she wouldn't even let Sara see what Petra kept hidden. So no matter how much Petra might talk like someone who'd take a guy to bed for no reason other than to release that pent up pressure, they both knew that wasn't going to happen. Not by a long-shot.

But Sara? That wicked edge burned in Sara's core, sharp and bright and dangerous. And, yeah, sex really was the best way to shut it down. The fastest, cleanest way that Sara knew to clear away that darkness that Petra saw but didn't truly understand. A darkness that always seemed to be seeping inside, getting into her head. Making her antsy until she craved an escape. One night, hot and hard, working things out. Opening up her head and taming that itchy, demanding need so that maybe—maybe—she could hold back those encroaching shadows for one more day.

But no matter how hard she tried, she never fought it back completely. It gave her an edge as a prosecutor—she knew that for sure—but that didn't mean she liked it.

"Oh, Danny-boy," Petra continued, her voice low enough not to carry, but plenty loud to irritate Sara. "Come over here, you delicious hunka-hunka man."

"Stop it."

"What? He can't hear me."

"Just drop it, okay? Dan's a great guy. But he's not *my* great guy."

Petra tilted her head, studying her. "Does that matter?"

Sara peered into her drink, both hating and appreciating how well her friend understood her. "Usually, no." She looked up to meet Petra's steady gaze. "But Dan's a friend. Not a good idea."

She meant what she said. She liked Dan. He was smart and funny, and he'd left a corporate career to become a public defender, something she admired even if her own passion was prosecuting the bad guys. But she wasn't looking for a fling with a friend, and she definitely wasn't looking for a relationship. And even if she were, Dan wasn't ... well, he just *wasn't.*

"I guess you can tell him that yourself." Petra said, with a glance toward the front of the bar. "And this is *so* not my fault."

Sara turned to see Dan push a lock of cornsilk blond hair off his forehead as he walked toward them.

"Busted," Petra said under her breath as Sara forced a smile and waved.

"Can I join?" he asked once his long strides had brought him to their table.

"Sure," Sara said, putting two twenties on the table. "But I was just leaving."

"Whoa, whoa, whoa," Petra said. "I thought I talked you out of—"

"*Petra.*" Before their food had arrived, Sara had told a very disapproving Petra that she planned to go meet with a witness tonight. Considering that the witness had come out of nowhere, Petra's concern was understandable, especially when Sara had brushed off Petra's offer to go with her. "I'm a PI, remember? Meeting mysterious witnesses is part of my job description. And you need backup."

But Sara had been steadfast. The wit had reached out to her, then convinced her he was legit by sharing details of a crime that hadn't been released to the press. A crime wherein four teens had been found in the storage room of an abandoned convenience store, their necks ripped open. Which was a crime about which Sara was very, very interested.

Once he'd cast his line and hooked her, he'd insisted she'd come alone. For a moment—one brief moment—Sara had almost told him to go to hell. But she hadn't. She needed answers.

So, yeah, Petra was right to disapprove. But Sara was going anyway.

"Hot date?" Dan asked, his easy smile doing little to hide his disappointment.

"No. Just work. A witness who keeps crazy hours." She stood. "I'm sorry, but I really can't stay."

"Come on, Sara," Petra pressed. "It's late."

"It's all good, Pet. I'm going to a Starbucks. Totally safe." She didn't mention that the Starbucks was right next door to the crime scene, and that her witness was going to take her down there. Nor did she mention that the guy technically wasn't her witness at all.

Petra shot her the kind of glare that in a superhero movie would have sliced through steel. Sara held her breath, willing her bestie not to call her out to Dan. Because she had to go. It was more than the crime. More than a potential prosecution. It was her life. Her past.

Her father.

And, yeah, she knew perfectly well that there was no way that whoever killed those kids could have murdered her dad. But the M.O. was the same, so of course she had to go. Because seventeen years of not knowing was killing her.

"—a chat and—"

She shook her head, pulling her thoughts back to the present as she realized that Dan was talking. "I'm sorry. I got distracted thinking about this case." Out of the corner of her eye, she saw Petra glare. "What were you saying?"

"Just that it's too bad you're leaving." Dan smiled, and she had to admit he was a good looking man. "I was looking forward to a drink and chat. With the both of you," he added, tossing Petra a polite smile that fooled no one.

"Maybe some other time," Sara said, thinking it was a shame that she didn't mean it. After all, Dan was an excellent attorney and easy on the eyes.

She stifled a sigh. Maybe she did need to stop this—not trying to learn about her dad's killer; no way was she stopping that—but overlooking potential long-term men because she was too busy seeking out the one-night, penis-enhanced version of an intense therapy session.

She had issues. She knew that. But at the end of the day, it wasn't about her terrible childhood trauma or her emotionally distant mom or the memory of her father on the sidewalk, blood pooling around him from the puncture wounds on his neck.

It wasn't about any of that psych stuff that therapists used to weigh you down.

No, it was about the job. About justice.

There were monsters out there. Murderers. Rapists. Drug dealers. They hurt people. Stole lives. Destroyed families. Sara knew that better than anyone.

She didn't need a relationship. She needed retribution. Justice. *Closure.*

And with every lowlife she put away, she came one step closer.

She didn't need to a full-time guy in her life.

All Sara needed was her job.

Luke answered his phone on the first ring, certain it would be Serge. "Tell me."

"You were right, "Serge said. "She's got something planned. Meeting a witness at a Starbucks."

"Did she notice you?"

"Of course not. Besides, why would she notice me? You're the one who got yourself tagged."

"I don't know that for certain," Luke said, though he suspected it. He'd been foolish. Stepped out of the shadows only once to get a better look. She'd turned, met his eyes, and the recognition on her face startled him.

He hadn't told Serge about that when he'd asked his friend to watch Sara tonight. He hadn't wanted to admit that it was possible that Sara had actually clocked him more than once. That Luke had been so enraptured by her that he'd been foolish. Careless. That he'd risked everything by almost getting seen.

"Where's this Starbucks?" Two months ago, she'd met with a witness in Inglewood. No, not a witness, because the stoner she'd talked to had no part to play in any case being investigated or prosecuted by the local authorities. She'd gone on her own, following some lead she'd turned up herself, completely oblivious to the danger she was circling. A danger much more potent than anything associated with a simple murder.

Her father's murder had been anything but simple.

Most egregiously, she'd gone alone, and it had taken every ounce of Luke's strength not to reveal himself to her. Hell, not to take her by the shoulders, stare into those beautiful green eyes, tell her what a damn fool she was being, and then cut off her inevitable protests and questions with a long, hard, claiming kiss.

Every ounce of his strength.

One day, he'd lose that battle. One day, he'd reveal himself.

God help him, he wanted to.

He squared his shoulders and forced his mind back to task. "Serge? Which Starbucks?"

"Didn't say."

"Who was she talking with?" Luke asked. "Petra?"

"And that public defender. Cummings."

Luke cursed under his breath. Dan Cummings had been inching closer to Sara for more than a year now, and he feared that the attorney would one day break through her defenses. Just the thought made him growl, the sound low and rough in his throat.

Serge chuckled. "Tell me how you really feel."

Luke ignored his friend. "She's going somewhere dangerous. Otherwise she would have told them."

"Or she thought it was irrelevant."

"I'm not taking the risk. Follow—"

"Follow her. I know. Trust me, by now I now this drill."

"She's my responsibility."

"And that makes her mine as well. But is this truly about responsibility? Because by my count, Sara's a grown woman now. Your obligation to watch over her ended years ago."

"Sergius..." There would be no mistaking the dangerous tone in Luke's voice.

"Fine, fine. I'll follow her. You know there is nothing I wouldn't do for you, brother. But that doesn't mean I'm wrong. You need to take a step back. Get some distance. She isn't your problem or your responsibility. Not anymore."

"Isn't she?" The words came hard, full of bitterness tainted with a growing, familiar rage.

"If Tiberius finds out, it won't be pretty. We both know that. You might even find yourself facing a Shade. Or perhaps that's what you're hoping for. They take your memories of the girl, and they take all the pain and guilt along with it."

Luke's blood surged as his temper rose. "Do you truly think I'm so weak that I would want those memories gone?"

On the other end of the call, Serge hesitated, his voice low and serious when he finally spoke. "I'll keep her safe."

"Good. Go. I'll catch up to you," he added, unable to shake an unwelcome sense of impending danger. And then, before Sergius could argue or push Luke's buttons anymore, he ended the call. He slid the cell phone into his back pocket, then left his study. He found Melton in the kitchen, engrossed in a recipe book featuring pastries of every kind imaginable.

"You never cease to baffle me."

Melton looked up, his eyes wide with surprise, his bristly gray hair sticking up as usual. "Sir. I didn't hear you come in."

Further proof that his butler-house manager-executive assistant had been fully absorbed, lost in a world drenched in confectioner's sugar and creamed butter.

"I hope you don't mind. It's only that I—"

"It's fine," Luke assured him, looking around the massive, high-tech kitchen. "Nice that the room gets some use."

"You are going out? Is it the prosecutor?"

"It is." He glanced up, as if looking through the ceiling at the bed chambers above. "You will let me know if...?"

Melton didn't need to hear the end of the sentence. "Of course."

"I couldn't survive without you, Melton."

"I believe you have that backward," the little man said, his back straight and his chest puffed out. "But I appreciate the sentiment." He cleared his throat. "Sir?"

"Yes?"

Melton squared his shoulders. "Do be careful. I fear that Tiberius asks too much of you."

"He doesn't," Luke said firmly. As far as Melton knew, Luke was still under orders to watch over Sara. He wasn't, as Serge had reminded him only moments before.

And yet Luke still watched. Even if Tiberius ordered him to pull back, Luke knew he wouldn't. He *couldn't*. Not now. Not when he'd come to know her. Understand her.

Crave her.

He craved her with a ferocity beyond any he'd known before, a longing that made his blood burn and his reason fail.

It was, Luke admitted, a humbling thought. He liked to believe he had better control over himself. But it wasn't true. Not where Sara Constantine was concerned. She invaded his thoughts. Made him want. Made him need.

And, yes, he would have her. Rules and orders be damned. Somehow, some way, Sara Constantine would be his.

Sara knew she was being reckless. She was twenty-five years old, and for most of her life, she'd been chasing a shadow. The mysterious someone who had killed her father. Who had left him bloodied and broken for her to find.

Even then, the irony hadn't been lost on Sara. Her father had been fascinated with supernatural lore. Vampires and werewolves. Demons and fairies. The spirit world. Reincarnation. Mysticism and magic. Folklore and Hollywood horror. If it wasn't supposed to exist within the bounds of the real world, he'd been obsessed with it.

Sara's mother had never understood his fascination with those stories, both ancient and new. Everything from Babylonian tales to whatever the current television season's sexy vampire drama happened to be. Her father was into all of them, and he told Sara the absolute best bedtime stories.

Even then, she'd known that telling tales of scary creatures who lived in cemeteries and preyed on humans was probably not the best bedtime ritual for a little girl, but she'd loved it anyway. He'd made the universe seem rich and fascinating, with rules and mythology all its own, and she'd listened, enraptured, every night as he told Sara stories while her mother fumed in the other room, frustrated with Frank Constantine's obsession with the stuff of fiction.

He'd told her once that he loved the mythology and folklore because it was an allegory for the dangers of the real world. She hadn't understood what he meant, and he'd explained that when the humans won in the stories, it was saying that people could win against the bad guys in the real world, too. And when the humans lost, it was a reminder that there are real dangers all around us.

And then those real dangers had found Frank Constantine. Some freak who was probably just as obsessed with the idea of vampires decided to play the role, and he'd left Frank on the sidewalk on Sara's eighth birthday, his neck punctured, then ripped open into two ragged wounds.

The universe really did have a dark sense of humor.

Frank's death had left Sara with a distant, frustrated mother, who had made no secret that she didn't have a clue what to do with a child, and Sara had vowed to grow up and find the bastard who murdered her father.

Big words for an eight-year-old, but Sara was a determined and focused person, even back then. And though she'd never before wanted to follow in her mother's footsteps, she told her mother at her father's funeral that one day she was going to be a prosecutor, too. One day, she was going to put away bad guys like the kind who killed her father. And maybe one day, she'd even prosecute Frank's killer.

She'd been as good as her word. She'd finished college, gone to law school, then become a prosecutor. And she loved it. Not only because of the possibility that someday she might avenge her father's death, but because of what the job meant. Now she was standing on the proper side of that line between light and dark, good and evil.

She was at the frontline, and she was fighting the good fight.

And, yeah, she knew it was risky, but that's who she was. She'd looked death in the eye that night when she'd found her father's still-warm body, and she'd been terrified.

But now Sara was the vampire hunter from all her dad's stories, the avenging angel, the fairy godmother. She wasn't a scared little girl anymore. She was the woman who stared down death and told it to go fuck itself.

Which was exactly why tonight she was driving to a Starbucks located right on the border of gang territory in South Los Angeles. The witness had told her about a gang he'd had a run-in with. A gang that he swore had killed those teens, and which had been around for years, always going for the neck. And sometimes the members even ritualistically drank the blood.

That's what the wit had said, anyway. But Sara had a feeling the wit had been trying to freak her out.

If so, it had worked.

Sara shuddered as she pulled into the parking lot and killed the engine of her battered Toyota. The witness hadn't gone through proper channels. He'd actually approached her outside of Probation when she was walking there after a long day at work.

The sun had just set, and he'd slipped out from the shadows, startling her. He told her he had information about one of Detective Emerson's cases. Sara had protested that she didn't know anything about the case, and she wasn't the assigned ADA. But then he'd told her about the neck wounds. About the bloodlettings. Finally he'd pressed a piece of paper into her hand, then slipped back into the night.

She'd unfolded the paper to find a time and place and a message in scrawled handwriting. *Meet me. You'll see. I can tell you where to find them. How to bring them down.*

She'd almost ignored it. But she'd buzzed Emerson to ask about the case. Just two colleagues chatting about the job. That's when she heard that the case had been reassigned. It was no longer a state matter. It had been transferred to the Feds. Specifically, Division 6, the Los Angeles-based, covert arm of Homeland Security.

And that was really freaking weird.

So now here she was, reckless and stupid though it might be to stick her nose into something that Division 6 had claimed.

She knew she should have told Porter, who could have informed Homeland of the potential witness. But she hadn't. She wanted answers for herself. Hell, she needed them.

For years, she'd been searching for her father's killer, and this was the only lead she'd had on any sort of vampire-style gang, cult, whatever, in years. She had to follow it. What if this gang had been in existence when her father had been killed? What if they'd been behind his death?

Maybe that's what the witness meant by *You'll see.*

She glanced around the parking lot, looking for her contact. But all she saw was the coffee shop and the eerie moving shadows cast by a partial moon and a cloudy night. She started to get out of the car, then glanced at the clock on the dash. Not yet eight-fifteen. She'd wait a bit longer before stepping out.

She considered going to the drive-through for a caffeine hit, and only then noticed how dimly lit and quiet the Starbucks was. She looked more closely. No movement inside. No cars in the drive-through. Just one car with a flat in the parking lot.

She snatched her phone, pulled up the app for the coffee shop, then cursed aloud when she saw that the place had closed fifteen minutes earlier.

Her chest tightened. Maybe she shouldn't have come. Or maybe she should have brought Dan. But he wouldn't understand. The fact was, no one did. Not even Petra, who at least knew that Sara had issues. About that, Petra was right. Because "the issue" was the man who'd killed her father.

She'd find him. She'd find the son of a bitch if it took her whole life. And she would put him away.

So yeah. She was right to come. She was here. There might be answers. And she wasn't backing away now.

Newly resolved, she pushed open the door of the car and stepped out. As she did, she saw a figure slip around the corner of the building.

Him.

She hesitated, then walked toward him. There was dim illumination coming from the interior of the building, and she paused in one of the squares of light that glowed on the asphalt.

He stopped walking.

Shit.

Sara stood her ground. She knew what he wanted—for her to continue toward him. That way, his face would remain in the shadows.

"You're the one who wanted to meet," she called to him. "So here I am. Tell me what you want me to know."

No answer. Instead, he turned and started walking away from her.

"Stop!" The word was out before she even realized she was speaking, and she'd already stepped outside the light. It was like crossing a dimensional barrier. She'd gone from safe to vulnerable, and she knew it.

Then again, when hadn't she been vulnerable? She'd walked with eyes wide open into undeniable danger.

The man turned, facing her again, but still cloaked in darkness.

She drew a breath, asking herself if it was really worth risking her own life to find out what happened to her father. The answer came easily: *Yes.*

She had to know. The question had haunted her entire life. It was a dark, hollow spot in her soul, and it was getting bigger. It was as if a piece of her was missing, and if she didn't pursue this, she would never fill that maw.

"Fuck it," she whispered to herself. She had her handbag over her shoulder, and she reached into the outside pocket, feeling the cool metal of the small Ruger she kept there. She'd been going to the range since she was a child. Her mother, who back then had been working as a prosecutor, had wanted her to know how to handle a weapon. Deborah Constantine kept guns in the house because of the kind of people she worked to put away. Sara did the same now, knowing that it was better to be safe. To be prepared.

Right now, she didn't feel quite prepared enough. She swallowed, then took two steps toward him.

"Follow," he said, then turned and started walking, circumnavigating the Starbucks until he disappeared behind it. She followed. What the hell, right? She was all in now.

She hurried to catch up, then rounded the side of the building only seconds behind him. But he was gone. Just gone.

She looked around, confused, her eyes trying to see into the deep shadows. But all she saw was the industrial trash bin and one car on rims. It had probably been there for months.

Where the hell was he?

She frowned, peering into shadows and trying to see more clearly. But the only illumination came from a dim yellow bulb on the back of the building that didn't reach all the way to the trash can.

She was alone. She felt her stomach tighten. Felt that tingle in her limbs. Fear. Awareness. Hesitation. Was this a mistake?

Oh, dear god, of course this was a mistake.

Her heart pounded as she cursed her own stupidity. She turned, intending to hurry back to her car, then found herself face to face with the witness. The clouds shifted, and a stream of moonlight hit his face. His eyes were dilated and his pupils seemed to glow red in the light.

The corner of his closed-mouth lifted in a sinister smile, and she saw a flash of white teeth as he whispered, "Bitch."

She stumbled backwards, cold shock filling her body. A trap. It had been a trap all along.

But why? Why would he lure her there? She wasn't even on the damn case.

It wasn't a question to which she'd ever know the answer. This man intended to kill her. Maybe that hadn't been clear before, but it became certain when he burst forward, then grabbed her arm, yanking her toward him. He'd moved fast—unbelievably fast. So quickly, in fact, that she wasn't sure how he got the knife at her throat. But it was there. She could feel the cold, deadly blade and forced herself to stay absolutely, perfectly still as he held her head in one hand and the knife in the other.

His eyes seemed to look right through her, still glowing red. A trick of the light? Some sort of drug reaction?

Not that it mattered. His eyes were the least of her worries.

"Do you think this is how I'll kill you, bitch? Do you think we haven't figured out who you are? Fucking abomination is what."

Sara whimpered, suddenly realizing that her hand still held the Ruger, and she knew her only choice was to fight or die.

She chose to fight, and in one swift move, she leaned back, pushing against the hand holding her head in place as she tried to gain a few precious inches. At the same time, she pulled her hand from her purse and fired point blank into his chest.

He dropped her, and she fell backward onto her ass, the gun still in her hand.

And then he lunged for her.

Despite the hole in his chest, he actually lunged for her. She fired again, and he kept coming, then lashed out and knocked the gun from her hand, sending it skittering across the pavement.

He was like a wild thing, and she knew he had to be pumped up on PCP or something—so high he was functioning despite the pain and bullet wounds that should have killed him. Or at least immobilized him.

She must have missed the heart. But how had she missed it?

Not a question that needed answering. Instead, she scrambled to her feet, turning to run, only to realize he'd maneuvered her against the Dumpster. Her gun was gone, and he was still ridiculously, impossibly fast. She couldn't outrun him.

But she had to try.

Thrust forward by a massive burst of fear and adrenalin, she shoved him, then bolted forward.

But it didn't matter. She got maybe twelve inches before he was in front of her again. *How? How had he moved so fast?*

He smiled, and the dim light and her fear played tricks on her because those white teeth now looked like fangs.

Vampire!

"Run all you like, bitch. The chase is the best part."

No. No, fear was making her think crazy thoughts. Evil was real, but her father's stories weren't. They were myth. Folklore. Not real. They couldn't be real.

Her thoughts spun out at lightning speed. This was about the gang. The ones that pretended to be vampires. Her witness-turned-attacker didn't just know about it. He was part of it.

"Please." Her mouth was so dry, she barely got the word out.

"Begging now? That's good, too. Think I like that even more than the chase." He inched closer to her, and she backed up until she hit the trash bin and there was nowhere else to go. She tried to slide sideways—just far enough so that she was away from the trash. She'd turn and she'd run. Hell, she'd sprout wings and fly.

But it didn't matter. He thrust out his hand, his long fingers curling around her upper arm. "Don't worry, Abomination. It will only hurt until you're dead."

She heard a whimper and realized it came from her. "Help!" she screamed, hating the fear that was flooding through her. *"Help!"* she bellowed again, this time wrenching her arm free and managing to turn. *Free.*

She started to run, only to choke from the pressure of her collar at her throat as he grabbed the back of her shirt and yanked her toward him.

This was it. He'd have her. Arms around her. Neck exposed. He'd kill her now. Just like someone had done to her father.

And then—suddenly—the pressure on her neck was gone, and she tumbled forward, landing hard on her knees.

She rolled over, turning in time to witness a huge shadowy form slam her attacker against the trash bin. The attacker's pale face glowed in the dim light from the moon, his eyes still reflecting red, and Sara could see both his fear and his hate as he snarled at Sara's savior, who still held him tight.

She trembled but started to stand.

"Stay down."

The voice came from behind her, and she twisted around to see a tall man with spiky blond hair stride past her, a black jacket to match his black jeans.

"I'll take over," the man in black said to the huge man holding her attacker.

"Where the hell were you?" The huge man's voice was harsh, yet still silky smooth. Sara tried to see his face, but it was obscured by shadows. "You were supposed to keep her safe."

"Our friend here wasn't alone. I got jumped by his two buddies."

"And they are…?"

The man in black shrugged. "Dust."

The bigger man made a low growling noise. "Careful," he said, turning his face slightly as if indicating her. Though why either of them needed to be careful of her, she couldn't say.

She wanted to get up and race back to her car. But self-preservation told her to do as told and stay down. They'd only catch her. And neither seemed in a particularly good mood. So far at least, they'd only helped her. She wanted to keep it that way.

The larger man thrust her attacker at the man in black. "Take him. Make him talk. And Serge—watch your temper. I want whatever answers you can squeeze from him."

"Understood," the man named Serge said. Then he gripped his prisoner's arm and led him past the trash bin and down the alley until the darkness swallowed them.

Which left her alone with the man who'd saved her. Strangely, that wasn't a comforting thought.

She licked her lips, then slowly climbed to her feet. "Thank you. I don't know why you were here, but your timing was impeccable."

"What the hell were you thinking coming here alone?" He turned toward her, his face becoming clear as a cloud drifted away to reveal the moon, letting its full light illuminate his features.

Whatever shock she'd felt upon hearing his chastising tone disappeared as she saw him clearly. That stunning face. Those amber eyes that shone like gold. That angular jaw. *Her stalker.*

"You. You've been following me. Why?"

"More accurately, I've been saving you." He took a step toward her, and she had to will her feet not to back away any more. He wouldn't hurt her; he'd just proven that. "And I think the better question is why the hell are you here?"

"I came to do my job," she said, trying for casual, but the lie was unconvincing even to her own ears. "And I was armed. He must have been wearing a vest."

"Which means you weren't actually armed, were you? Not sufficiently. Not against the likes of him."

Since he was right, she didn't bother to answer.

His head tilted slightly as he stared her down. He wore jeans and a pale gray Henley. He had muscular thighs and narrow hips. But his shoulders were broad, his upper arms huge. An all-around exceptional body, and she imagined that every inch of him was ripped. But it was his face that impressed her the most. The kind of beautiful face that populated the paintings of European museums.

Only his didn't have the untouched beauty of a painted angel. Instead, his exquisite face had the lines and scars of a man who'd seen the world. And his eyes—a spectacular shade of gold she could see even in this dim light—were more serious than a man of his age should have. Because he couldn't be much more than thirty. If that.

"Tell me why? Why have I been seeing you in every shadow?"

She saw the amusement on his face and expected him to deny it. Or, worse, to ignore the question. Instead, he said, "I was hired to protect you."

"Hired?" That made zero sense. "By who?"

He took a step closer, putting him only an arm's length away. "Does it matter?"

Her mouth was suddenly dry, and she had to force herself to hold his gaze. "Um, yeah," she said, her own heartbeat seeming to drown out the words. "Yeah, it really does."

He ran his finger through his wavy brown hair, worn long enough to curl around his ears. At the same time, he studied her, breaking their gaze to look her slowly up and down, his inspection affecting her like a physical touch. She stood completely still, determined to at least appear a lot cooler than she felt.

After a moment, he looked away, and she felt the sweet trill of victory. Except no explanation came.

Irritation won out over her discomfiture. "Oh, come on. I already thanked you for saving me, and I meant it. But you also owe me at least a few answers."

The corner of his mouth curved up, the motion so tiny that it could have been her imagination. "Do I?"

"Fine. Whatever. I'm going to find my gun, and then I'm going to go. But I meant what I said—thank you. I owe you a huge debt. And I work for the district attorney's office so if there's anything you need. Or cash if you'd like a more tangible—"

"No."

She frowned.

"I don't want your money or legal favors."

"Oh. Sorry. I didn't mean to offend you. I just wanted to tangibly thank—"

"There's only one thing I want." He took another step forward, putting him only inches away. She had to tilt her head back to even meet his eyes.

Sex.

He wanted sex. And the hard, brutal truth? She was still pumped up enough on adrenaline that she was practically melting from the mere suggestion.

No, no, no.

A little one-night stand action might be a fine way to battle back her demons, but she was always the one in control. Not so with this guy.

Then again, considering his danger edged toward deadly, she'd be a fool not to give him whatever form of payment he wanted.

She lifted her chin, forcing herself not to take a step back. To show no sign of weakness. "One thing? And what exactly is that?"

He reached out, cupping the back of her head as he moved closer with a speed that made her dizzy.

"Wait. I—"

But she didn't get the words out. They were cut off by the delicious pressure of his mouth closing over hers.

It started slow. A taste. A nibble. The slow burn of a candle inside of her, and damned if she didn't melt like a newly kissed teen on her first date.

One huge hand held her head in place as the other cupped her lower back. He urged her closer, deepening the kiss as it grew wilder. More intimate. As if he owned her and was staking his claim. The kind of kiss that was like fucking. Hot and deep, and firing every atom inside her. And despite the danger, despite the foolishness, she wanted more. She wanted everything.

She wanted *him*.

She pressed closer, moaning as she felt his erection hard against her, even as some bit of sanity forced its way into her head. She needed to pull back, not go forward. She needed answers. This was crazy.

What was he doing here? Why had he been following her? She had to know.

But she buried all those rational thoughts under the reminder that he'd just saved her. Why hurt her now?

Which, of course, was a bullshit justification for the fact that she simply wanted him. More than that, she wanted to take that edge off the way she did with so many men. Only none of them had ever truly satisfied.

It was the danger she craved; she knew that. But at their core, all the men before had been tame.

Not this man. He was wild. Practically feral. And damned if he didn't turn her on.

He broke the kiss, and she pulled back, breathing hard as she waited for him to kiss her again. Or, hell, to bend her over that broken down car and fuck her. She hated herself for wanting it so much, but she had to quell this need. This itch.

She pressed forward, intending to kiss him again, but he took her shoulders and gently pushed her back.

"You want more," she whispered, her voice rough.

"I do."

Relief swept through her, and she waited for him to draw her close again.

He smiled, but it didn't reach his eyes. In fact, he looked just a little bit sad. Then he took a step backward, then one more after that.

Her chest tightened. "You saved me. You deserve a reward." She mentally winced. She sounded needy and pathetic. Right then, that was how she felt. This man. There was something about this man.

"Did I not just have your kiss? That was reward enough."

"No, it wasn't."

His lips curved again, and he tilted his head in acknowledgement. "No, it wasn't. I want you, Sara Constantine. I want you naked beneath me. I want to hold you close. I want to kiss you senseless. I want to tease you until you scream, begging me to get lost inside you. I want it all, Sara."

"I—yes." She licked her dry lips, her body on fire simply from his words. "Yes, please."

"I want, but I cannot have."

"But—"

"Your father's murder ... it wasn't random."

Her body went from warm and aroused to ice cold.

"He was targeted. And that makes you a target."

The world seemed to tumble around her, scattering reality so that nothing made sense. She told herself to just breathe. To get it together. And when she finally did, her words were as low and as dangerous as she could make them. "Tell me who the hell you are."

"I think you know I won't hurt you."

"I don't know a damn thing. Except that wasn't my question."

"Why did you come here?" he asked.

"I'm the one asking the questions, buddy."

"You came to interview a witness."

"There," she said. "You see? You already knew the answer."

"You came," he continued, "despite the fact that the witness has nothing to do with your caseload. You came because you saw how your father died, and you've been chasing answers your whole life."

"Don't you *dare* talk to me like you know me."

"What if I do know you, Sara? What if I know you better than anyone else?"

"Who. Are. You?" She forced the words out, willing them to sound strong. To not reveal the slow build of fear ... and the twinge of guilty arousal that still lingered.

"Someone who understands you." He moved toward her again, and she caught his now-familiar woodsy scent. It was intoxicating. "Who understands why you go into the dark. Why you stare down what scares you most. You like it. You need it. Conquering that fear. Making it your own."

Without thinking, she reached out to slap his face. Because dammit, he was right.

He caught her wrist, his hand moving startlingly fast.

"Stay out of shadows," she snapped. "Stay out of my sight. Most of all, stay the hell away from me." With one solid jerk, she tore her wrist free.

For a moment, he only looked at her. Then he turned to walk away.

She almost released a sigh of relief, only to suck it back in when he paused to look back at her.

"I'll go, Sara. But staying away? I'm sorry. But that's not a promise I can keep."

CHAPTER

THREE

As far as Luke was concerned, the hardest thing he'd ever had to do was walk away. He'd actually held her in his arms. Felt her lips against his, her body melting for him, craving him. He could have had her right there. Stripped her naked and taken her under the light of the moon any way he wanted. He could have traced his fingertips over her breasts, then kissed her lower and lower until he could taste his fill of her. He wanted to gaze at her skin in the moonlight. He wanted to lose himself in her warmth. He wanted to hear her scream his name.

And yet he'd walked away.

Somehow, he'd found the strength to go.

Would that he were a weaker man...

Now, he shoved his hands down into the pockets of his jeans, circling the building so that he could make sure she got safely back into her car, while remaining confident that she wouldn't see him.

She got behind the wheel, then sat for a minute, her hands clutching the steering wheel, her eyes closed in what he assumed was a mixture of grief and fear. He wanted to go to her. To comfort her. But he knew he couldn't. And soon enough, she'd gathered herself, started the car, and pulled out of the parking lot.

He relaxed, only then realizing how great the effort had been to simply do nothing.

He heard the soft tread coming from behind. "Anything?"

"Nothing," Serge said, moving to stand beside him. He ran his fingers through his short blond hair. "I'll give the guy credit. That had to hurt. First he wouldn't talk, and now he can't. Can't do anything anymore, actually."

Luke nodded. "No more than he deserved."

"Traitorous bastard."

Luke quirked an eyebrow. "Did he say anything at all?"

Serge shook his head. "Nothing we hadn't already heard. He just spat the word abomination once more, then he shut up tight."

Abomination.

What the hell did that mean?

"Does it have to mean something?" Serge asked after Luke voiced the question. "She's Frank Constantine's daughter. He was a danger to all of us. It may not be accurate, but I can see why Abomination might be a designated nickname."

"That makes the girl a victim, not an abomination. She lost her father. And threat or not, the sins of Frank Constantine shouldn't be visited on the daughter."

"I can't argue with you," Serge said. "But you really think that's where that nickname came from? There's something we haven't been told."

Luke said nothing. But he knew his oldest friend was right. Some piece of the puzzle was missing.

Not that this was the first time they'd been left in the dark. Despite their high station, and the trust that Luke knew their leader had in them, there were still things that were kept quiet. Honestly, that pissed him off. But there wasn't a damn thing he could do about it right now.

"Did our little friend have any other cohorts?"

"Not that I could tell," Serge said. "Just the two that jumped me. If there were more, they stayed well-hidden and well-camouflaged."

"Maybe we'll get lucky and no one will realize they're missing for a while."

"This isn't feeling like a lucky kind of situation," Serge said. Once again he ran his fingers through his hair. "Listen, I can stand sentry at her house. Just in case there's someone else looking to hurt her."

"No. I will."

Serge tilted his head, his eyes narrowing. "You think too much about this woman."

"Do I?" Luke said the words casually, but the truth was he did wonder. In all the years he'd been watching her, was there ever a time that she wasn't in his thoughts? And maybe that was a mistake. After all, thinking about her stirred things inside of him and fomented impossible thoughts. Wild desires. Cravings he hadn't felt in ages.

He knew he couldn't have her. Knew he should listen to his friend and stay far, far away. But how could he, when as far as Luke was concerned Sara Constantine belonged to him? She just didn't know it yet.

That didn't matter, though. He felt it deeply enough for the both of them. It was as if she was a part of him, and he longed for her with a ferocity beyond any he'd ever known.

And, reason be damned, tonight he would go watch silently, standing sentry in the dark and protecting her from the things that hid within it.

Sara stood in her bathroom, her shoulder-length hair—still wet from the shower—slicked back from her face. She wore her robe tied tight around her, taking comfort in the way the soft terrycloth enfolded her.

What a horrible night.

She'd tried to sleep, but couldn't. All she saw when she closed her eyes was that freak attacking her.

She'd taken a shower to force him out of her mind, and it had worked. Now, instead of thinking about the creep who'd tried to kill her, she was thinking about the man who'd rescued her. A man who stood more than a head taller than her, and who had the strength to protect her. Whose broad chest and strong arms could hold her close and help her erase her fears.

His kiss had fired something inside of her. Something she didn't want to examine too closely. Something deeper and more primal than she'd felt with any man before. Those men had been about forgetting and fighting. About burning away the horror she saw in her job. About keeping away the danger she'd first seen as a child. About staring down that dangerous edge and winning.

But with her rescuer, it was different. It wasn't to dull that edge that she wanted him. Not completely, anyway.

Mostly, she just wanted him.

She shook her head, dismissing her thoughts. Clearly, she was still in shock from the encounter. Having some sort of victim bonding moment. She knew nothing about that man. Nothing other than that he'd been following her. And when you got right down to it, that was creepy as hell.

Or it should be.

The weird, undeniable reality was that knowing he'd been watching her—knowing that he was there to keep her safe—made her feel warm and protected in a way she hadn't felt since her father died.

With a soft curse, Sara dragged her fingers through her hair. She was losing it. Seriously losing it.

This wasn't the woman she wanted to be. Someone who mooned over a hot guy because he did a good deed for her. Except it had been so much more than a simple good deed. And no matter how much she wanted to deny it, something buried deep inside her had blossomed with that kiss.

"Well, hell," she said, to the world in general.

She heard the tea kettle start to whistle and left the bathroom for the kitchen, happy for the distraction. She killed the flame, then poured hot water into her mug and stood by the counter, waiting for the chamomile tea to steep to the perfect strength.

She was still standing there, trying not to think, because thinking was sending her thoughts in circles, when she heard the tap at her kitchen door. She about jumped a mile, her heart pounding in sudden fear. She hadn't asked her protector what had happened to her witness-turned-attacker when the blond man—Serge— took him away. She hadn't wanted to know. Because what she wanted to happen to him went completely against everything she stood for as a prosecutor.

It probably made her a hypocrite, but she really hoped he was dead.

But maybe he wasn't. Maybe he was right outside.

The tap came again. Louder this time. A full blown knock, and she drew in a breath, trying to ignore the icy fingers of fear that snaked up her back.

"I'm armed," she called, hurrying to the breakfast table to get the gun she'd retrieved from the parking lot. "So get the hell out of here and we won't have a problem."

She edged up beside the sliding glass door that led from the kitchen to the back patio. It had vertical blinds and she peered between the slats. The motion-detecting porch light was on, and she could see his profile. It wasn't her attacker.

It was *him.*

She froze as everything smart and rational inside her told her to dial 911 immediately. Her so-called protector had followed her. And she already knew he was dangerous.

But not to you.

No. *No, no, no.* She didn't know that for sure. Not really. He said he was hired to protect her, but that made no sense. Who could possibly have hired him? Certainly not her mother.

If he was that dangerous, he would've already hurt you.

Sara tried to quash the little voice. As far as she was concerned the man outside was dangerous in other ways, too. He made her feel too much. She'd melted under that kiss. Surrendered. And Sara was never the one who did the surrendering.

On the contrary, she liked the distance. The freedom that came with not caring if the men she took home to celebrate her victories or fight her demons never crossed her path again. With this man, though...

With this man, she was certain that she would care. And she didn't like that certainty.

But there he was, right outside her door. And now he'd turned, so that those golden eyes were looking directly at her through the window, silently compelling her to unlock the door. To fall into his arms.

And then, damn her, she was doing that, flipping the lock and turning the doorknob. She stepped back, pulling it open, then eased to one side, her chin lifting as she silently invited him in.

"Sara."

That was all he said, but the heat in his voice burned straight to her core.

She swallowed, trying to shake it off. "Still watching me? Protecting me?"

"Always." His low, growly voice rumbled through her. It was rough, the same way that she imagined his hands would feel against her skin. She looked down, afraid he could see her thoughts on her face. Only when she gathered herself again, did she meet his eyes. Then she nodded toward the door. "Close it. Lock it."

She expected him to make some comment about how she didn't need the locked door. That he could keep her safe. But he complied without argument, then turned back to her, as if waiting for further orders. The thought made her smile. "All right. You're here. Will you at least tell me who you are now?"

"I told you," he said, the low rumble of his voice doing all sorts of incredible things to her senses. "I'm someone who's protecting you."

"How do you fit all of that on a credit card?"

He cocked his head, "Pardon?"

"I was trying to get your name. You already told me the job."

The corner of his mouth lifted, the barest hint of amusement. "My name is Luke."

"Luke. I like that." She turned her back on him to go to the counter, the movement intentional. Designed to show him that she wasn't afraid. And maybe trying to convince herself of the same thing.

She picked up her tea before turning to face him again. "Do you want to tell me why you're really here?"

"I think you know."

She took a sip, trying to look casual. "Sorry. No idea at all."

He took a step toward her, then another, then one more, until he was so close that she had to fight the infuriating urge not to reach out and touch him. "Don't lie to me, Sara. That's the only thing I will ever ask of you. Don't lie to me. And I won't lie to you."

"You expect me to believe that?"

The corner of his mouth twitched. "It would probably be wise if you didn't."

One more step, and now he was only inches away. She was already backed up to the counter, and there was nowhere to go. She was trapped, her body hyperaware. She glanced down, realizing that she felt suddenly, strangely shy.

Screw that.

She forced herself to meet his eyes, then wished she hadn't. They were even more stunning in the light, with flecks of green flashing in those golden irises. They seemed magical, somehow. Like he could see all her secrets.

The thought unsettled her, and she lowered her gaze, her attention caught by his mouth. That wide, perfect mouth. Her lips tingled as she recalled the feel of them against her own. His was the kind of mouth that could do exquisite things to a woman, and as she imagined exactly what that might entail, a tiny moan escaped her lips and the tempo of her pulse increased. "We shouldn't," she said, meeting his eyes and holding his gaze.

She expected him to lie and say that she had entirely misread the situation. That he'd come only to make sure she was safe.

Instead he eased even closer, his bold fingers reaching for the sash of her robe. "You were disappointed before. You wanted more than a kiss."

She shook her head, "No, I didn't."

"I told you, Sara. Never lie to me."

"I don't even know you."

"But I know you." He lifted one hand from the sash, then traced his thumb over her mouth, the contact positively melting her. "Do you trust me, Sara?"

"No," she admitted. "But I want this anyway."

His lips didn't move, but she saw the smile in his eyes. A smile that turned to heat as she reached for his hand at her waist, her fingers running gently over his before tugging open the bow so that her robe fell open, exposing expose a strip of skin all the way from her neck to her bare pussy. She felt vulnerable. Exposed. And, exquisitely turned on.

She didn't stop there. With what she hoped was a sultry smile, she pushed the robe off her shoulders and let it fall to the ground, so that she stood naked in front of him, silently begging him to take her, even while a tiny voice in her head told her to back away. To run.

That this was dangerous. Ridiculous.

Intoxicating.

For better or for worse, Sara wasn't going anywhere.

"You are breathtaking," he told her, his voice tight, as if he was fighting back emotions. But she didn't want him to hold back at all. She'd taken the first step, and now she wanted everything.

Boldly, she moved even closer, and she heard that low, sexy growl as he brushed his fingertips over her bare shoulder. "You are incredible, Sara Constantine," he murmured. "Earlier tonight, I could practically smell your fear of the man who attacked you. But you weren't scared of me."

"I was," she admitted. "But I wanted you, too."

"Did you?" His fingers eased over the swell of her breast before finding her nipple and slowly teasing it.

She closed her eyes, biting her lower lip as she lost herself to the incredible sensation of being naked for this man. This stranger who she craved.

"I kissed you, and you wanted more, didn't you?" His other hand was on her waist, his fingers trailing toward her navel as he continued to tease her breast with the first hand. "So much more than a kiss," he continued, that wicked hand moving lower and lower, tracing lightly over the tender skin of her waxed pussy.

She reached behind her, steadying herself against the countertop as she closed her eyes and shifted her weight, opening her legs for him. Hoping he'd accept the invitation.

"Not just a kiss," he continued, his low voice seeming to reverberate through her body. "You wanted release. To work it out. To burn off the lust and the fear. You wanted to use me to get you through this night."

She kept her eyes closed, but she told the truth when she whispered, "Yes. God, yes."

"Good girl." He must have bent forward, because she felt his lips brush the still-damp strands of hair that brushed her shoulders. And at the same time that those words teased her imagination, his fingers teased her clit. The touch, so soft and gentle, was like a butterfly kiss, but it set off an explosion of sensations and a singular, violent need.

"Please," she murmured, spreading her legs even more. She opened her eyes, and found him looking back at her with a wild intensity that almost melted her. "Luke, please. Please, *oh!*"

She arched back as his fingers thrust deep inside her, her cry of, "Yes, oh, yes," cut off by the pressure of his mouth claiming hers. Owning her.

The kiss was long and deep, and only their lips touched. Their lips, and his fingers inside her. His tongue explored her mouth as she ground against his hand.

With his other hand, he grabbed her hair, forcing her head back so he could kiss her more easily, his tongue warring with hers until she was on the verge of exploding from the way he was playing her body like a fine instrument.

Soon, he lowered his mouth to her breast, his tongue dancing over her nipple. She gasped, her breath coming hard and fast. She was close—teetering right on the edge, but before that final crest of the wave washed over her, he pulled back, fingers and lips abandoning her.

"What's wrong?"

"You are forbidden fruit, my love."

"Love?" The warning bells that she'd been ignoring clanged louder. "You don't even know me."

"On the contrary. It is you who don't know me. But you? I know you, Sara. And I do love you."

She thought about the times she'd seen him and wondered how many more times there'd been. Dozens? Hundreds? "You don't know me," she snapped, pushing past him then starting to bend for her robe. But he was too fast. He snatched it up—then held it out to her with an apologetic tilt of his head.

She shoved her arms into it, then tightened the sash with one violent yank. "I think you should go. I won't lie and say I'm not attracted to you because, well, you pretty much know that I am. But I'm not going to bed with my stalker."

His cheek twitched as if he was trying to hold back laughter.

"Dammit, it's not funny."

"I'm not a stalker, Sara. And you're not scared of me."

That was true—she was long past fear and deep into both lust and a frustratingly unfulfilled longing. But right then what she wanted most of all was answers. "You say you know me? Great. I'm all ears. Tell me all about me."

"Very well." He'd moved back before to give her space, but now he stepped closer again. She wished he hadn't; it was hard to focus on his words when he was so close that she could imagine the way that hard body would feel in all her soft places.

But she didn't insist he step back. Instead, she just crossed her arms and stared him down. "Go on. Tell me what you know about me."

He hesitated, then moved to the other side of the kitchen. He leaned against the refrigerator, looking at her, and in that moment she felt strangely, uncomfortably, alone. "I know your father died when you were young. I know your mother has essentially checked out of your life. I know you're one hell of a litigator, and that you have a deep sense of justice."

He paused, his eyes roaming slowly over her body with such intensity it took all her effort not to reflexively tighten the robe again.

"I know what drives you, Sara. I know that every case is a stand-in for your father's murder." His voice was like a caress, so soft with compassion it almost made her weep. "And I know that you take far too many men to bed for all the wrong reasons."

Anger flared, erasing the melancholy that had eased in at the mention of her father. "Is that including you?" She said the words boldly, her voice tight to hide her confusion. He did know her. He knew her scarily well.

"No. When I take you to bed, it will be for the right reasons.

The answer came easily, with no hint of doubt, and Sara could feel the truth of it rushing through her, firing her senses. As if all of these questions meant nothing. They were just foreplay.

The thought made her smile, and beneath the robe, she felt her nipples tighten and her whole body go warm with desire. Foreplay, indeed.

"How do you know all of this?" she asked, trying to gather her wits.

"I told you. I was hired by someone who ... knew your father. He wanted to ensure your safety."

"So, what are you saying? I've had a series of silent body guards since I was eight years old?"

"Essentially, yes."

"Creepy."

"You don't like the thought of me watching over you?"

"If you're asking me if I like the idea of a Peeping Tom, then no, I don't."

It seemed as if she'd only blinked and he was back in front of her, so close she was intoxicated by his scent and craving his caress. "Make no mistake, Sara. I want you. But I have never crossed that line."

"Did you want to?"

"Are you asking if I wanted to see you with those men you let touch you? I think you know the answer to that question, Sara. No, I didn't want to see. But I did want to destroy every man you took to bed."

The words were hard and violent, and yet the truth in them touched something primal in her. Something she wasn't ready to confront. "I think you should go."

She said the words, but she didn't truly want him to leave. She didn't want it at all. She couldn't remember being this turned on by a man in forever, and yet this whole situation was wrong on so many levels. It was one thing to flirt with danger and bring home some random guy. But this man wasn't just a guy, he was like living flame. And if she wasn't careful, she could get very, very burned.

And yet, even knowing that, she trusted him.

What the hell was wrong with her?

"I'll leave if you want me to. But I don't think you do."

"Why?" She heard the sharp edge in her voice, and was certain he saw it for the camouflage it was. "Because you're the man I should be sleeping with? Not all those others?"

"Yes." Once again, he stepped closer. Once again, he opened her robe. She lifted her chin, but didn't protest. Not even when he slid his hands in and cupped her breasts, making her heart kick up in tempo and her mouth go dry.

"You should never have been with those men."

She pressed her hands over his, tightening his grip on her breasts, anger rising. "Why? Because I'm a woman. Does that mean I can't have a few flings to take the edge off? Men do it all the time. But I'm not allowed because I'm some little princess?"

"No," he said, his eyes hard on hers. "Because you're mine, Sara. And I think you know it as well as I do."

"The hell I am. I'm—"

He kissed her then, long and deep, and she melted into it, finally succumbing. Giving in to how much she wanted this kiss—and so much more.

When he finally pulled away, leaving her lips tingling and bruised, she heard herself whimper.

"Tell me, Sara."

She looked into his eyes, eyes that she could easily get lost in. She didn't even know him, but this felt right. It felt more right than anything ever had in her life.

"Who are you," she whispered again.

"Tell me you want this."

She considered denying it, but the truth was far too evident. "You already know the answer."

"I need to hear it."

"Why? Why not just take what you want. Maybe I'd like that."

"No. What I want, I will only value if it's freely given. I want all of you, Sara. I don't intend to be simply a way for you to scratch an itch."

Her head was swimming. "You still haven't told me. Not really. Who are you?"

"I have told you. I'm the man who loves you. I've loved you for a very long time."

"Oh." She knew she should be terrified, but the emotion didn't fit. Instead, she trusted him, foolish or not. She wasn't sure what she expected, but she knew with absolute certainty that he wouldn't hurt her.

No, what should terrify her was that word he'd spoken again —*love*. And yet she wasn't scared at all. It felt real and right and completely confusing.

She told herself that was because it didn't matter. Love was just a word, after all. And right then, not arguing with him about that silly word would get her what she wanted—his touch. His body.

She drew a breath, then lifted her chin. Then she shrugged her shoulders, and let the robe fall to the ground again. "Freely given," she said.

"Sara..."

She slid her arms around his waist, then lifted her mouth to his, surrendering to the kiss as her fingers followed the waistband of his jeans to his fly. She worked the button, lowered the zipper, and slid her hand inside to cup him. He was huge and hard, and when he growled—an actual, low, animalistic growl—she felt more feminine than she'd ever felt in her life.

With a soft moan, she broke the kiss, then leaned back to meet his eyes, the passion she saw reflected there both humbling and arousing her in a way she'd never experienced before. It made her feel wild, and when she stroked his cock and felt him grow even harder against her palm, the wave of sexual power that crashed over her made her gasp with ecstasy.

Boldly, she dropped to her knees, then teased her tongue along the length of him. She'd never particularly enjoyed giving head before, but as she drew him into her mouth—as she felt his fingers twine in her hair and heard his deep groan of pleasure—she wanted nothing more than to take him deeper and deeper, her own arousal heightened by the knowledge that despite his size and strength, in that moment, she completely owned this beautiful, dangerous man.

While her mouth teased and tasted, her fingers eased his jeans down so that she could slide her hands along the tight muscles of his lower back and then cup his perfect ass. Slowly, she dragged her fingernails over his skin, as he held her head, forcing her to take him deep and deeper until she knew he was right on the edge, and oh, dear Lord, she wanted to take him over.

He didn't let her.

Instead, he pulled back, his hold on her hair forcing her to stand as she whimpered from the loss of him. "Hush," he murmured, taking her by the waist and lifting her onto the counter as if she weighed nothing at all. Gently, he spread her legs, then stroked her inner thighs with his fingertips.

"Close your eyes," he ordered, and she complied, losing herself to the sensation of his rough fingertips on her sensitive skin only to gasp when she felt his breath on her clit followed by his tongue stroking and teasing her so relentlessly the pleasure felt unbearable.

She tried to squirm—tried to slide off that knife-edge of exquisite sensation, but he wouldn't let her. Instead, he held her in place, hands on her hips, his mouth on her sex, his tongue taking her so close, so close, so very close until her entire body seemed to explode into a thousand stars. And as her essence was showering back down to earth from the heavens, he thrust inside her, filling her completely, then taking her even further as they moved together, deeper and faster until they fell over the cliff together, this second orgasm eclipsing the first, until all she could do was cling to him, too limp to move or talk or think.

Gently, he pulled out of her, then lifted her as easily as if she was a child and carried her to the bedroom. He pulled back the covers, then settled her head on the pillow before sliding in beside her and covering them.

She closed her eyes, her lids too heavy to keep open, her body to used to move. But somehow she managed to find the strength to speak.

"Luke?" she murmured as he gently stroked her hair.

"Yes, my love?"

"You're right," she whispered. "I'm yours."

CHAPTER
FOUR

Luke spent the night watching her, relishing the miracle that was Sara. Some small part of him had feared that the reality of the woman wouldn't match his expectations, but that had been far from the case. Everything he'd ever craved about her, everything he'd anticipated her to be, she had proved it true ten-fold.

He'd waited so long, but she was truly his now, in every possible way.

Gently, he pulled the covers down, then watched shadows dance on her bare skin as the gentle glow of morning began to fill the room. Not harsh, direct sunlight, but a warm illumination that made her body glow as if lit by fire from within.

She was on her back, one arm above her head as she slept, her lips slightly parted. Gently, he pressed his palm to her breast, his cock tightening as her nipple hardened under his touch. He teased it, rolling it between his fingers, then releasing it as he bent over, desperate for her taste.

With the tip of his tongue, he played with her areola, feeling it pucker with arousal, her soft moan from the depths of sleep going straight to his cock. *God, he wanted her.*

And the beauty was that he had her. "I'm yours," she'd said, and there had been truth behind her words. Now, he wanted to make that truth even more real. Wanted to feel the reality of their bond. That she was his, just as he belonged to her.

Slowly, he moved on top of her, then bent his mouth to her breast again, his tongue playing with her nipple even as he traced one hand down her soft skin, finding the curve of her waist. He moved lower, too, his lips brushing her skin as he tasted his way down her body, his tongue dancing over her belly button, then lower still. He saw her skin tighten, her breath coming faster, her nipples like small pebbles now, both as hard as his cock. But still she slept, and he couldn't help but wonder about her dreams. Was she begging him to take her? Teasing him? Or perhaps she was she touching herself, imagining him watching.

The thought made him even more hard, and he slid his fingers between her legs, then groaned with need when he felt how wet she was. Wet and ready for him. And thank the gods for that, since right then he had no free will. There was nothing for him now other than being inside of her. He had to have her, had to touch her. Take her.

Had to claim her once again. Needed to take her to the edge, then watch her face as she woke with him deep inside her and they both tumbled over into the vast expanse of pure pleasure.

He straddled her, careful not to wake her, then teased her with the tip of his cock before easing inside her. He moved slowly at first, watching as her lips parted, as her fingers clutched at the mattress, and when he couldn't hold back any longer, he thrust deeper. Harder. Filling her completely until he could no longer tell where he ended and she began.

"Luke." His name on her lips as she swam back to wakefulness was the most potent aphrodisiac he'd every experienced, and it took all his effort not to come right then. Instead, he waited for her to fully rouse, then met her eyes as he exploded inside her, her cry of, "Yes, oh, yes," sending him tumbling into a sea of pleasure.

"I like waking up that way," she murmured moments later when he was by her side again, his fingers lazily tracing patterns on her skin.

"I'm very glad."

She snuggled closer, rolling over and hooking one leg over his thigh before taking his hand and sliding it between her legs. "Careful," he told her. "Don't start something you don't want to finish."

"No worry about that," she told him. "It's Saturday. As far as I'm concerned we can stay in bed all day. For that matter, maybe we should just stay here forever."

The word stung him, and he bent to kiss her shoulder so that she wouldn't notice the change. Because they couldn't have forever, and he knew better than most how swiftly time moved.

But that wasn't a conversation for today. Instead, he simply kissed her gently and whispered, "Yes, my love. Forever."

Sara woke with a start, her body realizing before her mind that she was alone in the bed. She rolled over, her hand stroking the mattress beside her. *Still warm.* He hadn't been gone for long.

She wanted to stay in bed, afraid that if she got up and went into the other room, she wouldn't find him there. What if he'd simply left?

The possibility was unbearable. She'd met the man less than twenty-four hours ago, and already the thought of never seeing him again made her want to break down and cry. Her, the woman who could so easily leave a guy's apartment, and who had no hesitations whatsoever about kicking them out of her place no matter how late the hour or how much they wanted to sleep over.

Not so with Luke. He'd walked into her world and turned it upside down.

Or maybe it was last night's attack. Maybe her reaction to him was some sort of psychological response to him rescuing her.

Except it wasn't. She was certain. This intensity between them wasn't the product of fear or gratitude, it was something deeper. Something even more primal. Something she'd never felt before. And oh, please, she hoped he felt it too. She thought he did, but what if she'd been wrong? What if he'd slipped out of the house, and simply disappeared back into the world?

She drew in a breath, bracing herself for disappointment as she got out of bed, then looked around for her robe, only to realize it was still on the floor in the kitchen. She went to her closet, and pulled on a pair of sweatpants and a threadbare T-shirt. Then she padded barefoot to the open door and stepped into the hallway, her head cocked as she listened, hoping for some hint that Luke was still around.

Nothing.

With a disappointed sigh, she made her way down the hallway. The house was built in the seventies, and had a boxy floorplan, which she liked. Unlike the more modern open style, this outdated house her parents bought that she'd grown up in had been perfect for hide-and-seek games with her friends, not to mention escaping her mother.

It was a house originally meant for a family. Her mother, her father, her. Possibly there would have been brothers and sisters had her father survived longer, though Sara tended to doubt it. Her mother had never seemed the type to want a child. As far as Sara could tell, Deborah Constantine never really wanted her.

Still, the house was familiar, full of memories that ran the entire spectrum of emotion, but lately Sara had been itching to leave. She was currently renting the place from her mother, but her father had left Sara a small inheritance and a hefty life insurance payout, and now she was considering buying a condo downtown. Both closer to work and away from her memories.

She passed the open doors to the other bedrooms, but found no sign of Luke. He wasn't in the living room or the den, either.

She paused at the swinging doors that marked the entrance to the kitchen. It was the last room, and she hesitated before entering, afraid she'd drown in the wave of disappointment if he wasn't in there.

But she had to know, and after drawing a single deep breath, she pushed through, only to exhale again when she saw him standing by the coffeemaker wearing only his jeans.

He turned to her and flashed that smile. The one that melted her. "Hey."

"Hey, yourself," she said. "I thought you were gone."

"Do you want me to be?"

She swallowed, realizing with crystal clear awareness the implications of answering honestly. Boldly, she met his eyes. "No," she said as she moved forward to slide her arms around his waist in an open display of need and affection that went against everything she usually did. Every wall she usually put up.

She closed her eyes and pressed her forehead against his bare chest. "No. This is what I want."

"Good. So do I." He stroked her hair until she lifted her head to look at him, then he bent forward and gently kissed her. As he did, she realized that she didn't feel his breath on her face, then had the odd thought that she hadn't felt it when they were making love either. Once or twice when he intentionally blew on her skin, teasing her into further wildness. But never a casual breath on her shoulders or her neck or tickling her eyelashes.

"—I hope that's okay."

She shook her head, trying to play back the words he'd just spoken. "I'm sorry, what?"

"I said that I made coffee. I hope that's okay."

"More than okay. In my world the making of coffee makes you just about perfect."

He smiled, and the mystery of his breath vanished in a puff of morning lust. "Do you have plans for the day?"

"That depends," he said. "I'd like to have plans here. With you. Ideally in your bed. Then maybe take you out this evening."

"I like that plan."

He reached out, toying with the hem of her tee. "Are you working today?"

"I told you last night. It's Saturday."

"And you usually work on Saturdays."

She took a step back, the tension returning to her body. "Right. I forgot. You've been watching me."

He reached for her hand. She hesitated, then extended hers, and he closed his fingers until her small hand disappeared in his large one. The difference was so dramatic that she almost felt like a child. Except this was not a man who made her feel childish things at all.

"That bothers you?"

"Of course," she said. "Wouldn't someone following and watching bother you?"

"I suppose it would. But, Sara, I won't apologize. And even now, I won't stop. No matter what, I will keep you safe."

"You keep saying that, but I'm twenty-five now, and nothing's happened to me that's blowback from my father's death."

"How do you know? Perhaps I've stood between you and an attacker."

"Perhaps?" She lifted her brows. "Have you?"

"Haven't I?"

"What? Last night?" She shook her head, not willing to entertain the thought. "That was a meeting with a potential source."

"On a case to which you have no connection."

She crossed her arms and stared him down. "That's irrelevant."

"It's not, Sara. He said he had information on the kind of case that fascinates you. Then he presented no information. Instead, he tried to kill you. And, if you recall, he failed because Serge and I were there."

He was right. No matter how much she hated that simple truth, she'd have to ignore reality to argue now. And Sara had never been one to shy away from reality. "Fine. You win."

"I am sorry, Sara. This is none of your making, and yet there are those who want you to pay the price for what your father did."

She took a sip of her now-cold coffee as she gathered her thoughts, debating if she even wanted to ask the question his words suggested. But she had to. No matter what her father might have been into, she had to know. She put the coffee down, taking a moment to gather herself before returning her attention to Luke. "You told me last night that my father was targeted, but you didn't tell me why. Tell me now."

For a moment, she thought he would remain silent. Then he said, "It had to do with the type of work he did."

"That makes no sense. He studied folklore. Stories about para-normal creatures. Supernatural fiction. Why on earth would someone want to kill him for that?"

"I cannot say. But I will tell you that initially my employer feared that you or your mother might be caught in the crossfire. Judged guilty simply by your proximity to him. He didn't want that to happen. So I was sent to watch over you."

She blinked as the meaning of his words hit her with full force. "You? You're older than me, sure, but unless you were guarding me at, what, eighteen, it couldn't have been your job all along could it?"

"It was. And yes. I am at least ten years older than you. Give or take," he added, with an odd little smile.

She moved closer and slid her hands along his shoulders and down his arms, enjoying the strength there. "I've never fallen for an older man before." She didn't add that she hadn't fallen for *any* man before.

"Well, you're definitely getting your money's worth with me."

"Huh?"

"Older," he said, amusement flickering in his eyes.

"Okay," she pressed. "What's the joke?"

His eyes widened. "Joke?" he repeated, his voice full of feigned innocence.

She rolled her eyes. Not a point that needed pressing. "At any rate, I kind of like it," she said with a tease. "The decadence of sleeping with an older man. Although I have to say, I think you're probably a much better bodyguard now than you would have been back as a teen or in your early twenties. Or were you this strong back then too?"

"I assure you, I was more than strong enough to do my job."

She lifted up on her tiptoes and kissed him. "I was just teasing." She cocked her head. "So were there attacks before? Or was last night the first?"

"No others," he said.

"Then why were you still watching me?"

"I told you. It's a job. And considering last night, it's good that I'm still on duty."

She moved closer, her body brushing against his. "Only a job?"

"I think you know the answer to that question." His voice was low with that rough edge that made her tingle in all the right places.

"I want to hear you say it."

"No, Sara. Not just a job."

Despite herself, she smiled. She wanted to play it cool, but the answer thrilled her more than it should. "It's definitely freaky, but I think I like knowing that you've been watching over me. Especially last night."

"I'm glad. I wouldn't stop even if you told me to, but I'm glad that knowing the truth doesn't upset you."

"It did." She closed her eyes as he enfolded her in his arms. "It doesn't anymore." She drew a breath. "I guess now I'm going to have to tell my boss about last night. Which sucks, considering the witness wasn't mine. He supposedly had info about a case that I'm not supposed to have anything to do with. That's not even with the DA's office anymore."

"What case?"

"A gang that killed four teens not long ago. Apparently they play like vampires, puncturing people's necks and then draining them of blood."

"Like your father died."

"Yes. Like my father."

"Your fascination with cases that mirror his is going to get you in even deeper trouble someday."

"You can't know that," she said. "But you're probably right. I'm either going to overstep at work and piss somebody off. Or I'm going to get too close to somebody who's dangerous. I know that. But it's a risk I'm willing to take."

"Why?"

"What do you mean why? He's my father. He was murdered. I don't have any answers. Why would someone do that to him? Murder him that way?"

"You can't tell me you don't actually have any ideas on that score."

She scowled, then moved to refill her coffee. "You seem to know everything about me, and I don't know anything about you."

"Do you want me to go?"

She just stared him down. For better or for worse, she wanted him. And he damn well knew it. "Would you? If I asked?"

"Of course," he said. "I want you, Sara, make no mistake. But I will only take what I want if it's freely given. Send me away, and I'll still watch over you, but I will also spend my hours dreaming of the day that I am invited back to your bed."

It was the perfect answer, and she felt her smile through her entire body. "I don't understand us," she confessed. "I barely know you, but I want you more than I've wanted any man, and that makes me very uncomfortable. Plus, I don't usually talk about this kind of stuff. I don't wake up after sex and have deep meaningful conversations with the men I fuck. That's not me."

"Perhaps not, but it is us. Maybe all you needed to open up was the right man in your bed."

The right man.

She fought her smile as she crossed the kitchen to the refrigerator. She pulled it open, then pulled out a bottle of water before shooting him a wicked glance over her shoulder. "Well, I don't know. Maybe I need to comparison shop. Find some security or law enforcement types with your kind of muscles. Just to be certain."

She heard the low rumble in his throat. That sexy growl that had already become like an aphrodisiac to her. He was at her side so quickly she would swear she hadn't even seen him move. "No."

She fought a delighted laugh. "No?"

He cupped her chin. "No."

She said nothing, mesmerized by the intensity of his eyes.

"You're mine, Sara. And I'm yours. And you already know it."

"Big words. The kind of words that can get you kicked out of a girl's house."

She wasn't fooling him, of course. He was right. She belonged to him. It was like something out of a movie—a lightning bolt. A connection.

Love?

She wasn't sure. All she knew was that he felt right. And they felt real.

Gently, he stroked her hair. "Say it." His voice was soft, but there was no mistaking the command.

"I'm yours," she whispered, then gasped as he pulled her close and kissed her so deeply she thought she would melt. "Oh, yeah," she murmured when their lips parted. "Definitely not kicking you out of the house."

Luke's deep chuckle rumbled through her body. "I'm very glad to hear it."

"Will you tell me something?"

"Of course."

"Why would anybody want someone who studied folklore and mythology dead?"

"What do you know about your father's work?"

She shrugged, then moved to the small kitchen table and pulled out one of the vintage-style chairs. "I've pretty much told you what I know," she said as she took a seat. "Paranormal lore. Research for some academic institution. He lived and breathed that stuff. He kept a journal. He was always reading. And he'd tell me amazing stories so vivid they felt real. Like we were living in a Lord of the Rings movie, but it wasn't hobbits and elves but vampires and demons and intrigue."

"Intrigue?"

"Yeah, he'd make up these complex worlds. He'd tell me that the vampires were mad at the werewolves. Or that the demons were meddling in vampire affairs. He'd say that the powers that be were going to have to set things straight. He'd create characters and play it all out like a movie. Or a TV show, I guess, because it kept going and going."

"And you enjoyed the stories?"

"Are you kidding? I loved them. My mother was furious with him. He used to tell them to me at bedtime, and she said it wasn't the type of thing that a father should tell his little girl. But I begged him to tell me. It was our time, and it was special."

"And the stories. Did you believe them? For that matter, did he?"

Her eyes went wide. "Are you kidding? Of course not. The stories were his passion, not his delusion. And even though I was a kid, I knew they weren't true. Trust me, Luke. I don't believe in vampires or demons or shapeshifters or any of it. But I do believe in monsters. That guy last night was one of the monsters."

She tilted her head, studying him. "How about you?" she asked, with a tease in her voice. "Are you afraid of the monsters in the dark?"

He didn't answer. Instead, she watched as his brow furrowed. As he stood up just a little bit straighter. She waited, and the longer the silence between them lingered, the harder her heart seemed to pound. "Luke?"

"Last night, I was the monster in the dark."

"No. You were the hero."

He nodded. "Be that as it may, the only thing that truly scares me is losing you."

"Oh." She met his eyes, feeling like she might drown in the passion she saw reflected there. "Luke, I—"

"How much would your world change if you learned that everything your father studied was real? Would that fascinate you? Terrify you?"

She searched his face, not entirely sure of the point of this game, but finding no answer. "Fascinate," she finally said. "But as for my world actually changing, I don't see why it would. I mean, if we're pretending it's real, then it's always been real, and I've always been living in that world."

With a shrug, she stood, then headed back to the coffee maker. "I mean, it's not like I'm bumping into vampires as I walk through the streets. Other than wanna-be's like the gang that killed those teens, I mean. So if they really are out there, I guess that means they keep to themselves. Just like in the movies."

It was the strangest question. And the really weird thing was that there was something about his tone of voice that made her think he might actually be serious. But that, of course, was ridiculous.

"Luke," she began, "why are you—"

CRASH!

Sara whipped around, to see the sliding glass door shatter as two men leaped inside. Or at least they seemed like men until she caught a look at their faces. Their eyes were blood red. Not the whites or the irises. But the pupils, just like last night's attacker. And they were wearing Halloween-style fake fangs. Except Sara didn't think they were fake at all.

"Stay behind me," Luke ordered, moving in front of her. He grabbed a thick wooden spoon from beside the sink, then thrust forward, slamming it into the tallest attacker's chest. Immediately, the intruder turned to a man-shaped blob of dust that lingered in the air for a moment, then fell into a pile resembling nothing more than large clump of dust to be collected and swept out the door on cleaning day.

What the holy hell?

She realized in that same moment that *she* was on the ground, too, her knees having gone weak, unable to support her anymore. As she stupidly gaped, one of the men rushed Luke, only to have Luke snap his neck, the action seemingly effortless.

Sara gasped, frozen with shock and fear, then full-on terror when the wobble-necked creature actually rose, fangs bared. "Dragos," he snarled at Luke, then lunged. Luke twisted, his body swooping down to retrieve the fallen spoon from the dust pile, then rising in one elegant motion to stab this vampire through the chest as well.

Vampire.

They were real. It was all real.

Even as the dust filled the air, a third vampire raced toward her, moving with lightning speed.

"*Luke!*" She screamed as the creature fell upon her. Sara slammed her head forward, making her ears ring and her entire body throb, but the movement kept his face away from her neck, giving her at least one more precious second to think. To fight.

Hell, to pray.

Luke started to bolt toward her, but another vamp leaped through the broken window, then kicked Luke in the back, sending him to the ground.

"No!" Sara screamed, as much in protest of the injury to Luke as against the other vampire who fell atop her, his fangs bloody.

"Won't you make a tasty dessert," it snarled, "you fucking abomination."

Her arms were thrust out, hands on his shoulders and her elbows locked as she tried to keep him away from her long enough for Luke to get to her, but the new vamp to the party was even bigger than Luke, and she was as worried for him as she was for herself.

No, she took it back. Definitely more worried about herself, especially now that the vamp had one hand around her throat and the world was starting to dim.

And then—miraculously—air flooded her lungs, and the pressure of the vampire's body on hers faded. She looked up, her vision clearing, only to be marred again by a storm of fine dust falling over her.

She scrambled to her feet, intending to head for the swinging doors. Maybe find something more useful than a wooden spoon with which to protect herself.

But as she approached, the double doors slammed open and the huge blond man from last night burst into the kitchen. *Serge.*

"Sara, get down," Luke called, now fighting yet another who'd entered her home.

Even as she wondered how they could do that without an invitation, she obeyed, dropping to the floor as Serge leaped over her, so high he almost touched the ceiling. She watched, mesmerized as Luke released the new vamp. It sneered, then lunged toward her again, only to be intercepted by Serge, whose back was to her. In one elegant move, he pulled a stake from his back pocket, then slammed it into the vampire's chest.

For one brief moment, relief crashed through her. *It was over.* Then another swarm of intruders flooded through the door, and Luke and Serge took up their positions again, with Luke sparing only one quick, sideways glance at her. "It's okay," he said, catching the stake that Serge tossed to him and springing into action.

It's okay, he'd said.

Too bad she didn't believe him.

CHAPTER
FIVE

S ara hated that she was right; it wasn't okay at all.

In fact, it was horrible, gut-wrenching, and confusing. Thankfully, only ten vampires came inside, if *only* was a word that could be used in the context of vampires. Sara watched, standing helplessly with her back pressed against the refrigerator, now holding a stake that Serge had thrust into her hand. She considered running forward and helping, but she knew damn well she'd only be in the way, distracting both Luke and Serge, who were fighting at the door.

Fighting vampires.

God. Oh, dear god.

As she watched, Luke ripped off one of the wooden cabinet doors. With just his hands, he broke it twice, making four thick stakes as effortlessly as if he'd broken a pencil. He fought like something out of a superhero movie, taking down four of the encroaching vampires in a flurry of motion that made Sara not only dizzy, but desperately thankful he'd been watching her.

Protecting her.

A vampire killed her father.

For what seemed like the millionth time in the last few minutes, the thought burst to the forefront of her mind.

Vampires are real, and one killed her father.

She rubbed her temples, racing thoughts and fears filling her mind, and she forced herself to ignore them as she tightened her grip on the wooden stake. She couldn't be distracted. One might get away from her two protectors, and if that happened, she needed to be ready.

Another went down, this one taken out by Serge, who used the carving knife that Sara had left in the sink a day ago to slice off the vampire's head. In a seamless dance, he used his other hand to drive a stake into the dead vamp's chest, as if two fatal blows were better than one.

As if it were a movie, Sara watched as that one's body melted into dust as well. Sara didn't know how Luke took out the next one, but when she turned her attention back to him, the body-shape of dust fell to a pile on the ground.

And that was it.

There had been more, but they'd scattered as their companions fell. Now her kitchen was dusty but empty except for her two heroes, and all the terror she'd been holding back—especially the fear that one of the invaders would kill Luke—rushed up inside her, the powerful combination of fear and relief pushing her to her feet and sending her racing toward Luke, desperate to feel her arms around him.

She didn't make it.

Instead, Serge caught her arm, pulling her to his side. "No," he said. "Not yet. Give him time."

She scowled at him, but he didn't notice. His head was bent, his eyes hidden so she could only see his forehead. *The hell with that.* She jerked her arm free, then raced forward, throwing herself against Luke and trying to spin him around. When he didn't move, she shifted until she was in front of him.

That's when she saw it.

His red pupils. His fangs. Smooth and sharp and deadly. She gasped, then backed away, only turning when she realized that she would bump into Serge.

She stopped, knowing with absolute certainty that he was a vampire, too.

"No. No, no, no." She shook her head, completely confounded by what was going on. By who these men were. By the fact that Luke....

She'd slept with him. More than that, she'd fallen for him. For the first time in her life, she'd opened her heart to a man. Lost herself with him. Wanted *him*, and not just the release of sex.

Hell, she'd even allowed herself a few happy fantasies that she could actually have a future with this guy. And happy fantasies were really *not* in Sara's milieu.

Had he messed with her mind? She'd read *Dracula*. She knew about being in thrall to a vampire. Was she now in thrall to Luke?

"Sara. Sara, Look at me."

She realized that she was standing still in the middle of the kitchen, staring down at the floor. She kept her head down, ignoring his demand, and desperately happy that she had the ability to do that.

"Sara, please look at me. Let me explain."

She wanted to tell him to go to hell, but she heard genuine pain in his voice. Slowly, she lifted her eyes to his, now golden once again. The fangs, too, were gone.

"Where did they go?"

"Most are dust. The last of them have left."

"No. Not that. Your fangs."

He hesitated, then said simply, "They retract."

"Oh." She was suddenly unsure how to respond. She hadn't expected the truth.

"You're a vampire."

"Yes."

"But you're warm." Even as she spoke the word, she felt like an idiot, and she glanced sideways toward, Serge, who raised his brows and looked amused.

"There are some things that folklore doesn't get right. We have blood. It circulates. And that makes it easier to walk among the humans. Were we drained, we would still survive, though we would be dried out, looking more like Nosferatu than Lestat."

Sara couldn't help herself; she smiled.

"Usually the blood moves slowly and our skin feels cold," he continued, then took one step toward her. "But when we are aroused..."

"Oh. Right." She glanced at Serge, feeling her cheeks burn, which was an absolutely ridiculous reaction. She cleared her throat. "Anyway, it's morning now. Daylight. But those vampires came in from outside and some escaped back into the yard. And none of them burst into flame."

"Yes. Young vampires can do that."

"Oh. So how old is young?"

"Most become sensitive to light around two hundred, and it becomes deadly around five."

"Oh." She probably should have expected numbers that large, but hearing them aloud seemed to shift everything into a new perspective. This man was a vampire. Truly a vampire.

She looked at him, then down at her hands. "I think I need to be alone right now. Can you two please go?"

Luke and Serge exchanged glances. "Well, actually, we can't. As you said, the sun's out."

Her mind spun as this new reality clicked into place. "Which means you're both more than five hundred years old?" She dragged her fingers through her hair. "I knew there was an age gap, but that's seriously crazy."

It was a ridiculous joke, probably borne of nerves, and she wasn't surprised that he didn't respond. Instead, he moved slowly toward her, as if approaching a skittish cat.

"I would have told you eventually. Perhaps I should have told you sooner."

She shook her head. "I don't know. I don't know when's the proper time to tell a woman you just slept with that you're a vampire." She cast a sideways glance at Serge, who she anticipated would be politely looking away, pretending to be thinking of something else. Instead, he was leaning against the wall by the swinging doors, arms crossed, looking for all the world like he was enjoying the show. "Um, do you mind?"

"Not at all. Please. Continue."

"Serge..." Luke's voice held a hint of warning, and Serge lifted his hands, not even trying to hide his amusement. Weirdly, his attitude calmed her. He and Luke were friends. Just regular guy friends who gave each other shit.

Luke cleared his throat.

"Fine, fine." Serge pointed a finger at Sara. "Don't stake him, okay? He can be an ass, but he's my oldest friend." He flashed his fangs, and she took a step backward toward Luke. "And I'd hate to have to kill you."

"*Serge.*"

Serge's lips twitched, clearly fighting laughter.

"You must forgive him," Luke said, once the other man had pushed through the swinging doors and disappeared from sight. Though Sara was quite certain he was still within hearing distance. "Or not," Luke said. "I'll leave that to you."

His casual, amused tone relaxed Sara even more, and though she knew he was doing it intentionally, she allowed some of the tension to flow from her body. "Your oldest friend?"

"We grew up together." He met her eyes. "We were changed together."

She swallowed. "When."

"A very long time ago." He took a tentative step closer, and she forced herself to stand her ground. She knew she shouldn't be afraid of him—if he wanted to harm her, he'd had plenty of opportunities, both before and after she learned the truth about him. But there was no denying that her reflex was to run.

"Sara, please." His voice was soft, gentle, and he extended his hand in silent invitation. She looked at it, wanting nothing more than to slide her hand into his and have him pull her into those strong arms and hold her tight.

She didn't. Instead, she shook her head slowly, fighting tears as she did. "I'm sorry. I   I loved everything about last night. After the almost dying part, I mean," she added with a tiny smile. "But this is too much, and even last night...."

She swallowed, looking down so that she didn't have to meet his eyes. "Even though I loved everything about it, we shouldn't have. *I* shouldn't have."

"Don't say that," he said, the plea evident in his tone. "Last night was precious to me."

"Me, too," she admitted. "But you know we can't—"

"We can," he said firmly. He took her hand, and she didn't pull away. "Everything I said last night I meant. You're mine, Sara. You have been for a very long time."

Hot tears trickled down her cheeks. His words should terrify her, but instead they filled her with warmth. Made her feel safe.

But those were only feelings. And she wasn't willing to let lust cloud her judgment. "You're a vampire."

"I am. And I have always known that you would learn the truth. I intended to tell you myself. I'm sorry you learned it this way."

"You're a vampire," she repeated. "A vampire killed my father. You said he was killed because of his work. Was it because he realized all those stories were real?"

She knew about the world now, too. Did that put a target on her back as well?

Luke said nothing, and she squared her shoulders, gathering courage for the biggest question of all. "Tell me, Luke. Why did he die? Who killed him?"

Luke glanced away, not meeting her eyes, and ice filled her veins.

"Oh." Her knees went weak, and he reached out to steady her.

She slapped his hand away, the burst of fear and anger giving her strength. "*You*. You. You killed my father? You took me to bed knowing that you'd killed my father."

"Sara..."

"You killed him and then you felt guilty leaving me vulnerable, so you protected me. And then last night you used me? You took advantage of me?" She still had the stake, and now she tightened her hand around it. "Do you think I would've slept with you knowing what you did? Hardly. I'd—"

"*I killed him.*"

Sara turned to see Serge pushing through the swinging doors.

Without thinking, she lunged at him with the stake, only to find herself plucked off the ground and pinned against the wall as easily as if she were a rag doll.

"Release her, Serge."

Serge didn't comply. Instead, he reached for the stake, tugged it from her fingers, then used one hand to crush it into sawdust as his other hand, positioned just under her ribcage, held her fast to the door.

"Dammit, Serge." Luke was at his side, moving so fast Sara hadn't seen him move.

"I owe you an apology," Serge said, "and sympathy for the loss of your father. But I was following orders, and it was my duty."

"Put her down."

That time, Serge complied. Luke moved to her side, but she scooted away, edging along the counter until she was across the kitchen from both of them.

"Someone ordered you to kill my father?"

"Yes."

"Who?"

"There's a hierarchy in our world as well," Serge said. "Rules. Laws. Codes. And those who break them are punished. I followed orders."

"Whose orders?"

"His name would mean nothing to you."

"And he just snapped his fingers and ordered my father killed?" The words felt like chalk in her mouth. "Why?"

"Frank Constantine worked in our world. He knew our secrets. Not just of the vampires, but of all preternatural creatures."

"All?" she repeated, her head swimming.

Luke didn't even pause in his answer. "Your father was going to reveal everything about our world," Luke said. "We would be hunted. And we would have to fight back. It would be war, Sara. And Tiberius couldn't let that happen."

She considered the name, realizing that unless his parents had strange thoughts about naming children, this vampire had probably been walking the earth since Roman times.

"Is this Tiberius despot going to have me killed?" She took a step back, suddenly realizing. "Did he send those guys to kill me?"

"He did not," Luke said, his voice full of certainty. "And as for telling you, there will be no blowback."

She crossed her arms as she stared him down, hoping she looked more confident and together than she felt. "And how the hell do you know that?"

"It's one thing to tell somebody I trust," Luke said, taking one small step toward her. "It's another thing for knowledge of our existence to make it out into the world."

"War," she said. "You can't be certain?"

"Of course we can."

She swallowed. He was right, of course. "This is a lot to take in." She bit her lower lip, then rushed into her next words, taking care not to look Luke in the eye. "You really need to go."

"Sara." Luke nodded toward the window.

"Right. The sun." She turned to look at Serge. "But you came in at the same time as the others."

"I've been in your garage since last night. I came in through your utility room."

She looked between them. "You thought this might happen."

"Thought, no," Luke said. "But I knew it was a possibility. And I would do anything to keep you safe. Including pissing you off by staying right here."

She wished she could regret every moment of last night, but despite his strange revelation that he was basically Dracula—despite the truly horrific battle that had taken place right in this kitchen—all she really wanted was move to closer and let him hold her. She'd never felt a connection this intense with any man, and now all her heart wanted was to sink into that bliss.

Her head, though...

Well, her head told her to walk away and never look back.

As if he could read her dark thoughts, Luke moved closer, then reached out to gently stroke her hair. She told herself she should jerk away. Instead, she leaned into it, letting his huge hand cup her face with such tenderness it made her want to cry.

"I don't know what to do," she whispered. "I don't know how to feel."

"I know. And I am truly sorry. But know this—I will always treasure last night. I will always protect you. Perhaps I was selfish, but I had no ulterior motive for bedding you. No motive other than to finally have the woman who already held my heart in her hands."

She closed her eyes, fighting fresh tears. She shook her head, wishing all the pieces of this new world would fall in place so she could see more clearly. "Why all of this firepower for me? And why now? My dad was killed almost two decades ago. And I don't have anything to do with this world. Or at least I didn't until last night."

"Why now?" Luke repeated. "I don't know. But as for why you, blood is important in our world, and you have Frank Constantine's blood."

"Oh." She thought about what Luke had told her about her father planning on revealing their secrets. As far as the vampires were concerned, her father had been a traitor. And she was being painted with the same brush.

She ran her fingers through her hair, then moved to the coffee maker. Not because she needed the caffeine—she was brutally awake. No, she just needed to move. To think. To somehow wrap her head around all of this.

But she couldn't.

She'd slept with a vampire.

Other vampires had broken into her home and tried to kill her.

And last night, one had lured her to a dark parking lot and almost done just that. Neither Luke nor Serge had said as much specifically, but she knew damn well it was true.

When she looked up from her thoughts, she found Luke staring back at her, his eyes reflecting both concern and warmth. *He was a vampire.* She wasn't sure if she'd truly processed that little fact.

He was a vampire.

She knew that was true. She'd seen it with her own eyes. He was a monster. A beast who lived on blood. A dead man walking, literally. And yet right then, all she wanted to do was go into his arms.

When the hell had she become so impulsive?

And didn't that win the award for stupid question of the decade? As far as sex was concerned, she'd always been impulsive. The men she picked up. Those hard hot moments when all she wanted to do was get the images of death out of her head. The memory of her father on that sidewalk. The murders and assaults she saw every day in her job. Impulsiveness had been her refuge. Her way of flipping her middle finger to the universe. She took risks. She survived. And that was one more fuck you to an uncaring universe that had wrenched a kind-hearted man away from his eight-year-old daughter.

And now here she was standing next to two men who were killers. One who had killed her father and another who had definitely killed, and many times over, too. She knew it, because that was a vampire's nature.

This was a wake up call. And she needed to answer it. She squared her shoulders. "I really need you both need to leave. Now."

"Sara...."

"I'm safe, right? The ones who ran, they won't be coming back?"

"They might be back, but they'll regroup first. But Sara, I'm not going to leave you."

"Protect me all you want. I'd be a fool to argue about that. But I need you to leave." She forced the words out. Forced common sense to speak instead of her heart. Somehow, she made the words come. But she couldn't quite manage to meet his eyes as she spoke.

"Sara." He stepped closer, then reached for her hand.

She took a backward step, shaking her hand. "I told you what I want. Please don't insult me by arguing." She watched his face, but his expression was totally unreadable. He could be hurt. He could be angry.

Hell, he could be bored.

Didn't matter. This wasn't about him. It wasn't about *them*. It was about her. "I mean it. You can stay in the garage until nightfall, but this is over. Whatever there was between us, it ends now. I can't do this. I can't," she paused searching for the words, but she couldn't find them. "I can't do this."

"You can send me away," Luke said, this time moving so fast that she couldn't pull her hand away, and she felt herself immediately swept away by the sensation of contact. Of his surprisingly warm skin against hers...it was electric. Intoxicating. And oh, so seductive.

She closed her eyes, forcing her mind to stop spinning and think rationally. He was intoxicating? Well, that was all the more reason to send him away. Never do anything important while drunk, right?

Firmly, she pulled her fingers from his, then watched as he squared his shoulders. "Very well. I will go. But it won't change anything. You are mine, Sara, and I love you. Nothing can change that. Not even death or time. And certainly not sending me away."

The words seeped into her, warming her blood. But she refused to let him see it. She knew she was right; they had no future. How could they? She turned, certain that Serge would be there, too, but the other vampire was gone, presumably into the garage.

"You're a vampire," she said, facing Luke again as she conjured the cold, hard words. "What could you possibly know about love?"

His eyes went flat. His expression unreadable.

She'd hit the bullseye. And she hated herself for it. She bent her head, studying her bare feet as she forced herself not to take back the words. "You're immortal, right? You'll get over me. I'm just a blip."

"You are not."

"I should be." She swallowed, then faced him. "Tell your boss I don't need someone watching over me, and even if I do, it shouldn't be you. Tell him to send someone else. It—it will be easier for you that way."

Easier for both of them.

She blinked back tears, hating herself for being so emotional. For feeling as though she'd known him forever when she barely knew him at all. But she knew enough. Knew that he had dark secrets. Knew that he was a kind of danger that she had never encountered before, despite having gone home with men who were dangerous in their own right. But this one. Oh, how he moved her. And right then, the thing she wanted most of all was to take back everything she said and pull him close.

But she wouldn't. *Couldn't.* Instead, she moved toward him, lifted herself up on her toes, and kissed him gently. "I won't forget you, Luke. But I can't be with you."

Luke paced his living room as Serge looked on, arms crossed and one brow raised.

"You need to walk away, my friend," Serge said after Luke had made ten more trips back and forth across the room.

Luke stopped, then shook his head. "I cannot."

"There will be other women. Hell, there will be hundreds of other women."

In a flash, Luke was at his friend's side, his arm under his neck as he pinned Serge to the wall, the fury that had propelled him now raging in his veins. "There is only her."

"Anyone this close needs to be kissing or fucking me, and nothing personal, my friend, but you aren't my type."

Luke backed away, his heated blood still boiling.

"Ah," Serge said, shaking his head as amusement flashed in his eyes. "You really are well and truly fucked, aren't you?"

"What the hell are you talking about?"

"I didn't realize before. I thought she was simply this century's pet. Like the tavern wench in the thirteen hundreds who shared your bed for a decade."

Luke remembered the woman. Sweet Agnes. A widow who lost her children to the fever. Even after her family had been five years gone, she'd still been lost in grief and despair when Luke met her. He'd taken her under his protection. Bedded her. Fed from her. She'd craved the feel of his fangs, seeking to punish herself for being the only one in their household to have survived.

He'd kept her close, forever fighting the urge to drain her fully. He was her protector. And as long as she lived, she was also his redemption for the countless lives he had taken in those early centuries when he'd wandered the continent, feeding at will, taking lives and destroying families. Those horrible years before he had encountered Tiberius, and the vampire leader had taken him in, then taught him how to tame the beast inside that had been freed centuries before when he had first changed.

"Sara is no serving wench."

"No," Serge said, his voice hard with meaning. "You, my friend, are in love."

Luke had said as much himself, of course, but having Serge acknowledge it, too, was like being slapped in the face with the blinding force of truth.

In all of his many years, Luke had shared his bed with many women. Some for only the pleasure of a night. Some who he invited into his home as well as his bed. Some who provided no more than a blissful moment of release and forgetfulness.

He had cared about them all, but Sara was different.

Luke had felt love only once before, and he had been human then. His wife. His daughter. They were in his heart. His blood. And losing them had been so painful he had vowed never to love again. For centuries, he had shielded his heart, unwilling to open himself to the pain of loss once again. And loss would be inevitable. Even were he to love another of his kind, eternity was long, and he did not trust the power of a lingering human emotion to last throughout the centuries anymore than he trusted fate not to steal his mate away. Bad luck mixed with one stake, and even a preternatural mate would be lost to him forever.

As for falling in love with a human? Well, that brought only the surety of pain upon their mortal death. Claiming a human as a bedmate and food source, as he had Agnes? He would permit himself as much. But the bond of love? Actually taking a human—or any of another species— as a true mate? That he could not bear.

At least that's what he'd thought before Sara.

She was in his blood. His heart. Every cell of his body. It felt as if she had lived within him for centuries, and for him to have found her across all the years and miles was a miracle.

He couldn't lose her. Were she a vampire, he might be tempted to wait. To give her time to feel for him with the same intensity as he felt for her.

But if she were a vampire it wouldn't be a problem. Because all that was keeping her at bay was his own vampiric nature. And that was something he could not change.

"You could just change her," Serge said, the comment so on-point it seemed as if his friend had been reading his mind.

"No. I could not."

Serge shrugged. "She's strong. She'd survive."

Luke shuddered, not nearly as certain his friend. He didn't have the chance to tell Serge as much, though, because his friend was still prattling on.

"She'd be pissed, sure," Serge continued, "but she'd forgive you, and even if it took a century, what would that matter if love were at the end of the journey?"

Luke raised a brow. "Sergius, my friend. You sound almost poetic. When did the thought of love ever move your heart?"

"It doesn't. But our friendship does. You want her. Take her."

It was tempting, Luke couldn't deny that. But no. He couldn't. Not even if she asked. The risks of losing her during the change were too great. Most did not survive, too overwhelmed by the physical and emotional torture that was never revealed in ridiculous human television shows. He had lost his beloved Livia that way, and that final death of his sweet daughter had broken him for centuries. He would not take the risk again.

And even if there were no risk?

Even then, he doubted he could do it. There was a value to the finite nature of life. And while he would rather turn to dust than live out the rest of his days without Sara, even were she to beg him for the change, he didn't know that he could do that to her. To reduce the magnificence of the world by expanding it for millennia. To take away her life. To put inside her the horror that came with the change.

"Fair enough," Serge said after Luke explained his thoughts. "But then you need to move on. You need to leave Los Angeles."

"Leave her?" He shook his head, "No. You heard them. That vampire hoard called her *Abomination*. Until I know what that means —until I know that she's no longer in danger—I'm not going anywhere."

Serge sighed, but nodded. "Very well. We'll find out."

Luke shook his head. "No. I will."

"Luke..."

"I am not pushing you away, my friend. But I need your help with something else."

"Anything. You know that."

Luke did. Serge was like his brother. Hell, he was closer than a brother. "I need you to take Tasha. Take her home with you to New York. Take her to all of the shows she wants."

"And what is it that you will be doing that you need your ward out of the way?"

"I can't be here to watch her and get Sara back. I need to be with Sara. I need to see this through. I need her to understand." He basically just needed her. "And I can't ask Milton to take on the responsibility. He's in charge of the house. Not in charge of a seventeen-year-old girl."

Serge chuckled. "Tasha is over five-hundred years old. She's hardly a child."

Luke met Serge's eyes. Held them. His friend nodded.

"Let her see whatever shows she wants. Take her anywhere in the town she wants. But, Serge, do not let her out of your sight."

"You think I don't know that?"

Of course Serge understood. He'd been there when Luke had changed Tasha. When they'd realized how much of a mistake that had been. He loved the girl like a daughter, but in his clearest moments, he had to admit that it would have been better all those years ago to let her perish, just as her family had.

"And what will you be doing while I'm escorting your ward down The Great White Way?"

"I'm going to convince Sara. I'm going to convince her that she is mine."

"It would be better to walk away, my friend."

Luke shook his head then turned to face the window. It was dark now. They'd left Sara's garage the moment the sun had set. And it had taken all of Luke's strength not to go back into that house after she had ordered them away.

Now, he pushed the button that operated the mechanical blinds. They rose, and moonlight streamed in. It was a crescent moon, but the night was cloudless and dark, and he watched as the light rippled on the small waves at slack tide and the dunes cast eerie shadows across the sand.

"I mean it," Serge said. "You need to wipe this woman from your mind."

"I would if I could. God knows it would be better for her. But I won't. I can't."

"And this is why I never have and never will fall in love," Serge said, his voice soft as he stepped to the window next to Luke. "It makes you stupid, my friend."

Luke chuckled. "I suppose it does."

Serge tilted his head, studying Luke. "Tell me this, then. If you love her, shouldn't you abide by her wishes and simply let her go?"

"Perhaps," Luke admitted. "But I cannot. And if that makes me a selfish bastard then so be it. I've been called worse."

"I figured you would've called me last Friday," Petra said. "At least to tell me that you hadn't died in a parking lot somewhere."

Sara winced. "I'm so sorry. I didn't think."

Petra frowned as she shot Sara a sideways glance. They were settled on one of the benches in the grassy area outside of the courthouse, and Sara flashed an apologetic smile that did nothing to quell Petra's scowl.

"I was worried," Petra continued, her finger tapping the side of her to-go coffee cup. "I mean, yeah, I checked on you to make sure you were alive, because that's what we kick-ass PIs do. So the worry faded. And I appreciate you finally answering my text last night, but come on, girl. You not only didn't check in, you didn't tell me a thing."

"Like I said, really sorry. I just—it was a weird weekend."

"Yeah? So tell me about it. Did you talk with that witness?"

Sara set her own coffee on the bench beside her. "The witness was a bust," she lied. "He never showed."

"Oh. Well." Petra's brow creased. "I was planning on yelling at you again, which I still should. But instead I'm going to say that I'm sorry. I know you were hoping ... well, honestly, I don't know what you were hoping. It's not like Homeland would let you on the case. Did you think you were going to magically get some insight into your dad?"

"Maybe. Yes. I don't know." She picked her coffee back up again, and idly scratched at the label, desperately wanting off the topic of her father. "I really am sorry I didn't call. It didn't even cross my mind, which makes me a terrible friend. But, well, the truth is...." She drifted off with a shrug, then forced out her next words. The truth, and yet still a lie. "I hooked up with a guy."

Petra's eyes went wide. "Seriously? Someone you met at the Starbucks?"

"No," Sara lied. "No, I met him later."

"Well? Go on. Tell me everything." She shifted position, bringing one leg up and tucking it under her as if settling in for a jolt of vicarious sex.

Not terribly surprising. Without getting graphic, Sara usually debriefed Petra on all of her nighttime escapades. It fascinated Petra, who was the polar opposite of Sara and wouldn't even dream of having sex on the first date. Or the second. A moot point, really, since as far as Sara knew, Petra simply didn't date.

And as for Sara, it gave her a second bite at that apple. A chance to examine more closely the why of those sweaty nights. Why had she needed a guy in her bed? What was she ignoring or trying to work through? Because it was never about the guy. Never even about sex. It was about that edge. That itch. That burning need that she didn't understand, but was like a constant, grasping thing that, no matter how hard she tried and how many men she slept with, was never truly satisfied.

And then there was Luke.

She hadn't slept with him to take the edge off. On the contrary, he *was* the edge. The burning need.

With him, she'd felt whole.

With him, she'd wanted more.

And yet she'd sent him away.

Because he's a vampire.

True. But right then, she couldn't seem to remember why that mattered.

"Sara?"

Sara blinked, then looked blankly up at Petra, whose eyes went suddenly wide. "Oh, wow," Petra said. "You like this one." She wiggled as if giddy. "Now you really do have to fill me in. What's he like? What's he do? How *exactly* did you meet?"

Sara wasn't about to tell Petra the truth about Luke. Not his name. Not the fact that he was the guy she'd seen watching her on more than one occasion. And certainly not the fact that he was a vampire.

Now that she sitting in the sun with her bestie, breathing fresh air outside of the office of her very normal job, it was harder and harder to wrap her head around that reality. And yet she didn't doubt it. Not for a second.

At the same time, she couldn't get him out of her head for even a second.

Damn it.

"Earth to Sara. Come on. Don't leave me hanging."

"He's just someone who was visiting one of my neighbors," she said, the lie coming surprisingly easily. "That condo building at the end of the street. They were having a party."

"And you got invited how?"

"A guy I know who lives there was walking by when I was getting out of the car. He told me I should swing by. So I did. I'd had a shit evening with the witness not showing, so I wanted to get it out of my head. I met him there, and, well, you know."

"I don't, because you're not telling me," Petra said, a tease in her voice. "Guess I'll have to find something sexy to stream tonight, because you, my friend, are no use to me at all."

"Sorry, not sorry."

Petra laughed, then leaned forward. "Are you going to see him again?"

"I don't think so."

"But you like him. Really like him."

"I do," Sara admitted. "Probably more than I should."

"What the hell does that mean? How can you like someone too much? That's the goal, isn't it? To find someone you like—even love—and have him love you back? Oh," she added, her voice turning somber. "It's not mutual?"

"Actually, I think it is."

"Then what is the problem?" Petra demanded. "I mean, okay, fine. Don't give me the details, but at least tell me why you're punishing yourself. And him. You like him. He likes you. And we both know you work too much. You should have a life. And that includes the possibility of a relationship"

"Said the pot to the kettle?"

"My situation is completely different, and you know it," Petra said, tugging at one of her gloves.

Sara winced. "Sorry, I didn't mean. I just wish you wouldn't worry so much about your condit—"

"This isn't about me. We're talking about you and the sex god. I mean, you haven't been in a relationship in, well, *ever* as far as I know. So why not test the waters?"

"I just don't think it's a good idea."

"And again, I ask, why not?"

"Because I think he's dangerous." Sara winced. She couldn't believe she blurted that out. She truly hadn't intended to. But at the same time she did want to talk. Petra was her best friend. And, as much as she hated to admit it, she needed perspective. Because all she wanted was to beg Luke to come back. But she'd let him go for a reason. An important one.

And even if she'd been wrong, she had no idea how to get ahold of him.

What if she'd made a terrible mistake?

"Wait, wait, wait. Dangerous? How?" Petra reached out and took Sara's hand. "Did he hurt you? I swear if the son of a bitch—"

"No. No nothing like that. He was wonderful."

"Then why dangerous?"

"It's just ... let's just say he's the kind of guy I go up against in court sometimes."

Petra leaned back. "You mean like as a defendant? Not a defense attorney."

"Defendant. Yeah."

"Holy shit." Petra dragged her fingers through her midnight black hair. "Does he have a sheet? Is he being investigated for something? Did you run him?"

"Nothing like that. He's clean now as far as I can tell. I ... I even think he's reformed. But there are ... things in his past. Things he told me. And I'm not sure I can date a guy like that. Can I?"

"So he told you these things he's done. You didn't already know and called him on it?"

"No. I had no idea."

"And you believe he's reformed?"

"I think so. He says so."

"Do you believe him?"

"Yeah. I do." She hadn't realized that truth until she said the words. But she did believe him. He'd protected her on more than one occasion. And he had been so sweet and tender in bed. So how could he be the monster that word—*vampire*—conjured?

She didn't want to believe it, she realized. She wanted to trust him. Wanted to lose herself in his arms again. Already, she felt his loss profoundly, as if there was a Luke-shaped hole in her heart.

She swallowed. "I do want to see him again," she admitted. "But I don't think I should."

Petra leaned back, then took a sip of her latte as she stared at Sara.

"What?"

Slowly, Petra shook her head. "You do realize you're being a huge hypocrite right now?"

"Excuse me?"

"Aren't you the one who volunteers with juvenile offenders? Kids with rap sheets longer than *War and Peace*, but you tell everyone who'll listen, including them, that they can change. That they don't have to stay criminals. That they can be better than their upbringing. Better than their past. Better than their bad habits."

Sara's mouth went dry. "Yeah. I do say all of that."

"So is that all just bullshit? Because you're not saying it about this guy. So why the hypocrisy?"

Sara only shook her head as she pictured Luke's fangs. And the blood. And her father, dead on the sidewalk.

But Luke hadn't killed him. And Petra was right. Sara didn't paint every defendant with the same brush. So was it fair to run so far from Luke?

He's a vampire. You're supposed to run from vampires.

Except her father hadn't. He'd been fascinated by that world. He'd worked among them. And the father she remembered was always happy. She'd never once seen a hint of fear.

And, yes, his job had killed him, but that was hardly unique to the preternatural world. If what Luke and Serge said, her father had put himself in a very bad position. But he hadn't been categorically afraid of vampires. Or any of it.

If Frank Constantine had walked in that dark, unseen world, then why couldn't Sara?

"I can practically hear you thinking," Petra said. "But I can't quite make out any of the words. So fill me in, okay?"

"I was just thinking that you are making a whole lot of sense."

"Yeah?" The pleasure practically dripped from Petra's voice. "Well, that's what I do. Solve other people's problems while I ignore my own."

Sara laughed "God, I love you. Every time I wonder why you're my bestie you say something like that and remind me."

"Oh, please. You never wonder why I'm your bestie."

They shared a smile. "Yeah. You're right about that."

"So you're going to give it another shot with this guy?"

"If I can. I may not be able to find him."

"You'll find him. He was in the neighborhood. It was a party. Someone must know him."

"Yeah," Sara said. "I'll figure it out." Maybe she just needed to stand on her porch and call his name. Maybe he was still out there watching her. Protecting her.

Petra glanced at her watch. "I need to head out. I've got a client meeting in about an hour." She stood and threw her drink in the trash as Sara did the same. "You'll find each other. I know it."

"What makes you so sure?"

Petra laughed. "Hello? Every rom-com and romance novel in the world. And trust me, I've read or watched pretty much all of them."

"Then I guess you must be right."

They parted ways at the courthouse door, and Sara buried herself in work for the rest of the afternoon. But once she was home and safely in bed, Petra's words came back to her.

She wished her friend was right, but this wasn't a rom-com so much as a paranormal romance. And she'd already tried to find Luke to no avail. She'd stood on her front porch at sunset, feeling like an idiot as she called out, "Luke! Luke, please come back!"

She told herself the neighbors would assume she was calling a dog, and she told herself it didn't matter. All that mattered was him hearing her voice or getting her message.

All that mattered was being back in his arms.

She tried again every hour until almost midnight, then she gave up and went to bed. She set her alarm for five, intending to wake up before dawn and try one more time. Then again at sunset.

And every night forward until she found him.

Somehow, she'd find him. She had to believe that.

She closed her eyes, letting herself get lost in the memory of him. Wishing she had the reality, but taking comfort in the imaginary feel of his hands on her body, his mouth on her breast. She slid her hand down between her legs, letting that glorious pressure build, telling herself he was inside her. That he was right there, his body heavy on hers, touching and teasing her until she was close, so very, very close, and then he'd thrust inside her, filling her. *Claiming her*.

Her eyes fluttered open as she tried to visualize him above her. His face. Those eyes.

And then there he was.

Not inside her, but standing at the foot of the bed, his lust-filled eyes on her face.

It should be creepy as fuck, but it wasn't. Instead, it was wildly erotic. The danger. The exhibitionism. She should be ashamed that his intrusion turned her on even more, but it did. Her body felt on fire, every cell hyperaware.

"Luke," she murmured.

"Shhh. Don't stop." He reached down and gently pulled the sheet away so that he could see her. The press of her tight nipples against her tank top, her hand in her sleep shorts.

She was so wet now, her fingers slippery, but she did as he asked, touching herself as they locked eyes. As she imagined it was his hand teasing her clit, sliding inside her core. Him that she was grinding against, wanting him harder, deeper.

With a sigh, she arched back, closing her eyes, holding the image of him watching in her head as her body tightened, release edging closer and closer. When she felt the mattress shift, she forced herself not to look. Not even when his hands stroked her inner thighs. Not even when his fingers teased the baggy sleep shorts to the side, and he replaced her fingers with his mouth.

She moaned, her hips moving as his tongue teased and tormented her, bringing her closer, but never over that edge. "Please," she begged. "Luke, please, please fuck me."

And then she heard the tear of material as he ripped the shorts off of her. She laughed, understanding that he was claiming her. Silently telling her that she was his. That he could take what he wanted.

The thought turned her on even more, though how that was possible, Sara truly didn't know. And then he was inside her, his cock filling her as one hand slid under her tank to tease her breast and his mouth closed hard on hers.

She reached up, her fingers sliding into his thick hair as she held his head in place, wanting the kiss deeper and harder, just like his cock. "Yes," she murmured against his mouth. It was the only word she knew, and soon even that was lost to her as she felt her entire body shatter, the sensation seemingly never-ending as he drew it out longer and longer until she was squirming beneath it, trying to close her thighs, begging him to stop because she couldn't take it anymore.

Then that warm, sweet glow as the orgasm faded and she was curled up against him, her cheek pressed to his chest as he gently stroked her back.

"I guess this means you weren't angry with me for coming inside," he said, making her burst into laughter.

"I probably should be, but I'm not. I thought you were my imagination at first." She slid her hand down, tracing the thin line of hair down his lower abdomen until she found his cock and felt it harden in response to her touch. "This was much, much better."

She tilted her head up, her sigh as he kissed her turning to giggles as he rolled onto his back and pulled her on top of him so that she was straddling his waist. "How did you get in?"

"I've watched you enough that I've memorized the key code on your front door."

"Oh." She should probably be more careful. Luke she didn't mind. Some of the defendants she'd put away who were now out on parole were a different story. "That's not actually what I meant, though. I mean without an invitation."

"Are you saying I'm unwelcome?"

"Funny man," she said, sliding down until she felt his cock against her ass. She wiggled against it. "You know you're very welcome."

"Careful, or this is the end of our conversation."

She considered wiggling some more, but she wanted to talk with him even more than she wanted round two. "Was that enough of an invitation, then? Just the fact that I wanted you? For that matter, how did those others get in? The ones who attacked us?"

"The invitation lore is a myth. Mostly, anyway."

"Mostly?"

"There are more than just vampires in this world, Sara. And there are some spell casters who are capable of making mystical barriers designed to keep other creatures out. They were more common centuries ago, and humans would pay for their services to secure their homes."

"Humans would pay? They just knew about those spell casters? For that matter, they knew about vampires?"

"Many did, yes," he told her. "But since the world has become modern, we creatures have moved deeper into the shadows. Few humans believe that preternatural creatures are real, and only a rare few know that such barriers are even possible. Even if an invitation were needed as your mythology believes, it wouldn't matter. In this modern world, humans spend an extraordinary amount of time outside after dark, which means there is less need to break into homes in order to feed."

"Is that what you used to do?"

"If I said yes, would you send me away?"

"No. But, well, how do you survive now? I mean, you do need blood, right? Or is that a myth, too?"

"Not a myth, and there are ways. But is this really what you want to be talking about now when you are naked in my arms?"

"Maybe not," she conceded. She licked her lips. "Why did you come back?"

"Because this is where I'm meant to be. At your side, Sara. In your bed."

Her whole body tingled, and she couldn't deny the heat that settled between her thighs or the tightness of her breath. She wondered if he could smell her arousal. She hoped that he could.

"But I told you to leave."

"You did."

"And yet you came back, even knowing I wanted you gone."

"Yes." He reached up and stroked her hair, and she was struck by a sudden sense of how large he was. Those broad shoulders. The strength in his arms. He could break her with a flick of his thumb. He could kill her with a kiss of those deadly fangs. She knew all of that. And she wasn't the least bit scared. On the contrary, his size and strength made her feel safer than she had since the death of her father.

She didn't realize she was crying until he used the pad of his thumb to wipe away a tear. "What troubles you, my love?"

"Nothing," she whispered. "It's only—you came. I wanted you to, but I didn't know how to find you. I even called for you. Did you hear?"

He shook his head, those golden eyes lit up like shining stars. "No, but that doesn't matter. I will always find you, Sara. And I will always keep you safe."

SEVEN

Perhaps Luke had been this content in some far, distant past that had dimmed in his memory, but he didn't think so. The calm, sweet happiness that flowed through him felt like a new experience. A rebirth. A revelation.

Love.

He'd been terrified coming back to her, ready to beg and plead for her to give them just one more chance. To fall to his knees and confess the depth of his need for her.

He'd come expecting the challenge of winning her over. Instead, he'd found a miracle.

She was his.

She truly loved him, the depth of her passion as deep as his own. And while he knew that challenges lay ahead for them, with Sara by his side, he was confident he'd have the strength to face them.

"What are you thinking?" he asked, gently stroking her soft skin. They were side by side in bed, her hand on his hip, his fingers caressing her side. They both craved the connection, the breach they'd crossed to find each other again still fresh in each other's minds.

"About your world," she told him. "Even living in the shadows, I don't understand how humans don't know."

"A combination of reasons, I suppose. We cling to the dark, as you said. It is in our interest to stay hidden, and to the extent we fail, most humans are more than willing to make up easy explanations for things they don't understand. But there are other methods of ensuring we remain off the radar of humans."

"Like what?"

"Wild stories with dubious explanations are always a possibility. And if that doesn't work, there are ways to ensure that a human who has glimpsed this world and understood what he saw retains no memory of it."

Her hand stilled on his hip. "Humans like me?"

He stroked her hair, tilting her head so that she was looking straight at him. "No. Never. I wouldn't allow it."

"What exactly is *it*?"

He exhaled, not wanting to tell her. Not wanting her to have so intimate a peek at the wizard behind the curtain. Not yet, anyway. And yet he also knew that he owed her the truth. And between the two of them, he had promised himself that truth would always win out. "There are different species of demons," he told her, "and each has unique talents. Some can take memories."

He felt the way her body tightened. "Amnesia?"

"Selective," he explained. "The Shades get inside your head, and they can pluck the memories out. Like picking fruit."

She shuddered, her body shaking against his. "So they just leave a big hole? What happens to the people? How do they function?"

"If they take an extended period of time, then yes. I believe that would be staged as head trauma. Amnesia. Some bullshit like that."

"That's horrible."

He nodded. "I don't disagree."

"And if it's not a long period of time?"

"Then they pick and choose. You might remember going to visit your friend, but not the encounter with a demon as you walked back to your car."

Her forehead creased. "If that's true, then it's possible I saw Serge kill my father. I could have seen it, and they might have erased it."

Luke cringed, hating the direction of her thoughts. "I don't believe that's the case. But why don't we leave this unpleasant subject for another time?"

"Luke..."

"Please, my love. We'll have plenty of time for me to show you the dark areas. But if I'm introducing you to this world, let me start with the delights."

"You already have," she teased, running her hand lightly along his body. "Many, many delights."

He laughed, then caught her hand and kissed it. "You make a good point. But there are other pleasant things as well. Demons whose kiss can give the gift of communicating with animals. Others who walk through your world disguised as magicians, with no one the wiser that they are using actual magic."

He loved how that made her smile. "That seems a bit like cheating."

"Not at all. Don't magicians claim that it is all real?"

She shrugged. "I suppose so." As he watched, her brow furrowed again, and the corner of her mouth curved down into a frown.

He laughed. "Tell me. What are you pondering now?"

"You're starting to know me far too well."

"Never," he said, pulling her close for a quick kiss. "But I shall spend every moment we having striving to know you fully."

"I like the sound of that."

"So?"

For a moment, she looked confused, then her expression cleared. "I was just thinking about criminal cases. Surely a lot of murders were actually committed by creatures in your world. Like those guys who attacked us. If one had killed me, for example, what would happen? The cops would search and not find the killer? Or do the human police sometimes arrest a vampire or demon and not even know it? Or—"

He pressed a finger over her lip. "It's complicated," he said. "But for the most part, we prosecute our own."

"Oh. How?"

"For now, let's just say that your Mr. Porter isn't the only lead prosecutor in town."

"But how do you arrest a vampire? I mean if Bram Stoker was right and vampires can turn into mist...."

"Sara."

"Sorry," she said, her laughter delighting him. "I'm just fascinated. Is it true? Can you turn into mist?"

He fought a smile. "It's true. And to answer your next question, there are ways to prevent that. There is balance in the world, after all. No creature is without weakness."

"What ways?"

"Are you familiar with hematite?"

"I think so. A mineral, right? Used to make iron?"

"It is. And in its pure form, it can bind a vampire."

"In that case, we need to get some. Having you bound and at my mercy, forced to obey my every—*hey!*"

He moved like lightning to roll her on her back and straddle her, then bent over and whispered in her ear. "I'm already at your mercy, Sara."

"Oh," she said, her voice turning low and husky, the heat in it intoxicating as she squirmed against him, sending desire spiraling through his blood. "In that case, let me tell you exactly what I want you to do...."

Sara woke in terror, yanked from the bed, then held fast by a thick arm around her waist and another around her neck. She tried to cry out as she saw no less than five huge men dressed all in black stand guard as Luke struggled in chains now attached to her walls. But his movements were sluggish. He seemed drugged, and only his eyes looked clear.

Eyes that looked at her with pain. And, yes, with fear.

Hematite.

"*Luke.*" She tried to shout the word, but the pressure at her throat was too intense. Instead, she let her gaze dart around the room, unsure what she was searching for, but praying that she would see something that could help them.

He heard her, though, and it was as if her voice was a switch. He fought like a madman, tugging at the chains, every muscle straining against his bonds.

"You know better, vampire," a voice from behind her said.

She twisted around, unable to see who held her. But a few feet away, she saw two cloaked figures so tall that their heads almost brushed the ceiling. They seemed to be only half in this world, solid and translucent all at the same time. One of them nodded at her as if in an ironic greeting. "Vampires are strong," he said, his voice only inside her head. "Until they are made weak."

He turned away, attention returning to Luke as Sara felt her knees go weak. It didn't matter. She was being held so tight by her captor, there was no risk of her falling. "Please," she whispered, but the word barely escaped her throat. And no one was listening to her anyway.

No one except Luke, who met her eyes, his filled with so much pain it broke her heart. He held her gaze, and the love she saw there quelled some of her fear. Then he turned away, his expression growing tight with fury.

"Why are you here?" Despite the emotion she saw on his face, his voice was weak, as if he had to push it out from beyond a wall of water.

"We have been sent." The dark figures spoke in unison, their voices ominous. "This woman—this human—you cannot have her."

"The hell I can't," Luke countered, the raw emotion in his words so palpable it broke through the drugged haze.

"Luke!" The name echoed in the small room, and it took a moment for Sara to realize it came from her. Immediately, the pressure against her neck increased.

He met her eyes, and she saw the pain and anger reflected there. But it was the fear that chilled her. She'd never seen that emotion on his face, not even when the vampires had attacked in the kitchen. And seeing it now killed the tiny bit of hope she was clinging to. "Luke," she repeated, but this time, she had no voice.

"I won't let them hurt you," he growled, his voice so fierce it rumbled through her.

"This ends now," the dark creatures said.

"Who sent you?" Once again, Luke's voice was sharp, his emotions battling back whatever hold they had on him. But it wasn't enough. Sara knew damn well that it wasn't enough. "Who the hell is pulling your chain?"

"That is none of your concern. All you must do now is make the choice. Her death or your memories."

Sara gasped, the words hitting her like a thousand shards of ice. "No," she blurted, or tried to. She could barely catch her breath from the pressure at her neck. But Luke heard her anyway, and when he met her eyes once again, the tiny bit of hope in her heart faded. He was as trapped as she was. Serge wasn't anywhere nearby to help. And these creatures—Shades, she now realized—held the power to steal him from her forever, simply by taking his memories of her.

The thought was unbearable. Even worse than the death, because at least then she wouldn't know what she had lost in that dark abyss of nothingness. But death wasn't really on the table. She knew what Luke would choose. Hadn't he told her he would always protect her?

Hot tears streamed down her cheeks. "No," she croaked, her voice barely audible. "Please, please no."

But no one heard. Or, if they did, they didn't care.

She saw the tears in his eyes through her own blurry vision as he looked at her, then whispered. "Never forget that I love you, Sara. Even if I don't remember, it's inside me."

She tried to struggle. To scream. All to no avail. And the Shades moved closer to him, then closer still.

Her chest ached with the force of her sobs, and as she tried to breathe, the pressure at her neck loosened just slightly. She could speak! And she scrambled to think clearly. To find some brilliant combination of words that would make them stop. And then, without even realizing she was going to say it, she blurted, "Take *my* memories instead!"

The Shades stopped.

Luke froze.

Everyone in the room looked at her, and the reality of what she'd suggested hit her with full force, but she wouldn't call them back. "Please," she begged as tears ran down her face. "Please take mine. Not his. Just mine. Take them and let him go."

"Sara, my love, no."

She nodded, lips pressed together to hold back her sobs. Only when she'd gathered herself did she try to speak again, thankful that the unseen captor behind her was allowing her to do so. "It's the only way. Don't you see? I'll be gone in a blink of an eye from your perspective. But you can live for ages. And that means that I will, too. I'll live in your memory."

"Sara—no. The thought of you not remembering what we had—"

"Is far less painful than the thought of living my life without you. Please, Luke. Please understand. And remember."

"No. No, Sara, please, no," he begged, but the Shades nodded, and Sara knew this was the best way. The only way.

"This is acceptable," the Shades said in unison. "But understand this changes nothing. Court the human again, and we will take your memories, Lucius Dragos. Your memories, or her life. Perhaps both."

He said nothing, but Sara saw the anger—and the pain—on his face.

"Say that you understand."

"I understand, you sons of bitches."

The Shades ignored the insult as they walked toward her. She held her breath, her eyes fixed on Luke, her vision blurred by her tears.

But for one brief moment, she saw his face clearly. And as the Shades reached out to touch her, he whispered, "I will never forget you."

And then her world went black.

"I saw him again," Sara told Petra as they walked down the hill toward Probation and Happy Hour with their friends.

"Who?"

"The guy. The one I've seen a couple of times before. He was in a doorway, mostly in the shadows."

"You saw him just now?" Petra asked, turning to look over her shoulder. "Let's go see what he wants."

She considered it, but didn't want to spook him. Weirdly, she liked knowing he was watching her. It should have been creepy. Instead, he felt like a guardian angel.

"No. Let's just catch up with the others."

"Glass of whiskey with your name on it?"

"Pretty much," Sara admitted.

"What did you do last night? Did you try to track down the guy from the party?"

Sara shook her head. She remembered telling Petra about the guy she met at the condo near her house, but honestly, she couldn't even picture him. "I just had a lazy night. Stayed home. Did nothing."

"Sounds fabulous."

"You'd think," Sara said. "But I still feel like I've been put through the wringer."

"Nothing drinks and friends can't cure."

"You speak the truth." But even as she spoke, she didn't quite believe it.

Something was off.

And sooner or later, Sara intended to figure out what it was.

THE END

Don't forget to visit kirajamesauthor.com to sign up for my Elite Reader Group, so you don't miss any news about this or other series! (Not to mention bonus scenes, character tidbits, and more!)

And please leave a review at Goodreads, Amazon, and your favorite vendor!

XOXO
Kira James

About the Author

Kira James is the semi-secret paranormal pen name of a *New York Times* bestselling author. As such, she lives mostly in someone else's head. Which, frankly, isn't such a bad deal, and definitely saves on rent.

You can find her at https://www.kirajamesauthor.com

Be sure to sign up for Kira's Elite Reader Group so you don't miss any news about this or other series! (Not to mention bonus scenes, character tidbits, and more!)